PROTECTOR OF MERCIA

BOOK 5 THE EAGLE OF MERCIA CHRONICLES

MJ PORTER

Boldwood

First published in Great Britain in 2023 by Boldwood Books Ltd.

Copyright © MJ Porter, 2023

Cover Design by Head Design Ltd

Cover Photography: Shutterstock

The moral right of MJ Porter to be identified as the author of this work has been asserted in accordance with the Copyright, Designs and Patents Act 1988.

All rights reserved. No part of this book may be reproduced in any form or by any electronic or mechanical means, including information storage and retrieval systems, without written permission from the author, except for the use of brief quotations in a book review.

This book is a work of fiction and, except in the case of historical fact, any resemblance to actual persons, living or dead, is purely coincidental.

Every effort has been made to obtain the necessary permissions with reference to copyright material, both illustrative and quoted. We apologise for any omissions in this respect and will be pleased to make the appropriate acknowledgements in any future edition.

A CIP catalogue record for this book is available from the British Library.

Paperback ISBN 978-1-83751-209-6

Large Print ISBN 978-1-83751-208-9

Hardback ISBN 978-1-83751-207-2

Ebook ISBN 978-1-83751-210-2

Kindle ISBN 978-1-83751-211-9

Audio CD ISBN 978-1-83751-202-7

MP3 CD ISBN 978-1-83751-203-4

Digital audio download ISBN 978-1-83751-205-8

Boldwood Books Ltd
23 Bowerdean Street
London SW6 3TN
www.boldwoodbooks.com

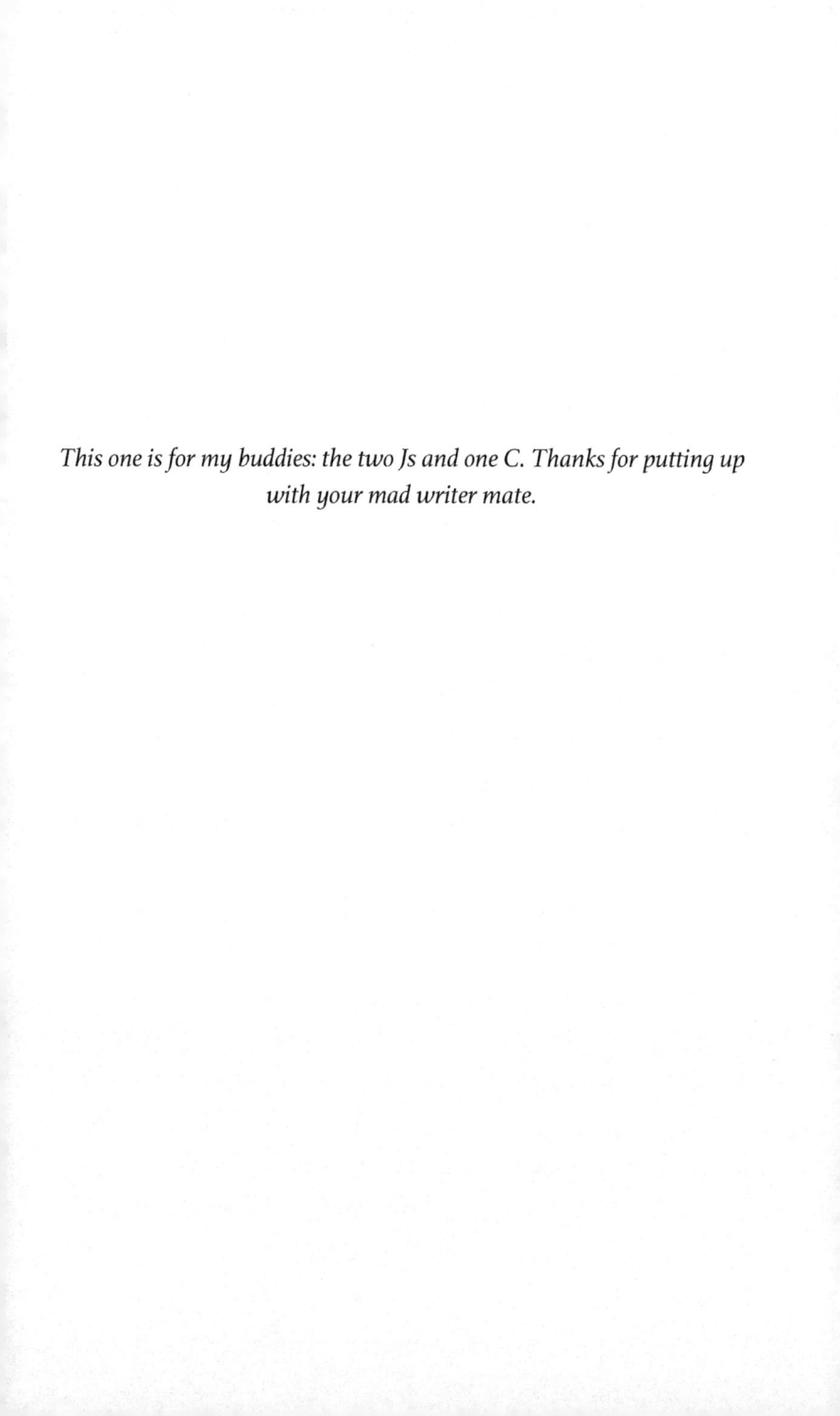

This one is for my buddies: the two Js and one C. Thanks for putting up with your mad writer mate.

Designed by Flintlock Covers

CAST OF CHARACTERS

Icel, orphaned youth living in Tamworth, his mother was Ceolburh
Brute, Icel's horse
Cenfrith, Icel's uncle, brother of Ceolburh and one of the Mercian king's warriors, who dies in *Son of Mercia*
Edwin, Icel's childhood friend, although they have been separated
Wine, Cenfrith's horse, now Icel's alongside Brute
Wynflæd, an old herbwoman at the Mercian king's court at Tamworth

The Kings of Mercia
Coelwulf, king of Mercia r.821–825 (deposed)
Beornwulf, king of Mercia r.825–826 (killed)
Lady Cynehild, Beornwulf's wife
Wiglaf, king of Mercia r.827–829 (deposed) r.830–
Queen Cynethryth, Wiglaf's wife
Wigmund, Wiglaf's son, married to Lady Cynehild, sister of Lord Coenwulf
Ecgberht, king of Wessex r.802 onwards, r.829 in Mercia

The Ealdormen/Bishops of Mercia
Ælfstan, one of King Wiglaf's supporters, an ally to Icel
Ælflæd, Lord Coenwulf's sister
Ælfred, ally of Lord Wigmund
Beornoth, one of King Wiglaf's ealdormen
Hunberht, an ally of Lord Wigmund
Muca, one of King Wiglaf's ealdormen
Sigered, a long-standing ealdorman who's survived the troubled years of the 820s
Sigegar, Sigered's grandson
Tidwulf, an ally of King Wiglaf
Wicga, ally of Lord Wigmund

Rulers of other kingdoms
Athelstan, king of the East Angles
Ecgberht, king of Wessex

Ealdorman Ælfstan's Warriors
Cenred, Mercian warrior
Goðeman, Mercian warrior
Kyre, Mercian warrior
Landwine, Mercian warrior
Maneca, Mercian warrior
Ordlaf, Mercian warrior
Oswy, Mercian warrior, once an ally of the queen
Uor, Mercian warrior
Waldhere, Mercian warrior
Wulfgar, Mercian warrior
Wulfheard, Mercian warrior, Ealdorman Ælfstan's oath-sworn man
Bada, Wulfheard's horse

Those living in Kingsholm
Coenwulf and Coelwulf, the sons of Lord Coenwulf and Lady Cynewise
Cuthwahl, Lord Coenwulf's warrior
Deremann, Lord Wigmund's warrior
Eadburg, living in Kingsholm, her mother cares for young Coenwulf and Coelwulf
Eadweard, Lord Wigmund's warrior
Forthgar, Lord Wigmund's warrior
Lady Cynewise, sister of Lord Coenwulf
Mergeat, Lord Wigmund's warrior
Osmod, Lord Coenwulf's warrior
Tatberht, Lord Coenwulf's warrior
Wulfred, Lord Wigmund's warrior

Those living in Hereford
Æthelbald, rogue living in the woodlands
Hywel, rogue living in the woodlands
The Wolf Lady, forest-dweller

Those living in Chester
Æthelgyth, tavern keeper
Godfrith, a young boy
Oswin, tavern stableman

In Northumbria
Wulfnoth, a lord

Those living in Tamworth
Cuthred, training to be a healer with Wynflæd
Eahric, commander of the king's household warriors
Gaya, previously a slave woman with a talent for healing, now freed
Theodore, previously a slave man with a talent for healing, now freed
Wynflæd, a healer

Places mentioned
Eamont, in the north-west, the site of a famous meeting in 927 (if you look at maps of Saxon England, you'll find precious few names on the north-west side of the country)
Hereford, close to the Welsh borders, in Mercia
Kingdom of Wessex, the area south of the River Thames, including Kent at this time, but not Dumnonia (Cornwall and Devon)
Kingsholm, associated with the ruling family of King Coelwulf, close to Gloucester, home to Lord Coenwulf
Lichfield, close to Tamworth and one of the holy sites in Mercia
Londonia, combining the ruins of Roman Londinium and Saxon Lundenwic
Tamworth, the capital of the Mercian kingdom
Winchcombe, the home of a nunnery associated with Mercian royal women
Wroxeter, close to the Welsh borders, in Mercia

THE STORY SO FAR

Icel has retrieved Lord Coenwulf, with the aid of his fellow warriors, from the Viking raiders on the Isle of Sheppey. But in doing so, three men have died, and on returning to Kingsholm, Lady Cynehild, while birthing her second son, has also met her death. But not before finally revealing the truth of Icel's identity as the unacknowledged son of the little lamented King Beornwulf of Mercia, dead for seven years. At the same time, Lady Cynehild has forced Icel to swear an oath to protect her sons and to ensure that they, unlike Icel, will one day claim their birthright as king of Mercia.

THE MERCIAN REGISTER
AD833

In this year, King Wiglaf of Mercia and King Athelstan of the East Angles forged an alliance against the Viking raiders ravaging the kingdom of the East Angles and swore with oaths to always be allies. The Viking raiders captured the Isle of Sheppey but were soon driven from it by men of the Wessex king, King Ecgberht.

1

WINTER AD833, TAMWORTH

'You knew.' The words shoot like seax strikes from my mouth. I've been holding them tight for too long. I should have come to Tamworth from Kingsholm sooner. It should have been the first place I came to when Lady Cynehild first told the truth of my birth – when she told me that my father was King Beornwulf, the king of Mercia who died fighting against the kingdom of the East Angles seven summers ago.

Wynflæd watches me, eyes filled with sorrow I don't want to see. Has she always pitied me? Was our friendship little more than the sympathy of an old woman? Was she training me to become a healer, like her, because she knew I could never claim my birthright?

'I did, boy, I did,' she confirms, her old, thin lips downturned, her eyes hard and flecked with flint.

'You should have told me,' I cry, wishing traitorous tears didn't fall from my eyes. I'm glad young Cuthred isn't here. We're alone in her workshop, and I'm grateful for that. I could have come upon her when she was busy tending to one of the frail within Tamworth. But for once, luck has favoured me. If Cuthred saw me crying, I don't know what I'd do. The rain that's drenched me on my journey here hasn't helped – making it appear as though I'm wreathed in sorrow.

'Why?' I watch Wynflæd as she settles before the hearth, holding out thin, almost translucent hands towards the leaping flames. It's cold, I realise that now. The heat of my fury has driven me onwards, despite the turning season. I sniff, and all I can smell is the scent of wet horses and churned mud. I stink of the cold. 'What good would it have done?' Her words are far from apologetic. I suck in a much-needed breath, seeking some sort of clarity. Why have I come to demand answers from her? What's drawn me to this place? Is it that she's the only person who knows the true identity of my father? Is it that she's my only family, or is it something else? Why am I here?

'I would have known the truth.' My voice is roughened by sorrow. I realise, at that moment, my fear. She must hear it.

'We kept you safe.' Her reply is barely heard above the rain drumming outside. No one is about in Tamworth. The streets are awash with running water and mud. Why then, I consider, does she whisper, even now?

'I wouldn't have been safe?' The words are stark, and I feel my forehead furrow.

'You're the son of a king.' I think she'll leave it there. But she turns away, looking down at her hands before she speaks again. 'The son of a king many blame for the current state of affairs in Mercia. You would have also been blamed.'

'Why would I? I wasn't his son when he was king. I was born before he became king and before he even thought of becoming king.'

'Ah, you've been made to think as the holy men would have it.' Those words spit with more ire than the snapping of the twigs in the heart of the fire. 'A son is a son. In the eyes of some, you would have been throne-worthy, an ætheling. It wouldn't have mattered to many. It still won't.' There's a caution there, one I don't like to hear.

I shake my head, and water pools from my cloak and down my nose. I lick it. I'm thirsty and angry.

'You can use it, you know.' Now I understand all those tales she told me of long-ago kings. I understand her too well, and a shiver of hope and dismissal ripples my spine. She didn't train me because she felt pity for my lost birthright. No, she kept me close so that, when the time came, she could make me Mercia's king.

'I'm no king,' I counter, saying those words enough to assure myself that I speak the truth. I am no king. I'll never be a king. I don't want to rule. I want to be Icel the healer. But I'll be content with Icel the warrior of Mercia. And yet, I'm angry as well. I would have known the truth of my birth. Those decisions should have been mine to make.

'You're an eagle, not a sparrow,' she counters, her words angrier. I eye her as I finally slip the sodden cloak from my shoulders and allow the water to stream onto the floor. There's a hook where other cloaks rest, and I place it on one, ensuring I don't make the others as wet as mine.

'I'm nothing.' I settle before her, sinking gratefully to the stool and the heat of the fire. Running a hand through my black hair, my eyes alight on the scar there, the one that does mark me with Mercia's eagle. But it is Mercia's, not mine.

'You're the son of a king.' She reaches towards me. Her skeletal hands are a too vivid reminder that, should I want to claim Beornwulf as my father, I need to do it quickly before she breathes her last, and there's no one to stand as witness to my claim. But who would accept the words of the old healer woman? Mercia is at peace with itself, almost. Mercia has recovered from the years of uncertainty, the years of too many kings, one after another, falling beneath the blade of the king of the East Angles, Athelstan, the king-killer. Mercia is whole and needs to be, for enemies surround her. Wessex to the south, the kingdom of the East Angles to the east, the Welsh to the west, and the Viking raiders who scurry along rivers, killing and taking people and treasure without thought, leaving bloodshed in their wake.

'I'm the son of my mother, who died birthing me.' I force those words through my tight throat. I've witnessed how my mother died. I watched Lady Cynehild fight her bloody battle on the birthing bed, one she lost, for all her youngest son lives and, I hope, thrives. Her youngest son. Coelwulf. What will his life be like? Who'll protect him from the horrors of who he is and what he did?

'You're the son of Beornwulf, king of Mercia. You have a royal name, for all many have forgotten that.' Once more, the intensity in those words belies the slightness of her frame, the cold etched onto her features as though it were a permanent tattoo emblazoned there with needle and ink. Wynflæd is old, tired and weak. I see it all laid bare before me. What if she doesn't survive the winter? I've always been alone, but I'll be even more alone if she's no longer here.

Edwin isn't my friend. I've shamed the men of Ealdorman Ælfstan's warriors by taking them to the Isle of Sheppey. King Wiglaf's rage is intense. We've all been punished for that act of disobedience, for all we rescued a man who would have died otherwise. Lord Coenwulf, a traitor to Mercia. A man who thought to ally with King Ecgberht of Wessex, or at least, that's what we believe was to happen.

What sort of man is Lord Coenwulf? He wasn't worthy of Lady Cynehild when they married to cement his bargain with King Wiglaf. He was her second husband. In turn, she had been my father's second wife.

Lord Coenwulf will make a poor father to young Coenwulf and Coelwulf, two motherless boys, yet his sister is wed to the king's son, Lord Wigmund. One day Lady Ælflæd will rule Mercia by the side of her husband. I foresee only that she'll be as fearless as the wife of King Offa. She'll not be cowed by a bishop or enemies. She'll be magnificent, for all her husband is a weak, mewling man who'd sooner offer his sword to the enemy than defend his family and kingdom. There is no love lost between myself and Wigmund. We've butted up against one another too many times in the past.

And Lady Ælflæd, I believe, suspects my true identity after her journey to Budworth to pay her respects at my uncle's grave on behalf of Lady Cynehild. Not from witnessing my uncle's grave, but from gazing at my mother's. We can never be friends if that's the case. Not now. I understand so much more since Lady Cynehild informed me of my identity. I wish she hadn't.

'You'll protect Mercia.' Wynflæd's still talking, and I try to listen to her words. 'You'll become her king. No fool, such as young Wigmund, will be able to do what you can. You must.' She almost ends with a shriek. But I'm shaking my head, looking at the fire, focusing on the blue heart of the flame, which should presage warmth but which reminds me only of the frozen world beyond the workshop. Rain might have turned the settlement of Tamworth to dark mud, but winter threatens. When the rain stops, the cold will arrive, and walking anywhere will be dangerous. Outside, it's white, blue, pale pink and mauve. It's the winter when it's light for a small part of the day and dark for all other times.

'I'm a warrior and a healer able to stitch battle wounds, nothing more,' I counter quickly, swallowing against the spark of hope that Wynflæd's assertion places in the fire of my belly. What could I be if I only had supporters? Could I rule? Could I govern better than King Wiglaf? Perhaps not, but yes, certainly better than his son and the collection of sycophants who've tied themselves to Wigmund, and his mother, Queen Cynethryth, the despised Ealdorman

Sigered amongst them. Surely, Sigered should be dead by now. He's old and twisted, but in his heart, not in his body.

Wynflæd's cold hand on mine douses the flames more quickly than an iron blade at my throat. 'Your uncle Cenfrith wanted this for you.'

But I'm shaking my head. My uncle didn't want it for himself. He certainly wouldn't have wanted it for me. He kept me safe. He did his duty. He could have told me himself if he'd wanted me to know. He could have built a collection of ealdormen and warriors around him, but my uncle was a loner. He always thought of Mercia and me, but not in the way Wynflæd thinks. He didn't want me to rule it. I know that for sure.

'My uncle didn't.' I cut her short. 'I don't want it, and anyway,' and this is the pillar of my argument, 'I can't have it. I'm oath-sworn at Lady Cynehild's wishes.'

'Oath-sworn?' Wynflæd's hooded eyes narrow, thin tongue licking at her dry lips. 'Oath-sworn,' she prompts when I offer nothing further.

'To her sons. Coenwulf and Coelwulf. They have a claim to the Mercian kingdom, a stronger one than mine.' Before I'm even aware of what she's doing, Wynflæd is on her feet, her shoulders tight, her stance rigid.

'That bitch.' The words thrum through her body, for all they're hissed with disgust. I feel my forehead furrow at such a reaction. Lady Cynehild and Wynflæd have long since reconciled. I thought them friends, not enemies. Wynflæd rounds on me to bend and grip my hand in her two hands, looking down at the scar from the seax blade when I tried to heal my uncle in the woodlands close to the border with the Welsh kingdoms. It feels as though it were a lifetime ago.

Her cold white fingers trace the edges of the wound. It's long since healed, but it's marked me more than anything else. This makes me Mercian. This makes me an eagle, but it's only skin-deep. It doesn't meet my heart.

'She never wanted you to have anything.' Spittle follows those words, her fingers continuing to trace the scar. I want to pull my hand back and cover the markings with my gloves, as I often do. But her grip's fierce. Her strength surprises me. 'She wasn't your friend, and you're not bound by an oath given to the conniving bitch. Your claim's stronger than her infant sons. You're the son of a king. Her sons are the sons of a son of a king. And what, she's bid you ensure her son is king one day?' Now her words are deathly quiet, the menace making me shiver. I finally snatch back my hand and cover the markings by clenching my fist. 'She would have you fight for her sons when she wouldn't fight for you? She would have you lay down your life to enforce an entitlement that will bring you into conflict with others and a claim that will do you little good but bring more scars to your flesh?' Wynflæd paces as she speaks, no longer whispering. Outside, the sound of the thunderous rain intensifies. I look down, noticing where water encroaches through the doorway. There should be straw there to absorb the water. Something to stop it from getting close to the hearth and compromising the ring of stones in which the wood snaps and crackles, a cheery counterpart to an unpleasant conversation.

'I gave my word,' I murmur. 'She asked, and I gave it.'

'And did you give it before you knew the truth of your birthright, your destiny, or after?' Her eyes blaze into mine.

I shake my head. I won't answer that.

'She was a conniving, lying she-devil until her last breaths.' My sharp intake of shocked breath has Wynflæd laughing. 'You thought her your friend. You thought her last moments a desperate request for you to shield children, æthelings that her disgraced husband will be unable to should King Wiglaf even allow him to live after what he's done? Did you think to feel pity and sorrow for a dying woman? Well, I assure you, she was clearer in those final moments than at any time in the last ten winters. She makes you a protector when she tried to force your uncle to send you from his protection? She demands from you everything that she denied you when you were a boy and needed others to ensure you gained what was rightfully yours.'

Wynflæd's eyes are wild, her fury bringing a glow to her skin that won't have been there since the warmth of the summer. She's enlivened, bold, and very, very scary.

'You won't do it,' she barks, the words a screech louder than an eagle chasing its prey. 'You'll not do it. The boys will become nothing. Their parentage will be forgotten. They'll have no one to speak for them. Had I known her intentions, I would never have allowed you to grow close. I would never have gone to her aid when the birth of her first child approached. I would have let her, and that child, die had I known of this.'

I hang my head low, tears threatening to spill once more. Her harsh words astound me.

'Your uncle would not have wanted this. He esteemed Lady Cynehild but only because she was, for the duration of her first marriage, complicit in keeping your identity a secret. Your father, had he lived, wouldn't have expected this from you. I can assure you of that.' Her words crack with fury.

I came here to tell Wynflæd of my anger, to demand answers, to seek some understanding of the part she willingly played in concealing my identity, but this meeting will be more than that. I know it. Perhaps she fears it too. She asks me for something I can't give. I'm no king. I have no right to rule Mercia, whether I will it or not.

I came here to lay my anger at her feet, but instead, she turns her rage on me.

'I can't deny my oath,' I speak into the silence, my words

resounding as though thunder echoes outside, along with the tumultuous downpour. 'I gave my word, admittedly, before I knew the truth of my father's identity,' I say, my voice softer now, not meeting her eyes. I'm not sure it matters. Had I known, I would still have been determined to protect the children. They are like I once was before I became a warrior. They are weak and powerless, and soon, I imagine, they'll lack even the protection of their father. 'I gave my word, and those children are defenceless. I'll protect them.' I speak slowly. I want her to understand. As she kept me safe throughout all these years, I will do the same for those children. To not do so would make me a weak man, no matter my anger at Lady Cynehild for her cruel use of the information she kept from me, or at my uncle for failing to tell me when he evidently knew. At my father for not acknowledging me and then dying before he could.

'Then why did you even come here?' she crows, rage filling the workshop where I spent so much of my childhood. 'Why did you come here if you were only going to disappoint my dreams of many winters?' Her chest heaves as I finally look at her, meet those familiar eyes, and see all that has been consistent until now in my short life.

I stand.

'It was to say goodbye.' And, without looking back, I unhook my dripping cloak and stride from the place.

Wynflæd makes no effort to stop me.

2

'Icel.' My name rings through the damp air from the too-familiar voice, but head down, my cloak failing to shield me from the rain, I push onwards. I tense, fearing that Wulfheard will encourage his stallion, Bada, to race towards me, regardless of the mess of the flooding road. Only when long moments have passed do I appreciate that Wulfheard has made no attempt whatsoever. Perhaps he thinks I'm not whom he thought I was. Maybe he doesn't care.

Tears sting my eyes afresh at this new betrayal, but I don't turn Brute's head and encourage Wine onwards, even when she tries to fight the leading rein and respond to Wulfheard's words. They must know one another of old. Fleeing from Wynflæd and Tamworth has brought me out in the teeming rain. I've taken Wine with me, my uncle's horse. If I never return to Tamworth, I must take responsibility for the animal.

Unbidden, my thoughts tumble to the day of Lady Cynehild's death. My life has changed beyond all recognition since then. I thought of myself as one person, but I'm another, and I'm far from reconciled to it. I consider if this is how my uncle felt when my mother died birthing me. At least he had my father, but then, my father never claimed me, or so it seems. For, had he called me his son, then I'd have long known whom he was and, perhaps, even known him better than that.

My father. A king. The idea is outrageous, and yet, so much makes sense now. Lady Cynehild's interest in me, or lack of interest, would be a better way of describing it. She always hated me, and yet she watched everything I did. She was my father's second wife, once he became king and was expected to birth an heir. Did Lady Cynehild hope I'd falter? Did she wish for me to make mistakes and embarrass the father I didn't know I had but that she did? I struggle to understand her thinking. The conversation I once overheard between her and my uncle during that cold winter rumbles through my mind. She wanted me gone from Tamworth. She wanted my uncle to hide me away, whether because of her failure in regards to an heir for the king, or because when she did have a child, she didn't want another with a prior claim. I wish I could hate her for that.

But it's my father that I hate. He should have claimed me as his son, no matter what. Why didn't he? I was a motherless child, and he cast me aside. Yes, I realise he kept me close and denied his second wife's desire to be rid of me, whatever her reasoning. And he ensured I had what was required, but I needed to know him. I was deprived of truly knowing him. There are so many questions I'd ask him, given half the chance. I'd know why he took the kingdom of Mercia from the rightful king. I would know why he rode to war against the might of the kingdom of the East Angles without so much as a backwards glance. Didn't he even consider the possibility he'd meet his death there? Didn't he think he might make me an orphan if he met his death?

Why? It's the only word that resounds in my head. Why?

'Icel.' The cry is harsh and filled with fury. 'What the bloody hell are you doing?' I look up, rain falling into my eyes to mask the traitor tears that fell when I was feeling sorry for myself, and meet the furious gaze of Wulfheard. Bada drips with rain, pooling onto the broken surface of the stone-built roadway, the gutters so alive with the downpour that they rumble as loud as a river.

'Go away,' I growl at the older man, trying not to see the flash of pain in his eyes, the betrayal in them, and the confusion.

'What do you mean, go away? I'm your commander. You do as I order you to do. Where have you been? Or rather, why do you have Wine and Brute? It's obvious you've been to Tamworth so where are you going now?'

'Leave me alone.' The words are leaden in my throat, but I must say them all the same. Despite everything I've just thought.

'What's the matter with you?' Wulfheard reaches across the gap between us and grips my arm. I shake him off, feeling the heat of his fingers on my chilled arm.

'I said, go away.' I speak slowly, emphasising the words as I knee Brute forward. Only Wulfheard keeps pace with us; Bada, head down, obeying his master's commands.

'You've been like this ever since Lady Cynehild died,' Wulfheard continues. I wish he'd leave me alone. 'You left Kingsholm without a word to anyone. I see you've been to Tamworth to collect Wine as well. Where do you think you're going.'

'To Kingsholm.'

'Why would you return to Kingsholm? The king's furious with Lord Coenwulf. As soon as he's well enough, it's believed he'll be banished, and the king will confiscate all of his lands. They even say that Lady Ælflæd, will be given the settlement in her own name.' The reminder of Lady Ælflæd, Coenwulf's sister and the wife of the king's son, is an unwelcome one.

'And what of his sons?' I meet Wulfheard's eyes now, seeing the furrow of his eyebrows, and the rain that drips from his nose.

'What of his sons? They're nothing to you.'

'They're Lady Cynehild's sons,' I cry, even though I want to hate her too. She's denied me of so much and now expects me to give it freely. And because I'm a man of my word, I can't refute the final oath she extracted from me.

'The king will care for them. After all, his son is married to their aunt. Their grandfather was once a king, their great-uncle as well.'

I shake my head. I know what will happen to them. I foresee it only too well. It happened to me, and it'll happen to them, no matter the intentions of Lady Ælflæd. She's a strong-willed woman, but she's the wife of the king's son's. One day she'll be queen. Someone, and possibly she's already realised this, will highlight how destructive the boys could be to her son's claim to rule Mercia.

And Lord Coenwulf's a ruin of himself. If I thought him an arrogant, quick-to-rage man when I cared for his father's horse after his father died an old man, he's ten times worse now. He's wrecked.

'The king's son will do all he can to eliminate them. They are but small children. Should they die, no one will think of them. Should someone get their hands on them, one of the other ealdormen, then they'd be a sure way to counter the power of King Wiglaf and his family. Those children are in danger.'

Again, confusion swamps Wulfheard's face. But he doesn't deny my argument, and that hardens my faltering resolve.

'Why should that concern you? What aren't you telling me, Icel? I'm your friend.' The final word's plaintive. I dip my head and focus on my hands, resting on the reins. My gloves are wet through. I can feel the dampness on my skin.

'You're my commander, as you said, when I ride with Ealdorman Ælfstan's warrior band. You're not my friend. You have never been. King Wiglaf and Ealdorman Ælfstan bid you train me to defend myself, and I don't deny that you did a very good job of it, but I'm not one of the warriors. I'm the Lord of Budworth. I should take up that position now.'

'And yet, you head towards Kingsholm and speak of the sons of Lord Coenwulf.' Wulfheard's response is once more rational. I'm aware that he thinks much more clearly than I do.

Silence falls between us, broken only by the sound of heavy rain falling and the rushing water in the blocked drainage channels to the side of the road.

'There is that as well,' I confirm, meeting his eyes, ensuring mine are firm and offer no flicker of my inner turmoil.

'Icel, what's going on?' The booming voice of Oswy cuts the air as he brings his horse into view. I'm aware that the rest of Ealdorman Ælfstan's warriors have halted their journey. All I need now is for Ealdorman Ælfstan to appear.

'Nothing. Leave me alone.' The words aren't easy to say. I've fought beside Oswy, and he's battled to protect me. I healed him and made him whole once more.

'Why's Wine with you?' Once more, confusion covers the other man's face. Wulfheard and Oswy's bewilderment is understandable, but I'm not accountable to them. My oath is to the king.

'She's my horse,' I huff, wishing this was over. The winter days are short enough. I need to resume my journey.

'If you're Lord of Budworth,' Wulfheard demands, and I can tell he's trying to be reasonable, 'why aren't you going there? Why do you head south?'

'I'm going to speak for Lord Coenwulf before the king.'

'The king knows what he plans to do. He's just waiting for Lord Coenwulf to be well enough to leave Mercia before banishing him. Don't tie yourself to Coenwulf. He's no friend of yours.' Wulfheard's words are lucid and sensible, and they echo Wynflæd's when speaking of Lady Cynehild.

'It's the children I must protect,' I retort, aware that my voice screeches with defiance. I sound like a child, not a warrior and lord of Mercia.

'Icel, it's not your role to protect those children. The king will see it done, no matter what happens to Lord Coenwulf. Do you plan on leaving Mercia with him? I don't think you want to do that.'

'The children will remain in Mercia,' I argue. 'I'm sure of it. And they must have protectors.'

'Their aunt will guard them and their other aunt, the young one, I forget her name. They'll be like brother and sister. And anyway, why is this yours to concern yourself with?'

'Lady Cynehild.'

'What of her?' But I can hear the suspicion in Wulfheard's voice. 'What did she say to you as she died? Why were you even there?'

'I...' But I can't find the words. I hate her, miss her, and yet must abide by her wishes simultaneously. Conflict undulates through me, but I know what's right. I need to give voice to my oath to her, and yet I can't. 'I must be there.'

'Ealdorman Ælfstan's there. He'll speak for the children.'

'Ealdorman Ælfstan's position is as untenable as Lord Coenwulf's. Both men will be banished, Coenwulf for his treason, and Ælfstan for going to get him.' Ælfstan is the ealdorman of the Magonsæte, to the north of Kingsholm, an unruly area at the best of times with its borders close to the Welsh kingdoms. The king will want a loyal man as his ally there.

'No, they won't.' Wulfheard dismisses my concerns. 'King Wiglaf needs Ealdorman Ælfstan. The attack on the Isle of Sheppey by the Viking raiders shows how conniving those bastards are. While the king might be furious, he understands we were protecting Mercia with our actions. The same can't be said for Lord Coenwulf. His warriors are all dead, his wife as well. And he's an embarrassment to the king. He must act to protect the union forged between the two families. Better to forget about Lord Coenwulf and focus on his sister, and the children.'

'I think you'll be surprised just what the king thinks.'

'Why, what have you heard? What do you know, Icel? It's not as though you're deep in the king's confidences or even allowed to speak with him other than when you rescue him from the enemy. King Wiglaf wants your blood, not your mind.'

'Perhaps, but all the same.'

'Then very well. Do what must be done. The men and I are sent to Worcester to escort Lady Ælflæd to Kingsholm. Think about what I've said, and I'll see you when we return.' With no more words, Wulfheard turns Bada back towards the road, but Oswy lingers, his gaze keen.

'These women, Icel, they know their worth. Lady Cynehild. The queen. Lady Ælflæd. They make demands on men, and we strive to fulfil those requests, but in the end, we're not their creatures. We know what's right and wrong, as with you and young Edwin. I knew the queen was wrong to belittle your accomplishments. I stepped aside from her control. I don't pretend it wasn't awkward, but it was the right thing to do. I can't deny that she glowers at me whenever I see her, but that is her problem, not mine. Icel, you know the right thing to do more than anyone I've ever known. Tread carefully, my friend.' And with that, Oswy leaves me as well. I linger, against my wishes, watching my fellow warriors ride on, until they disappear beneath the thick clouds, and then, heart hardened, I encourage Brute and Wine onwards to Kingsholm.

I need to reach Kingsholm. I'll add my voice to those few who demand leniency for Lord Coenwulf. I must align myself against the queen and Ealdorman Sigered, even more than now. And I know I must also see what Lady Ælflæd intends to do with regards to her nephews. Will she be swayed by her husband, Lord

Wigmund, the king's son? Or will she be honourable, as I hope – though I fear I think too highly of her. With everything that's happened, she too might be desperate to distance herself from her brother's actions.

Oswy's right. These women are ambitious, and they don't care if small children are cast aside in their efforts to maintain a hold on power.

And that's what drives me.

It's not love for Lady Cynehild, for I think, in the end, she didn't love me. Ultimately, she saw me as a means to an end, in much the same way that Wynflæd does. She thought I'd be king. Lady Cynehild hoped the very opposite. Why she told me the truth, with her final words, I don't know. Was it to tie me even more tightly to her children when she knew she was dying? Did she know her husband would be cast aside? So many questions. And no answers, only the silence of the grave.

But those children? Well, they're like I was as a child. Almost orphans, with one parent living who can't protect them, even if he wanted to.

I'll be the shield between Coenwulf and Coelwulf that their father can't be. Even if that brings me into conflict with the king, his wife, his son and Lady Ælflæd. Even if it means I can never wear the warrior helm of Mercia's king which, by my birth, I should be entitled to do.

3

KINGSHOLM

'My lord Coenwulf.' King Wiglaf's words are rich and booming. He speaks as the king of Mercia for all he's in the hall of Coenwulf, heir to his father who ruled as King Coelwulf and, by rights, the man who should be king.

Coenwulf is a ruin of the man he used to be. I thought him bitter and twisted when his father died, and he alleged I killed his father's horse, an accusation for which he later apologised. But now he's truly broken. He might well have wed Lady Cynehild as part of an accord with King Wiglaf. It might have been a union neither had wanted and yet, in the time since her death, I know he loved her. And I know he loves his children, even though he can hardly bear to gaze upon them.

And King Wiglaf? He's grown in stature and command in the years since he became king. He's not the man who ran from the might of King Ecgberht of Wessex. No. He's Mercia's warrior king. He's the man who's now held that position for longer than the two kings who ruled before him.

He's powerful. He's respected. And he knows it.

I eye him warily. I've learned to admire King Wiglaf. As a

warrior, he inspires his fellow men. As a king, he's to be esteemed. As a man, he's beset by an over-powerful wife and a useless son. I suppose a man can't have every advantage before him, and Wiglaf certainly doesn't.

And now he must contend with the matter of Lord Coenwulf, a man sworn to him, and yet who was captured by the Viking raiders while agreeing to meet King Ecgberht of Wessex in secrecy.

King Wiglaf has given Lord Coenwulf time to recover from his wounds gained on the Isle of Sheppey and from the death of Lady Cynehild, but it can never be enough. I don't believe that Lord Coenwulf will defend his actions. I almost think he wishes himself dead.

'My lord king.' Lord Coenwulf cannot bow low for fear of falling, and yet he has two of his warriors, one of them my old childhood friend Edwin, to either side so that they can support him all the same. His leg was badly broken by the Viking raiders and allowed to mend at an odd angle. Our rescue of him wasn't gentle. On our journey through Kent, I was forced to re-break his leg and set it correctly again for fear he'd never walk without a limp. It's been slow to heal. Too slow. He might always limp, despite my attempts to prevent it.

The hall at Kingsholm is the fullest I've ever seen it – more of Mercia's noblemen and women crammed into that small space than should be possible. I've found a gap not far from the door to the rear, but I can see well enough. Not that I truly wish to witness this. I would not observe the ruined man cast even lower, but King Wiglaf must punish him. I believe Queen Cynethryth is even more eager to abuse the broken Lord Coenwulf. Now that Lady Cynehild is dead, Queen Cynethryth has only her daughter by marriage, who could possibly claim as much respect as her. Cynehild and the queen were always far from allies. I contemplate whether she exalts in Cynehild's death. Perhaps, I consider, if the child had died as well as the mother, she might. She's a cruel woman, always with both eyes on the future and not just on the here and now. She must see the threat the young boys are to her grandson.

'You may sit,' the king announces, his hand flicking to show servants should bring the lord of Kingsholm a chair upon which to perch. If they don't do so, he'll fall, despite the support of his warriors.

King Wiglaf's dressed in his finest clothes, gold and silver shimmering from his fingers and tunic. His cloak is thick, and a collar of finest white fur lines it. His boots shimmer at the end of thick woollen trews. He wears no warrior helm, but a fine coil of gold slithers through his greying hair, revealing he's king here and no one else. His wife, the queen, sits to his left. She's bedecked in so much finery that I fear she'll tumble if asked to walk far. The weight of the shimmering jewels at her ear and throat must be cold against her skin. Her face is twisted, her silver threaded hair visible beneath the gauze material that covers it. She might look regal, but anger exudes from her. Fingers tapping against the side of the wooden chair she sits within, Queen Cynethyrth can't take her eyes from Lord Coenwulf.

She'd do better to mask her thoughts. I see them too clearly, and so will everyone else.

In the distance, the wail of a child splits the air. I half turn, wincing, before I stop myself. The babe is well, perhaps hungry or dirty, but well. I don't need to leave this place to protect him and his brother. In my self-appointed role, the women caring for the motherless boys are far from welcoming to me. In this, it seems, I lack all of the empathy I once knew when Wynflæd shared her secrets of healing with me.

The sound has heads turning, all apart from mine. The king catches my eye, a perplexed expression on his face. He didn't expect to find me here. He's not alone. I didn't expect to find me here either. No doubt he assumes I'm with Ealdorman Ælfstan's warriors, or perhaps even at Budworth, my estate. But not here, in Kingsholm.

'You've been called to answer to the charges brought against you.' The king quickly returns everyone to the present, talking over the wailing of the babe. 'That of treason.'

The word falls heavily and awkwardly, but the king hasn't finished.

'We must separate the unfortunate outcome of your attempt, your capture by our enemy Viking raiders, from what you intended, which was to speak with the king of Wessex, another enemy of Mercia. For all your wounds would perhaps be seen as punishment enough by some, I can't agree with that. Tell me, Lord Coenwulf, what did you hope to achieve?'

'My lord king.' Coenwulf's voice is frail and little used. 'I was sent word that King Ecgberht of Wessex wished to speak with me regarding the borders between Wessex and Mercia. As you know, there have been difficulties that extend far beyond the reach of the River Thames and include that of the Wansdyke. The land boundary is unruly and has been particularly so since King Ecgberht's incursion inside Mercia. I thought it warranted my attention.'

The words are deceptively bland. They mask the problems on the southern border, where no river exists to act as a natural divide, and instead there is the Wansdyke. As I understand it, thanks to Wulfheard long ago, it's similar to Offa's Dyke, which divides Mercia from the Welsh kingdoms. It's a ditch and a slope, the slope facing northwards, as though to stop any from attacking that way. I don't know who built it. Perhaps the giants who constructed Londinium. If not, then Saxons, like me, under the guidance of a king, long ago, in the far reaches of memory and history.

'And you decided to do so without referring the matter to me?'

Again, the words are bland. Both men are trying hard to remove the emotion from the meeting. King Wiglaf feels betrayed. I'm not sure that Lord Coenwulf can feel anything but sorrow for his dead wife and fear for his children.

'I did, my lord king. I knew you were close to Lundenwic. I hoped to contact King Ecgberht, determine his intentions, and seek your advice. It wasn't my objective to act with deception.'

'Hum.' That single word fills the hall. I look up, catching sight of the many eagle-headed shields displayed on the hall's walls above the king's head. Kingsholm has long been the home of Mercia's kings: Coenwulf and then his brother, Coelwulf, both the first of their names. The men who once walked these boards throughout the last thirty winters and warmed themselves before the hearth knew their worth. I still struggle to understand why King Coelwulf relinquished his rights to the kingdom of Mercia. It doesn't help that I know my father, King Beornwulf, was the cause of it.

My father. The thought sends a tremor of fury through my body. If he were here now, I'd kill him. I've no doubts about that. Perhaps Lady Cynehild as well. Both kept their secrets. Of my uncle, I can't decide. Grief for his death makes it impossible for me to hate him, not when, of all those who knew my true identity, he was the one who cared for me the most.

'I've heard a different version of this event.' Of course, I should have expected Ealdorman Sigered to add his voice to the proceedings. The worm is entirely that. I can't be alone in watching the look of smug satisfaction that crosses Queen Cynethryth's face at those words. Ealdorman Sigered is attended upon by his grandson Sigegar, one of Lord Wigmund's allies. Indeed, Lord Wigmund's allies seem to fill the hall: I've seen Ælfred and Hunberht. No doubt there are more of these men and women that I don't recognise who've cast in their lot with Lord Wigmund.

'I'm aware of that, Ealdorman Sigered.' The king isn't to be moved from his interrogation of Lord Coenwulf.

'Then you'll hear me speak,' the old man demands petulantly. He's standing, only just visible above the shoulders of those who sit. He gets smaller each time I see him, shrivelling up like a summer apple during the winter months. No doubt, he'd taste as bitter.

'Indeed, Ealdorman Sigered. Please share what you think you know.' The king speaks with suppressed frustration. I can't believe the ealdorman fails to hear the censure in those words, but he presses on, all the same.

'I've been informed, my lord king, that it was Lord Coenwulf who made overtures of friendship to the Wessex king. Not the other way around. He meant to ally with the Wessex king. His new marriage and the birth of his son had reminded him of all he'd lost.' I perceive a flicker of unease cross King Wiglaf's face. The words of Ealdorman Sigered are eminently feasible. King Wiglaf sees that clearly. If Ealdorman Sigered lies, he's making it as probable as possible.

'And you have witnesses to these accusations?' King Wiglaf speaks quickly before any murmur of unease can begin. My fists clench with outrage, revealing my unsuitability to be in King Wiglaf's position, even if I can claim just as much right to rule as Lord Coenwulf and his sons. Perhaps more right than King Wiglaf, even.

'Alas, only two, my lord king. Lord Coenwulf's men were all murdered by the Viking raiders, as I'm sure you remember.' I feel my forehead crease at those words. All but Edwin, and Edwin is loyal to Lord Coenwulf. He'd never speak out against him. Who then levels the accusation?

'And they'll speak?'

'She will, my lord king, yes. And so will he.' Now my heart stills.

My mouth's too dry to swallow. I fear I know who'll be brought forth by Ealdorman Sigered, and I'm not mistaken. Ealdorman Sigered means to lay the most damning evidence against Lord Coenwulf first. I'd hate him, but his planning earns my grudging respect. The damn bastard has survived for decades at the Mercian court. He means to continue to do so.

Lady Ælflæd. She's the wife of the king's son. She's Lord Coenwulf's sister and the aunt to his two small sons, and yet I notice the smirk of triumph on the queen's face and also on that of her son's. Lord Wigmund is a maggot to grind beneath my boots if only I had the opportunity. But I'm devastated that Lady Ælflæd steps forward to denounce her brother. I thought her better than this. I knew his actions would be an embarrassment, but this is too much.

I eye her. She is, as ever, beautiful. My heart thuds loudly in my chest. At this moment, I know I love her, and yet I loathe her as well. More and more, I'm realising the double-edged blade that love and hatred can be.

She shimmers with the wealth of her position, for all her face remains pale. I'm not convinced she's recovered from the birth of her child yet. She need not have travelled to Kingsholm. And yet she did, as soon as she could. It was her that Wulfheard and Oswy escorted to Kingsholm when I last saw them. Well, her and her husband.

'My lord king. I'll speak of my brother's ambitions to drive a wedge between the ancient realm of the kingdom of the Hwicce and that of the rest of the kingdom of Mercia.'

She talks without inflexion as she stands before all assembled. I can't believe what I'm hearing. She sounds nothing like the girl I once knew who berated her brother for his anger towards me. I've been aware of her at Kingsholm, but only in passing. We've managed to avoid one another. She's been secluded with her sickly son. I've been no company for anyone. Wulfheard and Oswy didn't stay, and neither did they approach me. I'm strangely grateful they left me alone.

Perhaps she now seeks a means of gaining revenge against her brother for such a poor marriage that even the progeny brought forth from it fails to thrive. Perhaps. Maybe she's just been turned by her husband's and his mother's wishes.

I can only see Lady Ælflæd's back, shoulders rigid, where she faces the king. Her brother makes a pitiful figure in comparison, his back to me as well, but his shoulders bent on the chair he's been allowed to sit upon. He quivers with the pressure of the trial. If he could, I imagine he'd whimper, as his son does from far away.

I open my mouth and then snap it shut once more. What can I do? I don't know the truth of the allegations. Yet they taste like ash on my too-dry tongue.

'It is specifics I require,' the king tries. I see his eyes flickering between the two. What must he see? What must he surmise from this unexpected discord between the two? Lady Ælflæd is a mother now. Her child is the future king of Mercia, provided Mercia stands united and not divided against its external enemies and its internal ones. Does King Wiglaf wish to bring Kingsholm and the Hwiccan territory more firmly under his command? And if he does, is that through the persuasions of Lady Ælflæd, or would he rather use other means?

'Then, we'll call on Ealdorman Sigered's remaining witness.' Lady Ælflæd is gracious as she inclines her head to her father by marriage, who is also king. I don't miss the look of gratification on Queen Cynethryth's face at her daughter-by-marriage's words.

I don't recognise the man who stumbles to his feet, bowing before he's upright. I thought I had a fairly good grasp of the men and women who made Kingsholm their home, but this man's unknown. It doesn't help that I'm trying to decide who he is just from his back. His hair is long but not unkempt, brown and uninspiring. There's no grey there. He's broad of shoulder and stands upright with a warrior's arrogance.

'My name's Eadbald.' His words are slow and laboured. 'I was once a member of King Coenwulf's loyal household warriors. Now, I'm not.' The words hide much. Where has he been for the last decade since King Coenwulf was removed from the kingship? Has he been inside Kingsholm?

'And you have an eyewitness account of events?' King Wiglaf's poise is assured. Perhaps I shouldn't be surprised that a man who can make decisions in the heat of battle can contend with family discord being played out before him, while the great and good of Mercia watch on.

I eye some of those others, as they sit, avidly watching these events. I know many of them, but there are some new faces. Where, I consider, have they come from? What stone have they crawled from to seek the attention of the king, or his queen, or his son?

'I can, my lord king, for I was the one who was sent to treat with King Ecgberht.' A gasp of outrage floods the hall, no doubt from the men and women of Kingsholm. I look to Lord Coenwulf's back, but he doesn't indicate how he takes the news. I want him to deny the words. I even seek out Edwin amongst the crowd, but he's no longer visible, having left Lord Coenwulf when he was settled on a chair.

I don't believe the lies. But if Lord Coenwulf doesn't speak out for himself, then everyone else will. Lady Ælflæd, and this man that I don't know, denounce him. And with no one decrying the poisonous rumours, which I'm sure they must be, things can only go poorly for Lord Coenwulf.

'My lord Coenwulf, do you have anything to say against such a statement?'

'I don't, my lord king.' I can't believe Lord Coenwulf will allow himself to be treated in such a way. I think of Lady Cynehild. She'd not have allowed her husband to conspire against Mercia. I'm sure of it. But what can I do? I know nothing.

'Then tell me, Eadbald. Where did you seek out King Ecgberht in Wessex?'

'My lord king,' the man queries.

I nod along with King Wiglaf's determination to get to the truth. Queen Cynethryth's face is mutinous for a moment until she remembers to clear it of her anger at her husband's dogged determination. I notice that she stills her son's hand on the chair beside her. His unease is evident.

'I travelled to Winchester, my lord king.' Eadbald doesn't even hesitate. King Wiglaf is far from done.

'And what did you think of Winchester, my good man?' This could almost be two men talking over ale and not discussing the life of another and whether or not treason was intended. 'Is it like Tamworth? Filled with churches?'

'Of course, it is, my lord king. Many churches in Winchester. All of them raised to our heavenly father.' I see Bishop Æthelweald nod as though he expected as much, despite the people of Wessex being enemies of Mercia.

'And they're dedicated to St Peter, as our church in Tamworth, or St Chad, as our church in Lichfield?'

'My, my lord king,' Eadbald stumbles, and now I fix my gaze on Bishop Æthelweald. He's also seated on the dais but further from the king. Does he know the dedications of the churches in Winchester? Does he know to whom the people there pray? Will he mouth those words to Eadbald? I'm convinced Eadbald has never been to Winchester. I can't imagine any man walking into Wessex-held territory when Mercia and Wessex are acknowledged enemies. They hate one another for the violence of Londonia and, before that, in Tamworth and on the borders with the Welsh. 'I didn't frequent the churches, my lord king.' Eadbald tries to equivocate, but I can hear the uncertainty in his voice. Is this, then, how the king will prove that Eadbald is lying?

'Is there not a church dedicated to the blessed Mary?' Queen Cynethryth interjects too quickly. And I sigh heavily. She's determined in her endeavours to oust Lord Coenwulf.

'Of course, my lady. How could I forget?' Eadbald is all bows and sycophantic. I want nothing more than to pummel him to the ground. My fists are so tightly clenched that I can feel my blunt nails digging into my skin. Damn the bastard and the bitch.

'St Mary's. And it is close to the king's residence?' While Wiglaf shows no outward sign of annoyance at his wife's interference, he persists.

'No, my lord king, far from it. And, of course, I didn't go to speak to the king himself, but rather his ealdorman.'

'And the man's name?'

'Was Ealdorman Wilfhardi.'

I sigh. This is no help. Ealdorman Wilfhardi is a name familiar to all in Mercia and Wessex.

'What terms did you carry?'

'A desire to ally against yourself, my lord king.'

'In what way?' The king's becoming ever more persistent.

'Against you, my lord king. To allow King Ecgberht to reclaim Mercia.'

'On what terms, though? What did Lord Coenwulf demand to turn traitor on his king?'

'Um, my lord king, I don't know. It was written on vellum, and I can't read.'

Once more, the king cannot break through Eadbald's façade. I wouldn't be surprised to discover someone has paid him to state all this. I would be even less surprised to discover that someone was Ealdorman Sigered.

Yet, what frustrates me more is that Lord Coenwulf refuses to speak for himself. Why isn't he defending himself before the king? All can see that King Wiglaf wishes him to dismiss the argument.

'Lord Coenwulf, what did you hope to achieve by allying with the Wessex king?'

'It doesn't matter.' The words are so soft, I only just hear them. I see others turning puzzled expressions, one to another, as though unsure whether they heard correctly.

'Repeat yourself so all can hear,' the bishop demands unctuously.

'It doesn't matter.' The mumble is barely louder than the first time.

I don't take my eyes from King Wiglaf's face. A flurry of emotions can be discerned in the tension of his shoulders and the way his fingers drum over his knees. This isn't what King Wiglaf wishes to hear. Far from it.

'Lord Coenwulf, I give you the opportunity to defend yourself for the final time. As it stands, I'll be left with no choice but to banish you from your home and Mercia. You'll be cast out if you've committed treason against the Mercian kingdom and the Mercian people.'

Silence thrums through the hall. I detect the resignation in King Wiglaf's posture. This isn't what he wanted to happen. Indeed, none thought it would be necessary, as Wulfheard argued with me when we last met. The king might have spoken of the need to separate the outcome from the intentions in his case, but all feel sympathy towards Lord Coenwulf. All, it seems, apart from the queen, her son, Ealdorman Sigered and Lord Coenwulf's own sister.

I feel compassion for Lord Coenwulf. He was tricked, and he was stolen away. Lady Cynehild, no matter how I hate her behaviour towards me, was a good, loyal Mercian. Her husband wouldn't have committed treason. She would never have asked us to retrieve him from the Viking raiders on the Isle of Sheppey if that had been his intention. It would have been better for him to die there than to face this. I want the king to be kind to Lord Coenwulf. But the poisonous words of Lady Ælflæd, the political astuteness of the queen and the desire of Ealdorman Sigered to please his ally, the queen, mean that the king has lost that option, especially as Lord Coenwulf won't defend himself, as he should.

Perhaps, if Ealdorman Ælfstan was here, or even others of the ealdormen, the king would have some support. But Ælfstan's been forced to return to his ealdordom of the Magonsæte, due to rumbles from the Welsh, while Tidwulf is in Lundenwic, and Muca is on the borderlands with the kingdom of the East Angles. If I didn't know better, I'd see the queen's hand in that as well. She's isolated Lord Coenwulf.

'Then my decision is this. As is the way of our people, you'll be banished from Mercia for a full seven winters. If, after that time, you still wish to return, you may petition me, provided no further crimes of treason have been uncovered. In your absence, Lady Ælflæd will command Kingsholm and your younger sister, Lady Cynewise.'

'My lord king.' Even now, Lord Coenwulf doesn't attempt to deny the sentence. Once more, the cry of a distressed child rings through the air. The queen leans towards her husband. I see him shake his head at whatever she says, but her words are persistent, as are those of her son. Indeed, Lady Ælflæd rushes forward to offer her support for the queen and her husband, as does another man, one I don't recognise but who seems to be high in the king's favour. Who is he? Why don't I know who he is? Dread grows in my belly, worse than anything I've ever felt.

And then the king breathes deeply and slowly exhales, somehow making sense of those who now bend his ear, demanding something else as punishment for Lord Coenwulf.

'My lord, as an assurance that you'll not enter into negotiations with the enemies of Mercia, and on the advice of Queen Cynethryth, my son and his wife, and Lord Beorhtwulf, your sons will remain behind to act as surety for your good behaviour.' It seems I know the man's name now, but whom he is, I still don't know. Not that I don't miss the similarity of his name to that of my father's. I would look at him further, determine if he might be somehow related to him, but instead, my heart constricts. Not that it's anything compared to the animal roar of outrage from Lord Coenwulf. I thought him dead inside, but that's not the case in the matter of his sons. Not at all.

4

'I'll care for your sons.' Lady Ælflæd's voice lacks all sincerity as I listen – when I shouldn't – to the conversation between her and her brother.

The king's gone, alongside his entourage, swept back to Tamworth with the first flakes of snow to fall this winter. His parting words were that Lord Coenwulf could recover until better weather. But then he'd be expected to be gone, per the terms of the king's sentencing of the traitorous fool.

'You will not. You have your son, and your ambitions are rampant. I want only my sons.' Lord Coenwulf's voice is a howl of agony. His physical wounds are healing. His mind isn't. I know that Theodore and Gaya grew increasingly worried about him while they lingered, to care for his sons and him. They should have returned to Ealdorman Tidwulf, but like me, they played dumb to the messengers sent to seek them out, until it was impossible to ignore those demands and the command of Lady Ælflæd herself.

Lord Coenwulf isn't the man he used to be. I fear for him as well, even more now there's only me here who thinks kindly of him.

'My son, Wigstan, will need supporters when he's old enough to rule. What better than his cousins?'

'No, you conniving bitch.' The malice is impossible to ignore, and I have some sympathy when Lady Ælflæd hisses in response.

'I'm no bitch,' she counters. 'I know the worth of my blood, and I'll use it.'

I'm unsure if it's her brother's erratic behaviour which makes her act as she does, or if she's truly changed.

'You've let the queen into your thoughts, haven't you? Don't deny it. Only from someone as callous as her would such a statement be considered acceptable. You spoke against me, and you lied when you did so. Why, sister, why?' It's clear that Lord Coenwulf has made a decision about his sister. I want to deny his words, but her next comment assures me he's no doubt correct.

'You're no man,' Lady Ælflæd hoots. 'And more, your sons will be my creatures when you're gone. They'll not know you, should you ever be allowed to return. They'll think of me as their mother and my husband as their father. You'll be nothing to them.'

'They'll be coming with me.' Lord Coenwulf's cry is anguished. His hatred has evaporated in the wake of his desperation.

'The king, the queen, my husband and Lord Beorhtwulf, says they won't be, and he has men here to ensure your compliance with that order. There's no one to help you, brother, especially not me. Kingsholm's mine. From here, my son will one day rule.'

'Your son must survive to rule first,' Coenwulf counters. I wince at that harsh retort, but it is the truth. The child, Wigstan, isn't strong. Compared to the shrieks of Coelwulf and his mighty lungs, Wigstan is a wounded lamb, barely able to bleat. Yet Lady Ælflæd has ejected Gaya and Theodore from Kingsholm. She didn't take kindly to their attempts to help. I said my farewells to them, and they smiled and embraced me. Theodore's parting words continue to resonate with me. 'This isn't your fault, young Icel,' he assured me, Gaya nodding along. The wisdom in their eyes tore at me, and yet I couldn't agree with them. I am oath-sworn. I am bound to the children.

'My son will thrive once this blasted cold weather has ended. Unless, brother dearest, that's a threat.'

'No threat, sister. I've heard your exhortations to God. I've heard your promises. Perhaps, if you wanted a son who would be strong and able to lead as his grandfather does, and his other grandfather did, you should have found someone less wormlike to take to your bed.'

The sharp slap of skin on skin assures me that Lady Ælflæd has taken her revenge on her brother for such words. But the slap doesn't bring the conversation to an end. Lord Coenwulf hasn't finished yet.

'Lord Beorhtwulf is no friend of yours,' he adds, the bitterness of the words easy to hear. 'You have more to fear than just the threat from my sons.'

'Lord Beorhtwulf is a man of honour. A friend to my husband.'

'Lord Beorhtwulf has his eyes on the kingship, just as much as your husband does.' I'm startled to hear this. 'And, he has the claim to it as well.'

'He is no ætheling?' Lady Ælflæd retorts. I can imagine the haughty expression on her face.

'Neither was your husband's father. Think on that, sister, dearest.'

I hurry away from the side of the hall, eager to not be caught creeping and listening once more. While few within Kingsholm question my presence, Lady Ælflæd is one of those that does. I'm as eager to avoid her now as I was once eager to be close to her.

Time has made strangers out of both of us. She no longer speaks to me or offers a confidence. She's the wife to the king's heir. The mother of the king's heir, heir. And she knows it. We move around one another. I'm overly alert to her presence. I am overly alert to staying away from her. I don't wish to be forcibly removed from Kingsholm, as Gaya and Theodore were.

Hastily, I scamper through the frozen puddles towards the dubious shelter of the stable. Inside, I can see the heated breath of horses and other men as well. In one of the empty stalls, a collection of warriors, oath-sworn to Lord Wigmund, play games of chance, fight and drink. It upsets the horses, but they won't be told.

I move aside, keen to avoid them, only to collide with Edwin.

'Icel.' His greeting is far from warm, but we're almost friends once more. Almost.

'Edwin, it's a bitter day,' I respond quickly. If I can conclude our conversation and sneak from the stables, then the men of Lord Wigmund won't see me. But it's a futile effort, and with a soft sigh, I hear the movement of wood on wood, and two heads appear above the stable door.

'Ah, Icel, we didn't hear you come in,' one of the men calls. He's angular and bright of cheek, a thick, bushy moustache almost half inside his wide, flat nose. I know why his nose is so flat. He likes to fight, does Eadweard. He relishes the cut and thrust of a good bare-knuckle battle. Why, I don't know. It's not as though he's good at such fights. Perhaps he was when a young man, but those days are long behind him. I think him older than Wulfheard now.

Edwin mouths 'sorry' to me, but it's not his fault. I should have thought more before coming this way. Eadweard and his foul-mouthed collection of friends are usually found here, banished from the hall by Lady Ælflæd, although Lord Wigmund keeps them close.

'Young Icel,' his comrade, Wulfred, echoes, as so often happens with the pair. It's almost as though they're one person, but with two heads – as I've heard is possible. Although their bodies are entirely opposite. Wulfred is short and wiry, lacking all hair, none on his head, none on his face. He doesn't even need to shave.

'You said today would be the day you'd join us,' Eadweard taunts. I've been determined to avoid this collection of warriors. Without my one-time friends at my back – Wulfheard, Oswy and Ealdorman Ælfstan – I've no desire to come up against these six men. All of them are dirty fighters, and it wouldn't bother me so much if they were good at it, but they're poor warriors, resorting to underhand tactics repeatedly to achieve the outcome they want. Wulfred isn't above tripping anyone who almost overpowers Eadweard. Eadweard is happy to thump an enemy of Wulfred's across the back if it appears he won't win the day.

'I must see to my horses,' I counter quickly. It's not a lie.

'But we've no one to fight, young Icel. And we'd like to fight you,' Eadweard whines, his tongue poking at some mark on his face. No doubt, he's cut himself shaving or has a bruise from an earlier fight. 'Edwin can help you, and you can join us then?' Eadweard suggests.

'Perhaps,' is my noncommittal response. I don't want to have anything to do with these men. I beckon to Edwin to join me and walk away, ignoring the catcalls and shouts of derision. I certainly don't respond to the suggestion that I'm too scared to fight Eadweard. I know how this small group conducts itself. And I intend to stay as far away from them as possible.

'Sorry,' Edwin huffs. He still suffers from the wounds he gained on the Isle of Sheppey. His left arm has yet to recover its strength, and his face is no longer smooth and free from scars.

'It's not your fault. I should have gone the other way.' I'm angry at myself, and my tone's short, even to my ears. 'Sorry, Edwin. I was... well, I was listening where I shouldn't have been.'

'Lady Ælflæd?' he questions, and I nod unhappily.

I can no sooner explain what's happened to her since we last met than I can wake the dead. She's a mystery to me, and her brother is right to term her a bitch, for that's what she's become. Or so it seems. I keep trying to excuse her actions, but she snaps at all and sundry. She rules Kingsholm like a vixen, and no one can do right for her. It'll be better when she's gone, only I don't foresee that happening anytime soon. The only person to whom she shows any care is her young son, Wigstan, and he's not appreciative of her gestures. She and her husband might be of one mind with regard to Lord Coenwulf's punishment, but I've never seen a tender look pass between them. I think she hates him as well.

'I hope she becomes a kinder mistress,' Edwin murmurs. I've heard her berate him for his weaknesses since the events that saw him rescue her brother. She has no regard for Edwin, even if her brother would be dead without him. Perhaps that would have made everything easier for her. Maybe that's why she's so evil-tongued towards the wounded warrior.

'I don't see it. I think the queen has her fangs into Lady Ælflæd. She acts with the same regard for man, woman and child as the queen.' I can't forget what I've heard between her and her brother. Does her temper mask her fear, or is she truly so focused on holding Kingsholm that she's angry with her brother for his antics? As to her young sister, Lady Cynewise. I'm well aware that she does her best to stay away from her older sister. Lady Ælflæd wishes to ensure her position by making her young sister a mirror image of her, but Lady Cynewise refuses to conform. Their arguments have also become legendary. All the same, I admire Cynewise. I've heard her inform her sister that she's a twisted shrew. The slap from that encounter was visible on Cynewise's young face for nearly ten days.

Eagerly, I reach up and run my hand along Brute's black neck. He bucks his head at my touch but quickly settles. Beside him, Wine dozes in her stable, head bowed, where she leans against the wooden struts of the building. A welcome grin touches my cheeks to see her in such a way. At least she's comfortable here. She might be the only one of us.

'What will you do?' Edwin has been asking me this for the last few weeks, ever since I made it clear I'd be staying at Kingsholm with Lord Coenwulf.

'I'll know when the time comes,' I murmur. 'What will you do?'

'I'm oath-sworn to Lord Coenwulf. I must escort him.'

'But where will he go? How will he keep you?'

'It doesn't matter. He's my lord, not Lady Ælflæd. There are few enough of his warriors left now. If I don't go with him, he'll be almost unaccompanied.'

I chew my lip as I reach for a brush to begin teasing the knots from Brute's mane. How he manages to become so unruly is beyond me. 'Lady Ælflæd will see him to the River Severn, and if there's no ship for him there, she'll force him into the water,' I argue, although I'd rather not think of her as capable of such.

'There'll be a ship. Its destination will be impossible to determine.'

'You sound so sure of this. Has Lord Coenwulf given you any assurances? Has he even spoken of it?'

'No.' Edwin hangs his head with the admission. 'He won't speak of when he must be parted from his sons.'

His sons. And this is the crux of my problem. I can't leave those children's side. When Lord Coenwulf is gone, no one will care for them. I'll be the person that does.

'And what of Eadburg?' Edwin and Eadburg have an understanding. She was overjoyed to see him returned to Kingsholm, and yet events since then have made it difficult for them.

'She can't come with me.' Edwin sounds mournful.

'I know that. That's what I'm asking. You tell me you love her, yet you'll leave her.'

'I'll have no choice, Icel. You know that. Her place is here, with her mother, the young lord's wet nurse. She won't leave her, just as you won't leave the children.' Edwin's words are reasoned and yet I fear for both of them when they're parted.

I sigh, scattering a cloud of dust released from Brute's coat. Coughing aside the sweet smell, I grimace all the same.

'I still believe you should convince her to go with you,' I try again.

'She won't leave her mother. She's adamant that seven years will pass quickly, and she'll wait for me.'

I shake my head. I know the truth of that, and Edwin's a fool if he believes it. Seven years is an eternity. In seven years, I've come from a boy to a man. Who knows what other changes will overcome me in the next seven years?

'You'll both find love elsewhere then,' I counter aggressively.

'No, we won't.' Edwin's lower lip juts in determination. 'We're in love and will remain true to one another. And anyway, we're talking about you, not me.'

'My place is with Lady Cynehild's sons. She made me swear to that.'

'But that means you must leave Ealdorman Ælfstan's warrior band and remain here with Lady Ælflæd.'

'I've already left it. And I'm not oath-sworn to him, but only to the king.'

'And the king will appreciate you playing nursemaid to the sons of his enemy?' Edwin taunts, eyebrows high.

I managed to evade the king when he was at Kingsholm. I'm hoping thoughts of me are far from his mind. I shake my head. 'No, the king won't appreciate it. But I don't believe the king truly wished to banish Lord Coenwulf. He tried hard to undermine the words of Eadbald and Lady Ælflæd. But Lord Coenwulf wouldn't help himself.' As I speak, I realise I'm gasping, the words flooding from me in a rush. I'm angry at Lord Coenwulf. I knew him when he was a man bowed low with grief, but now he has his sons. He should be prepared to fight for them. He should have told the king that he'd only depart with his children and not leave them behind instead of trying to bend his sister to his will now.

'Maybe,' Edwin admits with a long sigh. 'But the king made his pronouncement. Admittedly, he was coerced by his wife, son, Lady Ælflæd and that Lord Beorhtwulf, whomever he is.'

I'm pleased Edwin doesn't know whom Lord Beorhtwulf is, but it seems that no one else knows whom he is either. I've been unable to find out any more about him. That perplexes me, when I allow myself to think about it.

'Now we must follow those orders or face worse,' he continues. Edwin has evidently reconciled himself to what must happen, but I haven't. I realise that. I want something to occur to ensure Lord Coenwulf can remain with his sons. If that happens, it'll release me from my oath, I hope, for now.

'We must live with the consequences of our actions,' I confirm, wincing at the raucous sound of the warriors in the other half of the stables. If I'm to remain in Kingsholm, I'll need to do something about them, but do I need to ally with them? Perhaps it would be better to show them what sort of warrior I am. Maybe then they might leave me alone. But that's not to be done today. Today, I'll tend to my horses and consider the words of Lady Ælflæd.

I still can't believe how much she's changed. She's become twisted and warped. Is this, I think, what happens to women who marry into the ruling family of Mercia? Certainly, Lady Cynehild, when the wife of King Beornwulf, was far from kind to me. Did her ambition make her bitter? If so, then could I do with separating Lady Ælflæd from the grip of her husband and his mother? If not, she'll never become the girl I once knew, whose horse I once healed, and who spoke to her brother of me and occasioned an apology from him. She'll become as ambitious as the queen, if she hasn't done so already. Her behaviour towards her young sister is already unacceptable.

But Lady Ælflæd and I were children then, untried in the way of kingdoms and politics. Perhaps we've simply grown into the man and woman we were always destined to be – the thought is far from comforting.

5

'Icel.' I turn at the sound of my name, squinting into the fog behind me. It's not a good day to be riding, but I needed to escape the confines of Kingsholm. Everywhere I look is someone whose loyalty I suspect.

'Edwin.' I squint into the whiteness of the cold cloud, not sure if he called me or someone else did. The fog distorts all sound, and I don't even know where he's hailing me from.

'Icel.' The word once more, even though I've not moved. Beneath me, Brute breaths evenly. We've hardly been for a gallop, but instead a careful trot through the shockingly familiar landscape turned strangely haunted, with blackened twigs and branches threatening to pull my cloak free from my head. The air is thick with dampness, and Brute's black and white coat is drenched.

'I'm here,' I call, wincing when my words echo too loudly. I toy with gripping my eagle-headed seax, but here, so close to Kingsholm and with someone calling my name, I must think it's an ally.

Only then, I realise it isn't, as Eadweard and his cronies emerge out of the gloom.

'Ah, there you are,' Eadweard announces, as though he's found treasure. A gleam lights his eyes.

Now I wish I'd allowed Edwin to accompany me, although I denied him, knowing that it still pains him to ride. I'm alone, out here, with Eadweard, Wulfred, Forthgar, Deremann, Mergeat and the other fool whose name I don't know. Whatever's about to happen between us has been in the planning for some time. I've avoided the gang's reach for much of the winter. It was going to end, eventually.

'We thought to join you,' he calls, his voice rich with disdain. 'Fellow warriors should ride together when their winter captivity becomes too much.' He smirks, but his flat nose is bent once more. He's been fighting with anyone who'll try their luck against him. I don't want that person to be me, but if I must, then I must. I'm not sure I'll be able to overpower him, but I'm content to try.

'Then you're welcome. I plan on riding to the river and back again.'

The river isn't far from Kingsholm, but I'm taking a long route, heading towards Gloucester itself, before doubling back on myself. I wanted some solitude, but I'm not to get it.

'Then we should race.' Wulfred chuckles.

I eye him, noticing how water drips from his nose and down onto his chest. It might start to rain soon, and then the fog will be banished.

'It's too dangerous,' I caution. I'll not risk Brute on some stupid game.

'Chicken,' Wulfred whispers.

'If you like,' I counter, not swayed by such a disparaging term, encouraging Brute onwards at our steady pace, overly aware of the men close to my back. I lick my lips, tasting the fog's moisture and the thin line of sweat beading in my black moustache. I shouldn't have called out to these men. I should have remained hidden from them.

'No, no, Wulfred, Icel's correct. It's too dangerous. A gentle trot, nothing more. To the River Severn and back to Kingsholm. It sounds ideal.' Eadweard's delight makes me worry once more. Close to the river, and with the fog as thick as it is, no one will see if we descend into a fight. They won't come looking for me if the six should decide to overpower me. Only Edwin would even notice my disappearance – well, perhaps he and Eadburg, the woman he loves and the daughter of the woman who acts as wet nurse to the children at Kingsholm. They'd miss my unwelcome, loitering presence.

Indeed, it's because of them that I'm here. Eadburg's mother banished me from the children, accusing me of upsetting them with my stink and clank of iron. I didn't argue with her. The children upset me as well, with their constant demands and frailty. Should someone think to end their life, it wouldn't take much. That chafes at me every day. I swore to protect the children. And I must. But I sense betrayal everywhere. I only left because Edwin was there with Eadburg. He might still be weak, but he can stab with his seax. The two are love-struck, and that turns my stomach as well, and I'm aware jealousy is the cause.

I listen to the jangle of harnesses as the other horses follow Brute. Brute, head outstretched, lacks all concern. His gait is smooth, moving at a pace that allows him to ensure the placement of his hooves on the slick ground. I swallow, tasting the saltiness of my sweat. The silence between us grows, and it's far from comfortable.

'They say you fought at Lundenwic,' Eadweard calls from atop his grey stallion. The animal's light-footed despite its bulk. If it came to a race, I don't believe it would stand a chance of winning against Brute. But that's not going to happen. Not today.

'I did, yes, and inside Londinium.' I thought all knew of my battle antics, but perhaps not. I thought all knew of my endeavours for the king, but that must be my conceit. I didn't realise I had any until now. 'Were you there?' I think to ask. They must have been, surely.

'No, we were in Tamworth, protecting the queen and Lord Wigmund.'

Ah, of course, they're the sworn men of Lord Wigmund. Why would they have been close to the threat of actual violence? I consider them once more. Are they fierce warriors, or do they just look the part?

'They also said you healed some bastard Wessex warriors,' Wulfred continues, the edge to his voice impossible to ignore.

'I did, yes, they helped me, and I helped them. Not that it matters. They're all dead now.'

'And against the Viking raiders in the kingdom of the East Angles? You ensured Peterborough remained in the hands of the king?'

I sigh softly, hoping they don't hear me. 'I did, yes. With Ealdorman Ælfstan and his men.' Perhaps it would have been better had Uor not spoken his words to the scop song in praise of my antics.

'And then you went to the Isle of Sheppey to retrieve a traitor, leaving the River Thames open to attack from the enemy?' This comes from Eadweard once more, and now anger infuses his words.

'I did, yes. I retrieved Lord Coenwulf at the request of Lady Cynehild.'

'What a conniving cow she was,' one of the other men calls, Deremann I think, and the others chuckle darkly. The grip on my reins stiffens. I don't like to hear others call the dead woman names even if I think it on a daily basis. 'And that wasn't on the orders of the king?'

'No, it wasn't,' I confirm, gently guiding Brute with my knees. Ahead, I can hear sounds coming from inside Gloucester. I can't see the settlement, but I relax at knowing I'm not alone out here with these six men. I might even make an excuse to go inside the settlement. Perhaps it's a market day despite the fog and gloom?

'And now the king is keen for you to know the full fury of his wrath.'

'The king is, is he?' I counter, turning to observe the leering glower on Eadweard's face but without making it too obvious that I distrust him.

'He is, yes, you little shit.' Before I can react, someone lunges at me. I find myself scrabbling for my reins but knowing I'll fall all the same. The ground veers upwards at me as I land, face down, on the damp grass, coughing aside the force of the impact, even while someone pummels my back.

I wince at the impacts. I should have donned my byrnie, but I didn't. I have my cloak and my weapons belt, but nothing else. No shield. No helm. I thought to use the weather as my protection. And these men mean to batter me. I hear the tread of others dismounting and coming to join the fight. I try and force myself upwards, but Wulfred, for all his slight build, has pinned me to the ground with his legs. Every time I think to catch a deep breath, he thrusts his fists, in tight formation, one-two, one-two, into my back.

I'll be black and blue tomorrow. Should I live until then.

I sense Brute's unease as he veers backwards and then forwards while one of the men tries to take his reins, only I'm still holding them in one hand. I need him to run away. Perhaps even summon help from Kingsholm. With effort, I unclench my left fist and turn my body to allow the leather straps to come free with Brute's actions.

'Go,' I huff, while it feels as though all six men beat me. I see Brute's hooves move out of sight at a quick trot and then consider my enemy.

We're all men of Mercia, but we're not all allies. I replay Eadweard's words to me. This, then, is at the command of Lord Wigmund, or so I assume. I can't genuinely imagine the king setting thugs on me, not when he owes his life to me.

With supreme effort, I suck in a deep breath and then expel it as I force myself to roll free from Wulfred, who still traps me on my back, the damp grass quickly reaching my skin. But, with my hands free, I meet his punches with some of my own, catching sight of the smirking face of Eadweard. I want to rip that expression from his face, lips and all if need be.

When Wulfred deflates before me, thanks to a punishing blow to his nose, I jettison him from my body and surge upwards. Crouching, Eadweard rounds on me, still smirking but with his eyebrows furrowed now. He didn't expect me to put up much of a fight, despite the stories he's heard of me. He kicks out, aiming for my cock and stones, and I just manage to close my legs and turn aside from his attack. With my right fist, I smack his nose. It's hard to miss such a target, and he howls with pain, blood pouring over his thick moustache and down his chest.

But Wulfred's back on his feet, and he leaps at me from behind, his arms circling my neck and pulling me backwards. We land in a crack of bones, and I'm on the bloody ground again. Well, I nearly am – Wulfred's beneath me. I can feel him growing still. Perhaps the damn arse has knocked himself on a stone. Perhaps he's just winded.

Two more of the men come at me. Æthelbald's younger than the others, perhaps the same number of winters to his name as me. He swings with deliberation, economical with his movements, as he reaches down to grab me by the shoulders and haul me upwards. It's my turn to kick out, trying to land a blow on the man whose name I don't know. His nose drips with a stinking cold, and its bright red illuminates him better than any brand. But he skips out of my snaking leg and hooks his own around mine, preventing me from standing.

Eadweard joins them, and it's all I can do to pull my arms around my head and protect it, curling around the hurt of my belly.

Six men against one. Well, five, for I do see when I open my eyes that Wulfred is silent on the ground. If he's dead, this will go very badly. I hope he lives. I don't want to be held accountable for protecting myself from six of my fellow warriors when I was doing little more than taking a ride out on a fog-shrouded day.

My thoughts turn inwards, the pain from the blows becoming less and less, and at some point I lose awareness of where I am, the view around me turning black.

When I wake, everything aches. I'm lying on my back, looking upwards at the still fog-shrouded sky. I don't know how long I've been unaware, but I hear the sound of something close by and reach for my seax blade on my weapons belt, only to feel a thousand different hurts and, worse, to realise my seax isn't there.

A nose comes into view, a questing tongue as well, and I sigh. It's Brute, returned to me. I turn and see that I'm alone. I spare a thought for Wulfred, hoping he still breathes. But it doesn't help me. Everything aches, I can only see a little out of my left eye, and it hurts even to raise my hand to run it over the swelling. My lips are thick and coated with something that I think must be blood.

'Arse,' I exclaim, but even that hurts. 'How long have I been here?' I ask Brute, but get no response. He doesn't lick me any more but watches me from along his long nose, a look of confusion in his familiar eyes. 'Did they hurt you?' I exhale, and when he doesn't move, I take it to mean he escaped as I intended but has since come back to find me. If he thinks I'm going to be able to leap into his saddle and take him back to a warm stable and food, then he's very much mistaken.

I shiver, the cold seeping into my bones and beneath my cloak, drenched from the grasses upon which I lie. It could be worse. I could be on the road, in the gutter, or even lying on a pile of horse-shit. I sniff, but my nose is blocked, and instead a wracking cough floods my body. I'm forced to sit upright, despite the pain, or choke on whatever makes me cough.

'Ahhh,' I growl when I can manage words again. Tears drip from my eyes, unbidden, and I lick them from my swollen lips. But the thought of standing is beyond me. I look down at myself, seeing my swollen nose beneath my eyes, and notice the rips on my tunic. My cloak only remains over half of my body. No wonder I'm so damn cold. I try to pull it tighter, but my arms refuse the request, and all I accomplish is to make myself pant, which makes my chest hurt.

'Arse,' I exclaim again, closing my eyes and almost wishing the voice of Wulfheard would appear from the fog. But it won't. He's far from here, close to the king, with Ealdorman Ælfstan. I've made it clear that I want nothing more to do with them. Yet I'd welcome them now. They'd capture Eadweard and his thug friends and see they were punished for what they've done to me. If I return to Kingsholm, or rather, when I do, I'll find nothing but recrimination. No doubt, they'll blame me for what's happened between us. Is my reputation so immense that people will believe I started a fight with six men and expected to triumph?

Not that I have a choice. I've vowed to protect the children of Lady Cynehild, and I will do so. It won't be long until the weather is good enough that Lord Coenwulf must leave his family holdings and begin his seven winters of exile. How he'll cope, I've no idea. He adores his children. He spends more time with them than any other father would do, rarely letting them out of sight. I consider how much he suspects his sister might imperil his children, or whether it was just angry words exchanged between the two. I know that I fear for them. And not just from the queen and Lady Cynehild. There are others. I'm still wary of Lord Beorhtwulf, and even of Lord Wigmund's men. If they can beat me as badly, what could they do to two small children?

Reaching up, wincing at the same time, I reach for the small silver eagle sigil that my uncle bid me return to Lady Cynehild, and which she then gave to me.

It speaks of my heritage as a member of the select few who could rightfully claim the kingdom of Mercia as theirs to rule. Why I wear it, I don't know. I should bury and hide it so no one can suspect my true identity. Yet I think to one day give it to the sons of Lady Cynehild. I think it should be theirs, not mine. But they're mere babes. What if something does befall them? Would that enable me to pursue my claim?

I shake my head. Dismiss the thought. I don't want to be a king. I don't even want to know that I could be king. I close my eyes again, determined to blot out the pain in my body and the hurt in my mind.

Do I wish my uncle had told me? Do I wish that my father had claimed me? If he had, would I have led a life like Lord Wigmund? Pampered and adored by his mother. Kept safe from any hurt or ill that might befall him. Held back from fighting to keep Mercia safe.

I'm denying all that only, unbidden, a stray thought threads into my mind. If I'd been named as an ætheling, throne-worthy, then perhaps I would have been wed to Lady Ælflæd, and not Lord Wigmund. And if that had happened, she'd never have become the conniving, politically astute woman she is now. Perhaps, we might even have been like Edwin and Eadburg.

Once more, a stray tear falls from my closed eye. I don't want to know this. I want to return to when my commitments were much easier. All I needed to do was protect Mercia from her enemies with my sword and seax and nothing else.

How I wish that were all I need to do now.

6

'Bloody hell. What happened to you?' The voice of Cuthwalh on the gate at Kingsholm startles me awake. It's darker than pitch, and I've hardly been aware of Brute's steady hoof falls. If not for him, I'd never have made it here. It took until night had fallen for me to get myself into the saddle. I don't know how long it'll take me to dismount.

'Viking raiders or Wessex scum?' The other man demands, his eyes peering into the darkness as he hastens to close the gate after Brute has walked inside the settlement.

'Just some friendly Mercians,' I wince through my thick lip and aching body.

I feel every single thump and whack that was laid on me.

With the gate shut behind him, Cuthwahl comes closer to me, a brand in his hand making me cringe away from the bright flames.

'Um, so you were involved with those damn fools then, were you?'

'They're here?'

'Aye, came back before noon. They didn't say much. One of them was slumped in his saddle, but he's awake now. You took on all six of them?' I eye the other man. Cuthwalh is about my age, no more and no less. He's newly come to the service of Lord Coenwulf, since so many of his men were killed by the Viking raiders who took him to the Isle of Sheppey. He's much broader than I am, yet I've watched him with the other warriors. He'll make a good fighter one day. 'They were asked what happened to them, but they were wary about it – passed it off as a little fight with a drunk man in the tavern in Gloucester. I can see why. Do you need help?' He's following me to the stable, and as Brute slows to a stop, aware I can't ride him beneath the low-hanging doorway, Cuthwalh must realise this isn't going to be easy.

I don't want to ask for help, but it's that or sit here all night, getting even colder than I already am.

'Yes, if you could,' I grudgingly admit. 'Even if it's just to keep me on my feet when I slide down Brute's side.'

'Wait a moment.' Hastily, Cuthwalh finds a place to put the brand so that we still have enough light to see by, and then he braces himself close to my leg and Brute. 'When you're ready,' he calls. I take a deep breath, prepare myself for the agony of what's about to happen, and try to force my right leg over the back of Brute's saddle.

It's torture. My chest and leg hurt, and sweat beads down my forehead before I'm even halfway there. Damn, they beat me badly.

'Take your time.' Cuthwalh's tone is patient and filled with understanding. 'Will you demand justice from them?' he continues. My leg still hasn't made it to where it needs to be. I'm considering just falling to the ground, arse first. It's got to hurt less than trying to dismount as usual. Beneath me, Brute's patient, but I'm not.

'Ow,' I huff through tight cheeks, blowing them wide with effort. Finally, my leg comes free and, as I feared, I tumble to the ground, my left leg just about straight, my right leg still far from where it should be. If not for Cuthwalh, I'd be on my arse. But his strong arms keep me upright, and with Brute to the other side, I finally stand, the pain too great to allow me to do more than just breathe for a long moment.

Cuthwalh steps aside slightly when he trusts me to stay upright. I finally hobble towards him, away from Brute. My face is sheeted in perspiration, my legs are trembling, my lips are wobbling with pain, and my chest is so tight it hurts to take even the smallest breaths.

'My thanks,' I eventually manage.

'Here, give me the beast, and I'll take him into the stable. You need to get into the hall, warm up and rest.' I open my mouth to argue with Cuthwalh, but Brute's already moving away, the promise of hay and warmth making him surprisingly placid.

'My thanks,' I wheeze again, my eyes on the hall. Eadweard, Wulfred and the rest of their group of men will be inside. They clearly never intended to tell anyone of what happened between us. Did they hope they'd left me for dead? Did they attack me for the fun of it, or did they, as Eadweard intimated, do so on the orders of the king, or rather, Lord Wigmund? The thought makes me consider Cuthwalh's words. Should I seek justice? I could demand that Lord Coenwulf finds against them, but of course, Lord Coenwulf is unlikely to care, and the men aren't answerable to him, anyway. They owe their oaths to Lord Wigmund, who still makes his home at Kingsholm, ostentatiously, to ensure that Lord Coenwulf doesn't misbehave before he's banished. But all know it's more that, here, Lord Wigmund is far from Tamworth and can imagine he rules as king.

Laboriously, I make my way to the hall, where the door guard, Osmod, allows me entry.

'My thanks,' I whisper. And he grimaces at seeing the state I'm in.

'I'd say the other bastard looks worse, but I'd be lying,' he murmurs, only to quickly stifle a yawn.

'Aye, well. I didn't put up much of a fight in the end.'

'Over there,' and he points to the banked hearth. I'm grateful to see a space for my weary head. My position here is far from regular. I've no dwelling to call my own. I'm not one of Lord Coenwulf's warriors, so I have no place in his bunkhouse either. But I'm not alone in sleeping in the hall, especially not at this time of year, when the hearth is kept burning all day and night long.

Wincing but trying not to shriek with my movements, I limp to the spot and then appreciate I have another problem. It's all but impossible for me to get down on the ground with the agony I'm in. Just like dismounting, this will be excruciating and almost undoable. Gritting my teeth, aware that I don't wish to wake everyone from snoring, I stretch my right leg out before me, my arms reaching for the wooden boards beneath me. And still, they reach. Normally, it would be easy to tumble to the floor, wrap my cloak around me, use another to cushion my head and be asleep in no time. But tonight, I'm sweating and shivering by the time I'm finally prone. Every ache and sting makes itself felt all over again.

I can't even wrap my cloak around me, and it remains bunched beneath my back. I'd fight it, but I can't. Instead, and as uncomfortable as I am, I close my eyes and welcome the warmth. Tomorrow will be soon enough to contend with all my injuries.

Somewhere close by, a child's fretful cry splits the air. I nod in sympathy, reminded again of why I'm enduring this. The child needs me. Of that, I'm sure.

I'm woken by a boot kicking my chest. Pain stabs down towards my legs, and bile rises in my throat. I only just manage to turn aside, to stop the vomit from staining my ripped shirt.

'What are you doing here?'

I meet the angry eyes of Eadweard. From outside, the noise of the settlement waking is easy to hear, the cry of the disturbed chickens, the cockerel with his loud call, the banging of the blacksmith and the humming of the monks. I want to close my eyes and sleep, but I don't trust Eadweard. He's a nasty piece of work, as he showed yesterday.

'I thought we made it clear you weren't welcome here,' Eadweard continues, bending low so no one else can hear the conversation. 'You almost killed Wulfred.' My eyes flicker to my eagle-headed seax, on his weapons belt. He shouldn't be wearing it in Lord Coenwulf's hall. He shouldn't have it at all.

'It was nothing to do with me. He should look where he punches,' I counter, wishing my chest wasn't so tight and I could get up without looking like an aged man. My bruises are making themselves felt. My tongue feels like it's been dipped in dandelion flowers, fuzzy and unwieldy.

'You little turd.' Eadweard launches himself at me, but somehow I manage to scamper away from him, just pulling my legs clear from his unwarranted attack.

'Lads,' a ripe voice calls from the door. I catch the eye of another of the new Kingsholm warriors striding towards us, I think his name is Tatberht, with big meaty fists and a face that looks set to punch and ask questions later. 'This is the lord's hall, not a fighting den,' he shouts. I can feel the eyes of everyone on us, although I can't see that much from my place on the wooden floorboards.

Eadweard stands abruptly, forcing himself upright from where he's almost fallen to the floor. His face is a rictus of fury.

'He almost killed Wulfred yesterday,' Eadweard hollers at the gate warden.

'Well, I'd say there were enough of you to fight off one man,' Tatberht, counters, standing between us, forcing Eadweard to step away from me. I realise how close I am to the hearth as heat suffuses my face. I've been cold all night, and now I'm too bloody hot. 'Now, get out of here, and I don't want to see you until I'm no longer the gate warden for the day.'

With a final backwards glance that assures me this argument is far from finished, Eadweard strides from the hall. As he goes, I hear the scamper of other booted feet and appreciate that he wasn't alone. I consider where Wulfred is.

'Osmod told me about it all, and Cuthwalh,' Tatberht informs me, offering me his hand so I can stand upright. 'We don't want them sort here,' he mutters, but I'm struggling to stand and can't answer straight away.

Only when I'm upright does he step away from me.

'You look like you've been chewed up and spat out by an eagle,' he offers with half a smile. 'I suggest you get yourself cleaned up and sorted out before Lord Coenwulf sees you. And Lady Ælflæd. With her temper, she might lay the blame at you, not at the feet of Eadweard and his lot.'

'My thanks,' I pant, gratefully sinking onto a wooden bench, just far enough away from the fire that I can feel its heat but not sweat from it.

He walks away, and I envy such ease. It'll take me days to get fully back on my feet. Abruptly, I'm aware of someone watching me, and I turn to meet the appraising eyes of Lady Cynewise.

'Lady Cynewise,' I cough, wishing my voice was steadier. She looks like her sister, Lady Ælflæd, only much younger. It's strange to call such a youngster 'lady' but that's what she is. I'm pleased she no longer wears the marks of the slap her sister gave her.

Lady Cynewise nods but, licking her lips, says nothing else until she opens her mouth. 'You need something for the bruising and something to take the swelling from your lips.'

I'd laugh to hear her assessment of me, almost the words of Wynflæd but from a mere slip of a girl. I consider how she knows this and realise it must be because she's needed to make use of the same remedies herself.

'Do you know what those things are?' I ask as she hands me a beaker of water which I drink eagerly.

'I do, yes. I've been studying them. The monks don't realise I'm learning as much as I am. They think only men should know how to heal.' The disgust in her voice has my lips curling wide. 'Theodore and Gaya were teaching me before they were forced to leave on my sister's instructions.' Her tone is filled with remorse. I miss the two healers as well. They were a steadying presence, and somewhere I could go to step away from the scrutiny of those who mean me ill. 'I'll go and find yarrow, woodruff, and wild carrot,' she announces as though I'm testing her. 'And also some garlic and nettles to add to the pottage for you.'

'So, you'll help me? To feel better?'

'I will, Icel, yes. But you smell really bad. Perhaps you could go for a bath first, and I'll prepare a poultice and potion for you.' With those words, the trace of the older woman she'll one day be disappears, and once more, she's just a young girl. She must be about ten winters old, perhaps not quite as old.

'Apologies, my lady.' I try and bow but hiss at the stab of pain elicited along my shoulder blades.

'There's no need to bow to me, Icel. Just do what I say.' And with that, she threads her way through the people in her older brother's hall and ventures outside, once more sounding as though she's the lady of the settlement. I smile and fill another cup of water from the waiting jug before slowly getting to my feet. I'm reminded of when I first met Ælflæd, and she knew how to tend to her horse, or at least how to do some of it. The daughters of the late King Coelwulf, the first of his name, appear well educated and very sure of themselves. I consider why, then, Lord Coenwulf is so very different to them.

The bite of the sharp wind has me shivering and frantically trying to gather together the remnants of my torn tunic as I venture outside. But it's impossible. I need some water to clean myself with, and also some new clothes to wear. My clothes are in the stables with Brute and Wine, so I limp that way, cursing every step that makes me shudder with agony.

Inside, the stablemen are busy with their tasks.

'Hail, Icel,' Pega calls to me while Hatel veers backwards out of one of the stalls and looks me up and down. 'It's true then?' Pega questions me. 'You got into a fight with Eadweard and Wulfred, and the rest of 'em.'

'I think it would be better to say they got into a fight with me.'

Pega's face is rueful. 'A right pair of arseholes, them two,' he mutters. 'Best avoided.'

'I was trying to avoid them. I was far from Kingsholm at the time.'

'A pity they're men of Lord Wigmund,' Pega continues. 'It would be good to have them gone from Kingsholm. They do nothing but cause trouble with their fighting and gambling.'

Pega follows me to where Wine and Brute await me, both heads over the doors of their stables as I labour towards them. From the way Pega and Hatel talk of the other men, I can at least be assured that they're not hiding in the stables today.

'You stink.' Pega echoes young Lady Cynewise, wafting his hand in front of his nose. It must be bad if he's aware of it even over the redolent smell of horses and their shit.

'I'm just getting some clothes, and then I'll do something about the smell.'

'And the bruises and fat lip?'

'Yes, those as well.' He opens the door for me, pushing gently against Wine, who watches me with her intelligent eyes. I consider if the two horses have exchanged stories during the night. Does she know what's happened to me?

'Here.' Pega proffers me my sack of clothes. I take it gratefully, wishing it weighed less. 'I'll tend to your mounts for you, today only. I can't have others seeing me do this for you more than once. Now, away with you, and when I next see you, I hope you'll be only one shade and not every colour of the rainbow.'

I reach out and rub the noses of Wine and Brute and then retrace my steps. I do consider why Pega didn't bid me stay where I was and get my clothes for me, but I don't say anything. He's being too good to me as it is. The stablemen must also avoid Eadweard, Wulfred and the others. Too often they're in the stables, upsetting the horses, and they think nothing of causing problems for the stablemen. Pega's right. They are arseholes.

I go to where the water's stored in huge oak casks, brought here from the river, not far away. Some are for drinking water, and others can be used for anything and added to by leaving the top off the cask's covering and letting the rain fall into it. For now, it's half iced over, and I know that the shock of the cold water will be unpleasant. And will probably hurt like hell.

Pulling my tunic clear, glancing at the array of colours covering my thick chest and the fine down of black hair over it, I plunge my head directly into the cask, seeing stars, my heart pounding with the shock of it all. I stay there longer than I want to, and when I straighten up, I wash my face with my hands, forgetting about my lips. For a moment, pain surges through my body, and I sway slightly and grip the top of the cask to steady myself.

'Good god,' I exhale when I think I can manage rational thought again. 'Good god,' I repeat, pulling a clean tunic over my head after I've run my hands under my armpits, inhaling the familiar smell of horse and hay.

Only then do I retrace my steps back to the hall, smelling better but bitterly cold from the water and the wind. I hardly focus on what's happening around me, content to let the sounds of everyday life wash over me. The gates to the settlement are wide open. People come and go as they wish, leading horses and carts laden with goods to trade. Yesterday's fog has lifted. The days are still long enough to allow men and women to continue their usual tasks. In a few short weeks, it'll be impossible to travel further than to Gloucester without the need to seek shelter elsewhere for the night before returning.

I return to my seat and drink more water, wincing as my chest brushes against the wood of the table before me. There's no sign of young Lady Cynewise. Just as I'm considering gathering my own supplies to help my aches and pains, she appears in the doorway, head downcast, an array of items in her hands. Jars, leaves, scruffy old weeds, or so they appear, and a swathe of white linen. I try to rush to her side, but instead I only manage to knock myself against the wood of the table once more and clatter back to the stool, breathing heavily, eyes downcast.

A crash of clay on the table before me has me lifting my eyes. Lady Cynewise appraises me with the cool eyes of a much older woman. The similarity to Wynflæd astounds me all over again. There must be seven decades between them and at least as many kings. I'd shake my head, but that would hurt.

'At least you smell better,' she assures me, nimble hands gathering together what she needs.

I'm aware of one of the servants hovering close by, a slim hand covering her mouth as she watches Cynewise. I catch her eyes, and they dance with amusement but also respect. Certainly, she doesn't try and stop the youngster. I consider if she's her nursemaid, but surely Cynewise is too old to need a nursemaid. I think to ask Eadburg, when I next see her. And I must check up on the babe and his brother. I've not seen them since the day before yesterday, for all I'm here to ensure they're protected.

'Here.' A murky mixture is presented to me, the sharp smell of birthwort making me want to gag. The scent is too reminiscent of death and decay. 'Put that on your bruises,' she orders me. I want to advise her that perhaps it needs a little more agrimony to drive away the noxious smell, but her face, beneath the façade of someone who knows what they're doing, belies some unease.

'My lady,' I say, and unwillingly scoop the mixture and put it over my shivering chest. The welter of colours there is fiercely illuminated against my pale skin and dark hair covering. She shows no embarrassment at my semi-nakedness; another trait that will make her a good healer. Wynflæd never seems concerned by any body part presented to her, whether intimate or just a grazed elbow.

'Let me help you do your back,' she offers. I shudder away from that and eye the servant woman. Luckily, she's seen my problem.

'My lady, I'll do that for you. You don't want it on your hands.' Soft hands slowly begin to rub the awful-smelling treatment into my back. The servant's hands are cold, my skin is cold, and the lotion is cold and stinks, yet somehow it soothes me.

Lady Cynewise doesn't even watch. Instead, tongue sticking through her thin lips, she begins to work on the next part of her tonic for me. She moves to the hearth, spoons a selection of the pottage into a smaller container and begins to add nettles, far from finely chopped, and garlic, far from finely sliced, into her bowl. I watch her carefully. She seems too small to handle the huge cooking pot, but she manages it well enough.

I eye her cutting knife and quickly realise everything is roughly chopped because it's about as sharp as a branch. Perhaps I might sharpen it for her, or if not, find something more suitable for the task.

'You're done.' The servant quickly steps aside as she speaks.

'You smell like the charnel house,' she winces in sympathy, and I nod. Her eyes stray to Cynewise and once more they sparkle with joy and some trepidation. 'She knows what she's doing, but only the hounds have been subject to her ministrations so far.'

'She does know what she's doing, yes. I have some skill in healing as well,' I offer, although whether I'm reassuring her or me, I'm not sure. Either way, I can already feel the salve taking effect. I find I can breathe more deeply, and my chest isn't as tight as throughout the night.

Not for the first time, I consider how I allowed myself to get into such a state. I should have fought them off harder, even if there were six of them, and I was alone. Even Brute could have become involved, but I sent him away rather than risk him. I regret that now.

'Eat this,' Cynewise commands me. I notice the servant leaving the hall, no doubt to wash her hands clear of the smell.

'It smells good,' I offer, and it does, much better than my skin. But I'm not going to tell her that. She watches me, eyes serious, as I try the first spoonful, which is far too hot. Hastily, I swill more water into my mouth and push the bowl away from me.

'I'll eat it when it's not quite so hot,' I explain, wishing my tongue didn't burn to add to my other miseries.

'Hum,' Cynewise says, eyeing her collection of supplies. 'I think a linen around your chest will help, but I think you smell bad again. I thought you'd washed?'

'I did, yes, all of me. It was cold.'

'Then why do you smell now?'

'Ah, um. Perhaps there's too much birthwort and not enough agrimony in the salve.'

A flicker of uncertainty covers her face, bright eyes shimmering. I fear she might cry. But she doesn't. Instead, she knocks her forehead with her hand, shaking her head.

'Of course. I could think of no reason to add the amount of agrimony they suggested, but it's to counter the smell, isn't it? Agrimony smells of the summer, whereas birthwort smells like death and yarrow more like farts.' She grimaces. 'Sorry. Why didn't you say anything?' Now her eyes are accusing. I appreciate that I've erred in not telling her. 'I've had more than enough of people tolerating what I'm doing as though I'm a babe in the cot and not someone learning how to heal. I know, I know that a girl of my position shouldn't be concerned with healing people, but it's my passion.' Fury covers her face.

'I thought you did a very good job,' I offer, and then hiss sharply. 'Sorry, I didn't mean to sound condescending. I learned about healing from a young age too. But the woman who taught me always let me make mistakes to learn more from them.'

'Well, she was a mean old hag then,' Cynewise announces, elbows on the table, her head in her hands. 'She should have helped you rather than hindered you.'

'I think it did help,' I offer. 'She's a wise woman.'

'She still lives?' This astounds her.

'Yes, at Tamworth. Haven't you heard of Wynflæd? I thought she visited here?'

'Oh her, the really, really old woman? She came with Theodore and Gaya once. The monks disapprove of Theodore and Gaya. They spoke to my brother about banishing them from Kingsholm, but Lady Cynehild was adamant they came. And now, the monks blame them for what happened to Lady Cynehild, and so they've been banished on my sister's orders. I do miss Lady Cynehild.' The words erupt in a gush and with a quiver of her chin.

'I do, too,' I agree.

'What will happen to my brother?' Cynewise demands to know.

'He'll leave here, as the king instructed.'

'But where will he go?' Her voice is plaintive, and no longer assured.

'I don't know, but I'm sure he'll be safe and return soon.'

'It isn't fair.' Small arms cross over her chest, her lower lip jutting out angrily. 'My brother shouldn't have to leave Kingsholm. This is his home, and his children are here. I'm here.' The last ends with a shriek.

I'm not sure what to say to her. I refuse to offer reassurance I don't feel myself. She's right to be worried.

'And my sister, Ælflæd, has become horrible ever since she married the king's son. And her son, well, he's not well at all.' The words erupt in a rush. I can tell she's worried. 'I've told her that Theodore and Gaya should tend to him, but Ælflæd will only let the monks close to Wigstan. What good will prayers do for the poor thing when he struggles to drink his mother's milk?'

I feel my forehead furrow at this. I was aware that Wigstan was failing to thrive. I didn't know it was failure to get enough nourishment that was the problem. Perhaps then, this accounts for Ælflæd's difficult nature. I know I should stop trying to find excuses for her, and yet I do, all the same. 'What do you think ails him?'

'He can't suck as well as he should, or my sister's milk is no good. I've heard the monks talking about it. They seem to believe that prayer will aid him. Theodore and Gaya knew what to do but my sister didn't like what they said, and the monks overruled all they said.'

I lapse into silence, considering her words. I can't say I've ever heard of something like this, but I'm aware that babes can struggle in their first months of life. Some think it's God's will, but I've been taught to heal. Sometimes, I know it's just something lacking in the mother's diet or even the babe. Wynflæd would have suggested lots of meat for the mother. I consider whether Lady Ælflæd would have eaten well while carrying the child. But then, I didn't see her throughout her term. I can't say one way or another.'

'Then why were they banished?'

'Lord Wigmund doesn't want to admit there's anything wrong with his firstborn son, and my sister, she's desperate to keep on the right side of him. She's fearful that what my brother did will cause her to be cast aside by the king's son.'

'It seems as though a lot's happening,' I murmur, aware there's much there for someone as young as her to worry about, especially when the death of Lady Cynehild must still pain her, and she and her sister are such opposites.

'The other baby is doing really well.' Lady Cynewise perks up. 'Young Coelwulf eats enough for two babies. Oh, and the poos he does. They stink.' A smile drives the worry from her face.

I hold my tongue, keen to see her happy.

'Come on,' she says. 'I need to put this around you, and then I'll make another pot of salve for you. One that doesn't reek like the charnel house.' Sprightly, she hastens to the task, humming merrily to herself as I try not to wince and groan at the reminder of my bruises.

Much later, she leaves me, bundling up all her supplies, with the aid of the returned servant, and hastens from the hall.

'I'll check on you tomorrow,' she says. 'Now, eat your pottage, and get better soon.'

I chuckle. If she could order me well, then she would. But her words about the two small babies, Coelwulf and Wigstan, concern me. Coelwulf is hale and hearty. Wigstan, the son of the ætheling, isn't; and Lady Ælflæd is remiss not to seek aid from Theodore and Gaya when they have such a wealth of experience. They have far more knowledge than the monks. A tendril of fear coils in my belly.

7

'Bloody hell. Have you shit yourself?' The voice of Eadweard rouses me from where I'm dozing by the hearth. I take a tight breath and meet his taunting gaze. 'I thought only the young and old shit themselves,' he continues. His eyes are bright, his face twisted with desire to belittle me.

'And those who meet their death on the slaughter field,' I counter.

'And you'd know all about that? Wouldn't you?'

Sitting upright, from where my head's been slumped on the board, allows all kinds of agonies to sizzle up my back and down my chest, making my heart thump too loudly.

'Not the shitting myself bit, no, but killing to protect my king? I'd know all about that. Would you? In fact, I did it with that very seax you hold there, and which I'd have back, now.'

I'm in no mind to argue with Eadweard. He beat me with the aid of his friends yesterday. I'll seek my vengeance one day. For now, all I want is my seax returned to me. He has no right to it. If anything, it shows how well he beat me, as opposed to what he's been telling everyone about me overpowering them. If I'd overpowered them, how would I have lost my very distinctive seax, with its eagle emblem made from twisted metal?

The taunting smirk slips from his face as his allies encircle him.

'Why are you here?' he demands to know, his hand reaching for the seax.

'I'm getting warm before the hearth.'

'Why are you here, in Kingsholm?'

'It's none of your concern, Eadweard. But know this, I'm not going anywhere.' I see his fist clench as though he might start a fight with me once more, and I tighten my body to hold myself firm against more punishing blows. 'Return my seax to me, and I'll do nothing further to counter your attack on me, on one of the king's well-known warriors, a man who fought to protect his king's life.' I think Eadweard will argue with me. Certainly, he looks prepared to. I notice, with a wry look, that Wulfred only carries a slight bruise to his cheek, where my head must have hit him as we tumbled backwards. Other than that, and slightly pale skin, he doesn't look as though he's been in a fight.

Only then Lord Wigmund appears in the hall. I've no idea where he's been for half the day. I don't much care.

'Eadweard, a word.' The king's son beckons him closer. Uneasily, Eadweard slips the seax from its place on his weapons belt and places it before me while, trailed by his collection of allies, Ealdorman Sigered's son amongst them, Lord Wigmund strides to the raised dais and seats himself there, ordering food and ale for him and his allies.

I try and make myself as small as possible, as I scoop up my seax, relieved by the familiar weight and feel of the blade in my hand. I'm keen to avoid Wigmund's scrutiny, and some of the others. I have no formal place here. None at all. And with so many months since Lady Cynehild's death, I can't use that as an excuse any more. The rest of the warriors who rescued Lord Coenwulf left months ago. The fact that I linger must be noticed by more than just Eadweard and his cronies.

I would ask Lord Coenwulf for a more permanent position, but he won't be here much longer. No, I just try and keep out of sight as much as possible, spending my time with Edwin and the rest of the warriors of Kingsholm. If it came to it, they could ask me to pay for staying here, eating their food, and sheltering under the hall's roof. I'd have the coin to pay, at least, for while I'm here, in Kingsholm, my estate at Budworth remains under the care of my reeve. He's sent messages to me on a number of occasions, and coins as well. I don't fear for the place, but I don't wish to visit there, not now I know the truth of my identity.

With trepidation, I apply the new, less smelly salve to my chest and what parts of my back I can reach, and then pull my tunic over my head. The linen bandage is more of an encumbrance than an aid, but I don't remove it. If I have to fight Eadweard and his men again, it'll provide another layer of protection from their feet and fists.

I try to hear the words of Lord Wigmund, but it's impossible. The men speak quietly, plotting something that will undoubtedly enhance their prestige, but such politicking is of no concern to me. When some of the Kingsholm warriors - Osmod, Cuthwalh and Tatberht - meander outside, I hasten to join them, merging with them so that I don't catch the eye of either Lord Wigmund or Eadweard.

Once outside, I'm not sure what to do with myself. I find myself close to the building where the small children are cared for, the very same room where Lady Cynehild breathed her last. Aware I won't be any more welcome than usual, I open the door and enter all the same. No one questions me. No one bars my way. There are no wardens, and raucous laughter means my entry is unnoticed. Peering through the wicker screen that divides the door from the smaller rooms, I chuckle to hear young Coenwulf's joyous voice as he giggles while playing with his nurse. I see Eadburg there as well, holding the smaller Coelwulf, although he sits upright, watching his brother with a fierce expression. Coelwulf is desperate to be playing with his older brother.

I seek out the other child, Wigstan, but he's not playing or sitting. Indeed, I suspect he lies in the arms of another of the women, sitting closer to the hearth, murmuring a soft song to the child. I can't think there can be much difference in age between the two small babes. My heart constricts, fearful that perhaps Lady Cynewise's worries are well founded.

I'm not foolish. I'm well aware that not all children are born to flourish and grow to adulthood, but despite Lady Ælflæd's sharp words, and my fears for the person she's become since wedding the king's son, I wouldn't wish such sorrow on her.

Before I'm noticed, I once more slip from the hall, my mind swirling with thoughts, as I make my way to the church and the monks. Never one to think the power of prayer can work unaided, I still offer some words to our Lord God, as Wynflæd might well do, hoping that some good might come of it for Lady Ælflæd's child. Unbidden I consider if our son would have been healthier if we'd had children together. But then I banish the thought. Lady Ælflæd and I are not even friends, and perhaps, we never were.

8

AD834

Lady Cynewise sobs quietly as she stands in the crowded yard outside the hall, watching her much older brother mount up. The weather has changed, the scent of summer is in the air. It'll soon be Eastermonað. Lord Wigmund and his warriors, headed by Eadweard and Wulfred, have demanded it's time for Lord Coenwulf to begin his exile. There's recently been a visit from Lord Beorhtwulf. No doubt he came to add his weight to the decision of Lord Wigmund and Lady Ælflæd to have Lord Coenwulf leave.

No one stands with young Lady Cynewise, not even the servant, who I know is called Gode. All is chaos and angry shouting. I've watched Edwin and Eadburg tearfully part from one another; Edwin, Cuthwalh, Tatberht and Osmod preparing to escort Lord Coenwulf wherever he goes. I decided not to listen to Lord Coenwulf take his leave of his children. That parting will have been bitter and double-edged. When, or rather if, Lord Coenwulf returns to Kingsholm, his children won't know him. They may as well be named orphans now.

Lady Ælflæd has shown herself to be no ally of her brother. She's taken regal command of the children, trying to banish

Eadburg and her mother from their side, but there the women refused to be cast aside. They are, Eadburg said, their carers, placed there by Lady Cynehild, before her death, and have no intention of leaving the children with no one to care for them. While they might hold their places for now, I'm once more suspicious of Ælflæd, especially with her weak son. My prayers did little good for him. The monks prayers are equally ineffective. He needs an experienced healer. One more skilled than me and young Lady Cynewise.

I could weep for what's happening, but I'm as powerless as Lord Coenwulf. The king has been petitioned, and while I think he'd retract his judgement, Lord Wigmund is staunch in demanding the older man leave, and he's supported by others. He has the encouragement of his mother in this, and also Lord Beorhtwulf. The queen doesn't like Lord Coenwulf, and she's not alone in that, for all she brokered the marriage union between him and his wife.

'Take care of yourself,' I murmur to Edwin, mounted on his horse, his face streaked with sorrow.

'And you as well. I suggest you leave this place. With Lord Wigmund in command, you'll only end with more bruises to your name. Return to Ealdorman Ælfstan and his warriors.'

I nod but shake my head sadly. I'm not as angry with them as I once was, our time apart making me appreciate that I miss all of them, even Oswy and his toxic arse. But I have a new oath now, and one I can't easily ignore. 'Don't worry about me, Edwin. Just go carefully. Don't allow Lord Coenwulf to enter into any alliance which the king will use as an excuse to extend his exile or even make it permanent.'

'Then, if you're determined to stay, care for Eadburg for me, her mother and the other children. I fear for them all.'

I reach up and grip Edwin's forearm, feeling his strength there, for all mine is greater. As he's healed, our friendship has also mended. It's felt good to have one friend within Kingsholm throughout the long winter 'I'll do as you ask. And soon, the time will run its course, and we'll be reunited.'

'Perhaps, but if you go to Tamworth, let my mother know this was my choice. It was the honourable action to follow.'

'I will, I assure you.' And with that, Edwin turns his mount, and together with three other men, making the party a total of seven, the horses leave the sanctuary of Kingsholm. I know they plan to find a ship to take them to Frankia or perhaps to one of the Irish kingdoms, but still, I'm fearful. Although, well, at least Lord Coenwulf hasn't sought sanctuary from King Athelstan of the East Angles or King Ecgberht of Wessex. That would have caused enormous problems, and would have ensured he was never allowed to return to Mercia.

I stand and watch the horses' tails until they disappear, and only then realise that only Lady Cynewise and I remain. She still cries, clutching something in her hand.

'My lady.' I walk to her, thinking of taking her hand and offering her some comfort. Furious eyes greet mine, her face red and splotchy with tears. I snatch my hand back. She's not a child to be comforted, for all her next demand is filled with childish sentiments.

'I want my brother back.'

'I know you do, but alas, he must win the king's regard by fulfilling his punishment.' I try to keep my voice even. She's furious. I recognise the emotion too well.

'The king's a horrible man, and his wife is worse,' Lady Cynewise shrieks, startling me. I turn quickly, hoping no one has heard the outburst. Should Lord Wigmund hear, I've no doubt he'd punish the young girl. Should her sister hear, the punishment will be even worse. Should word get back to the queen, I dread to consider what could befall her.

'You don't want anyone to hear you say that,' I murmur. This startles her, and her mouth falls open in shock.

'You didn't berate me for saying it.' Her words are surprised. I consider how many others have tried to stifle her anger and fear and failed to do so, by denying her thoughts.

'No, I didn't,' I confirm, holding her gaze. Now her eyes narrow, and she looks me up and down, perhaps seeing me for the first time since she aided me after I was beaten black and blue by Eadweard and his allies. Her ointment helped me until I could make my own. All the same, it was near enough two weeks before I could mount easily, and all that time, I felt the gaze and the threat from Eadweard. Even now, two months after he beat me, I imagine he plots his next attempt on me. I've ensured I'm never alone, even in the stables when tending to Brute and Wine. I'm aware that will become more difficult now that Edwin, Tatberht and Osmod have left Kingsholm. I can't rely on Haga and Patel getting involved with bloodthirsty warriors.

'Are your bruises all gone?' she queries.

'Yes, thank you. You helped me. You have my thanks.'

Her eyebrows arc. 'Then I knew what I was doing?'

'You did, apart from the problem with the birthwort.'

She grins and uses the cloth she's clutching to wipe the snot from her nose, pleased with my acclaim for her skills. 'My brother gave me this. He said it was my mother's.' Abruptly, she's recalled to what's just happened.

This surprises me. The cloth is as fine as gossamer, as finely spun as a spider's web. I would have expected it to perish in the years since her mother's death, but it seems not.

'I don't remember her. I'm like my nephews. They won't remember their mother either.' Her voice breaks as she speaks. I appreciate that she is another like me. I didn't know my mother. I certainly didn't know my father. Neither, it seems, did she, and certainly not well.

'Perhaps not, but you can tell them stories of her.' I hope this makes her smile. I know I would have appreciated stories of my mother, but mention of my mother was more likely to be met with denial. Not even Wynflæd likes to speak about her.

'I can, can't I?' She looks pleased with the suggestion as we begin walking back to the hall, her tears for now forgotten, as her hand snakes inside mine. Such an action comforts me as well, which I find surprising. I didn't expect to find someone who thought as I did, but Lady Cynewise and I are more alike, for all over a decade separates us in age.

The smell of cooking meat fills the air, reminding me that Lord Wigmund has ordered a feast to celebrate the banishment of Lord Coenwulf. Lord Wigmund's a damn fool, and yet I won't refuse the food. Only then, there's a clatter of horses' hooves, and I turn, expecting to see Lord Coenwulf's return.

But, of course, it's not him. He has determined to face his banishment honourably. Despite his sorrow at leaving his children and his home. Instead, I meet the surprised face of Wulfheard and, behind him, Oswy and Maneca, mounted on their horses.

'What are you doing here?' we ask one another simultaneously.

9

'The king sent us to protect Kingsholm. He knew that Lord Coenwulf was leaving today. Have we missed him?' Wulfheard demands, looking around as though Coenwulf might just appear out of thin air. Behind him are more and more familiar faces. I thrill to see them, even while being careful not to show them how pleased I am that they're here.

'Yes, he left just now. This is his sister, Lady Cynewise.'

'Good day, my lady.' Wulfheard surprises me with his respectful greeting for one so young. 'The king's aware of reports of Viking raiders close to the borders with the Welsh kingdom of Gwent. He's sent my men and me, or rather, Ealdorman Ælfstan's men, under my command, to ensure the king's son is protected, and of course, Lord Coenwulf's children as well.'

'Well met.' The poise of Lady Cynewise doesn't surprise me. She knows whom she is well enough. Her brother might be gone but she's still the daughter of a previous king of Mercia. 'Lord Wigmund is in the hall, celebrating the departure of my brother.' For all the words are laced with tight fury, they remain polite and courtly. I can see Cynewise knows what's expected of a Mercian woman of high birth. I detect the work of Lady Cynehild in her iron resolve, impressive for one so young.

At that moment, a roar of appreciation erupts from the hall.

'Then perhaps, the king's son might think to have men on gate duty.' Wulfheard's lips twist. I see he's about as pleased to be here as an injured man about to have his wounds cleaned with vinegar. 'Maneca, Cenred, dismount, and have the gates closed. Stay on guard until I can sort this mess out,' Wulfheard huffs, his eyes dancing with fury. His gaze sweeps over me, although it lingers for a moment too long, and then he looks to Cynewise.

'My lady, if you could take me to the hall. I'll inform Lord Wigmund of our arrival.'

I don't miss the smirk of triumph on the young woman's lips.

'I'll be having words with you later,' Wulfheard promises me. I watch him go and then look up at Oswy. He evades my gaze. I feel a tremor of unease. I was angry when I last saw Oswy. Angry and fit to fight anyone. He won't know why, and I can't tell him why. The moment elongates for too long, and then he jumps down, throws his reins over his horse's head, and engulfs me in an embrace that stinks of the sharp, biting wind, horse, sweat and the familiarity of Tamworth. I could weep.

'We've missed you in Tamworth,' he announces, stepping back and appraising me to see if I've changed while we've been apart all winter.

'Yes, we have,' Cenred confirms, dismounting as well. I still await some other comment, some slight, but it doesn't come. Indeed, all the men approach me, offering words of greeting, and I feel an unusual smile on my lips. From the hall, I'm aware of the joviality of the situation draining away, the crash of doors being flung open, of furious strides over the courtyard before the hall.

Still, through it all, I feel enveloped in warmth from my friends. For a time, I even consider why I left them. With them, I can forget all about Lady Cynehild's dying wish, of the oath she bid me speak before breathing her last.

All until a small boy's giggle and a babe's chuckling permeate my thoughts.

I turn, eyes wide to see young Coenwulf, the older boy, reaching up to touch the noses of the milling horses. Eadburg's there, her cheeks tear-stained, as the look of hope slips from her face. She must have believed Lord Coenwulf, and more importantly, Edwin, had returned to her.

'Eadburg, come meet the warriors of Ealdorman Ælfstan. They've been sent to protect Kingsholm now that Lord Coenwulf's begun his banishment.'

I think she'll shake her head and walk the children away back to her mother, but instead, gripping the babe tightly, she briefly curtsies and comes to my side.

I keep half an eye on young Coenwulf, the older boy, but Oswy's down on one knee beside the diminutive child. I can hear him murmuring about the horses. I never expected to see such a thing.

'That's Oswy,' I inform Eadburg, 'and this is Kyre, Landwine, Waldhere.' I make hasty introductions. Those on their feet stand a little taller, admiring her fine appearance, marred only by the red of her eyes and the splotchy cheeks that shine pink in the bright daylight. She is a fine-looking woman. Edwin is lucky to have found her. I only hope they can survive the coming seven years apart.

I continue my introductions while Maneca and Cenred quickly pull the double gate closed and adopt a position of belligerence on the viewing point just to the side of the gates. I can already hear confused voices from outside Kingsholm. I don't think the gate will remain closed for long. There are too many people working in the fields and about on errands, but as always, Wulfheard has worked quickly to ensure all know there are warriors inside Kingsholm once more and not the useless turds of Eadweard and his cronies.

'They're your friends?' Eadburg asks me, just to be sure.

'Yes, Wulfheard, he's in the hall at the moment, taught me to fight. Oswy helped me as well. And I've stitched up all of them from one wound or another.' A look of confusion touches her face while the babe reaches out as though he too wants to touch one of the horses. She steps closer, but Kyre intervenes.

'Here, the child's heavy. Let me hold him for you. Come on, young man, come and meet Bada. She's Wulfheard's horse and likes littlies.' Hesitantly, Eadburg passes over the precious burden, and abruptly I realise that while I've exiled myself here, to Kingsholm, I've had little to do with the children I'm supposed to be guarding against whatever might harm them.

'Icel, I don't understand why you're here when your friends have only just arrived.' I can hear the confusion in Eadburg's words.

'Don't worry, Eadburg, I don't either, not really. But here's where I must be.' I shrug as I reply. I speak the truth.

But our pleasant exchanges don't last long.

'Get out of here.' The furious voice of Lord Wigmund sends chickens shrieking, and Eadburg instinctively moves to grab hold of both small children. But Oswy holds firm to young Coenwulf while Kyre grips Coelwulf tightly. 'You're not welcome here. And you should leave.'

Behind a furious Wigmund, I see Wulfheard, a frown on his familiar face, his hands resting in a warrior's stance, close to his weapons. In contrast, Eadweard, Wulfred and his allies spill from the hall, grinning with delight at this new development. They're no match for Wulfheard. In fact, if anything, seeing them beside him, I realise what pathetic figures Eadweard and Wulfred make.

'My lord, as I advised you, we're here on the king's instructions.' Wulfheard's words aren't shouted but carry well all the same from where he stands, close to the hall.

'And I'm the king's son, the ætheling, and don't require additional warriors within my own home.'

I'm not alone in wincing at the reminder that, by right, Lord Wigmund is now the master of Kingsholm, although, actually, the king placed it in the hands of his wife, Lady Ælflæd.

'Your gates were open, my lord, and there are reports of Viking raiders and other disturbances along the borders with the Welsh kingdoms. The king, and the queen, both ordered us here. Ealdorman Ælfstan will arrive shortly as well.' If Wulfheard hoped the mention of the queen would sway the matter, he's to be mistaken.

Now Lord Wigmund's face turns purple with rage.

'I don't need someone to stand as my nursemaid. I'm the king's son, a husband and a father. I know how to defend my settlement.'

'But the gates, my lord?' Wulfheard is persistent, and I suddenly appreciate that he has much experience dealing with difficult lordlings. How he doesn't sigh, I don't know.

I notice Lady Cynewise emerging from the hall, and I note her wide eyes as she absorbs what's happening, no doubt keen to avoid the scrutiny of her sister. Even Lady Ælflæd joins the arguing, emerging from the building where the children are cared for. Compared to the chunky child in Oswy's arms, young Wigstan is about half his size and twice as difficult, as he twists in his mother's arms, his cries continuous. A string of wet nurses have tried to tend to him, but he refuses all of them, preferring his mother to all others. Lady Ælflæd, as bitter as she can be, is always tired and lacking in sleep, thanks to her son. He's an awkward and unhappy child. I've heard Eadburg and her mother discussing it at length. Again, I'm aware that Theodore and Gaya would have been able to do more for Ælflæd than her monks and their chanting. Even Wynflæd would have been able to calm the child. There are always remedies but Lady Ælflæd is led by her husband and his mother, the queen. And they both believe they know best.

'What is this?' Lady Ælflæd asks, her words snapping tighter than a war banner in a stiff breeze. She's pale in the bright daylight. While she and her brother have parted on bad terms, this must be difficult for her. Or at least, I hope she has some regret for what's happened. It would perhaps help if her husband showed some regard for her, but he's announced, to all who'll hear, that his wife's no good to him while she tends to their child. They don't share a bed. In fact, they share little but the rule of Kingsholm, and even that's uneven. As such, there'll be no sibling for Wigstan anytime soon.

'My lady, the king has sent my men and me to guard Kingsholm while you and the king's son are in attendance. There are reports of disturbances on the borders with the Welsh kingdoms and some suspected incursions from the Viking raiders. Your gates were wide open.' I'm impressed that Wulfheard has the patience to repeat himself once more.

'Then why are we all arguing about this?' She fixes her husband with a fiery gaze. He subsides, lips tight with fury. 'Find yourselves somewhere for the horses. But you'll have to sleep in the main hall. There are no spare beds to be found anywhere.'

This seems to amuse Lord Wigmund, who turns, his cloak swirling around him, and marches back to his aborted feast, trailed by Eadweard and the others, who don't use all the room in the bunkhouse now that Edwin and his allies have left to escort Lord Coenwulf, despite Lady Ælflæd's words. For a long moment, no one else moves, but then Wulfheard speaks.

'Men, tend to your horses. If there's no room in the stables, then we'll arrange a temporary paddock for now.'

'I'll take the boys,' Eadburg announces, holding out her hands. She grips the babe tightly, for all I can see he's heavy to carry, even with her hip jutting out to one side to take his weight, while young Coenwulf slips his hand into hers, a joyful look on his bright face. I fear he'll ask after his father, but as they turn, and make their way to where Lady Ælflæd still watches, eyes narrowed, and my fellow warriors start to lead the horses away, I can hear Coenwulf chattering away about the 'big' horses, and how much he likes them. I don't miss the strange look on Lady Ælflæd's face as she eyes young Coelwulf. Does she wish her son was as hale and hearty? I imagine she does, but I also detect another emotion there. Is it hatred or jealousy, or the cold-hearted musings of a woman who knows her son might not survive but that he has two cousins with a claim better than his?

I feel the smile at young Coenwulf's chattering draining from my face, and then Wulfheard's before me, obstructing my view of Lady Ælflæd.

'Right, Icel. It's time me and you talked.' Without waiting for my agreement, he grips my arm tightly and pulls me towards where Cenred and Maneca watch for trouble from outside the gate. He doesn't so much as spare a glance for Lady Ælflæd, and I'm pleased to see Lady Cynewise slowly back away so as to avoid her sister's scrutiny.

Wulfheard forces me up the steep steps that lead to a lookout position to the left-hand side of the gates, I watch Maneca and Cenred slip their way down the stairs.

'Cowards,' I murmur under my breath, but I don't think they hear me. My heart's hammering in my chest. This isn't going to be a nice conversation.

'Ealdorman Ælfstan has forced this godforsaken commission

on us because he wants to know what you're doing and when you're returning to Tamworth.' He turns, looking over the landscape surrounding Kingsholm, which is suspiciously flat, the sound of the River Severn close enough that we can hear it. Should it flood, as I know it does, some fields will be inundated, but hopefully not Kingsholm itself.

'I'm not coming back to Tamworth,' I say softly.

'That's what Wynflæd told me. Why?' The fact he's spoken to her of me is a surprise.

'I have to stay here, as I said, guard the children.'

'Why does this fall to you?'

'Lady Cynehild made me swear.'

'And who does she think the children need protecting from?'

This is the question I don't want to answer. Wulfheard doesn't speak, either. When he once more faces me, his eyes flash with respect.

'It's a heavy burden for you. But, if Lady Cynehild suspected the king, the queen, or their pestilent son was a threat to her children, why didn't she do something about it before she died?'

I know my mouth hangs open in shock at his words.

'Really, Icel, you're not the only one with a mind and eyes in your head.' Wulfheard shakes his head at me and waits for a response.

'I... well, I don't know. Of course, she died somewhat unexpectedly. Neither did she, I imagine, think the queen would ensure her husband was sent into exile.'

'Perhaps not, but she was always astute.'

'I was here, and so she laid the oath on me.' I add nothing further. I'd sooner forget why. I'd sooner forget the rest of her admission to me, although the silver eagle hangs heavily around my neck.

'Ealdorman Ælfstan's wary of Lady Ælflæd. He says there are

reports that the child she shares with Lord Wigmund is weak and won't survive. As such, until she grows ripe with another babe, the future rule of the Mercians could well be in jeopardy. And, of course, following the last decade of unrest, there are others who think to have a claim to the kingship as well. I'm sure you're aware of Lord Beorhtwulf, as he was in Kingsholm when the king banished Lord Coenwulf. He thinks himself a contender for the kingship of Mercia as well.'

It's good to know Lord Beorhtwulf has come to the attention of Ealdorman Ælfstan and Wulfheard. But I address the issue of the babe, young Wigstan. 'Lord Wigmund is only as young as me. He'll live forever, especially as he seems unable to lift a blade to protect Mercia.'

'Perhaps, Icel, perhaps, but that makes him as weak as the child dependent on his mother's milk to thrive. And Lady Ælflæd will realise this. At the moment, should something happen to her husband, men and women will look to the claim of her brother and not to her. After all, Lord Coenwulf is the son of a king, and he now has sons. Do you know where Lord Coenwulf's gone?'

'No, he took ship this morning. That's all I know. Some said it would take him to Frankia, but I don't know the truth of that.'

Wulfheard is decidedly unhappy about this. 'With Lord Wigmund here and not with his father, Lord Beorhtwulf is gaining in popularity. I've even seen Ealdorman Sigered whispering in corners with him, and all know Sigered was fiercely loyal to the queen.'

'Who is Lord Beorhtwulf? No one in Kingsholm knows.'

'He claims descent from King Beonred, the ill-fated king who ruled for a year only between Æthelbald and Offa last century.' Wulfheard sounds like Wynflæd now, filling me with details of a past I know little about, and in fact, that few will know about, as it's near enough eighty winters ago.

'Then he also claims kinship with King Beornwulf?' The words leave my mouth before I can stop them.

'Aye, he does, but it's so distant, not even the bishops can decipher it,' Wulfheard states, unaware of why I'm asking such questions and why King Beornwulf's name is so readily on my lips.

I chew on my lip, running my hands through my thick beard and moustache. It's kept me warm through the winter, but perhaps it's time to trim it back.

'Then we have many people thinking to claim the kingship of Mercia, and all while King Wiglaf yet lives.'

'We do, yes. Ealdorman Ælfstan cautions us all to be wary. That's why he's stayed at Tamworth, now that affairs in his ealdordom are settled. He doesn't wish to leave while there's so much unease. The king and queen are still unhappy with one another after he was forced to banish Lord Coenwulf when he didn't want to do so. And he's right. All the queen has accomplished is to allow this Lord Beorhtwulf to make an impression on the men and women of the witan. And Lord Beorhtwulf is well oiled and knows how to gain the ear of everyone. I've seen him at work. Few are immune to his charms. And, unlike Lord Wigmund, the king's son, he at least has the look of a warrior about him.'

I breathe deeply, inhaling the cold, fresh scent of the coming spring. I can't help thinking, although I don't want to, that if I made my true origins known, then I too could cause problems for King Wiglaf. If this Beorhtwulf, whomever he is, can claim some tenuous link to a previous king, I can do the same. Only, I really don't want to do so. Wynflæd could speak for me, and all would trust and believe her, I don't deny that, but she would also then be threatened, and not just by the queen, but by any who would think to dispute my claim. I want to ask about her, but I can't bring myself to ask the question, *Does she still live?* I'd sooner think that she does, than know that she doesn't, and surely, when mentioning her earlier, Wulfheard would have told me had she died. Hopefully, one day, I'll be able to reconcile with her, but not yet.

But, as though to prove the point, the pitiful cry of the small child, Wigstan, echoes through the air once more. A reminder that, for the time being, the future of Mercia depends on the life of a child whom everyone fears will die before reaching his first name day.

10

'You're coming with us,' Wulfheard informs me, his legs wide, hands on his hips, brokering no argument. 'We have to ride the borders and ensure all is well.'

'But—' I start.

'I don't really care,' Wulfheard continues, as though I've not spoken, 'why you think you shouldn't. Brute needs a gallop. He's kicking his stall to pieces in the stables. And you need to get away from the crying babes and the presence of Lord Wigmund and those he surrounds himself with.'

Wulfheard only arrived yesterday with the rest of Ealdorman Ælfstan's men, but already I can tell he's restless. The gale of last night won't have helped. With the shrieking of wood, the crash of objects fleeing across the settlement, and the constant draft through the wattle and daub walls, everyone feels twitchy for all the storm has dropped away. The lack of the howling wind means everything seems strangely calm and quiet.

'Fine,' I capitulate, hurrying to Brute's side. Wine watches me with knowing eyes but eagerly pulls at the hay in her stall. She's content. Brute isn't. I'm reminded that Wine is a much older horse.

Perhaps it's time to send her to Budworth to be cared for there. Here, I spend too much of my time shovelling shit from the stalls, refusing to allow Pega to do it on my behalf, now that I'm able once more, after my beating. Perhaps, I consider, the next time I receive a message from my reeve at Budworth, I'll arrange for Wine to return with them.

Brute doesn't make it easy. He fights me when I try and saddle him, biting my ear and huffing into it, bashing my back with his long head.

'Do you want to go out?' I eventually exclaim in exasperation, even as Wulfheard calls through the door.

'Hurry up, Icel. Today would be good.'

As though understanding those words, Brute finally allows me to place his saddle, having been forced to loosen off the straps beneath his belly because he's grown fatter during the cold, dark winter months.

I lead him outside and, mounting up, with only a small argument, I join Wulfheard and Oswy as they wait to be allowed to leave the settlement. Sadly, Eadweard and Wulfred are on gate duty, and they take their time so that Wulfheard leaps from Bada's back and opens the gates wide himself. They've not been forced to this duty throughout the long winter, when Edwin, Osmod and Tatberht were usually prevailed upon. But Lord Wigmund, unhappy with Wulfheard's arrival, has assigned them the task. I'd smirk about it, but I don't wish to have anything to do with them.

'If you're this slow when I get back, then you'll be on mucking-out duty for a week,' Wulfheard informs the two men. Neither looks concerned. 'And don't think Lord Wigmund will do anything to intervene. He'll be quieter than a mouse now that I'm here and in overall command,' Wulfheard continues. I'm not convinced that's correct, but there's enough truth in it for both men to look contrite, even while Eadweard arches his eyebrows at me.

'Got your friends to help you, young Icel?' Eadweard taunts. 'I can beat all of them, just like you.'

'I doubt that.' Oswy rides his mount too close to Eadweard, making him step backwards, right into a ripe pile of green horseshit. 'I can pummel your face so your nose lies so close to your face, it'll be no good for breathing through.' The menace in the tone brings a wry smile. It's good to have Oswy beside me, even if it's only for now.

Outside the gates of Kingsholm, Wulfheard turns Bada's head towards the river. There's a bridge within Gloucester, but Wulfheard doesn't go that way, instead heading northwards, which surprises me.

'I thought there were Viking raiders?' I murmur.

'There are reports of Viking raiders,' Oswy informs me, and something in his tone makes me doubt those reports. What is Ealdorman Ælfstan playing at? If there are no Viking raiders, how has he got his warriors assigned to Lord Wigmund?

Beneath me, Brute's restless, and only when we have a clear sight of the river, the fields only just beginning to turn green, apart from those within which the spring crop is slowly becoming ready to harvest, does he eagerly stretch his legs. Quickly, we pass the place where Eadweard almost beat me to death, and I realise I've not been this far outside the settlement since then. I bend low over Brute's shoulder and allow him to set the pace.

Around me, the thunder of hooves assures me that the others do the same.

The thrill of the speed loosens the tension from my shoulder, and by the time Wulfheard calls for us to rein in, I feel more myself than I have since Lady Cynehild's death. How I wish she'd kept the knowledge she knew to herself. I'd never have known, and that would have been acceptable.

'So, men.' Wulfheard beckons us close to him, the horses

pawing at the ground, seeking out the few growing strands of grass. 'As you can imagine, our purpose here isn't quite what as it appears. Yes, we must ensure the safety of Lord Wigmund, Lady Ælflæd, and the children, but the ealdorman also commands us to be alert to any indication that all is not as it seems. Now that Mercia has countered the threat of Wessex, if only for the moment, and the aggression of the kingdom of the East Angles, if only for the moment, some grow impatient with the same ruler for the last four years. The ealdorman expects trouble from Lord Wigmund and certainly Lady Ælflæd, and also from Lord Beorhtwulf.'

'What of Viking raiders and Welsh unrest?' Maneca queries, his tone ensuring we all know the idea of playing politics is far from appealing.

'They somehow seem the lesser threat at this time,' Wulfheard admits. I can see it costs him. Mercians should be loyal to Mercians, but of course, my father wasn't loyal to his king. He undermined and then usurped Lord Coenwulf's father. In doing so, he undoubtedly planted the seed that others could do the same.

'I'd sooner run my blade through a Wessex bastard than have to listen to the titters and whispers of those who should know better.' Cenred sounds aggrieved.

I look to Oswy. His clenched hands on his reins show his fury. He's been forced to play this game before. No doubt he thought it was done with. 'Why is nothing ever just accomplished and left as it is?' Oswy questions angrily, assuring me I know his thoughts well.

'Every generation thinks it knows best,' Wulfheard announces, although he's not happy about it. 'We might all be old – well, apart from Icel – and we might all have seen enough to sicken us for one lifetime, but these new ones, who've never been sorely tried, think it little more than a game of kingdoms. As though it were tafl and not people's lives.'

I shudder at Wulfheard's doom-laden tone. I'm not used to seeing my fellow warriors looking so concerned. But then, the enemy they might now face isn't one that comes at them, assesses their weaknesses and strengths, and strikes to undermine them. No, this enemy is something less tangible, hard to grasp and even harder to keep hold of. How else, I realise, was my father's identity kept so secret?

'Then every generation deserves a whack behind the ears from their mother or father, and to be brought to heel. They must understand that good men have died for this stupid fascination with who will rule,' Oswy continues.

'If only they had our wisdom,' Wulfheard muses, and we're all silent.

'So, there are no Viking raiders or unease on the Welsh border?' I ask, just to be sure.

'Oh yes, there are rumours of them, all right,' Wulfheard assures me. 'And those are easy enough to contend with. It's the other whispers we must be alert to. Now, tell us, Icel, who is that woman you spoke to with Lord Coenwulf's children?'

'She's taken,' I hasten to inform them all. 'She and Edwin, they have an arrangement, and although Edwin's gone with Lord Coenwulf, she's sure, as is he, that seven winters will pass quickly, and they'll be reunited.'

'She has a mother, though,' Cenred calls, his approval evident. 'And she's a widow.'

Wulfheard smirks but then faces them all. 'We cause no trouble here. We don't need any women. We can amuse ourselves well enough by riding out and fighting amongst ourselves. I don't want to pull you apart from one another and give Lord Wigmund any opportunity to complain to his father or bloody mother.'

'Where's the queen?' I query instead.

'She's currently in Winchcombe, so not far from here. Worse

luck. She and the king are largely separated, but she thinks to have some control over the nunnery there, as Lady Cwenthryth did before her. I wish her luck with that.' I try and bring to mind who Cwenthryth was and then recall she was the daughter of King Coenwulf, the first of his name. I think. She took command of the nunnery where her brother was buried and used his sainted status to add to the troubles in Mercia following her father's demise. She's been dead for some years. Perhaps all the Mercian women are meddlesome, not just the queen and Lady Ælflæd.

'So the king has a disaffected son, wife, and this new lordling, Beorhtwulf, all vying for power, and scattered over Mercia. Isn't that dangerous?'

'Yes, it's very dangerous. That's why we're here. Ealdorman Tidwulf has men with the queen, and in Tamworth, Ealdorman Beornoth keeps his gaze on Ealdorman Sigered as well as Beorhtwulf, whom he's not related to although they share name elements. Sigered is more slippery than a Thames-caught eel. But enough pessimism. Come, we'll ride the boundaries and see what can be seen.'

With that, Wulfheard urges Bada onwards, and the other men hasten to hurry, which makes Brute rush to the front. My horse, catching me unawares, streams onwards, and the landscape, notably flat, passes swiftly before my eyes. In the distance, I can see the Welsh hills, not that they ever come any closer. We'd need to cross the River Severn at one of the bridges to do that.

When Brute eventually slows, I turn him and peer back the way we've come. To the south, hills rise, leading onwards to where I know Wessex must be, while to the west, the hint of cloud suggests the sea isn't far either. Wulfheard's the first to catch me.

'I see he's as well behaved as ever.'

'Nothing changes there,' I confirm.

'Tell me, Icel, I didn't want to ask inside the walls of Kingsholm, but Lady Ælflæd seems greatly changed.'

'She is, yes, I suspect she wishes to be queen more than her brother ever wished to be king. Her son is a poor feeder and lacks strength, or so I've heard. I think she worries he might die, and of course, she does have to live with the odious Lord Wigmund.'

'Perhaps,' Wulfheard muses, but I can see his mind is busy, mulling over all that might be the cause of the current unease running through Mercia. 'Never one to believe a fight can solve everything, I think if, this summer, we have an attack from one of our many enemies, then Mercia will unite, and all will be well again.'

'I doubt you'll get your wish,' I caution him. The Viking raiders, having been attacked on the Isle of Sheppey, haven't been sighted since, at least not close to the River Thames or even to the north, where they might sneak along the River Trent. As for King Ecgberht of Wessex, it's understood that he still struggles to contain the unease from the Viking raider attacks. I can't see that he'll direct his gaze to Mercia anytime soon. Mercia, I fear, will tear itself apart without the aid of any external force.

11

'Wulfheard.' The sharp command of Ealdorman Ælfstan echoes above the clash of training weapons inside Kingsholm, and every man there turns to eye Ælfstan, mounted on his horse.

'My lord. We didn't know to expect you yet,' is the immediate reply from Wulfheard who, cheeks puffing, strides towards his oath-sworn lord, his weapon lowered. 'It's not yet midsummer.'

'Well, I'm here, and now we're commanded to Londonia. Viking raiders along the River Thames. Ealdorman Muca sends word to the king.' Whether Ealdorman Ælfstan approves of this or not is impossible to tell. I note that he rides with two men I don't know. Has he taken on men to replace those lost last year, or are they about some other business?

Such news that the enemy has been sighted should fill me with trepidation, but I'm a warrior, and this is what I do. Anything has to be better than enduring the sour atmosphere at Kingsholm. Young Coenwulf and Coelwulf thrive. Young Wigstan, I believe, is slowly starting to gain on Coelwulf, which cheers me even if his mother remains contrary in her treatment of all, including her young sister.

Lady Cynewise has become somewhat of a friend to the men under the command of Wulfheard and also to me. But that's not what makes the atmosphere so difficult. No, that's been caused by the arrival of Queen Cynethryth from Winchcombe with all of her demands. It would have been better for all, including her son, had the queen remained in her manor but she's determined to ensure all know her son is the king's heir, even if neither the queen or his son are with the king.

'When do we leave?' Wulfheard calls to Ælfstan, a very public conversation so that neither of them have to repeat themselves again.

'Tomorrow morning. The queen brought her warriors with her. I carry instructions that she's to remain here, with the king's son, until such time as the Viking raiders are removed from the River Thames.' Now I understand whom the other two warriors are. They must be from the king to the queen, or just the queen's men, encountered on the road by the ealdorman.

Such an accounting is well given, and I nod, conflicted already, despite my urge to be clear of Kingsholm. It's been a long half a year here. I've no true bed to call my own. I'm heartily sick of living from day to day not knowing where I can place my possessions or rest my head each night. It's been easier since the arrival of Wulfheard and the others. But only just.

'And don't think you're not included, Icel,' Ælfstan's calls to me, as though able to hear my thoughts. The command is hardly privately given. 'The king has personally demanded that you're included.' My heart sinks at that, but it's not surprising. I can't help but see the queen's hand at play in this. She was dismayed to find me at Kingsholm when she arrived, just shy of a month ago. I found her watching me. I didn't know she'd sent word to the king.

And yet I gave my oath to Lady Cynehild. Surely, I try and

equivocate, I must be fulfilling it by ensuring Mercia remains whole.

'My lord.' I incline my head towards him and note that the tension eases from his shoulders at my easy response. I don't want to leave the children. Even though I hardly see them, at least I'm close if they need me. But equally, I know I must leave Kingsholm. My presence here has outgrown any grudging acceptance it might have initially earned. Eadweard and Wulfred understand to keep their distance, but that's more down to Wulfheard and Oswy than anything I've done. If my fellow warriors leave, and I'm left with Eadweard and Wulfred, I realise I'll be beaten close to death again. Equally, the queen and her son are overly aware of me. Lady Ælflæd, I fear, sees nothing but her son, and her perceived failure, and that of her brother's treason. She wouldn't know whether I was here or not, and that saddens me even now. I've spent so long trying to avoid her, and yet I now realise I needn't have bothered. She doesn't see me. I could have been sat before her for the last half a year, and she still wouldn't have acknowledged my presence.

Later that night, I seek out Eadburg. She and I have become friends in Edwin's absence. It's strange how much easier it is to like him when he's not here. Yes, Edwin and I had been thrust together inside Kingsholm, but all the same, I didn't always find his presence as easy as when we were children. We mended our friendship, but it wasn't quite the same.

'There's still no word from Edwin,' Eadburg frets, as I watch her tending to the children's clothes, needle in hand, ensuring the tears are repaired.

'I don't think there will be, either. Lord Coenwulf knows that his safety depends on no one knowing where he is.' Eadburg and I have had this conversation almost every day since Edwin left.

'Perhaps, but the same can't be true for Edwin, Cuthwalh, and the others who went with him,' she protests.

'If they're all still together, then yes, it must.'

She sighs unhappily at my oft-spoken phrase. She accepts it, and yet, I imagine, late at night, that it taunts her all the same.

'How are the children?'

This question makes her smile. I'm sure, as young as she is, that she must wish to be a mother herself. 'Coenwulf is learning his letters with the monks. Coelwulf's sitting and rolling unaided now. He's a quick boy to learn. And Wigstan is getting there,' she offers with a soft smile. I think all of the women have a soft spot for Wigstan, who's battled through no end of hardships as he appears determined to defy the odds and survive his first year. They don't appreciate his mother, but Wigstan has finally begun to accept the presence of others who care for him, allowing Lady Ælflæd some respite. No matter what people might say about him, he's certainly a fighter. 'And, of course, Lady Cynewise is always with the children, for all she's really one herself.'

I've found occasion to send Lady Cynewise herbs I find on my travels beyond the confines of Kingsholm. I've brought her fennel, yarrow, wild onion, young beech leaves and watercress. I know she still practises on any who'll ask her opinion. She's much better with people than the monks, who think they know all there is to know about healing. Not for the first time, I think she'd have been helpful in Ealdorman Tidwulf's desire to write a leechbook, and she'd certainly have benefited from the presence of Gaya and Theodore. I've still not managed to find her a sharper blade. I really must look for one in Londonia.

'Then you're happy all will be well when we leave?'

Now Eadburg's face twists. 'Provided the queen doesn't interfere. She's only ever birthed one child but believes she knows better than my mother, who birthed six of her own children, and assisted with almost every other woman's child within Kingsholm. She was the woman who tended to the old king's wife, and ensured that Lady Cynewise survived the loss of her mother.' Outrage sparks those words.

I nod. 'Yes, she's somewhat overbearing,' I try and mollify.

'But yes, Icel. Don't worry. Fight the Viking raiders, and all will be well when you return to Kingsholm. Will you be returning here?' Her question's edged with worry.

'I will, yes. Wine's remaining behind. Pega says he'll see to her needs, but I'm sure she'd welcome some attention from young Coenwulf.'

'Of course. She's so gentle with him. I don't think it'll be long until he needs his own pony to ride.'

'You can never start them too young,' I confirm, and then we part. I return to my horses to ensure all is as it should be. I can't say I'm excited to be riding to Londonia and a possible fight with the enemies of Mercia. But I'd sooner face them than the ones within Mercia, who work to undermine all that King Wiglaf has achieved. My opinion of him continues to evolve and change. I admire him for all he's done, and yet wish he was a little more alert to the antics of his wife, son and Ealdorman Sigered. And Lord Beorhtwulf.

King Wiglaf seeks Mercia's enemies at her borders and along her rivers. I'm not sure he's correct to do so.

* * *

I lean over Brute's shoulder, raised in the saddle, trying to make it easier for him as he nears the summit of the huge hill Ealdorman Ælfstan was determined we crested. For all there's another way that misses the hill, the ealdorman wouldn't listen to the complaints of the horses or the men.

'A viewpoint such as this should be examined in detail,' he said obdurately. Now, Brute is the first to near the top of the hill. I know the others are struggling behind me. I did almost consider dismounting and know that others have done so, yet Brute pushed on. He's the most stubborn horse I've ever met.

Finally, as the terrain levels out, I turn and look behind me. Seeing a vast distance to the north and west is possible from here. The hills of the Welsh kingdoms are easy to pick out, as is the patchwork quilt of fields before me. Everything looks tranquil, even the river threading through the land from the sea, all along the River Severn. I'd hoped to search the shoreline for seaweed for Lady Cynewise, but that will have to wait. Perhaps Ealdorman Ælfstan was correct after all. Maybe a permanent watch should be kept here, alert to any possible dangers from Viking raiders using the sea.

'Good God.' Wulfheard is next to arrive, his neck streaming with sweat, where he walks beside Bada, who, head down, looks exhausted. I can see Ealdorman Ælfstan walking beside his mount as well, and determine to hold my tongue when he arrives, although I doubt others will do the same.

The furthest away is Oswy, his horse ploughing ahead of him while, back bent to the slope, he almost crawls on hands and knees.

'It's like the hill on the Isle of Sheppey,' Wulfheard huffs, his face bright pink with the exertion.

'Only five times as long,' I offer resentfully, not wishing to be reminded of the fight and the men we lost there. Sometimes I feel like the others have forgotten all about those who've fallen in the name of Mercia. But then, one of them will say something, a soft word or two, a cup of ale raised in their memory, and I appreciate that we all carry wounds we keep hidden deep in our hearts.

'Was it worth it?' Wulfheard calls to the ealdorman when he finally arrives. The tone's sharp, and I think the ealdorman will be angry, but instead, he grins, more rictus than joy.

'At least we can say it was indeed worth it,' he calls to Oswy and others still struggling. 'It would have been crap if we'd arrived here and the clouds had descended, and we couldn't see anything.'

He makes a fair point, and as the men collapse to the ground, the horses panting and covered in sweat, I realise we'll be allowed to rest and drink in the view. I swig water from my supplies and look at my fellow warriors.

The years are starting to show on many of them. There's no one here younger than me. I thought the ealdorman would replace those he lost at Sheppey, but he hasn't. Perhaps it would be too much like hard work to whip men into shape so that they fitted with the motley collection of warriors.

The ealdorman is the most changed of all. When I first met him, he was a young man, perhaps with not many more winters to his name than I have now, but time and the fighting we've been forced to endure throughout the last seven summers has left him with physical wounds. His blue eyes are still as bright as ever, but the odd fleck of grey can be seen in his brown beard, and sometimes, when no one's looking, he walks with a slight limp. And, beneath his tunic, I know his chest is criss-crossed with scars from long-since-healed injuries.

Oswy finally emerges only to collapse onto the green tufted grass, his chest heaving beneath his tunic. He started the climb with his byrnie in place, so I hope his horse now carries it, or he'll be retracing his steps. He's a tall man, although I overtop him now. His blond hair masks the streaks of silver that are only visible beneath the bright light of the noon sun. For once, he has no black eye, and his nose is straight. How long that will last is impossible to know. Probably until we encounter one of the Viking raiders or he gets enticed into a fight with someone. Beneath his clothes, his flesh is hard with muscle and the scars of his battles. One of those scars I healed inside Londinium.

'How about it, men, a lookout point, just here?' Ealdorman Ælfstan calls to them.

'As long as we never have to stand a watch,' Maneca huffs. He's on his feet and is recovering more quickly than the others, but it's not that quick.

'The horses need watering,' I call to anyone who'll listen, leading Brute towards where I can hear the rush of tumbling water. Here, a light breeze plays with my dark hair, and I'm grateful I took the time to trim back my beard and moustache. Brute drinks eagerly, for all he seems little concerned by what he's just endured. The other horses follow him without their riders, and I walk amongst them, using a handful of long grasses from the side of the brook to wipe the white foam from their backs, shaking my head at the same time. The men should be here, doing this. Not me.

Eventually, they stagger towards me, even the ealdorman struggling, until they realise it's cooler here, away from the sun's heat, with a collection of branches serving as a shade.

'I think we should move on after we've eaten,' the ealdorman confirms. I look down and smile. All of them have overextended themselves this morning – the damn fools.

Later, as the day begins to close in around us, the horses and men, still languid in their movements, are called to a halt by Wulfheard.

'We sleep here tonight and press on tomorrow to Londonia. It'll take us another three days to get there.' This he directs to Ealdorman Ælfstan. It should have been possible to reach Londonia in three days if we'd taken the other route, and not the four that it now will. There's no response from the ealdorman as we settle for the night. Above my head, the sky's cloudless, stars shimmering brightly as the others grumble and groan, and only when soft snores fill the air do I close my eyes, finding comfort in being with my allies once more and, more importantly, being absent from the oppressive atmosphere inside Kingsholm, where the queen, and her son, plot for when he must become king in the place of his father. I can't see it will happen, but what do I know of politics and kingships?

12

'Where have they been seen?' Ealdorman Ælfstan directs the question to Ealdorman Muca as they greet each other before the hall in Londonia. It seems little has changed since last year when we were here. Although, of course, Frithwine, Æthelmod and Brithelm aren't with us, so there's not likely to be a bloody fight.

'Towards the coast. At least five ships, and sometimes as many as ten.'

The ealdorman looks unhappy at the news.

'They've been disrupting what trading there is at this time of the year when the river levels are so low. The men and women have been vocal in their complaints.'

'So, no fighting, just pillaging?'

'We've found two settlements that have been abandoned, close to the mouth of the river. We found no bodies, so we must assume the inhabitants ran away before they were fired by the enemy.'

'And you have men on watch duty?'

'Yes, we do, and Londinium still possesses a contingent of warriors who use the fort's high walls to watch the river, but the enemy aren't fools. They know to stay out of sight and pick off the ships one by one.'

'Do we have warriors in the ships?'

'Not at this time, no. I don't know many warriors who like to be on a ship, and the traders aren't keen to have a Mercian warrior in there with them. They think one will be no help, although some of them have started to move in convoys, finding safety in numbers.'

I listen with half an ear, eating the fine bread and pottage handed to us after four days of travelling here. Affairs in Londonia sound less fractious than last year, but I can see why Ealdorman Muca wanted reinforcements from the king. The trade that does take place in Londonia is important to Mercia. If the traders stop using the route, even during the summer, then Mercia will suffer, and so will the king's finances.

'And Wessex?'

'Nothing from them. The traders are happy to visit their shore as well as ours. They bring little news, even when I ask specific questions.'

'It's early in the season,' Ælfstan muses. 'Perhaps this is just the beginning, or maybe they've decided on different targets for the remainder of the year. Any news of Lord Coenwulf's whereabouts?' I listen more carefully now. I'd not realised it was something that anyone was genuinely interested in.

'Nothing. It's as though he's disappeared. How was the queen when you saw her?' Ealdorman Muca speaks as though he doesn't truly want the answer.

'Demanding, as to be expected.' Ælfstan lowers his voice. 'There's no sign of another child yet for her son and wife. She grows impatient with Lady Ælflæd, for all she only managed one son with the king. At least it appears as though the child, Wigstan, will survive, after all.'

The two men move aside to discuss matters of taxation and

trade, and I stop listening, a pit of unease in my belly.

'What's the matter with you?' Wulfheard queries later when we're preparing to sleep before setting off again in the morning.

'Nothing, really. Just thinking.'

'Well, I'd do less of that if I were you, Icel. I really would. It just seems to get you into trouble.'

* * *

For two months, we ride ever eastward and then back towards Londonia. First one way and then another. The weather gets steadily hotter, the routes familiar beneath the horses' hooves, but we don't see even one Viking raider ship in all that time. The settlements we pass are mostly intact. As Ealdorman Muca said, one or two closer to the mouth of the River Thames have been abandoned and burned. But almost everywhere we visit, the inhabitants are busy in the fields or ensuring their defences are in good condition. Ditches are dug deeper, or at least have the filth of the winter removed from the stinking water lying in the bottom of them, while the ramparts are repaired and the gates made to hang straight where they might have dipped on hinges that creak and complain from the damp winter weather.

'Nothing's happening,' Oswy calls in frustration, far from for the first time. We came here to counter the enemy, but they're non-existent. Whatever ships were plaguing the traders have disappeared as though they were never here. Six times we ride past the location where we first fought the Viking raiders last year, and six times we come to the location where we returned from our foray to the Isle of Sheppey. My skin changes colour beneath the unrelenting heat, but I've no wounds to try and heal other than the odd splinter or knife wound from cutting onions and herbs for the pottage.

The land's hot, the crops ripening, and for once we don't get rained on. We keep our canvases rolled tight on the back of our horses' saddles, and we all grow even more restless than we were in Kingsholm.

'There's nothing,' Wulfheard presses the ealdorman. Ealdorman Ælfstan hasn't remained with us for the entire time. For a month, he kept to Londonia, closeted with Muca, as they discussed court matters.

'No, there isn't,' the ealdorman quickly agrees. 'It's almost as though there never was anything, and we've been summoned here by little more than whispers. Muca fears a substantial attack may be launched against Londonia, but I don't understand how. Surely such an undertaking would require some degree of organisation that I don't see at work here. Not even a scouting vessel. I think the Viking raiders have learned from what happened to them last year. They mean to stay clear of Mercia, and perhaps even Wessex, for they've no way of knowing we retrieved Lord Coenwulf last year. They might believe it the work of the Wessex king's son.'

'Then we should leave,' Oswy says quickly.

'And go where? Wouldn't you sooner be here than stuck in Tamworth or Kingsholm? I assure you, the queen continues to cause problems if the reports Muca are receiving are correct. Better to stay here, away from the rumour and gossip.'

And so we do. All summer long. For four months, from Eastermonað to Weodmoað, including the most pleasant of all months, Liða, we ride the riverbanks, learning the settlements by name, and recognising people in all of them, who provide us with food and ale, in exchange for our assistance in constructing new defences for them. All of us are shaded by the sun, refusing to wear our byrnies when we ride because they rub against our hot skin. The ealdorman stays with us on some occasions but, on others, remains in Lundenwic or even in Londinium, taking his place on the ancient high stone ramparts, where he says he can see us, no matter how far away we think to be from his scrutiny. He says it to ensure we stay alert, but we don't need such a threat. We've all fought the enemy too many times. We don't fear to do so again.

Time and again, my thoughts turn to Edwin, Lady Ælflæd and the two children. I hope Edwin is well, that young Coenwulf and Coelwulf thrive, and I even hope that Wigstan continues to do well. My feelings towards Lady Ælflæd are ambiguous. She married the king's son. She knew what she was doing. And now, no doubt, she must share his bed once more in the hope of carrying another of his children. I'd pity her if I didn't feel so angry at her for speaking out against her brother. I consider Lady Cynewise as well. I pray that she continues to learn and spend her time with Eadburg and her mother, and that I remember to find her a sharp cutting knife for her herbs before we return to Kingsholm.

Only when the weather takes a decided turn for the worse and the harvest is collected in are we allowed back to Londonia.

'Icel.' The ealdorman beckons me closer, his face revealing nothing of his inner thoughts, as I enter the hall from which Ealdorman Muca controls Londonia for the king. Ealdorman Ælfstan has been absent for much of the last month. I know he planned to travel to Tamworth and seek out the king, and see what was happening amongst those lords not deployed by the king to ensure Mercia was defended.

'What is it, my lord?' I murmur, realising, as he moves away from the rest of the returning men, that this is something he wishes only to tell me.

'I've heard some worrying reports of what's happening at Kingsholm. I know you'd want to know.' Immediately, my stomach fills with unease.

'What sort of reports?'

'The queen, her son, Lady Ælflæd.'

'What of them?'

Now the ealdorman looks away, not wishing to meet my eyes. 'And Lord Coenwulf's children.'

'What of them?' My voice has grown cold.

'I don't know, not for sure, but I thought you should know. I fear. I fear that they mean to take some sort of irrevocable course of action against them now that Wigstan is so much more hale. You know, of course, about Lord Beorhtwulf. I believe they mean to take actions to limit those with a claim to the kingship of Mercia, and they mean to start with the youngest and easiest to contend with. The king will hear nothing against his wife, son and grandson, but Lord Beorhtwulf speaks with all the confidence of a man who knows what's really happening. Of course, he might intend to undermine the queen, I just don't know. It worries me, Icel, it really does.' The ealdorman looks plaintively at me.

'No,' I gasp, all of my previous worries and fears descending upon me. I don't want to suspect Lady Ælflæd of such thoughts towards her nephews, and yet I can't deny that it's not the first time I've feared for them. I'd hoped that Wigstan's better health would prevent the need, but perhaps it's not enough. Once more, I'm reminded of King Offa. He was stringent in disposing of those with any link to the kingship. As such, it's a wonder that Lord Beorhtwulf, and his kinship to King Beonred, has survived to the day. Indeed, it makes me consider that Lord Beorhtwulf might be full of shit with his claims.

'Return to Kingsholm as quickly as you can, if you wish. Wulfheard told me of your bond with them, because of their mother. I'll follow on tomorrow. I must conclude some business here, with Ealdorman Muca. But I'll come after you. Despite the king's denial, I would see what's happening with my own eyes.'

I nod, already resolved to a long journey north and one that will be too slow, even with Brute as my companion.

'It might all be little and nothing. Whispers from those who mean to smear the name of the king and his wife. But, well...' I can tell he doesn't want to admit this. 'There's enough potential for them to be true that we should ensure nothing ill befalls the children.'

'My thanks for telling me.' I turn aside, but he reaches out and grips my arm.

'Icel, whatever this means to you, do nothing rash. We'll be there in another day, two at most after you arrive. Nothing is happening here. The enemy, wherever they are, aren't about to attack Londonia.'

'I'll do my best,' I inform him, my thoughts already on Kingsholm, the threat of the Viking raiders disappearing, with the fear for the two boys. I don't like to think of what the queen might be capable. Even more, I don't want Lady Ælflæd to be implicated, either. But if it's Lord Wigmund, I wouldn't be surprised. The men he chooses to spend his time with – Ælfred, Hunberht, even Eadweard and Wulfred – lack all honour.

I speak to no one as I slip from the hall again, meeting a surprised-looking Brute in the stables. But he makes no complaint when I quickly saddle him and turn him westwards. While the peak of the summer is passed, there's more than enough daylight to keep up a steady canter, and then, when the darkness finally descends, the moon offers just enough illumination that we can travel at a steady trot. We pause for some rest after over a day's travelling, and then I urge Brute onwards. I don't take the hill route that Ealdorman Ælfstan insisted upon on the way to Londonia. It would only slow us. All the same, we manage to compress three days of travelling into just over two.

We arrive outside Kingsholm when the gates have been opened for the day and elicit no surprise from those who witness us passing beneath them. I note that there are no gate wardens once more. The queen and her son remain too confident of their safety.

'Icel?' Pega calls to me from the stables as I take Brute inside for some much-deserved rest.

I turn and meet his surprised eyes. 'Hello, Pega. How is everyone here at Kingsholm?' I try and keep my voice neutral, hoping he doesn't realise how exhausted Brute and I are. But Pega's face clouds at the question, and he steps close to me, so close that the bristles on his beard touch my ear.

'There's something foul afoot here. I worry for young Lady Cynewise and also for the two little lords. It's not been the same all summer with you and Wulfheard gone.'

'Thank you,' I murmur, surprised by his immediate admission.

'Icel, be wary. The queen's here although she and her son and Lady Ælflæd are preparing to travel to Tamworth on the king's orders. He's summoned them to attend a witan, but they mean to take the children with them, including Lady Cynewise, even though they'd be better left here. Why take such small children on such a journey, especially when two of them have never left Kingsholm before?'

'What? Why?'

Pega shrugs his shoulders, but I already understand too much. Away from Kingsholm and those who care for Lord Coenwulf's children, it'll be much easier for something to befall them. Different scenarios rush through my mind, and none of them are good.

'When do they leave?'

'Today, that's why I'm already saddling the horses.'

'Ealdorman Ælfstan means to follow me here. He should arrive in two days at most. When he does, tell him what you've told me. He'll know what to do.'

'And what will you do?'

'I'll go with them. I'll be their protector,' I announce, not even giving it a moment's thought.

'I suggest you ensure that Lord Wigmund, Lady Ælflæd and the queen don't see you. And Eadweard and the others. Not that it's easy to do. Your horse is unmistakable.' Brute lifts his head at those words, as though he understands them.

'I'll wait outside Kingsholm, and when they leave, I'll keep close, but not too close.' I appreciate he's right to caution me.

'Then go, and quickly.' I turn Brute, wishing I'd thought of this sooner. Quickly, head bowed, I walk Brute to the gate, mindful that I need to evade Eadweard, Wulfred, the queen and her son. Only when I'm once more outside do I take a deep breath. Hastily, I lead Brute to the far side of the road that stretches northwards and into a copse of trees, where we can hide away from those about to travel to see the king.

Eagerly, I wait and watch, the effects of the long days and nights of travel making it hard to stay awake. I allow Brute to doze but don't remove his saddle. The morning moves on apace, and the sun is blindingly hot for once, even though it's moving swiftly towards Haligmonað. I sweat beneath the trees, wishing I could sleep. I stand close to Brute, leaning against a handy tree trunk whose branches start high overhead. I listen to the cries of the men and women of Kingsholm. The shouted commands of those frustrated by one thing or another, and then I startle awake, much, much later, the sky already darkening, and curse myself for a damn fool.

The passage of the convoy north can be clearly seen in the piles of horseshit that splatters the road. I've slept through them leaving, and the fear in my belly hardens to one of sheer terror.

I've lost sight of the children.

'Come on,' I urge Brute, and together, with the blackness of a moonless, cloud-filled sky far overhead, we hurry after the sons of Lady Cynehild.

13

Somehow, I expect to catch them easily. But I don't. The road towards Tamworth is one I've travelled often, with Brute, and Wine.

I push Brute on, aware we've both had time to rest and that my horse never considers his physical limits until it's too late. Eyes wide, I keep alert, noting the drops of horseshit that splatter the road.

Overhead, the halo of shimmering stars moves on apace, and more than once I find myself fixated on one or another of them until the swoop of an owl or bat drags my eyes back to the road. And still, I can hear no sign of the party that's gone on ahead. I consider if they'll stop for the night in Worcester or if they won't make it so far. I didn't see how they intended to travel. Are the children on horses with an experienced rider, or are they in an ox-drawn cart with Eadburg and her mother? I remain alert, looking for signs of either.

All the same, I can't imagine the queen, her son and Lady Ælflæd wanting to camp by the side of the road if they've ridden. Yet I see nothing to give me an idea of where they might stop and so, at the crossroads, where a bridge leads over the River Avon and where I must decide, I glance down, eyeing the horse manure in the moon's glimmer. Which way from here? I wish I hadn't fallen asleep and had stayed alert. Indecision wars inside me, but I press on northwards towards Tamworth. Brute is steady beneath my feet, but I know we've travelled at a warrior's pace and not that of horses carrying children.

Yet the crossroads are too muddled. Anyone could have gone anywhere. There are signs of horses going towards Worcester, but equally, signs of them going towards Tamworth making use of the Fosse Way. Grimacing, I encourage Brute on, more watchful now. Any moment, I expect to encounter the party, sleeping on the side of the road, the smell of smoke alerting me to their presence. But there's nothing. Just a line of horse manure that continues onwards, alongside the occasional hoof print in a pile of mud, washed onto the decaying surface of the uneven road.

I know that Wulfheard would assure me that these roads were built by the giants who constructed Londinium and that they've survived for this long. Still, I can't help thinking, when the road slants to one side, or Brute has to sidestep some of the disturbed stones and gravel, that these roads could do with some repair work if they're to last another five hundred winters, or however long they've been here. Looking upwards, such a span of time seems small and inconsequential, but looking forwards, it seems as though it's been forever. Those men and women who laboured to hack through the hard-packed earth to carry the stones and pebbles to these places are not only long dead, their bodies will have become nought but dust and bones.

Caught up in my reverie, eyes on the heavens above me, I curse when I next glance to the ground. The telltale signs of horse manure have disappeared. Those small pieces that remain have been ground into the stones and surrounding grasses that think to claim the drainage ditches.

I lead Brute on, eyes peering downwards, but there's nothing.

'We've missed them,' I growl deep in my throat, and my horse is unhappy to turn back the way we've just come. I dismount angrily, jarring my knees, and retrace my steps, eyes on the ground. For what feels like half the night, I bend low, looking for what I seek.

'Where have they gone?' I huff more than once, trying to determine how I missed this change beneath me. Why were my thoughts on ancient people when my concern is for those living now?

'Where have they gone?' I repeat, fear suddenly constricting my chest. I don't want to think anything evil of Lady Ælflæd, but honestly, it's not her that I fear. The queen and her son are ambitious. Too ambitious. And they're not the only ones. Where are they?

'Damn it,' I exclaim, as the grey edges of dawn begin to tint the horizon. Brute follows me. His nose low, reins tied up behind his saddle. More than once, he bumps me, a question on his long, black and white face. But I've no answer for him. Not yet.

'Where have they gone?' I glower, fed up of repeating myself, standing to ease my aching back, pushing my hips forward to lessen the pain there. 'How have I missed them, and where are they going?' Frustrated and angry with myself, I reach for the saddle and help myself to a glug of water before leading Brute towards the welcoming gurgle of a nearby stream.

As he drinks eagerly, I look for signs of horse hooves, but there are none. The riders didn't come this way. Where, then, have they gone? Pega said they were travelling to Tamworth, but unless they've taken some strange route, they've not done so. Perhaps they only travelled some of the distance, turning off to spend the night in a manor somewhere or even visiting Winchcombe. That could, I realise, be my mistake. Or, perhaps, at the crossroads to Worcester, they went that way, keen to speak to the bishop?

'Come on,' I urge Brute, when he's drunk as much as he wants and I've given him some time to tug at the long grasses as well. 'We'll find them at Worcester, I'm sure of it.'

Brute's response is silence, but he does allow me to mount and hastens back towards Worcester, the river at our side offering a low burble of noise until we once more find the crossroads leading to the bridge over the River Avon. Here, with the help of more sunlight, I decide I made my mistake. It's obvious, or so it seems, that most of the traffic went towards the other settlement.

'At this rate,' I muse, 'it'll take them nearly a week to cover a journey we could make in two days at the most. But, of course, the queen is with them. No doubt she expects comfort, not speed.'

Ahead, the settlement of Worcester quickly comes into view, the fields under cultivation, hedges demarcating one crop from another, cows and sheep busy cropping the grasses for it's not yet slaughter month. Some say Worcester is an old settlement, but to me it looks like any other, complete with wooden halls and thatched roofs. But, not wanting to be distracted again, I glance downwards, time and time again, and just before I call for entry into the settlement itself, the smell of the river ripe in the air, I see a trail of horse hooves skirting the settlement. Forehead furrowed, I don't hear the woman speaking to me.

'Move your bloody horse, you great oaf of a man. I can't get my donkey through.' Her words are filled with venom as I peer down and down. She's diminutive, but with hands on hips looks as though she could flay me with her tongue.

Brute eagerly skips out of the way, and she goes to move to the fields and beyond. I consider what the poor donkey carries and where he's going, but call out.

'Is the queen in residence?'

'The queen?' The woman's shocked words assure me that she's not. 'The queen? Why would she come to Worcester? You daft beggar.' And away she goes, encouraging the pliant beast to walk beside her. As I watch, the beast pauses, and a virulent stream of shit hits the ground with a wet thud.

'So that's where all the shit comes from on the road,' I muse.

Ahead, the gates to Worcester are open wide, and I note that some sort of defensive structure encircles parts of the settlement but not all of it. Houses jut up against the ruins of the walls, and the gate really doesn't stop anyone from getting inside. A tumbled-down ruin to the side of it allows entry and exit for those with no goods to convey. I watch a handful of children spider their way over the ruins, chasing a small black and white dog, tail wagging, as it races onwards. They'll have fun catching the little terror.

So, the queen isn't inside Worcester? Where then might she be?

'Are you coming or going?' a grizzled man demands to know. He stands beside me, a wool hat covering sparse hair, his long nose almost touching his lips. His voice is rough, but his eyes are bright with interest.

'I was looking for the queen, but I hear she's not here.'

'The queen? Why would she come to Worcester? No, my lord, last we heard, she was at Winchcombe or Kingsholm with her son, and the king at Tamworth.'

'My thanks,' I call, turning Brute back towards the bridge that leads back to the Fosse Way.

'We've seen no one in these parts other than a group of riders who skirted the settlement yesterday, heading off towards Hereford, I think.'

I stop at those words. Riders? Hereford? 'Is that usual?'

'No, not really. Most people going to Hereford cross the River Severn at Gloucester. It's easier down there. They have to ask some of the river traders to help them up here. The river's wide and there's no bridge.'

'How were they dressed?' I ask the man. I can feel my forehead's furrowed, my eyes narrowed in confusion.

'Like you, my lord. Warriors, I should say.'

'I'm no lord,' I counter, only to shrug my shoulders. I am a lord. I just don't like to think about it.

'Go and see old Leofstan. He'll be upstream a bit. He'll know who they were. He can get information out of a stone, that one.'

I smirk at the rueful tone and dip my head to thank him for his help.

'That way.' He points, showing me where I can bypass the houses and the remnants of the wall on my way to the river. Eyes alert, I look to the settlement as the smoke of cook fires blights the early morning sky. Worcester is much smaller than Gloucester, the village closest to Kingsholm. At Gloucester, much of the old wall remains; inside it, the monks and nuns have built their church and keep very much to themselves. Outside it, the houses of the traders and farmers, complete with workshops and winter enclosures for those animals lucky enough to survive, spread over a wide area, not always close to the old walls.

Here, the buildings that don't belong to the church are pressed up tight to the embankment of the old wall, and there are far fewer of them. That said, the church is visible, its wooden struts and thatched roof peeking over the top of the decaying wall. I ride Brute slowly, mindful of the collection of grazing animals and the runaway dog and children that seem to pay me no heed. This is a place of few defences and even fewer people.

I follow my nose as much as the outskirts of the settlement to where the river is. Once there, I look across it. It's wide. The gate warden's correct to warn me. I can see two ships bobbing in the river and seek out Leofstan. It seems I need not worry that I won't find him.

'My lord.' His voice is firm and filled with command as he steps to the side of me, emerging from a slanting building, inside which I must assume he keeps his stores. There's no cloud of smoke, and neither can I smell it. It's not a dwelling. That's obvious.

'Leofstan?'

'Aye, my lord. Can I assist you in some way?'

'Riders, yesterday? They came this way?'

'They did, yes, off to Hereford, they said. I told 'em to go to Gloucester, but they were having none of it.'

'How many?'

'A dozen of 'em. They weren't happy about the river. Almost as though they didn't know it was here.'

'Did they, excuse the question because it's strange, have a child with them or another lord?'

'A child? Not that I can say. But there was activity on the river overnight. I heard it, but I didn't see it. Others might have crossed later on. It was a clear night. Still, I kept to my bed. But it's impossible not to hear. My home is there.' Leofstan points close to the walls, and I understand. The house, of firm construction, faces westwards, towards the river, but it's just far enough away that I'd not be keen to be roused from my bed to see what was happening. 'I knew it wasn't my boat,' he said. 'I sent it to Gloucester only yesterday.'

'And a lord?'

'Impossible to tell. They might have crossed later, during the night.'

Chewing my lip, I gaze at the view of the river. It's wide here, but nothing compared to the River Thames. Yet I don't know the river.

'Could I swim it with my horse?'

'Why would you want to do that? You're almost in the kingdom of the Welsh, and nothing comes from there but trouble. Mark my words.'

'I think the men are my friends,' I murmur. 'I'm keen to find them.'

'Your friends, are they? Well, I can tell you that one of them was named Wulfred, if that helps you. Had no hair on his head. Surly-faced bastard.'

'Wulfred? Yes, yes, that sounds like him,' I reply, but clearly too quickly. An arched eyebrow, and I think Leofstan is as good at getting the truth out of everyone as the man at the gate informed me.

'Then I can help you. Come with me downstream a little. There's somewhere that the river narrows even more. You'll stand more chance there than you will here. We need a bridge, but no one will part with the coin to build one. Not the bishop. And certainly not the traders, or to be honest, me. I make a living from ferrying people on to the far side of the river, but I give them the opportunity to use the bridge at Gloucester first.'

'Lead on.' I offer an attempt at a smile, but it doesn't touch my lips.

Unlike Leofstan, I know what lies to the west of the river. My uncle and I spent more than enough time close to Hereford. The Welsh kingdoms start some way off yet, but the woodland will be thick, and I'll be alone. And I don't understand what Wulfred and Eadweard are doing. Shouldn't I be turning my head to Tamworth? Only something about that doesn't feel right. I don't believe the queen, Lady Ælflæd and Lord Wigmund are going to Tamworth, not with the children of Lord Coenwulf. It seems they're not crossing the river here either unless they did so during the night. Where, then, are the children? It might be easy enough to hide young Coenwulf and Coelwulf, but not Lady Cynewise.

The strength of the sun gains in intensity, as I walk northwards, Leofstan content to hold his tongue. His gait is firm, for all his legs are more widely spaced than mine. Perhaps, I reason, it's a sign of the time he's spent on board his own ship. I know of mounted warriors who walk similarly, too used to being astride a horse.

'Here you go, my lord.'

I open my mouth to snap back my immediate reply, only to see his eyes shimmering with mirth before I gaze at the river before me. Here, trees grow close to the bank, a tangle of dying summer growth stretching into the river. But – and I smirk to see this – there are two trees, one on each side of the river, and their limbs just about meet and twist together. A bridge for small animals, and I can see where some slight children might think to try their luck.

'Down you go, and then just keep straight,' Leofstan informs me, his eye on the supplies on the back of Brute. 'Have you been to Londonia?' he queries.

'Yes, it's all quiet down there. No sign of the Viking raiders or Wessex warriors.'

'Hum,' he muses. 'This river here. It's been my livelihood since before I could walk, yet I sense its weakness. It's good for trade. It'll be better for those Viking raiders and their ships.'

I startle at that, eyeing him with surprise. 'It won't come to that, surely? The Viking raiders like to stay close to the sea, not the rivers, other than the wide expanse of the Thames.'

'Maybe not. When they tire of such easy targets as the markets and isolated monasteries and nunneries, they'll consider what else they might be able to reach quickly. I've even heard some tell that they lift their ships clear from the rivers when they run out and carry them until they find the next river.'

'No,' I exclaim, astounded by such an idea.

'Yes, my lord. And when you return to King Wiglaf, perhaps you could tell him of such concerns.'

'King Wiglaf?'

'Yes, my lord. I know one of the king's warriors when I see him. You might be alone, but your equipment and horse are of the finest standard. Not for you, a rusty spear or an axe fit for cutting wood, not men.'

'My thanks,' I offer him, suddenly wishing I didn't need to remove my byrnie and tunic to cross the river. But I'll sink if I don't remove my armour. At least, I realise, my body isn't criss-crossed with the many wounds that Oswy or the ealdorman would reveal.

'I'll watch you across. I can't be much help to you if you flounder, but I think your horse will keep you safe.'

And with that, bare-chested and without my boots, for they're tied to the saddle, I clamber down the riverbank, Brute beside me, trying to avoid all the twisting weeds of a full summer's growth, and a thistle, that rears up, almost head height.

Gingerly, I dip a toe in the water, shivering at the coldness of it. I think it's colder than the River Thames. A chuckle reaches my ears. Resolutely, I ignore it, encouraging Brute into the water, and I follow him, teeth clenched to fight off the breath-stealing cold.

Beneath me, my feet kick up muck and filth from the bottom of the riverbed, and I can feel what I hope are fish shimmering around my legs. Brute eagerly stretches out, and I follow him, staying near his saddle. The water's at least less turbulent here, and I don't feel the tug of the tide around my legs. Perhaps that only happens on the River Thames. I'm sure that if Uor were here he'd tell me all about different rivers, but for now, I focus only on the far shore. In no time at all, before my body can truly warm up in the water, I erupt onto the opposite riverbank, streaming water.

'Well done, my lord. Now, just follow your nose, and it'll take you to Hereford.'

I lift my hand in thanks to Leofstan as he begins his march back towards Worcester. In the distance, the settlement seems both smaller and bigger, the pall of smoke over it informing me that even a small population needs much wood to burn to provide food and keep warm, as well as to work at smelting and whatever trades take place close to the old walls.

Eagerly, I slip my tunic back over my wet back, forcing my byrnie over it as well. And then, feet white with cold, I wince at the unforgiving leather of my boots as I slip them on. Beside me, Brute drips, and I think I should dry him, but it's getting warmer and warmer, almost as though the summer intends to cling on and not allow autumn to turn the leaves a myriad hue of browns and oranges.

'Come on then, lad. Let's see what we can find.' In all honesty, I'm not sure why I'm here. I should be following the Fosse Way to Tamworth, but I'm not. I've never trusted Eadweard and Wulfred or the rest of them. They didn't journey south to help secure Mercia's southern border when it was under threat. No, they stayed at Kingsholm. So why have they finally left it? I'm determined to find out.

Slipping beneath the boughs of the trees that line the river, Brute travels ahead of me, head bowed, forging a path for me to follow. I'm reminded of the time I spent hiding in the woodlands hereabouts when my uncle fled from Tamworth as King Ecgberht of Wessex claimed it for himself. I haven't given much thought to the places I visited since then. For a moment, I fear that I might stumble upon spots we once camped, perhaps even where my uncle met his death.

Angrily, I force myself to continue. What's past is past. I need to determine what Eadweard and Wulfred are up to and what's happening to the children of Lord Coenwulf, and his sister, and perhaps then I might be able to rest and enjoy the peace.

Only, of course, that's not about to happen.

14

The first indication that I'm not alone is the sharp snap of a twig echoing through the treeline. I pause, trying to listen, but Brute hasn't heard it, and he presses on, head bowed, no doubt keen to be free from the trees.

'What was that?' I murmur, but of course, I receive no answer, and eventually I convince myself I've imagined it. Overhead, the interlocking boughs of oak and fir trees block out much of the light, but the strange sepia tones offer just enough visibility to see.

The bank of trees continues, with no sign of it ever thinning, not even the odd stump to assure me that I might be getting close to a place where the locals come to collect their wood for burning. Only then I hear another sharp snap of a breaking twig, this one followed by an exclamation of pain.

'Who's there?' I call, hand reaching for my seax, pleased I tied my weapons belt back in place after my dip in the water.

My words echo back to me, and for all I peer around me, and even Brute's come to a halt, I don't see or hear anything else.

'Whoever you are, know that I'm a warrior of Mercia, and I'm armed. I've killed many men.' My words sound pathetic, even to my ears, but I'll give whomever it is a firm warning. If they attack me now and die on the edge of my blade, they can't say it was entirely unexpected.

'Come on, lad,' I urge Brute on, hopeful that whoever follows me leaves me alone or that we reach a road or designated pathway before I have to shed blood. I distract myself by finding all the mushrooms that Wynflæd might once have asked me to hunt for her. I note the different coloured caps as I go, not bending to pick them but careful not to trample them. Brown, red, thin, curved, I see them all deep in the woodlands. The thought of Wynflæd brings with it sorrow. I left Tamworth on bad terms with her, and I've not yet returned to make my apologies. Perhaps, one day soon, when the mystery of Lord Coenwulf's sons has been resolved, I might visit her with a sack of mushrooms, some horseradish and burdock, alongside other herbs she might need to make my peace with her.

As angry as I was, I'm starting to consider why. What difference does it make to my life whom my father was? He was never really my father. My uncle raised me. Wynflæd and Edwin's mother aided him in that. I should be grateful to them, not angry because they kept such a secret from me.

'Ah, I thought it was.' The words startle me from my thoughts. Looking up, I feel my lips compress on seeing Eadweard, Wulfred and his other warriors in a semicircle, blocking my way ahead.

'Why are you here?' I demand to know. 'What's in Hereford?' I can't see their horses, and I know they've ridden here. So, this isn't all of their force. They've left the horses somewhere else. I strain to hear but can detect no sound of a crying babe or a garrulous small child.

Eadweard chuckles at my questions, revealing his front tooth's been knocked out, no doubt in a fight.

'What does any of this have to do with you, Icel?'

'Do you have Lord Coenwulf's children and his sister?' I persist. I'm convinced they do, but I don't know where.

'Why would we have them?' Wulfred smirks, licking his thin lips with a sliver of tongue. Those with him laugh as well, the sound ripe with derision.

'You left Kingsholm with the queen, and the children?'

'We did, yes, but now we're going to Hereford, on the queen's business.'

'Why are you taking the children to Hereford? What's there?'

'Icel, Icel. Why are you concerned with children that aren't yours? The queen said you would be. I doubted her, as you weren't even in Kingsholm when we left, but she was correct to send us this way. We've been aware of you ever since you crossed the river at Worcester.'

'Wait? What?'

'Icel, you're not quite as clever as you think.' Only now do I hear yet another snap of a broken branch, and I turn, startled to see the huge warrior from Tamworth behind me. Horsa's eyes are as dull as ever, but it doesn't matter because his arms encircle me before I can lash out with my seax as he crushes my arms tighter and tighter to my chest. For the first time in any battle I've ever fought, I wish I wasn't wearing my byrnie. It makes breathing even more difficult.

I kick out with my feet, but I'm like a child lifted by a parent besides the huge warrior. I can't aim a blow on his knees, and I quickly succumb to this unexpected attack, my breath stolen from me in the tight crush.

When I wake again, I'm trussed up like a dead boar, feet together, knees together, my arms above my head, with the rope looped around something in the ground, perhaps even a tree trunk. My mouth tastes of the carding comb. I try to spit aside the woolliness, but there's no moisture to aid me. I think I can hear the nicker of my horse, but in the dark undergrowth, I can see nothing.

'You should be pleased we didn't gag you,' a voice speaks out of the gloom. I'm not alone then. That's something. Not that I can see it'll help me.

'Why are you doing this?'

'Orders,' the voice replies. It's not Eadweard or Wulfred who speaks, but someone else.

'Whose orders?'

'What does it matter? Now, shut up, and go back to sleep.'

'I need to piss and drink.'

'Piss where you are,' the belligerent voice informs me. 'It's only going to be the first of many occasions. Water, I can aid you with. There's a beaker beside your head. If you can reach it, you can drink it.'

'Untie me.'

'No chance. We'll keep you here until we can let you go. No idea how long that will be, or how much of you will still be here by then. Boredom can only be relieved with a few nicks to my enemy.'

The voice, disembodied and coming from further away than I might think, sends a judder of fear through my body. 'Where's Wulfred and Eadweard, and the big man from Tamworth, Horsa?'

'None of your concern,' the disembodied voice again. 'Now shut up before I gag you, and then you'll be in a whole new world of pain.'

Biting my lip, I stop my questions from pouring forth. I should have asked about Brute, but I don't believe any man with half an eye to a good horse would harm him. Brute's more useful to them alive. I might not be.

Sniffing, I scent the damp of the water, and shuffle around, using my feet to drive me backwards so that my arms can bend. Then, I roll over, aiming for where I think a beaker of water waits for me. Licking my lips, I can all but taste it, but it seems impossible to drink the fluid.

Rolling once, twice, trying to ignore the twisting of my left arm, tongue extended, I feel the rim of a wooden beaker. At least it'll be light, I console myself, shuffling closer so that I can just about lift my head and clamp my teeth around it. Unable to sit upright, I have no choice but to force my head back, beaker between my teeth. River water pools into my mouth, but I can't swallow with my mouth open and, instead, it falls into my beard and down my neck, causing an unpleasant coldness. I release the beaker, returning it to its place, where it wobbles precariously. I think it'll fall, but it doesn't.

Swallowing, I get the idea of water, if not the full sensation of sating my thirst. But perhaps I shouldn't be worrying about that. The urge to piss is becoming a pressing concern. I don't wish to soil myself, but there won't be a choice soon. All the same, I try and find a comfortable position, working to ignore the stone or rock that presses against my back, and close my eyes, concentrating on slowing my breathing. When daylight comes, I want to be alert and ready to escape. I won't be kept a captive here. The fact that someone has ordered these men to detain me assures me that I'm correct to suspect the plans for the two sons of Lord Coenwulf. That I'm here, in some part of the woodland that stretches towards Hereford, assures me that Lord Coenwulf's sons and his sister aren't close by. I must escape before the evil machinations of the queen or Lord Wigmund, or even Lady Ælflæd, can take a course they'll have occasion to regret deeply and which will see me fail in my oath to Lady Cynehild.

But damn it, I need to piss first.

Disgusted with myself, I allow the warm liquid to leave my body and only then manage to sleep.

A kick wakes me, and then a face looms so close to me that I have to close my eyes because I can't move my head backwards.

'Wakey, wakey, you stinking turd.' The words are rough, spoken with harsh angles, but all the same, the man's Saxon. He slaps my face with a calloused hand, and I open my eyes once more, eyeing him with disdain. My trews have dried while I've slept, but the stink hasn't left me. And my arms. The agony is intense, painfully tingling, as I try to open and close my hands to get some feeling back into them, but they don't want to move.

'What's all the fuss about you?' the man asks again, and he moves back so I can get a good look at him. He's younger than I first thought, his hair a deep brown, almost black, a fine moustache and beard covering his chin and lower face so that only the thick slits of his lips are visible. They're pink, nearly red, and when he rears back and stands, I appreciate his average height. Probably smaller than me but taller than many others.

'Who are you?' I demand to know.

'None of your damn business.' I expect the reply for all it tells me nothing.

'Where's my horse?'

'He's well.' The response doesn't answer my question, although I hope it's true.

'I need to piss,' I demand, hopeful he might be kinder to me than the man who guarded me last night.

'Ah, well, do it where you are. You're no better than the beasts while you're here.'

'And where is here?'

'Here,' and he lifts his hands to either side of his body and extends them to the side, indicating the woodland. It's light beneath the trees, but not blazing sunlight, more the tones of brown and beige that I noticed yesterday.

'What do you plan on doing to me?'

'No idea, my friend. I'm just being paid to watch you, nothing else, nothing more. And feed you, I suppose.' The scent of smoke belatedly reaches me, and my belly rumbles angrily. 'If you want to eat and drink, you best shut up,' he responds at the noise, but there's humour in his words, not menace. All the same, I stay my tongue, trying to wake up more quickly and reassess my situation now that it's light enough to see.

I remain bound to the tree behind me. I manage to shuffle backwards on my arse, lifting my arms a little so that I can see what's surrounding me, which isn't much. The fire is far enough away from my feet that I can't kick at the flames licking around the wood. The man himself stands to the other side of the fire. He's dressed in a brown tunic and trews and no byrnie, but his weapons belt glitters with enough sharp edges to assure me it's a matter of choice, not for the lack of it.

I consider again whom he is and where he's come from. He must be a Mercian, but perhaps from far north, close to the kingdom of Northumbria. I've never seen him before. Admittedly, there are many Mercians I've never met. Still, I'd have thought, during my time fighting for Mercia, that I've encountered somewhere from everywhere in the vast sprawl of the kingdom over the middle of Britain. But it seems not. Not even when I went to Bardney did I hear a man with such an accent.

'Here. You can have one hand to eat your food and one hand only. If I see you messing around, I'll not give you any more. I'm only to watch you. Not to feed you. I don't think they care if you live or die, although I imagine you do.'

Swiftly, the man comes around my head. I feel him untying the hempen rope that keeps me supine. With relief, my left arm comes free, although it flops like a dying fish on the side of a river. My right arm is quickly retied, causing many sensations to ripple down my arm.

'This is for you.' He thrusts the bowl at me, rich with a fatty pottage, although I don't see any meat in it. I look from him to the bowl, wondering how to hold it when I have only one hand. He sighs softly, the glint of his brown eyes filled with frustration. 'Sit back, and wedge it between your thighs and your belly. That's the best I can do for you.'

With more care than I expect, he holds the bowl while I shuffle around and only then places it on my belly. There's no spoon, so I use my fingers, trying not to think of all the places they've been and how dirty the nails are. Eagerly, I scoop the too-hot mixture, burning my mouth in the process, but not truly caring. I need to eat. I must have the strength to win free when the opportunity presents itself.

He sits by the fire and eats as well. It's hard to hear over the chomping of my jaws, but I'm sure I can hear voices from not far away. And if not voices, then the chatter of hens. Perhaps, for all the trees in front of me seem to go on forever, behind me, if I could only see better, the woodland comes to a halt, and there's a settlement there. I consider whether it'll be a Welsh or a Mercian one. My captor's armed, so perhaps Welsh, although it could equally be that he's expecting trouble from someone thinking to seek me out. Whom that might be, I don't know. No one will know where I am. Pega will think me at Tamworth. The ealdorman will think me at Tamworth. How would anyone know to look for me to the west of the River Severn?

I eat, but even as I do so, a weight of fear settles in my belly beside the food. No one knows where I am. No one will look for me. There's no reason for these men to keep me alive, not if I threaten whatever Eadweard and Wulfred are assisting the queen with.

15

My arm's tied again, but only after I've been given the opportunity to shit as well as piss. The smell's noxious, and the warrior pushes my leavings aside with a branch, his nose wrinkled all the time.

'I didn't realise I'd be a nursemaid to you,' he mumbles, re-securing me. I wince as my right arm's pulled once more, my left having recovered its feeling, but I know it won't be long until it's gone again. My arms are held at an awkward angle above my head, similar to being in the second line of the shield wall. I grit my teeth, but it doesn't help with the pain. I console myself, thinking it'll be better when I can't feel them.

The day drags. The man doesn't speak to me again. No one joins him. He feeds the fire before him, slowly and with only so many twigs, as though there are no more to burn, for all we're surrounded by woodland. He adds more oats to the pot and some chunks of pork, which make my belly rumble again, although I know I won't get any of them. The smell drives me mad. I lick my lips time and time again. He brings me water every so often, holding the beaker before me to my lips so that I can drink more easily than last night. All the same, I never feel truly sated.

I piss again, hating the sharp smell of my body but unable to do anything about it. I do need a nursemaid, after all.

'So, we're just waiting here?'

'Yes.' The quick reply. I want to ask a hundred questions, but I don't. He seems content to leave me alone, provided I'm no trouble. As much as I hate to feel so helpless, with nothing further to give me an idea of what will happen, I decide that ignorance is better. I doze, even as uncomfortable as I am. I count the branches above my head, watching the light seem to bounce from curling leaf to curling leaf. I wish I'd not come alone and that I'd not been fooled by whatever happened outside Worcester. I should have stayed on the Fosse Way and turned Brute's head towards Tamworth. I should have waited for the ealdorman and Wulfheard.

I know why I didn't, and that shames me. I shouldn't have been too embarrassed to face Wynflæd once more. Whether she forgives me for my outburst last year or not, at least I wouldn't have been here, trussed up and helpless, being watched by a man who might sooner kill me should I become too problematic.

The man feeds me once more, releasing my right hand this time so that a thousand shards of metal seem to permeate my flesh. I've long since lost all feeling in my feet. No matter how many times I bang them on the woodland floor, they remain lost to me. My feet and legs are too tightly tied to allow any movement.

'My thanks,' I murmur, delighted to see a piece of succulent pork amongst the oats and onions of the mixture.

A grunt is my only response.

As night falls, I see a flicker of movement by the fireside, more shadows than anything, and the next voice that speaks is that of a different man. I'm sure I heard the other one call him Æthelbald, but I hold that tight. I don't want him to know that I know his name. I can't see him.

'You'll sleep and behave yourself,' he informs me in no uncertain terms. 'Today's gaoler is soft as shite. Hywel's too kind to everyone, but I'm not. I'll beat you to within an inch of your life if necessary. You just need to be alive. They didn't say that you had to be entirely alive.'

The voice is more that of a wounded bear, and I pull my legs up, trying to shield myself from an imaginary blow. I've eaten, and I've drunk well all day. I can't say the same will happen during the night. And I'm so uncomfortable and in so much pain that sleep's impossible. The movement of animals above my head startles me more than once, the thump of something landing on branches sends a scattering of curling leaves to settle on my face. The occasional spiderweb joins them. I twist and turn, but sleep evades me. Not that Æthelbald, if that's his name, seems to sense my unhappiness. He stays by the fire, feeding it twigs and occasionally a handful of dried leaves so that it flames brightly whenever the loud shriek of an animal sounds too close.

I'd not considered that there might be boars or wolves in the woodland. If one were to attack, I couldn't defend myself. That worry, added to everything else, keeps me awake long into the night until the depth of darkness begins to fade, and only then do I finally manage to sleep. And then, it's not for long. The man from the day before wakes me, as he did the day before. The routine of yesterday repeats itself. My lips are parched, no matter the water given to me. My arms are in a thousand agonies, and now, when I try to move them, it merely sets off a pain in my legs and feet. I've watched men and women die from many wounds and illnesses. I've never seen anyone lose their limbs because they were tied too tightly, but I'm sure it can happen.

Just before darkness falls, I call to the man, my voice broken, my throat dry and my tongue feeling too large for my mouth.

'Hywel, please, my legs, just for a moment or two. They're agony.'

He eyes me with sympathy and comes towards me. He doesn't seem to notice that I know his name.

'If you kick me, I'll stab you,' he menaces.

'I can't even move them,' I mumble. He nods, satisfied with my response, as he undoes the leg bindings. Unable to stop myself, I howl in agony, and his hand clamps over my mouth, his eyes wild with a threat. I nod, gather myself together, and try not to shriek as my foot also comes loose.

Somehow, I manage to move my legs aside. It's not easy. The action is slow and laboured, and I hear a whistle of sympathy from my captor, but he still ties me tightly once more, just as I've managed to regain the feeling in both my legs and feet. I know it'll not be long until I'm as helpless again, but my ears hear the sound of footsteps coming towards us, and my captor hastens to ensure his kindness isn't seen.

The two men speak in low voices, close to the fire. I can't see the man who watches me at night, Æthelbald. He's entirely unknown to me. If I ever escape from here, and I'm not sure I will, I might meet him anywhere and never know we spent this time together.

Hywel leaves without glancing at me, and the night guard hunkers down, feeding more fuel to the flames. Already, I can feel the chill of the coming night. I've survived without my cloak and been almost warm enough. I doubt the same will happen this night. If I could see the heavens from beneath the tree's bough, I imagine they'd be crystalline, not a cloud in sight.

The heat from the fire almost reaches me, but my face is far from warm, and for the rest of my body, it hardly seems to matter. My feet and legs have quickly fallen numb once more, and even though I try to move my fingers occasionally, they're also unresponsive.

I lick my lips. I need more moisture. I can't remember when I last pissed, and that's not a good sign. I've been fed a pottage without even onions to flavour it, and while it was palatable, it only made me more thirsty.

I close my eyes and try to think myself away from this place. Anywhere would be better than here, even fighting on the Isle of Sheppey to rescue Lord Coenwulf. I grimace at the reminder, a slow tear falling down my cheeks at the memory of Frithwine, and before him, Garwulf, losing their lives, fighting for Mercia. I'm weak and feeble. I'm no warrior; here, I've never felt more pathetic, useless, and bloody scared. If they were going to kill me, I just wish they would.

I open my eyes, and my breath blooms before me in the frigid conditions. The icy cold of the ground has numbed my arse and the rest of me as well. I'm nothing but a mouth to breathe with and eyes to see. But I can see more than the previous nights.

I focus on the stars up above. Their persistent glimmer gives me hope, even as I start to shake, each shiver an agony of a hundred tiny wounds. I grit my teeth, my chest rising and falling too quickly as I allow my fears to overwhelm me. Why am I here? More tears form in my eyes, and I can little afford to lose the moisture from my body.

Why am I here? Who'll miss me? Who'll even know of my death when I breathe my last, frozen to the core, strung out, ready for roasting over a pit?

And then I hear it. My eyes start open, and I shuffle backwards, my legs crying, my arse feeling like it belongs to someone else.

It comes again. A crack of a branch? No, it's the snuffling of a creature scenting the air. I glance towards the fire. It doesn't blaze as brightly as before. No, the flames have fallen to a sullen red, the soft shift of the ash dissipating as the final fuel is consumed, a faint shush in an otherwise quiet night. There are no night-time animals. There's no flapping of wings or hoot of owls. I can barely breathe. The man, I realise, is asleep, slumped on his side, his blades flashing in the glimmer of the moon and the stars, and something is coming.

And it's not a man, but a beast.

* * *

I watch the wolf. Its coat is flecked with white at the edges, or so I imagine, the lighter shades the only means of illumination. Its ears are alert, eyes flashing in the darkness. It scents the air. The sound should barely reach me, but it does in the sullen silence of the deepest night. The air is so cold that I can also see where it breathes. I stay still, trying to evade its detection, although it must know I'm there. I stink of my filth and shit. I'm stretched out, ready for it to rip my innards from me. I have no means of defence.

My guard's fast asleep, dreaming of a warm bed and companion, and not of the cold or the hunter that seeks fresh prey. I'm going to die here, and it won't be by blade but by teeth, sharp teeth that yank my flesh from my body. It won't be a clean death but one filled with pain and sorrow. My thoughts flick to the children of Lord Coenwulf, and his sister. I've failed Lady Cynehild. I've failed my uncle. Everything in my life has been a failure, and now it will end, and I can do nothing to stop it.

I can't take my eyes off the animal. It moves so quietly, disturbing neither flame nor guard, its eyes focused on the sleeping man. I hold out half a hope that the wolf will kill the man, and then be sated, and leave me to be found by someone else. The guard in the morning, perhaps. But do I want that?

I fear I'll never fight my way free. So, should I welcome the teeth of the wolf, its sharp jaw and animal urge to sate its hunger? I hear licking and realise the pottage has fallen to one side, and the animal helps itself to the vestiges of the meal. But without meat, I can't see the animal being content with that.

I watch, and I wait. A hundred thoughts tumble through my mind, none as horrifying as the sharp snap of jaws on flesh. I hardly dare look, but I force myself to it.

The animal's no longer grey and flecked with white. Dark fluid coats its snout as it turns, chewing with ferocity. I see the throat of the night guard glinting dully in the moonlight. The man didn't even know, but more importantly, how did the wolf know to take such a clean kill?

I listen to the sharp snap of teeth over bone. My bowels turn to fluid, staining myself once more. But the animal doesn't come towards me. I scurry backwards, desperate now to free my arms or my feet, anything so that I can defend myself. Then the animal stops, head canted to one side, before sitting back and letting loose a sound I don't ever want to hear, and certainly not at such close quarters.

The howl fills the night air: long, loud and clear of all fear. It's a cry of triumph and joy, of satisfaction, and to my horror, as I scream along with it, releasing all of my fear into the crystal-clear night sky, it's joined by others.

'No,' I sob, gasping for breath, my heart hammering, my chest rising and falling too quickly. 'No,' I mutter again and again, the sound ripped from my throat as the wolf savages my night guard. The other animals slink from the undergrowth, heads down, shoulders powerful, all of them grey but edged with white to give away their position on a night such as this.

I count them, one, two, and then there are six of them altogether. The tearing of fabric is loud in my ears, the snap of sharp jaws, the slicing of broken flesh. Vomit fills my mouth. I cough it aside or risk choking. I spit and swallow, but there's only the taste of the foulness of my last meal in my mouth.

I'll die here, somewhere beneath the trees. All that will be found of me will be my gnawed and white bones. I've seen enough bodies to know I'll be unrecognisable. Bad enough to die and have my flesh turn corrupt. But this way, there'll be no flesh left. I'll be dead and eaten. Wulfheard will never know what became of me. Wynflæd will go to her death believing I hated her, and what of those children, with no one to protect them?

I think of Edwin, of my uncle, of Budworth. Who'll claim it as their own? I've written no will. I've made no provision for a death I was arrogant enough to believe would never come. I think of the kingship, of Mercia, of what I might have been had I not become caught up in this foolhardy attempt to rescue children I share no blood with. When Brute is found, he won't be able to answer the questions of those who know I'm missing. No. I'll be lost for all time. And what will become of Brute, and Wine? Horses such as them need good grain and warm stables. What if no one protects them? Before Brute was mine he was known as foul-tempered and unrideable. I wouldn't want that to happen to him once more.

I murmur, soft words beneath my breath, surprised to realise they're the oft-repeated prayers spoken by the holy men in their sumptuous robes that keep the chill of winter from their bodies while they berate the rest of us from their pulpit.

I shudder. My eyes closing and then opening. And then closing at the horror of the scene before me.

One of the wolves knocks the woodpile, and flame springs afresh. They squeal and yip, pulling back from their feast, only to return. So much more is illuminated. I'm only grateful the man was asleep when he died, or his eyes would haunt me.

A raven lands, joining the wolves. They eye one another, but then all return to the feast. Another raven, and even, I notice, some other small creatures, all of them taking their fill, eating of the bounty the first wolf provided.

I'll be next. I know it. They'll eat, and then they'll realise they could eat yet more.

My fear turns to fury. I bend and twist, tugging on the hempen ropes that bind my hands, trying to work them loose, one-handed. The actions never worked during my imprisonment, but that doesn't mean they won't work now. I scrabble with my feet and legs, pulling them close to my belly, for all the movement is torture. I twist and turn. I try and find space between my legs to pull one foot clear of the bindings. Tears blind me, and my breath is faster and faster, the cloud of it almost obscuring the scene before me so that I see shadows and orange flames, bloodied muzzles and little else.

I twist and turn, and it's no good. I can't get free. Whoever tied me ensured that I'd never win free. I curse the man who aided me yesterday, who redid the knots even tighter than the original ones. I thought he did me a kindness but no, he's doomed me to my death.

The ravens fly away, all three of them, the softness of the man's eyes and lips in their bellies, or so I assume. The wolves continue to eat, but not the first one. No, he moves aside, his back legs lithe on a body forged for stealth and speed. He sits beside the fire, closest to me, bending to lick his paws and muzzle, looking little more than a pet dog or a hunting hound, and only then, when he's content that the first man's blood is gone from his fur, does he move towards me. His amber eyes glow as warm as the fire, and I scream. I can't stop myself.

The sound echoes all around the woodlands.

I scream and scream and scream, and the wolf is before me. His meaty breath on my face. His eyes are cold and appraising for all they echo with the warmth of the fire. And I close my eyes as his foul-smelling open mouth comes towards me.

16

The pain doesn't come. That surprises me but doesn't make me open my eyes. Perhaps, I think, my body's just too cold and broken already. I try not to listen to the wet sounds of teeth tearing at my flesh, of my blood spurting free from the confines of the blue ribbons running through my body. I try not to smell the corruption of my flesh, the stink of my bowels being opened and torn asunder.

And then the heat returns to my face, and I open my eyes, peering into the gaze of the wolf, its head canted to one side in confusion, a sliver of something that I fear is my flesh dripping from one side of its open mouth.

I rip my eyes from the gaze and stare down at my legs and feet. I expect to see my innards on display, the grey and red of the ropes of my belly trailing down my legs.

But I see none of those things. My forehead furrows. My legs are free. I bang them against the mulch of the floor, releasing the sharp stink of my piss with the movement. Tears stream down my face as I try to escape this wrathful enemy. The wolf moves towards me. I swallow, aware that my Adam's apple is a perfect inducement to severing my lifeblood there, but the animal, with a swish of its long black tail against my face, merely walks around me.

Ahead, the other animals still feast – well, four of them do. One of them has stepped aside and, in a parody of a man, sits beside the fire, warming itself in the glow from the flames as it licks the blood and flesh from its paws.

A wet tongue on my hand has me wincing, only then my arms collapse above me, freed from the confines of the rope.

'What?' I ask, the sound ragged and guttural. Does the wolf mean to make me run from here? Is he only interested if there's a chase?

Not that I can stand yet. It's agony just to bring my arms back to my side, to look at the whiteness of the flesh, which looks deader than the man the wolves are devouring.

'What?' I ask again. The wolf's returned to my side. He eyes me and then bows his head a little, as I hurry to undo the ties that bind my ankles, the wolf having released my arms and legs.

'How?' I stutter again, fumbling with the knots. I tried this. Not with my hands, admittedly, but how has an animal, who only moments ago mauled my enemy to death while he slept, managed to free me from my ropes? I feel my forehead furrow as the scent of meaty breath combines with my stagnant cloud of air.

Of course, the damn animal can tell me nothing. As much as I wish to scamper away, even if only up high, into the tree on which the ravens now stand guard, squawking one to another as though offering a commentary on what's happening below them, I'm frozen in place, and not just by the cold of the cloudless night. Winter's coming. This is a promise of that, but those thoughts are irrelevant. Why has the animal released me?

'Can I... Can I go?' I ask, my words firmer now, for all I stumble over the sentence. 'My thanks.' I push upwards, using my hands to extend my aching legs. My feet remain clubby appendages, and standing is agony. The wolf does nothing. Neither do the other members of its pack. I wince and stifle another cry of pain as I'm finally upright.

'Thank you.' I offer a bow to the majestic creature, and slowly begin to back away. I'm mindful of the tree trunk at my back and the boughs of the trees that hang low. I remember the sound of hens that I thought I heard. Perhaps there are people there, and they'll aid me. Even if they only tell me where I am, that will be enough.

'Thank you,' I murmur once more, feeling that I'll actually be free from the horrors of my confinement and the terror of the wolf attack. The animal observes me, and then dips its head and turns around languidly, its long legs loping back towards the remainder of the pack. Only then, when all six wolves are once more occupied, do I turn my back on them and race through the tangled limbs and increasingly tighter growth of trees that shields me from wherever the noise of the hens came.

I'm not quiet, far from it, my breath ragged, my limbs still causing me problems, as my feet refuse to work properly, occasionally losing their firm grip or just slipping from beneath me. I try to listen for any sign of being followed, but there's nothing. Not even the yip of the wolves as they call one to another. Neither is there any howling or the swift sound of paws over the soft surface of the woodland floor.

And only then – with my breath tight in my chest, my eyes open so wide that more than once pieces of twig have landed in them, half blinding me – do I erupt into a clearing. The smell of a smoking fire is rife in the air, the cries of hens exploding in a cacophony of riot, as though I'm the wolf and not running from it, and a figure steps into my path.

Long hair, beneath a fur-lined cloak, and a sharp nose are all that's visible.

'Get away from my hens, you monster.'

The voice is distinctly feminine, and I collapse to the ground.

'I'm not a monster. The wolf. The wolf released me.'

'Released you?' The incredulity in her voice is impossible to ignore. For a moment, I fear she won't believe me, and the axe, no doubt for chopping wood, that she holds menacingly takes on huge proportions in my mind. Have I survived the wolf only to be chopped down here?

'Well, sometimes he does that,' she confirms conversationally, arm slowly lowering, the disbelief in her voice gone. I want to ask more about that, but she hasn't finished with her questions yet. 'But why were you in the woodlands?'

'I was held captive,' I pant, my tongue dry in my mouth. 'Two men, they meant to hold me. I don't know if they intended to kill me.'

'So you're the Mercian that the fools were speaking about. I thought they were making it up, although they had silver coins to show for all their talking.' Only now does she fling back the hood on the cloak and eye me. I try not to startle, for half the woman's face is a mass of scar, pink, long since faded to red, one cheek slimmer than the other, the flesh pulled too tight. 'The wolf and its pack and I have something of an agreement,' she murmurs, holding my gaze as though testing me. 'It seems they've included you in that.'

'Are they more reliable than men who can be bought for silver?' I question.

She nods and smiles, her right cheek barely moving, giving her a lopsided expression. 'Come on. I'll feed you and help if I can.' Turning her back on me, she strides out, her legs so long I almost have to run to keep up with her. I look around me. This is a clearing in the heartland of the wood. Far ahead, the shush of trees swaying with the wind can be heard.

'You live here?' I ask.

'I do, yes. Safer here with the beasts than with men. But of course, some know of me. The charcoal burners and the woodsmen. That's who had you, I believe. Poor men, both of them. Eager to earn more, even if they have to hold a man against his will. Mind, the one wasn't beloved by the wolf pack. I imagine that's the one who was attacked. Damn fool, antagonising the beasts by taking their pups and skinning them for a bit of extra meat and fur to sell to men who only give half of what it's worth.'

Ahead, a dwelling appears, cleverly hidden behind a mass of what seems to be hedgerows but isn't. She shows me the way through, a sidestep here, a sidestep there, and then a small wooden gateway to keep the chickens in their pen and, no doubt, away from the hungry appetites of the wolves.

The hall is smaller than some but certainly large enough for a woman if she lives alone. There are also separate buildings, one for the grain, one for the animals, and another one that seems smaller than the others. Perhaps this is where the hens spend their winter months.

'Clean yourself there. I can't allow you inside when you stink of the midden.'

I notice the barrels of water where she points, and shudder at the thought of getting cold and wet, but I do stink, and it's making me feel nauseous. With little enthusiasm, I thrust my head in the barrel and then use a bucket to pour more over me. The woman has gone, and I'm grateful as I shiver and shudder.

* * *

The whiff of woodsmoke hangs in the air as she welcomes me inside through a finely hinged door to the hall. Here I gasp in surprise. The wall furnishings are elaborate, the embroidery showing wolves in all their guises, from vicious warriors to nurturing mothers, and she smiles again.

'They call me the Wolf Lady. It works to keep most of them away from me. I've no control over the wolves, but they aid me on occasion. Here, you look hungry and thirsty.'

She moves around the hearth, finding me water from a jug and then pulling a cauldron free from the fire, from which the most appetising smell I've inhaled in a long time emanates.

'Chicken. It's always chicken unless the wolf catches something else and brings it to me.' Once more she speaks as though she and the wolf do have an agreement. Again, I want to ask more, but I'm hungry and thirsty.

Eagerly, I drink and then eat the food. A low moan escapes my mouth as I savour the succulent chicken and pottage.

'This is fit for a king,' I exclaim, unable to mask my surprise.

'Well, no king is having it. But, tell me, what's your name?'

'I'm Icel, Lord of Budworth, which makes me sound more than I am. I wanted to be a healer, but now I'm a warrior, fighting for the Mercian king.' My relief at being free from my captors and the wolf makes me say too much.

'Do you know you're in the borderlands with the Welsh kingdoms?' she queries.

'I was seeking Hereford with my horse.' At the memory of that, I almost drop my bowl. 'Brute, I don't know where he is.'

'Brute?'

'My horse. The king gifted him to me. He's a beast, as the name implies.'

'Then I imagine he's recognisable?'

'Very.'

'I'll point you in the direction of Hereford in the morning. You'll find him there, no doubt. But why were you going to Hereford and why were you in the woodlands?' And now my arms hang limp, and I remember it all.

'I'm seeking two small boys and a young girl, but I fear I've been misled.'

'Are they your children?'

But I'm already shaking my head. 'No, but I gave my oath to protect them, and I've failed in that already.'

'Æthelbald and Hywel spoke only of a man, not children or even a horse.'

'You knew they held me captive?'

'I thought they were fools who spoke about things that could never be true. I apologise for that.' In the firelight, her savaged face is shadowed.

'How did you know them?'

'I pay them to help me sometimes with the planting out and harvesting. It's much work for one woman, and there are few who think to aid me, even when I can offer eggs and chicken in payment. I almost trusted them.'

'Then you know where they live, well, where the one who yet lives?'

'I do, yes, onwards to Hereford. You'll find them there. Well, you'll find Hywel, I imagine. Æthelbald will be the dead one.'

'What's your name?' I want to ask so much more, but her name will be enough for now.

'They call me the Wolf Lady, and you may do the same. My name is of little importance these days. No one remembers who I used to be, only what I am now. Now, enough talking. Get some rest, and then tomorrow, I'll point you onward. Hopefully, you'll find your horse, and your children, although I think your horse concerns you more.'

Her words unsettle me. I think she's wrong. I hope she's wrong. Or maybe I don't.

17

By the time I've walked to Hereford the following day, the wounds on my wrists and ankles are throbbing. The Wolf Lady escorts me only so far until the denseness of the trees once more gives way to the sky above our heads.

'Just follow the track,' she advises me.

'My thanks,' I offer, but she's already turned, seemingly dismissing me from her thoughts. I consider whom she once was and why she lives the way she does. But more than anything, I'm just grateful she assisted me and didn't sever my head from its neck with her axe. I'm also grateful that she and the wolf have such an agreement, and that, luckily, I seem to have benefited from that as well, even while Æthelbald is more than half-eaten.

Wincing and limping, I amble onwards to where a pall of smoke hangs low in the sky. In no time, I can smell food cooking and the overwhelming stench of many people living in a close community. I see the first building, a stone-built cattle byre, or some such, in a field filled with animals contentedly chewing beneath the pale blue sky. The night wasn't as cold as the previous one, but dew mars the visible grasses. Not that the cows seem to mind. And only then do I remember that only one of the men who held me a prisoner is dead. Will Hywel think to hold me captive once more, or will he hide away, pretend he had nothing to do with it? The sound of running water can also be heard. In the near distance, the river glints at me. I sniff, thinking I could do with dunking my head in it, but really, I must find my horse and my weapons. The eagle-headed seax my uncle gave me is gone. But surprisingly, the silver sigil remains at my neck. I'm grateful for that.

I recall asking my uncle if I could come with him to Hereford. He refused, saying Edwin and I should stay hidden. As such, this is my first sight of the settlement. It seems little different to Worcester or Gloucester, and like those two places, a river provides part of its defence, although not the same river as at Worcester and Gloucester.

This, then, is a border settlement with the Welsh kingdoms across the river. Facing the hills and the Welsh kingdoms, I appreciate how exposed it is. All well and good for the bishop to have his hall and church here but, not far away, I'm sure the Welsh must hunger for a bloody good fight. It makes me feel imperilled just thinking about it. I hasten my steps. The walls and river might only provide the vestige of protection, but it's better than being here alone. Without my weapons.

'Hail,' the call rolls. I meet the eyes of a guard and incline my head.

'Good day,' I offer.

'You been in the wars, my friend?' the man asks. He stands firmly, his stance wide, his feet planted, hand straying to where his weapons hang on his weapons belt. But I wish him luck with finding them, thanks to his overhanging belly. I wonder if he can even see his feet.

'A fight, in the woodlands,' I offer. 'They took my horse. Have you seen a piebald creature? You'll know him. He probably ate your hand.'

'That feisty bugger's yours, is it? Been giving the blacksmith a hard time. Hywel wanted new shoes on the creature, but you can't get near him.'

'And where might that be?'

'Follow the smell of burning ore and, of course, the cries of men trying to tame that damn animal. He's been kicking all night. I hardly got a wink of sleep.'

Despite it all, I grin to hear that. 'Apologies, my friend. But tell me, who brought him here, and did they happen to have any children with them?'

'It was that damn fool Hywel, and no, he came alone, which is unusual as he's usually found with Æthelbald. He told some tale of finding the beast roaming in the woodlands not far from the Wolf Lady.' He shudders as he speaks, and I begin to realise that the woman has quite the reputation. If nothing else, it'll guard her against others thinking to attack her. Wise women aren't to be feared, but sometimes, sometimes, it's good to stir up a little terror. Or so Wynflæd has always told me. 'In you go, and you'll be welcome to him,' he continues.

'And I must tell you that Æthelbald will never step foot here again.'

The man nods, eyes narrowing, and then he indicates that I should enter all the same. I consider if he thinks I killed Æthelbald. Whatever his reasoning, he's keen to have Brute away from Hereford, and I'm as eager to oblige.

'But tell me, what do you know about the Wolf Lady?'

His eyes narrow, and now I think he might refuse me entry, but he sticks out his chest and speaks instead. 'The Wolf Lady is one of ours. She lives how she lives, and we respect that, and so can you. If you go anywhere near her, I assure you, you'll regret it. She knows how to fight. And how to cook,' he adds, and I'm unsure what he means by that. But he clamps his lips tightly shut and I know I'm not going to get anything further from him. I nod, and walk on.

For a moment, on stepping through the gateway, I'm unsure where to go, and then I hear it and, grinning to myself, follow the cries of outrage coming from the northern side of the settlement. People gaze at me with some unease, but no one runs from me, which I take to mean I don't look that bad.

And then I see him. Brute, eyes wild, legs kicking, with a man to either side of him. His shrill cry makes me wince. I realise that many of the people, including the monks from the church just visible from where I walk, have come together to watch the spectacle.

'I say you take him back to where you found him,' a thin woman cries to the blacksmith, and the man, I believe, is Hywel. 'He's more trouble than he's worth, no matter how much you might think to get for selling him.'

'Brute.' I call his name, and the horse immediately stills as I forge a path through the crowd and come to a stop before him, hand extended. The groan of relief from the man I take to be the blacksmith is audible, as is the startled cry from Hywel.

'He's your horse, my lord?' the soot-stained man asks me, but it's more a hopeful statement.

'I lost him in the woodlands,' I counter, not tearing my gaze from Hywel. I'll say nothing for now, but I fully intend to have a conversation with him and soon.

'Then I'm glad you've found him. My stable's all but destroyed, thanks to his hooves.'

'He doesn't like many people,' I reassure, running my hand over Brute's long nose. His eyes watch me, the fury slowly dissipating. 'And did you find my saddlebags as well?' I ask benignly.

'Yes, everything that was on him,' the blacksmith confirms quickly. 'A strange collection of goods for a warrior.'

'Well, sometimes I tend to my fellow warriors' injuries, as well.'

I glance at Hywel again, eyes narrowed. I'm daring him to make a run for it, but he's been kind to me. Perhaps now, if I repay the kindness, he'll assist me.

'Then take him, and be gone. We could all do with some peace and quiet.' With that, the blacksmith turns aside, and I know the crowd's dissipating behind me.

I wait still, and Hywel stays as well.

'Now tell me,' I say softly, my voice filled with menace, 'who paid you, where they went, and what you were to do with me.'

'What's it worth to me?' he demands, chest puffed out.

'Your life,' I reply quickly. 'I'm sure that, round here, thieves are hung for their crimes. I'm not sure what happens to those who detain men and women against their will, but I imagine it'll be even less pleasant.'

His shoulders sag, and I see a younger man than I expected revealed to me.

'I'll buy you a meal from the tavern, and I'll tell you everything.'

'Very well, but I'm not going inside. Brute will also kick the tavern building down if I do so.'

That seems to satisfy him, and together we walk deeper into the settlement.

Small children watch Brute with fearful eyes as he takes my commands and parades beside me. He bristles with pent-up fury but, for now, seems content to behave. While it's warmer than the day before, the thought of sitting outside is far from appealing, but I have little choice.

'Get what you want. I'll have the same. But come back to me, or I'll hunt you down and ensure all know your true nature.'

He shrugs his shoulders and dips his head inside the dark

doorway. I consider watching him but instead find a bench to perch on, threading Brute's reins through the wooden legs. He has room to move, but not much.

'We'll be on the way soon,' I reassure him. I'm unsure when he last ate or drank, but for now, he seems content.

I'm holding a wooden beaker of ale in no time, and Hywel's sitting opposite me.

'Tell me everything.' He drinks deeply, wipes his hand on his sleeve and begins to speak.

'It was Æthelbald. He came to me and asked me to help him guard some soft Mercian lord in the woods close to the home of the Wolf Lady. He said I'd get thirty silver coins for my silence. I knew he was getting more, but thirty silver coins is a lot. I agreed. He didn't say much else, just that we were to watch you for a week and then let you go, but he said I could have your horse as well if I wanted him. Mean bastard. It was hardly a good bargain that I struck.'

'And you know Æthelbald is dead.'

'Yes, I went up there to relieve him and found only the remains of him and none of you. I already had the horse, but he seemed lame. That's why I took him to the blacksmith.'

'And these men, did Æthelbald tell you who they were?' I'm relieved to hear they had no intention of killing me. Still, why had I needed to be apprehended for a week? What had Eadweard, Wulfred and the others planned for me? Or rather, what was planned in my absence?

'No. I heard some Mercian voices, but I never saw them.'

'And my weapons?'

'You didn't have any when I found you. I take it the Mercians took them from you.'

I nod, unhappy with the knowledge, even though I suspected it all along. 'So, those Mercians aren't still around?'

'No, we've seen no new warriors of late. The bishop keeps some men for the border skirmishes but no one else.'

I wish I knew where they'd gone, but I can well suspect.

'My thanks for your honesty.' I stand abruptly, bending to retrieve Brute's reins. It's clear to me where I need to go. 'Here.' I place a handful of Londonia struck coins in his hand, the weight pleasing. 'You didn't kill me and almost kept my horse safe. You have my thanks. But now I need to return to Tamworth.'

Hywel's eyes glint at his prize, even as two bowls of pottage are brought outside by a small woman, beady-eyed, a look of displeasure on her face at seeing Hywel.

'He can have it,' I offer her. She gasps at seeing me, so perhaps I look more lordly than I feel, and almost curtsies, in the process slopping the fatty mixture over the side of the bowl. A hound at her feet hastens to lick the spillage. Hywel grabs both bowls eagerly to relieve her of the burden.

'You should eat, my lord,' she says to me. 'The finest pottage this close to the border.'

'I'm sure it is,' I reply, a tight smile on my face. If that's the finest, I muse, I dread to think about the worst. Still, it makes some of my road brothers' attempts seem better in comparison. 'If you hear anything else,' I bend low to Hywel's ear, 'seek me out at Tamworth or Budworth. I'll see you're well recompensed.' Hywel shivers and grins at the menace in my words. 'And don't keep Mercian warriors captive, you damn fool. You never know when you might just need one.'

18

I've never visited Hereford, but leaving and heading slightly northwards, I know a moment of recollection. I've been this way before, with my uncle. We might have kept as close to the trees as possible, but I recognise the ancient road and the view easily enough. That can only mean I'm not actually that far from where my uncle died. Brute, once free from Hereford, is pliable and eager to be on his way. Just for a moment, I consider going back the way I've come, keen to seek out the dead man and hunt for possible tracks that Eadweard, Wulfred and Horsa might have left on their way to wherever it is they're going. But I stop myself. Already I've lost valuable time. I can think of no reason why I might have been persuaded to venture this way other than by people who wanted me to think this was where the children were heading.

Fury stirs in my heart, and with Brute eager to kick the last few days of captivity from him, I bend low over his head and encourage him to ride as fast as his long legs will take him. Any sign of a limp has disappeared. I smirk at that. He thought of playing his own games with the man who took him. My horse is a clever beast. The River Wye quickly disappears from view, heading westwards into the hills, while Brute and I keep our gaze northwards. I'm not going back towards Worcester. I'll cross the River Severn in a different place or avoid it altogether.

I try and clear my thoughts from the memory of my uncle, but it's difficult. Every new corner turned seems to reveal another one of the places we journeyed to together. I think of Edwin as well. Where is he? I never thought to worry about him again, not after we became enemies instead of friends, but the last near-enough year has taught me I should be less hasty. Time heals, and we both need one another. Or we did. He's gone again. I wish I knew where he and Lord Coenwulf were. I should like to seek him out and tell him of my fears. He might think them unfounded, but I don't believe they are. I realise I miss Edwin. That revelation surprises me.

The day stretches on. I have no food, my saddlebags riffled for what I did have, which explains all that's needed about the men who took me. They were hungry. They didn't really want coins, just the means to feed themselves. My belly growls, but it's manageable. Time and time again, Brute and I walk to a stream or a brook, drinking deeply, and then resume our way. As night falls, the moon shimmers above my head, and I reach for my cloak, which was left in my possession in my saddlebags, and wrap it around my body. It's going to be cold, but there's enough moonlight to see by, and so I continue, for now. I know we'll have to stop at some point. And that moment comes when Brute slows to a trot and then hangs his head low, his chest heaving.

'Good lad,' I murmur, dismounting and hastening to remove his saddle so that he can drink from yet another stream. The rush of the water is fierce, and the feel of it on my fingers is chill. I consider whether I should stay awake or not and protect my horse to prevent us both being captured once more, but I dismiss the worry. I walked into that trap. They won't expect me to have escaped. There are still three or four days left of the week the men were to hold me captive. That's to my advantage.

* * *

The closer we get to Tamworth, having turned eastwards when we crossed the River Severn once more at Wroxeter, the faster Brute goes, and yet my fear only intensifies. I need to find Eadweard, Wulfred and their allies, alongside my weapons, but what exactly can I do? If I rush into Tamworth demanding to see the queen, Lord Wigmund and Lady Ælflæd with wild theories about the children and sister of Lord Coenwulf, I imagine even the king will dismiss me.

No, I need to be more subtle than that, but I'm not sure how. And then, as the following day draws to an end, the lights of Tamworth appear before me, having bypassed Lichfield along the way. I could have stayed there for the night and arrived fresh and perhaps even washed. I've changed my clothes from those I wore when forced to piss myself, but I have no others that are clean. I wrinkle my nose. I whiff of horse, sweat and the undergrowth where I was kept tied to the tree. Not even the barrel of cold water that the Wolf Lady allowed me to use could disperse the smell.

But the darkness gives me the cover I need. I won't exactly sneak into Tamworth, but at least few will see me.

I dismount and lead Brute along the walkway that allows entrance inside the settlement's walls. I find a smile on my face as I greet the king's warriors on guard duty. Not that they do much else but acknowledge me with the weary gaze of men who must stand guard duty throughout the long night. It's clear they recognise me, and just before the gates are closed for the night, I slip inside the too-familiar place, exchanging soft words with them, but not more than that. They don't know I shouldn't be here, that I should be tied to a tree. Neither do I ask after those I seek.

Hastily, I take Brute to the stable and leave him there, content with a bag of oats and a bucket of water, while the remainder of the king's horses sleep in their stables. Brute deserves some rest. I run my eyes over the other animals in the gloom, and content I don't recognise Wulfheard's mount, I leave once more. Wherever my fellow warriors are, they're not within Tamworth.

Cuthred hasn't seen me, for which I'm grateful. But now comes the more difficult part. I need to get to Wynflæd, make good on my accusations to her, and find out what she knows about what was planned for the children and sister of Lord Coenwulf.

I hear raucous cries from the king's hall and consider what feast is being celebrated. A firepit assures me that some huge animal has been roasted for the occasion. I lick my lips. Eating would be good, but I have other, more pressing concerns. I realise why the guard men were so unimpressed with their duty. No doubt, they've missed out on free-flowing ale and meat.

I decide against creeping through the buildings to reach Wynflæd's workshop, but I cover my head with my cloak to offer some camouflage as I stride towards it. It's not that I don't want to be seen, but it'll be much easier if I'm not. Outside Wynflæd's door, I pause for a moment, listening to discover if she's alone. I can hear Cuthred talking but little else.

Hesitantly, I bend and knock on the wooden door, and it opens immediately, offering the welcome glow of somewhere I think of as home. Cuthred's eyes boggle wide, and I appreciate that he's grown about a foot since I last saw him. I press a finger to his lips, and he stays his tongue but opens the door wide to allow me entry.

My eyes alight on Wynflæd, and she shows absolutely no surprise at seeing me. If anything, a swift look of relief assures me that I might be welcome.

'At last,' she huffs, as Cuthred quickly closes the door and once more surprises me by lifting a plank of wood across it to further ensure it remains locked. I feel my eyebrows furrow, and Wynflæd cautions me with her finger across her lips, just as I did to Cuthred.

She's aged in my absence, but her wiry strength hasn't left her. There might be more wrinkles around the corners of her eyes and lips, but she's lost none of her quickness of thought.

'Speak in whispers. This place is alive with rumours and gossip. Now, where have you been? I sent for you days ago at Kingsholm. I expected you three days ago, at the latest.'

'I didn't get your message,' I whisper back. 'But I was at Kingsholm before that anyway, my intention to follow them here.' I don't think I need to say more about whom I mean. 'But I was turned around at Worcester and led a merry dance across the River Severn until I was captured outside Hereford. If you believe me, and I scarce do, a wolf set me free.'

Wynflæd's face is a riot of emotion, but my final comment draws a smile from her. 'You met the famous Wolf Lady then?'

'I did, yes. You know of her?' I suppose I shouldn't be surprised.

Wynflæd nods, for a moment amusement in her eyes, that quickly fades as her thoughts must turn to why she sent for me. 'You suspect?'

'I do, yes.'

'Then you're right to. Cuthred has heard rumours. Some of Lord Wigmund's men arrived here three days ago and left very quickly with heavy saddlebags. What were their names?' she questions Cuthred.

He grimaces. 'Wulfred and Eadweard, and some others as well. Horsa was with them. Nasty pieces of work, all of them.'

I nod, unsurprised to discover that they came this way. 'They paid the men near Hereford,' I confirm. Cuthred hands me a beaker of water and then a bowl of pottage, and I eat eagerly.

'And they in turn were paid,' Wynflæd confirms.

'By the queen?' I announce, convinced she is behind all this. Yes, the warriors may nominally owe their allegiance to Wigmund, but I don't think him capable of this. But Wynflæd shakes her head, confusing me.

'By Lord Wigmund.' And again she shakes her head.

I'm forced to say the words I don't want to. I had hoped against hope that she wasn't involved. 'By Lady Ælflæd.'

When she shakes her head once more, I open my mouth to argue, but she hushes me. Cuthred, seeing my rope burns, has brought me a pot of salve, and Wynflæd's strong fingers massage it into my wrists. I won't tell her of my ankles, but I might use it on them when I know what's happening.

'There are very clever people manipulating the royal family, I assure you. I'm unsure of the true power behind it all, but I have my suspicions that Lord Beorhtwulf is involved. He's a wealthy individual, and he's grown in the king's confidence, but what's important is finding those small boys.'

'They came here?' I question, although I'm considering young Lady Cynewise. Wynflæd speaks of the children of Lord Coenwulf, not his sister.

'No, the boys never arrived, and Lady Ælflæd and her sister are most distressed about it all. Lady Ælflæd's son isn't yet strong. I know she hopes to have another child, but in the meantime, her nephews are æthelings, as well as her son. And Lady Cynewise is just as worried, so I've heard.'

'So, Lady Cynewise is here, in Tamworth?'

'Yes, why wouldn't she be?' Wynflæd queries, confused by my question.

'I thought she was taken as well.'

'No, she's with her sister, although she seems unhappy about it. They arrived together. I sent for you because the boys weren't part of the original travelling group, and a messenger was here, on Ealdorman Ælfstan's business, and he said he'd take my request to you.'

I nod again and then eye Cuthred and Wynflæd. 'She has the makings of a healer. While she's here, see if you can bring her into your confidence. As young as she is, I trust her.'

Wynflæd's thin lips part in a smile. 'I will. Thank you, Icel. I thought she was wise.'

'But that doesn't answer the questions of the boys. Has the king sent men to find them? Has Wulfheard set out to find them?' I ask hopefully.

'The king isn't concerned. He believes the children have been forced to stop along the way. They were separate from the majority of the riders, for they were in an ox-cart, not on horseback. He believes they'll arrive imminently. He shows little concern, and no, Wulfheard and the rest of the men haven't been seen all summer. Ealdorman Ælfstan was last here more than three weeks ago. But he was alone. I suspect the boys have been taken northwards to the lands of the Northumbrians, using this journey to Tamworth as a means of covering what's truly happening. It's wild country in Northumbria. They could be lost and never found.' Her words are edged with worry. It seems she's forgotten her rancour towards Lady Cynehild, or has decided the children aren't to be included.

'Then they live?' I scarce say it. All of my fears are in those three words.

'I believe so, yes, but only for now. I wish I knew all the details, but I don't.' Wynflæd sounds confident when she speaks. I take comfort from that.

'I can't just go riding through Northumbria. I hear it's huge. I'll never find them, and stand the chance of encountering the Northumbrian king's warriors.'

'Perhaps, but Cuthred heard a name whispered by those who

headed north only three days ago. He was collecting mushrooms for me. He's much better at it than you.' Her ability to berate me even now astonishes me. She winks and then exhales a name, 'Eamont.'

I furrow my forehead at her.

'That's where you'll find them. And it falls to you to do so.'

I nod, considering what I must do. But certainly, it seems I'm to visit Northumbria, whether I want to or not.

19

I leave while it's still dark. Cuthred has spent the grey light of dawn scampering through Tamworth, bringing me bread and cheese while I've borrowed some oats from the grain store. I considered heading towards Budworth, but I don't wish to imperil my people. And there are others, Eadweard and Wulfred amongst them, who might suspect, should I win free, that I'll go there. They wouldn't think to find me at Tamworth. I do need weapons, but again, Wynflæd seems to know better than I do. Cuthred brings me a seax, although not the sharpest, and an old byrnie, rust-stained and no doubt forgotten about by one of the old men who think to never fight again for Mercia. Alongside it is their shield, which is also in a bad way. How Cuthred knew where to find it, I'm unsure. The loss of my seax is a keen one. I know Eadweard will have it. He tried to take it from me once before. No doubt he's taken delight in stealing it again.

For now, I have two days remaining before they told Æthelbald and Hywel to release me. I need to make good on that time to get as far north as possible. It's unfortunate that I'll have to retrace my passage of the previous day, but there's little else I can do. Wynflæd assures me the place I must go to is in the north but on the west, not the east.

'But, are you sure they didn't merely take the children to their father?' I want to believe it's possible, despite my worries. The news that Lady Ælflæd is concerned for her nephews has me reconsidering my thoughts about her. Perhaps, after all, she does care about them, although I've seen little to assure me of that.

'Yes, I'm confident. I hear Lord Coenwulf's in West Frankia, a guest of King Louis. A messenger brought word from Edwin to his mother.' I startle at that, but it brings me some reassurance even while it increases my worry.

'What will you do when you find them?' Wynflæd questions me.

'I've no idea. But I'll do something.'

She grips my arm before bidding me goodbye. 'Those children are in peril, Icel. Always, and especially without their feeble father to protect them.' I feel my forehead furrow at her words.

'I know.' I murmur.

'Do what you must,' is her parting directive. I'm surprised by the way she reaches up, lips compressed so that I bend to her. She plants a kiss on my beard-fuzzed chin. 'And shave once in a while.' Unexpectedly, a tear slides from her eye, and I swallow against the thickness of my throat. Is this us saying goodbye again? She hasn't even spoken of my outburst last year. Does she mean for me to never return to Tamworth?

'I...' I begin, but she shakes her head.

'Go,' she urges me. 'Go. Lives depend on you.'

So used to obeying her, I'm out of the workshop without considering it, mounted, and on my way northwards before the new dawn even breaks in a welter of cold pinks and reds.

Only at the top of a small rise leading towards Lichfield do I stop and gaze back the way I've travelled. I hope to see Tamworth again. But more, I hope to see Wynflæd once more.

* * *

It starts to rain with the rising of the sun. It's cold and biting, reminding me that it won't be long until the weather becomes miserable, and we all want nothing but to shelter beneath our cloaks. Before that can happen, I need to find the children.

I didn't see the queen, Lady Wigmund or Lady Ælflæd at Tamworth, but I knew they were there, thanks to Wynflæd. Neither did I seek out young Lady Cynewise. I trust Wynflæd to have told me the truth of what's befallen the family. Creeping through the gate, the unmistakable cries of young Wigstan echoing through the wooden buildings, the irony wasn't lost on me that he was safe while his cousins are lost, and the king doesn't even seem to realise.

Huddled inside my cloak, miserable with the ice-cold rain falling into my face, I squint forwards, pitying Brute for having to endure. We pass the ancient settlement of Wall quickly, the place where my uncle, Edwin and I slept on that first night escaping from Tamworth. The similarities to my situation now and then aren't lost on me.

I thought I was done with sneaking around but evidently not.

As the day progresses, the clouds grow greyer and greyer. The downpour drenches me so that I'm so cold I fear it'll be impossible to dismount. I become so used to the susurration of the rain, and little else, that the noise of the trees I guide Brute beneath startles me. I turn, laugh at myself, and slowly dismount, every movement an agony. Of late, I feel I've been used hard. It isn't getting any better.

'Come on, lad.' I take him to the gurgling stream that's pulled me from the road, running with water, the ditches overflowing and sending a summer's worth of dry weeds cascading into every available dip and hollow that marks the ancient roadway.

Brute comes eagerly, and I stand with him, drinking, for all I can't imagine why I need any more water.

'Have you ever been north?' I ask my horse, muzzle dripping with water, his bright eyes glowing in the gloom. His silence is to be expected.

Pulling my gloves free from my hands – luckily, I'd not been wearing them when apprehended, and I found them in my saddlebags – my eyes are drawn to the scar there. I have the scar, but not the blade of my eagle-headed seax. For the first time, I consider why my uncle had it. Was it perhaps a gift from Beornwulf, my father? Was it maybe a promise that he'd acknowledge me one day? Chewing on bread that Cuthred collected for me, I consider. I hope the blade was my uncle's and had nothing to do with my father. I want it to have been Cenfrith's and not Beornwulf's. I also want it back. Not as much as the children, but the desire is there all the same.

Brute settles beneath the trees, undoubtedly grateful to be free from the heavy rain. I watch him, considering my path. It's been a miserable day, and I don't relish spending more time on Watling Street. The road, cut through the landscape, is exposed to the rain. Here, beneath these few trees, the worst of the rain is kept from my shoulders. It almost feels dry.

'Come, we'll stop for the night,' I encourage my horse, leading him away from the water and beneath the low boughs of an elongated fir tree. I have to lift it high, but once underneath, the heavy boughs spread from the tree much higher up, and there's room for us. I only just have to lower my head.

There are traces of others camping here in the past. The soft floor of pine needles is disturbed in some places, a circle of stones showing where others have risked a fire but left no wood for others to burn. Eagerly, I lift some oats from the saddle for Brute, leaving him to eat them while I slump to the ground, happy to be still. Since leaving Londonia, besides when I was tied to the tree, I've done nothing but ride my horse.

Before darkness descends, I inspect the rope-burn marks at my wrists and ankles and smear on more of the salve Cuthred handed me. It's not the same, applying it myself. Wynflæd's fingers might be thin sticks, but they're strong and gentle and know just the right amount of pressure to apply. I lack her skill.

My thoughts turn to the wolf. I'm exposed here, as I was there. I can't imagine I'll be lucky enough to evade another such wolf attack, but perhaps the rain might keep any such denizens away from me while I sleep. Resolved, I settle to sleep.

The following day, the rain has stopped, but in its wake, an icy blast of wind ripples the trees, sending even the great boughs beneath which I slept swaying from side to side.

'Bloody hell,' I murmur to Brute, emerging from the warmth of our night-time sanctuary. Another day of tedium and shivering awaits, and I'm far from happy. Mounting Brute, I gaze onwards. The sky promises nothing but trouble, and indeed, by late afternoon, the wind has brought more rain with it, no doubt from the hills to the west. We've met the road I once took on my journey to Bardney, to inform King Wiglaf of what was happening in the borderlands with the Wessex king as my uncle lay dying. I eye it uneasily. Despite having travelled it only a few days ago in the opposite direction, the memories of that first occasion remain with me, and I find it hard to banish those remembrances.

Shuddering inside my cloak, Brute, somehow sensing my unease, spurs himself onwards, the hope of a warm night driving him, although I can see nowhere that might provide the same. Not yet. Eventually, I pull Brute aside. I've seen no sign of habitation for a long time, and there's no hope of it ahead, but I can sense something out there, and so I direct him from the road. Soon a building emerges from the gloom. I can tell it's been long abandoned, but the roof still holds over at least half of it. And it's better than nothing. With my horse at my side, we enter it and prepare to sleep.

I don't know how much further I need to travel. All Wynflæd could tell me was that it was northwards. I know I'm more north than I've ever been in the past, but whether that's north enough or not, I just don't know.

* * *

It isn't, and a day later, Brute and I have come to the end of the road we followed. Ahead, I can just glimpse what I suspect is the sea and before it – well, quite some distance before it from my vantage point – is a busy settlement. I consider whether I should enter it, but my food supplies are running low, and despite Wynflæd's words, I've yet to see any sign of anything that makes me suspect I'm truly following the path of the lost children.

The rain on that first night washed away all traces of any advance made. The horseshit forced into the drainage ditches, and any stray hoof marks in the mud were lost as well.

'Come on,' I urge Brute. 'A warm meal and some oats wouldn't go amiss.'

I dismount at the gates, supported on either side by ruinous walls, and meet the gaze of one of the guards. He eyes me with feigned nonchalance as I enter.

'Is this Chester?' I call to him and receive a nod in return. I expect something similar to Londinium from the exterior walls but on a less grand scale. Certainly, the current inhabitants occupy the remains of some sort of ordered settlement, but it's more as though they squat amongst the ruins. Few of the buildings are entirely of stone. Instead, many have wood or wattle and daub reinforced wicker fences screening them from others. That said, it's clearly a busy trading day. The smell of meat being roasted, and other less pleasant smells, no doubt from a tannery, pervade the air as I walk along the roadway demarcated by walls running along its sides. It's a ruin, but one more lived in than Londinium. Yet the people here are less settled than those within Lundenwic.

The scent of the river carries on the breeze, but I make my way straight to an alehouse, or so I assume from the men and women converged around its door, sitting on benches.

A small boy runs to me, eyes wide as he looks up and up and up at Brute, who waits patiently, for all the noise of so many people in one place must disturb him after so long on the road with only one another for company.

'Show me the stables, and I'll take him,' I offer, a smile on my face for his unease at seeing a horse such as Brute.

'This way,' and he scampers before me. Not that anyone seems to note us. Well, no one but a woman whose eyes track me from beneath a thick mat of reddish hair. She sits at one of the few stools, and I consider whether she's looking for me or just a curious woman. I know to be wary.

I guide Brute into perhaps the most complete building I've seen so far, redolent with the smell of other horses and hay. He seems content enough, and I pull a silver coin from my money bag and offer it to the boy.

'Watch him, and you'll get another when I return.' His eyes alight with delight. I make my way back to the front of the alehouse, eyes downcast, seeking the woman. She still watches me, although her attempts are well covered by her hair. Only the tension in her shoulders assures me that she's well aware of my return.

'What can I get you?' a man asks me jovially. He has a thin face and a thinner body. His lips curl back over a collection of jagged, uneven teeth.

'Food, ale and water,' I reply, again reaching for coins to offset the cost.

He takes them eagerly, and I find a space to settle on the benches. It's cool, but not cold. The heat in the sun is pleasant after the days of freezing rain and winds, and I don't want to risk being inside should someone try and take Brute away. I've lost him once. I have no intention of making the same mistake again.

I try not to watch the woman as I absorb myself in the conversation between the men and women before me. They're traders, of that I'm sure. Their clothes are better than those who labour in the fields but not so fine as to arouse suspicion in those with half a mind to theft.

I'm not really listening to their words, just pretending to, but then something they say does catch my attention.

'Travelling north at this time of year...' is what permeates my hearing.

'And in this weather. Damn nobility. Got no sense,' a man informs another. 'Mind, I made a pretty coin from them with some of my furs. Top price for them. Told them it was mink, but it was nothing of the sort.' He chuckles, his bearded face alight with the joy of making a good sale. 'You'd think they had no idea of the weather conditions at this time of year. The women were shivering, and the children almost blue with cold.'

I find breathing almost impossible, even as I smile my thanks to the man who brings me what I ordered.

'It's dangerous, to travel so far north. Have you heard of the attacks on the Isle of Sheppey? I know the Wessex scum deserve all they get, but all the same. North of here, they were. Bloody fools.'

With a sense of panic warring inside me, I hastily eat my fill. I want to ask the man more, but equally, I don't want to arouse the suspicion of the woman who still watches me and whose motivations I suspect. Is she merely a thief, out to take what I have from me, or has she been left here to watch out for any sign of the children and their captor being followed?

'Where can I get supplies? Bread and cheese for me and oats for my horse.'

'I can do bread and cheese and some dried meat. The horse, you'll have to visit old Eomer, close to the gate. He keeps such for sale.'

'My thanks. I'll take what I can. I'll go and source the oats first and return here.'

'No need, my lord. I can have them with you in a few moments.'

I remain seated and only stand to return to Brute when I have three loaves of good bread and a round of cheese to add to my sack, alongside a linen that smells of pork. I thought of spending the night here, at the tavern, out of the elements, but know I must continue northwards. The trader has left, and I can't ask him more even if I wanted to, but I believe he saw the children, and perhaps Eadburg and her mother as well. I've given no thought to her, but of course, they will have travelled to Tamworth with the children. Or at least, that must be where they thought they were going.

Palming the coin into the boy's hand as I go to retrieve Brute earlier than expected from his warm stable, I have one more request from him.

'Take me to Eomer.'

'Of course, this way.' He skips ahead, his hand clenched tightly to stop him from losing his precious coins. I imagine he'll eat well tonight, or indeed, for seven days. All the same, his ragged appearance worries me. He has no shoes, and his tunic reveals more of his stomach than it covers. 'Here he is,' the boy grins.

Eomer is a trader of oats and other grains that the farmers must sell to him. His workshop is one of the better ones in Chester, the roof hanging low over the wooden and stone building, and from it, sacks of produce spill, some open, others securely fastened, and five young thugs with mean looking faces move amongst them, checking people who view the produce. Only when they hear the jingle of coin do smiles grace their aspects.

'My thanks. Tell me what's your name and where are your mother and father?'

The boy shrugs his thin shoulders. 'Don't have any. The monks shelter me for the night, and then I work where I can. My name's Godfrith.'

'Then take these, Godfrith.' I offer him another five coins. 'And get yourself some shoes for the winter, a tunic that fits and a cloak as well.' His eyes widen. I'm unsure why I've done this, but the thought of his thin bones shivering all winter worries me. 'Now tell me, where can I find the road that runs north from here?'

'You don't want to go north,' he says too quickly. 'It's wild country there. Even the traders take guards with them.'

'I can look after myself,' I try to reassure. 'And I have my horse. He can gallop very fast.'

'Perhaps, but all the same. I wouldn't. But if you must, leave through the gate here and follow the river. Eventually, you'll meet another road.'

'My thanks.' I smile and turn aside, bartering for oats for Brute, which I should have done before paying my young friend more, and only then manage to leave, passing the same guard from earlier. I glimpse movement from close by and realise the woman still watches me, having moved aside from the alehouse. I consider if she'll follow me and prepare myself for such an occurrence. I can see no evidence that she has a horse, and she'll need one. But perhaps the horse is hidden.

I don't have my usual weapons, but Cuthred and Wynflæd found me some with which to travel. I have the seax with a bone handle, that I've spent time sharpening, although it's still too blunt. I have no sword, but I do have an old and battered shield that might help me, provided my enemy is half-blind and unable to tell one end of a blade from the other. And I have the old byrnie as well. I miss my sword and my seax, but it's been a long time since those were the only ways I knew to kill.

Fighting with Oswy and the others has shown me that, sometimes, a good punch is all that's needed, provided I aim it well.

It's easy enough to pick out the river the young lad directs me to, and Brute shows no concern at having his rest curtailed. With my supplies carefully stowed away, we strike out once more. This time, I'm alert to any sign of others having come this way. The way is liberally supplied with horseshit and the sign of animal hooves and horses' hooves, particularly in the sometimes muddy spots that obscure what was once a much better-maintained trackway.

I listen carefully for any sign of being chased, but it's difficult to hear anything above the noise of Brute's steps. When the settlement has receded behind me, and I'm confident the way onwards isn't as tricky as I first feared, I speed Brute's passage. If someone is following me on foot, they'll struggle to keep pace with my horse, and if they're on horseback, they'll struggle as well. Brute, even at a canter, isn't slow.

Every so often, I risk looking behind me, but I can see no one rushing to follow me. I pass a few people, herding animals back towards their farm-steadings, perhaps from market day. The fields are brown and bare, their crops taken from them. But still, the words of the young lad don't seem to be true. He told me not to come this way. Perhaps he meant to dissuade me from travelling further north than the outlying settlements. Maybe he didn't want me to leave when I was so kind to him.

I'm unsure, but we go onwards until darkness covers the land again, and then I realise that someone is definitely following me.

20

'Hello,' I call into the growing gloom.

The roadway stretches clear before me, but behind it's more shadowed and twisty. Yet I know what a horse hoof sounds like, even one trying not to make too much noise.

'I'm armed,' I call again. I've no intention of being caught unawares. Once was more than enough. Eadweard and Wulfred left me feeling foolish and doubting my skills. But there's no reply. Brute stiffens beneath me but keeps up his steady gait. Not that he can do so forever. We've covered a great distance of late. He'll tire, and so will I. I don't know this landscape. I've no idea where I might be able to seek shelter or even hide away from whoever pursues me. The lack of a response assures me that they mean harm, unfortunately.

And then I have a thought. I hope it's just Eadweard and Wulfred who follow me. I wouldn't like to think it was a Viking raider, perhaps come ashore nearby using the river, as they've done with the River Thames and in the kingdom of the East Angles.

I reach for my seax, the unfamiliar handle settling uncomfortably in my hand. I don't like it, and I'll probably be more of a threat to myself than my pursuer, but it brings some comfort.

Darkness continues to fall, and after nights and nights of the moonlight being good enough to see by, it's eerily dark and quiet. I can see only some distance ahead, and Brute is stepping more carefully, keen not to injure himself. The sounds of the night slowly grow around me, the flap of owl wings, the hoot of the same birds, and the scurrying of animals who hunt at night. I'd welcome the sight of something more familiar, perhaps an eagle far overhead, but there's nothing.

Fear stalks me, as does my hunter, only for a large rock formation to veer upwards from nowhere, just as I'm beginning to worry we might need to travel all night long.

'Here,' I whisper, encouraging Brute off the road. He comes willingly, head bowed low, a sign of his exhaustion. The rock formation is bulky to my right-hand side. It easily hides Brute, who I keep close enough to me that I can mount if needed. I can poke my head clear from its side, but I can see no one. And so, a conundrum, should I wait for them to ride past or hide from them until the morning gives me the light I need to see? My lips twist in thought as I run my hand through my beard. Once more, it's unruly and needs cutting back, but now's hardly the time.

I grip Brute's rein and quietly follow the rock formation until I'm convinced we won't be seen from the road. I can't rightly tell, but from running my hand along it, I think it moves slightly back the further from the road I go, which will hide me. Hopefully.

The sound of the night swells around me, making it impossible to hear what my hunter might be doing. I lean against the rock rather than sit on the ground. Beside me, Brute drowses, also leaning against the rock, and his soft breathing lulls me so that my eyes close as well. I can't stay awake all night, despite my best intentions.

When I open them, at a nudge from Brute, dawn is lightening the horizon, and there's no sign of my pursuer. Forehead furrowed, I look ahead. In the far distance, I can see the orange glow of a fire, perhaps from others forced to stay all night outdoors. But other than that, the area is cast in shadows, dawn yet to steal its way across the unfamiliar landscape. I look to Brute as he nudges me again. He doesn't seem concerned, but neither is he entirely happy about something.

I look behind him then and feel along his muscly frame, but it's not a wound that unsettles him. I strain to hear, but there's no sound either. Only then do I hear whispers, little more than a soft shush, just out of true hearing. There's someone there, and if they're whispering, there's more than one someone, I must assume.

With Brute behind me, I follow the rock formation further. Above my head, I can sense there's some other mass there. Perhaps these rocks are part of a quarry or have fallen from a hillside. I keep glancing upwards, but until true dawn arrives, I can't see much more. The sound slowly gets louder and louder, and I realise that there's just one voice, and the words they say are repeated over and over again, every so often accompanied by a sob of such desolation that it almost brings a tear to my eye.

'Who's there?' The words are strongly feminine, and I'm sure I recognise the voice.

'Eadburg,' I gasp. She looks up at me from where she sits, huddled on the ground. She has no cloak, and her dress has been ripped, her hair in disarray, but it's whom she sits with that turns my stomach leaden. Her mother. Her flesh white and marbled, the horrifying black bruises of their captivity evident in the rope marks around her neck and wrists, and yet those wounds didn't kill her. No, a bloodied gash is visible, on her chest, and I stumble to my knees and envelop Eadburg in my arms.

She shivers and trembles. I realise that the words I've been hearing have been her soft prayers for her dead mother, the woman who was tasked with being nursemaid to young Coenwulf and Coelwulf. The woman who was wet nurse to the motherless child. My heart stills in fear, even as Eadburg shudders, her words muffled against my shoulder.

What have these people done to the children of Lady Cynehild?

And why have they murdered Eadburg's mother?

Eventually, Eadburg quietens beneath me. I wrap my cloak from my shoulders around her, gently pry her hands from her mother, and move her to one side. The body is cold and rigid, and so is Eadburg.

'How long have you been here?' My words, softly said, break the silence as though thunder rumbling from overhead. She flinches, eyes wild, and I can see the bruises that also scar her body. I shake my head. It's not really important. 'Here, I have food and water.' I place a piece of bread in one hand and my water in the other. 'You need to eat,' I urge her. She does so, chewing instinctively. I'm sure if I asked her, she wouldn't know what she was eating.

Brute's vigilant beside me. It's clear it wasn't Eadburg who followed me yesterday. Should I be alert to others close by? With the daylight, I glance all around, but there's no one nearby, not even when I step back, shivering in the brisk wind, craning my head as far back as possible to see if there's someone above us.

'They took the children away from us.' Eadburg's words startle me, just as I shocked her earlier.

'When was this?'

'Two days ago, I think. We made it this far, but my mother succumbed to the wounds they inflicted on her.' Her voice catches on saying that.

'I'm so sorry about your mother,' I murmur, and I am, but my thoughts are elsewhere. 'Where did you escape from?' I query.

'Somewhere towards the east. They took the children and then tied us up. We tried to win free. And we nearly made it but then we had to fight. My mother made me run for it, but I went back, and found her, later. I got her this far but I couldn't get her any further, and then, and then...' Eadburg gasps the words, unable to say them. I hold her tight and only when she's recovered do I ask my next question.

'Do you know who it was or where they took the children?'

'No. I didn't know the men. To start with, it was Eadweard and Wulfred, but only for the first day, and then others were responsible. They said we were going to Tamworth, but we never arrived there.'

I crouch before her. 'Would you be able to take me back to where you were held captive?' She's shaking her head before the words leave my mouth.

'No, never. I need to take my mother home to Kingsholm.'

'But we need to find the children.'

She nods miserably, the realisation that she must leave her mother here hardening her features. 'I think... I think they mean to kill them. Why else would they have separated us from them?' Her words are mournful begging me to deny them.

'When did they separate you?'

'Four days ago. We were tied up and couldn't escape for some of that time, no matter how hard we tried.'

I'm unsurprised by her statement that they mean to kill the children. My only real surprise is that, four days ago, they hadn't done so yet. Admittedly, they might have done so by now. I can see what they're thinking. Take the children far away where the blame can never be placed on them and where the bodies will never be found. I clench my fists in a fury, running my fingers over my eagle scar. I'm beyond furious, and not just because Eadburg's mother is dead. These people have no right to meddle in matters of the ruling family of Mercia. The only consolation is that I don't believe Lady Ælflæd is involved, not any more, not if Wynflæd's right when she says she's worried about the children.

'I think they were going north, anyway,' Eadburg murmurs. 'There's no point in going back to where we were captive. There were only two men there. The others had left with the children.'

'Then I'll bury your mother and continue travelling northwards. Will you come with me?' I ask her softly. I'm asking too much of her, but I can't take her back to Chester, not now.

'Yes.' The single word is flecked with rage and resolve. I offer her a sad smile. I can see why Edwin was so enamoured of her. She's not as soft as I thought she was.

'Is there any keepsake you wish to take from her?' I murmur. It's going to be difficult to dig a grave here, but there are more than enough rocks. It'll have to be a cairn for Eadburg's mother. At least, I realise, it'll be easy enough to find, should Eadburg wish to do so. She nods, words beyond her, and moves to her mother. I don't watch what she does. I hear soft kisses and know her goodbyes have been said, although her mourning will be long and hard.

I move the body away from the rocky outcropping just a little, and then, with the hard and unyielding rocky surface beneath her body, I begin to place stones and rocks of all sizes over her. Eadburg doesn't help, and I don't blame her for that. She stands with Brute, her hands on his piebald coat as every rock obscures her mother from view.

Standing, my back crying in pain, I offer her a mournful smile but know I can wait no longer.

'Come, mount Brute. He can take both of us, provided we don't push him too fast.'

Terror fills her eyes, and I wonder if she's ever ridden.

'He'll behave, I promise.' I only hope there's some truth in those words as her warmth settles in front of me, and I direct Brute back to the road we were following yesterday.

I lower my head as the cairn passes out of sight.

I hope this is the only such cairn I need to construct.

Already too many have died while the children of Lady Cynehild remain in the gravest of peril.

I must locate them, even if it makes me a powerful enemy.

I'll find them, I resolve, no matter what trouble it brings to my door. The children are too small and helpless to be part of this game of kingdoms between those who think to rule after King Wiglaf.

21

'Do you know where they were taking them, other than northwards?' I ask Eadburg much later. We've ridden a long way, but not quickly. Brute is firm beneath me, but I'm minded to dismount and give him a break from his heavy burden. He's all I have, and we might need to go a long distance yet.

'I don't think so, no.' Before me, Eadburg has spent time sleeping, finally trusting Brute won't bolt with her on his back. I've been alert, ready to defend us if necessary and, if not, to allow Brute his head so that he can get us away from danger. I look behind us every so often, but I can see no one following us. Still, I can't escape the feeling that someone is there, all the same.

The landscape's growing more and more rugged. To the west, I occasionally catch glimpses of the sea, but my focus is mainly on our surroundings from which our enemy could emerge and catch me unawares. I consider what Wynflæd said to me and what finding Eadburg has revealed to me, and I'm still unsure where to direct Brute other than northwards. I don't know where Eamont is. I didn't ask in Chester, not when I thought the woman paid too much attention to me.

But, at some point, the north will run out, although I imagine not for a long time. Uor and Wulfheard have ensured that I understand the nature of the place I call my home. I might live far from the coast, but nowhere in Britain is truly that far from the sea, not when it's an island.

I wish I knew who had the children. Like Eadburg, I suspected Eadweard and Wulfred, but of course, they were busy misleading me and making me follow them to Hereford, so that they could keep me tied up for seven days. I don't know where they are now. I didn't expect finding the children would be easy, but I didn't believe it would feel this impossible.

The landscape here is ragged. It makes the hills and woodlands of Mercia look tame by comparison. We've seen more sheep than we have people. But there is a roadway, and it stretches onwards.

'Aren't we in the kingdom of Northumbria?' Eadburg eventually asks me, her voice tinged with worry.

'I don't know. There's no marker to show where one kingdom begins and another ends. There are no banners proclaiming that one person or another owns this land.'

The words aren't comforting, but I've been thinking the same for some time. I know Chester is part of Mercia. I'm not sure what the land much further north is. Northumbria is precisely that, the land north of the Humber. While I've never been there, I know that the Humber doesn't run entirely across the kingdom. Like the River Thames, it ends before reaching the western side of the island, but still, the land north of where the Humber lies, regardless of east or west, it still Northumbria. Further north, where the Saxons no longer claim the land as their own, Stratchclyde and the kingdom of Atholl can be found, but that should be far ahead, or so I hope. Bad enough to be a Mercian in Northumbria. To be a Saxon in the kingdom of Atholl or Strathclyde will be much worse.

'If we're Mercians in Northumbria, will the locals not set upon us?' I pause then, mouth open to offer a swift denial, but I genuinely don't know the answer. I've been to the kingdom of the East Angles, to Wessex and, indeed, almost inside some of the Welsh kingdoms. I can't say I was entirely welcomed anywhere that wasn't Mercia.

'We'll see,' is all I can say. I'm not going to offer a reassurance that might not prove to be true. Silence falls once more, and when we stop to relieve ourselves and water Brute, I don't remount, instead walking beside my horse. For all I tell Eadburg to mount, she refuses, and instead we walk onwards.

It all seems hopeless. In this wild, untamed land, how can we find two small children apprehended by who knows whom and, no doubt, taken on fast horses far from where they think we'll look?

'I see smoke.' Eadburg's words rouse me from my wallowing, and I startle. She's correct. There's smoke up ahead, but as we walk, it's clear it's merely a cook fire in one of the dwellings beside the road.

Indeed, now I look, the land here is less wild and more tamed. There are fences built of wattle and daub, and the sounds of animals permeate my hearing. Yet, first, we must counter a collection of men and women who watch us with distrustful eyes. A shiver of fear ripples through my body.

'Good day,' I call to them, wishing my voice didn't catch on those two words.

Eadburg walks so close to Brute that he can hardly move forwards, but he does so, moving her unwillingly on.

'Good day,' a woman calls to me, her words rolling slightly but intelligible enough.

'We seek a party with two small children. Did they pass this way? Both blonde-haired, one not much more than a babe in arms.'

I keep my gaze on the woman. Her hair's streaked with white, but her eyes are bright and alert, and her back isn't bent or twisted by her labour. The dwellings are of firm construction and well maintained, fresh thatch on one of them. This is a prosperous place for all it seems far from Chester.

'What are they to you?' she demands to know, and I feel a spark of hope.

'My children,' Eadburg surprises me by sobbing aloud. Whether she means it or not, it's a good argument. Yet I'm unconvinced that the woman believes her, or those who come closer to us. A huge hound dog comes and sniffs my crotch, and I run my hand over his soft muzzle. He might be welcoming now, but an animal such as that is surely a hunter, like the wolf, and I'm convinced it could sever my throat with a well-placed bite.

'Then, yes, they passed this way. There were many of them. Finely dressed. Why do they want your children?'

'I'm the concubine of a king to the south, and they have a claim to the kingdom.'

At this, the woman spits to the side as though to ward off evil. Her reaction surprises me. 'Men are such fools,' she calls to us. 'They went by two days ago. I don't know where they were heading. I would suggest it must be Strathclyde, or somewhere such as that. The road will take you there. Follow it carefully. There are wild folk in these parts. They won't think to talk to you as we've done.'

'My thanks.' Eadburg lets forth a gentle sob, her anguish clear to hear.

'Good day to you,' I call, the dog backing away at the sound of a guttural cry from one of the men, no doubt its name.

I don't rush to leave the settlement, and I can feel we're being watched for a long time after the smell of smoke has dissipated.

'Do you think they spoke the truth?' I hiss to Eadburg.

'Why wouldn't they? We're not an army of men come to destroy their homes and livelihood.'

'Perhaps,' I counter. The thought of continuing for another two days, taking us further and further from Mercia, is unsettling. I've never been so far from home before. I feel exposed.

'What's Strathclyde?' Eadburg asks me later when we've stopped for the night beneath a spreading oak tree, the only sign of shelter as the sky darkens.

'A kingdom, like the Welsh ones.'

'Not Saxon then?'

'No, not Saxon.'

'Why would they go there? Wouldn't that be a risk?'

'I don't think they are going there. I just think they're going somewhere they believe no one will notice the two small children, or rather, notice when they kill them.'

Her gasp startles me. 'Is that what they mean to do?' she cries, for all she was the one to tell me that.

'I can't think why else they'd have stolen them away,' I counter.

'In my heart, I hoped they were taking them to their father.'

'No, he's in West Frankia. They mean to kill them, I'm sure of it.'

'Why? Because Lady Ælflæd's son is so weak?'

'I don't know. But their claim to the kingship is a good one.' I don't add that mine is as well. I've almost forgotten all about it.

'They wouldn't revert to the old line of the kings, surely?'

'They've done it before, or so Wynflæd would tell you. She knows a great deal about the ruling families.'

Eadburg's face, half-shadowed, looks increasingly unhappy. She hardly eats the bread and cheese I offer her.

'What will you do when you find them?' her voice calls to me long after I think she's fallen asleep. I've determined to stay awake, to provide some protection throughout the long night, although I know I won't be able to survive with none. 'There's only you.' Her words aren't reassuring.

'We'll retrieve them and return them to Mercia.'

'But we're so far from Mercia. There's no one to help us. We only have Brute.'

Her dire assessment of the situation is unnerving but truthful.

'But they don't have Brute. He's the fastest horse I've yet met. He'll get us back to Mercia.' And if not all of us, I think to myself, at least the children and Eadburg.

22

Another day passes with no sign of our quarry, and then, finally, as we're seeking shelter for another night, I hear an unmistakable voice. Young Coenwulf, his childish words lisping through the trees. Eadburg gasps and then thrusts her hands over her mouth to stop more sound gushing forth.

Here, there's a woodland that I thought was all but deserted, but the road surges through them. I don't know if the children are ahead on the road or just deep within the trees as well. The scent of smoke drifts in the air. Wherever they are, they've made camp for the night.

I look to Eadburg and she nods at me, reaching out and taking hold of Brute's reins so that I can slide through the trees and undergrowth, seeking out the children and whoever has them captive.

It's grown dark enough on the road to be unable to see far. Beneath the trees, with little light from the moon, it's even darker. I move quickly but then slow myself. I'll walk into their campsite without realising if I'm not careful. While the smell of smoke is pungent with damp, I can see no light from the fire to guide my steps. I'm grateful for that. Such brightness would blind me more than the darkness.

Around me, animals scurry in the branches, making just enough noise to mask my steps. Hardly daring to breathe, I continue, working my way around and under the reaching boughs of the trees. The childish voice has been shushed, I hope not permanently, and my hand keeps reaching for my blunt seax. Fury thuds in my chest.

While I can't hear young Coenwulf, I can detect the murmur of people talking one to another, the laughter of men sharing some sort of joke, and the more frantic reply of someone shushing them. The sounds guide my steps more than my eyes. And then I crouch low, using a long-since abandoned tree stump to hide behind.

The camp's before me, but far enough away that I won't be seen, provided they don't have guards this far out. Not that I think they will. There are no more than twenty or so people altogether. Their voices are distinctly Mercian. One of the men sits beside the smoking fire. Another figure, with their back to me – perhaps a woman with hair long enough that it moves as the head darts from side to side – sits beside him, a small shape beside them, Coenwulf, I presume. I assume young Coelwulf is in their arms. I can't hear what's being said.

I eye the men. They're the real problem. It's not possible to make out many details. There are enough horses for them all to ride unencumbered, and I also think several pack animals as well. This expedition has been well planned. There's no sign of the original ox-cart. Wherever that was left, it's far from here.

For a moment, I consider if I've got this all wrong. Are they just taking the children to their father but having to employ diversionary tactics to ensure King Wiglaf doesn't hear of it?

Only then I remember that they killed Eadburg's mother.

There was no need to do that. She would have happily gone with the children to be reunited with their father.

No, this is something else entirely.

I stay in place long into the night, watching the camp. They all eat, and then most of them turn to sleep, the children with the other figure. I'm still not sure if it's a woman or a man. Not that it matters. I did catch the shimmer of a blade at their waist when they stood to settle the children beneath a canvas to sleep.

Other than the children, everyone in the group carries iron at their waist.

Whatever else, they're expecting trouble. But what can I do? One man against their number?

Only when I can hardly stay awake any longer do I retrace my steps towards where I left Eadburg and Brute. My mind's a riot of fear and resolve. I've found the children, but how can I rescue them? Eadburg's earlier words were stark but true. What can I do alone?

Eadburg, leaning against Brute, where they both sleep beneath a tree, jolts awake when I return, her face pale enough to see even through the blackness.

'Are they there?' she demands to know, her whisper hoarse, as she stifles a yawn.

'Yes, but so are at least sixteen men and possibly a woman protecting them.' She slumps in defeat at that, and I join her on the other side of Brute. He looks at me but then closes his eyes again, no doubt sensing that nothing's about to happen anytime soon. 'Get some more sleep,' I urge her. 'I need some as well. I'm not going to be able to resolve this tonight.' She huffs unhappily but quietens, and I try to calm my breathing and think my way out of this.

What can I do? One man and a woman, with one blunt seax between them. Oh, and a shield, and a rusty byrnie. Against seventeen others. I counted carefully while I watched them. I feared there were twenty but the number is less. Not that it much helps. While I thought the figure with the children might be a woman, the more I've watched, the more I'm convinced that's not the case, which means the children have a warrior, not only guarding them but also taking personal responsibility for their care. I wish I knew whom it was. I'm grateful the children are still alive, but will they remain that way for long? And why all this nurturing for them? Why this huge distance? Why the skulking about taking them so far north? Why not just kill the children and hide their bodies? After all, they killed Eadburg's mother. Why not them as well? Although, of course, they didn't mean to kill Eadburg's mother, did they?

Sleep is long in coming, and when I wake, grit stings my eyes, and Eadburg is pacing the small space.

'It's our duty to get them,' she hisses at me, seemingly unaware that her footsteps are loud while she tries to speak quietly. Anyone close by would hear her movements and come and investigate.

'I know we must get them,' I counter. 'It's not that which worries me, but the how. I am but one man.'

'Well, you have Brute and me.'

'But no other weapons.' I try to explain my reasoning, aware this argument between us has changed. She was concerned to begin with about what I could do. I was convinced I'd be enough, alongside Brute. Yet now she tries to convince me that I am, when I fear the numbers facing us.

'If we sneak in under cover of darkness, then it won't matter.'

'They keep a watch at night,' I inform her.

'So, not all of the warriors, surely?'

I furrow my forehead then, considering how she knows all this. It's not exactly the discussion two lovers would share, but perhaps she asked Edwin about such things. 'And they might move on today.'

'They're not,' she announces staunchly, and my eyes narrow accusingly.

'You went to look? You could have alerted them to our presence.'

'Well, I didn't, and they're busy making pottage, and the children are being amused with games and a small ball. I think they're waiting for someone.'

'Who?' I demand, forgetting my fury at her.

'If I knew that, I'd tell you, but I don't.'

'If they're waiting for someone, then we need to get them before these other people arrive.'

'Exactly,' she counters, hands on her hips. She looks so like her mother at that moment, that I have to blink the shadowed image of the older woman that seems to settle over Eadburg.

'That still doesn't help with how,' I argue.

'No, but I think whoever it is, is travelling from the north, not the south.'

None of this makes sense to me.

'So, if we skirt around them, we might intercept whomever it is,' I muse.

'Why would we do that?' Her response is sharp.

'Ah, well, what if they've never met that person? We could pretend to be them and gain control over the children,' I counter.

'Would you kidnap small children for someone you've never met?' She makes a good point, and my spark of hope evaporates before it can genuinely settle over me. 'And they know me, anyway. They took me and my mother, alongside the children.' Her words are surprisingly bland considering her mother is now dead.

'So we need to retrieve them sooner rather than later,' I conclude.

'Yes, and we should hurry.'

'Why are they arriving today? Did you hear something when you were there?'

'I don't know, but we shouldn't leave them there longer than necessary.' Her words are stubborn, her chin jutting out.

'No, we shouldn't, but I can't just blunder in there. I need to have some idea of what we'll do.' A loud huff of annoyance erupts from her mouth. I'm about to demand to know what she'd do, only a look of worry crosses her face, and she scampers to my side.

I hear it then as well. There's someone walking around not far away. I don't know if they're coming from behind or in front. What if I've been shadowed here? What if the red-haired woman from Chester has finally caught me? What if it's one of the men who has the children captive?

'Damn it,' I exhale, hoping we've not been discovered either by those who have the boys, or by someone who's been tailing me. I don't want to be tied up again, left to feel useless while the children are once more taken from me.

I hold myself still, aware that Brute does the same, although his legs tremble where they extend to the side of him. He wants to stand but can't, not yet.

I grab his long nose, forcing him to look at me. His eyes are furious, but he doesn't buck against me.

A voice calls to another, and I wince, only to hear the reply coming from even further away.

'They've gone,' I mumble, releasing Brute so he can stand. He does so quickly, eager to be on his feet. I'm sure the voices came from ahead, and not behind, but the thought of the red-haired woman reminds me of my fears in Chester and when I first ventured north. What if there is more than one enemy out there?

My gaze settles on Brute. Perhaps he might hold some answers, but I can think of nothing.

I can't ride him through the campsite. They have more than enough horses to chase me, and I don't believe I can burden Brute with two adults and two small children at the same time.

All the same, my eyes appraise him, watching as he nibbles the growth beneath the tree.

Perhaps, I muse.

23

The day's long and tedious. I spend much of it hovering just out of sight of the campsite where the children of Lord Coenwulf are being cared for, even though they're far from Mercia. What I witness doesn't accord with Wynflæd's or my fears, but perhaps one of the warriors has a soft heart.

I watch carefully, with Eadburg out of sight behind me and Brute kept under the tree. I've not tied him to a branch. If he needs to escape, then he can. I won't have him taken from me by those who'd profit from selling him. If he senses danger, I rely on him to do what must be done.

For much of the time, my face is twisted in concentration, assessing my idea from as many different outcomes as possible. Will it work? Won't it? I'm beginning to think there's no chance when the weather offers me a helping hand.

The rain, as it falls, is loud, almost thundering. It's as though every single water barrel has been upended at once, the drumming of a hundred hooves or even the advance of an enemy. I find a smile on my lips, and Eadburg makes her way to my side, assurance on her face. For a woman terrified of Brute only days ago, I'm pleased to see how she's grown in confidence. No doubt, she's determined to secure the children and seek vengeance for her mother's death. I mirror her thoughts.

As darkness covers the land alongside the heavy rain, we move.

The men of the camp have sought shelter beneath canvases. Coenwulf and Coelwulf's voices are muted as they're swallowed beneath the bleached linen. I imagine the smell will be unpleasant.

Rain falls onto my head, the deluge so heavy that the reaching branches overhead can't stop its progress.

'Come on,' I urge Eadburg. I hear angry voices shouting one to another as the guards are forced from their shelter to stand outside, watching northwards and southwards. It'll be difficult to evade them, but I have my blunt seax. If I have to silence them, then I will, using whatever means necessary. Now that the meal for the evening has been consumed, and many of the bored men sleep, I can't think those with the unwelcome duty will be relieved by others happy not to stand in the rain.

All the same, I force us both backwards, watching where I step carefully, although the heavy rain does truly mask all sound. Without the torrent, I don't think my idea would have stood any chance of succeeding, but I'm more hopeful now. It might still fail, but it won't be from lack of trying.

Eadburg moves silently, having hitched her dress through her belt so that she can't trip or snag the weeds and thistles on it. Her face is set with determination. I've no blade to give her, and she wouldn't take it even if I did. She does have a stone to hand should she need to defend herself.

When I'm happy we've moved close enough while still being far enough away, I meet her eyes. She waits, and I continue to circle the camp. We can't see one another, but she has only to recite the familiar prayer always used in church, and she'll continue towards the horses.

The horses.

At the moment, the horses provide our enemy with an advantage over us. They undoubtedly have better blades and are better protected; no matter what we do, they'll also have speed. But without the horses? Then they'll struggle, so we must do all we can to disperse the horses before taking one or two to aid us and, only then, steal the children from beneath their noses.

Happy I'm approaching the horses from a different position to Eadburg, and with the words of the prayer concluded, I fix my eyes on where I want to go. The darkness is becoming all-consuming, the path I want to take slowly disappearing the closer I get. I keep my eyes ahead, trying not to bump into trees or trip over the disturbed ground, and certainly not fall down some burrowing animals' hideaway, but it's hard going. My eyes narrow and then narrow again. I hear one of the guards calling to another, his voice booming above the thundering rain. A reply comes back to him, and both continue with their duties. I know one was sheltering beneath an overhanging branch, but whether he's still there is impossible to tell.

The sound of hooves moving over the ground reaches my ears. The horses have no such protection. The rain coats them, and the animals are unhappy with that. I nod with satisfaction. They're making so much noise, it'll be another means of masking my place amongst them.

The smell of horseshit is ripe in the air. The animals have been penned here for too long, and no one has been caring for them. If they came this way, having lost Eadburg and her mother, whom they must think are both dead following their escape attempts, then they could have been here for five or six days.

Then I'm amongst the animals, my hand trailing along the back of one of the beasts until I reach its head. The animals are tied – loosely, admittedly, but not allowing them as much room as they'd like. They have no saddles, only the leading ropes. This will make it somewhat difficult. The ropes are twisted and threaded, the animals shuffling amongst one another. And that's why my hand follows the animal's body, head, and then the rope tied around a tree stump. I bend and begin to work the tight knot loose with fumbling fingers. Of course, the rope's damp and slick with rain, and it's too dark to actually see, but at least the horses haven't raised any alarm. I'm sure I can hear Eadburg's breaths, but I concentrate on what I'm doing.

We need to free the horses. Have them wander off beneath the heavy clouds and darkness of night, and then, then, we can grab the children, hasten back to Mercia, and return them to Kingsholm. After that, I won't be leaving it again. Not anytime soon.

I feel the knots give beneath my fingers, one horse and then another pulling loose on their ropes. I follow the cords, determined not to wound the animals by having them snag on branches. I loop the rope around my arms, following it back to the animal, and then hastily saw through the hemp with my seax. I could have done that first, but the animals need to leave slowly, not as one. The first animal, realising it's free, eagerly turns aside, forcing a path through the others as it seeks freedom, and, no doubt, respite from the rain.

The second animal is slower, and I wait for it to move on before tracing the rope to another. I'm aware that Eadburg must be with me, but I can't see her. I do hear the soft thud of hooves beneath the thundering rainstorm. I hope it rains all night long. That way, we can accomplish what needs to be done.

Slowly, the herd of horses begins to dissipate. It's so dark that I lose sight of them immediately, but I can just hear them moving further and further from the camp. While the rain's masking our movements, it's also making the horses unwilling to take their chance at freedom. I fear they might find somewhere to shelter beneath the trees and simply stay there.

When I've released six of the animals, I feel a cold hand on mine and meet the blazing eyes of Eadburg.

'They're not going far,' she cautions me in an exhalation.

'Damn it,' I reply, grimacing at the realisation.

'We carry on, all the same. We can release them and then chase them further from the encampment.'

'We need to be careful. One of the guards has been this way once already. He didn't notice anything, but I'm sure he will.'

I don't know how long the tasks take us. It feels like more than half of the night, and I still need to retrieve the children, but I can't hurry any more. The ropes that hold the animals are twisted and refuse to yield to my fingers. The horses are sluggish to rush away, but we can't move to the next part of our plan until this is complete.

'We should move more quickly,' I whisper. She disappears, leaving me with the curious nose of a horse and its warm breath on my cheek. 'Come on then,' and I follow the cord to where it's tied and release it.

Two more of the animals follow, and if my calculations are correct, then that should be more than half of them. That was my part in this, as well as keeping hold of two more animals so that Eadburg could ride with one of the children. I want a spare, just in case the other animal goes lame. We can't afford to be caught with the children and have no means of escape.

I can't tell if I've chosen two horses that will be good to ride in the darkness, but I grip their leading ropes and begin to move aside. The press of horses has long since dissipated. Eadburg has one more horse to remove, as far as I can tell.

Moving backwards, my shoulders tense as I feel the scrutiny of someone. I turn, but it's too dark to see anything. The two horses walk into me, forcing me onwards or risk losing them. The sudden slap of slack rope rings loudly in my ears. Sodden footsteps come my way. My heart pounds too loudly. I know we'll be discovered, and we're not ready yet.

'Who's there?' a voice calls, filled with menace.

'Me, you bloody fool,' a disarticulated voice responds, and the steady stream of someone taking a piss fills my ears.

Once I've heard the steps backtrack, Eadburg hastens to my side, and together we merge back into the treeline, encouraging the milling horses we encounter.

'Can you take them back?' I ask her. This wasn't part of the initial idea, but with the horses reluctant to leave of their own accord, I must make sure they move off.

'What?' she exclaims, snapping the ropes from my hands.

'Lead them back to Brute, and wait for me,' I urge her through lips that hardly move as I try to stay quiet.

'Get the children,' is her parting shot as she merges with the trees. There's no time to argue with me. Even if she's uncomfortable with the animals, there is no other choice to be taken.

Hastily, I reach out and find the other animals. Three of them stand tightly together. I encourage one of them to move onwards, and the other two follow, but the first stops again. I step to it and encourage it once more. However, no sooner are the other two moving than it stops for a second time.

'Come on,' I growl, deciding to lead one of the animals instead. I'm not aware of other horses close by, but three is more than enough for the enemy to chase us once I have the children. The loss of the horses is sure to be discovered soon. I still need to find the children, and that element of this rescue is even more dangerous. Abruptly, I stop and peer backwards. I can't tell which way I've come. I peer into the gloom, but everywhere is murky and damp. I can't even find horse hooves in the forest floor because it's too dark to see them.

'Damn it,' I exclaim softly. I try and retrace my steps, but one of the horses follows me.

'Go away,' I urge the animal. 'Go that way.' But the horse is stubborn and stays where it is. I waver and then determine to strike out the way I think I need to go. I could tie the horse to a tree, but I don't want to. It could be stuck here forever, dying of thirst and starvation, and I can't do that.

On I go, sure I must have missed the campsite, aware that every time I think I've lost the horse, it reappears, its head hanging low, its hoof beats surprisingly soft over the damp forest floor. And then, when I think I've made a huge mistake, I finally see what I need to see. Ahead, the campsite emerges from the dark dankness, and the horse is still with me. Perhaps I can use it after all.

24

The campfire coughs and spits as the rain falls into it. The light it emits is little more than enough to illuminate the ground beside it. But it does show me that no one moves within that small area. Whoever has the unfortunate task of keeping watch doesn't do so from the fire. They must be elsewhere. Not beneath one of the canvases, but perhaps under one of the trees.

I squint into the gloom, wishing I could see more, but aware that now is the time to act. Whatever happens next, it's the opportunity I need to retrieve the children.

I gaze at the horse, head bowed, beside me. It makes no noise. I find its presence comforting.

I intended to scamper between the canvases and trees and retrieve the children on foot. But I have a horse now. I eye the animal. I consider if I recognise it. Is it perhaps an animal from Kingsholm, or have Eadweard and Wulfred's part in this endeavour entirely ended? Does it know me? Does it, more importantly, know the children? It might prove much easier to take the children if they recognise the horse or at least if Coenwulf does. Little Coelwulf will be far too young to identify the animal or even me. And that's a problem. While I've sworn to protect the children, I've done so from a distance, more often than not, unwelcome inside the hall where they spend the majority of their time. Young Coenwulf might simply believe I'm another bad person come to steal him away. He might kick up a fuss. But I can't risk Eadburg here, not with so many warriors carrying iron.

I can protect myself and hopefully the children, but not Eadburg as well.

The beating of my heart slows as I consider my options. I strain to detect the voices of others, but I can barely hear the snoring of those who do sleep. The fire hisses as a sudden deluge tumbles onto it from the branches overhead.

I can't wait any longer.

On stealthy feet, I slide onto the horse's back. The animal's smaller than Brute, perhaps similar to Wine, and easy to mount. With my upper body lying along the damp animal's long neck, my trews even more drenched now, I knee it forward.

'Come on,' I whisper. And it moves out from the shelter of the trees and between the canvases. The animal must be able to see more easily than I can as it avoids all the ropes supporting the canvases, and the seething fire. I direct it towards the canvas I believe the boys are inside from my observations during the day, and then slip from the beast's back again. I'm not waiting to see if anyone hears me. Instead, I duck down to hack through the bindings tying the canvas door closed with my blunt blade. I lack the time to fumble through the toggles of wood. The smell inside the tent is as noxious as I thought it would be, the pig's fat used to proof the tent against the rain mixing with that of bad breath and flatulence and it's impossible to see anything.

I wince as the snoring rumble ceases, only to resume almost immediately.

On my hands and knees, I enter the confines of the canvas. My clothing creaks with the dampness and my trews are too tight around my knees. I look forward, but I can make no sense of the shapes in the gloom. There's no light to see by, none at all.

And then, white eyes greet mine, and I realise I'm being watched.

'Coenwulf,' I whisper, against my better judgement, surprised that he's awake. With hearing like that, he'll one day make a fine warrior to sneak up on his enemies.

'Who are you?' he asks, his words far too loud with his childish shock at being woken in the night.

'I'm a friend of Eadburg's. I've come to take you home.' My words are so soft I'm not sure he hears them. But he must.

'And Coelwulf?' he demands.

'Yes, yes,' I whisper. 'You need to be really quiet. Where's your brother?'

'Here, beside me.'

I can hear Coenwulf moving but can't see what he's doing.

'He's really heavy,' I hear next. My hand has reached for my blunt seax, convinced that we're being too noisy and the warrior who cares for the children will wake. But I can't expect the youngster to carry his brother unaided. Rearing back to waddle into the tent on my feet, my arse almost touching the floor, I make my way to where I think Coenwulf is.

I feel a sodden lump and realise it's his brother. He stinks of piss and shit, and I wrinkle my nose. It's not just the horses that these warriors neglect.

I pat the furs that cover him and, determining which end is which, I scoop him into my arms and turn to leave the tent.

Coelwulf stirs in my arms but doesn't wake.

'Follow me,' I urge his older brother.

Coenwulf hesitates.

'I'll take you to Eadburg,' I promise him hoarsely. I'm convinced that my antics must have been discovered. Yes, the drumming rain has covered our conversation, but I'm sure we're noisier than that.

'What about my toys?'

'We'll leave them, for now.' I try and sound as reassuring as possible, even though I want to do nothing but roar at him to hurry up.

And then I hear a sound I've been fearing.

'Go back to sleep, you little runts,' a heavily accented voice demands as they roll over in their sleeping furs.

Coenwulf stuffs his hand in his mouth but still emits a squeak of fear.

I look down at the sleeping child in my arms, wincing at the movements coming from behind me. I can't let this man discover what I've done. He'll rouse the entire bloody campsite, and even having a horse to speed our escape might be useless to me.

Slowly, I place the sleeping child back on the ground, reaching for my seax. But Coenwulf remains behind me. Should the man realise he's not alone with the children, it'll be easy for him to grab Coenwulf. I can't risk that. I must take both children back to Kingsholm. I can't sacrifice one for the other.

Fear makes my arms leaden and my movements too slow.

'Where are you, you little shit?' the voice asks again. I can sense Coenwulf's shaking. He might not recognise me, but he knows whoever has him captive isn't his friend. Slowly, I turn my head and lift a finger to my lips to urge him to silence. I don't know if he sees me, and I don't appreciate the shriek of my damp clothes as I move. I still can't see where the man lies, but I need to find him.

Slowly, hardly daring to breathe, I turn on my knees, mindful that I might kick Coelwulf. I'm wedged between the two children, and the opening to the tent is so damn close, but I can't risk it. This man must die.

Coenwulf has his wide, frightened eyes fixed on mine. His

hand is still in his mouth, trying to stop his whimper of fear from escaping. I can sense the man's hand moving, no doubt feeling for where the children slept. He might expect Coenwulf to move in his sleep, but not Coelwulf, whose soft snores still reverberate through my damp boots.

I beckon Coenwulf to me, but he can't move. Urgently, I reach out to him. I don't want him to see this. It might be dark in here, but he doesn't need to witness my killing his captive. He's but a child. He has no idea of what men will do to one another in the name of war and politics.

His thin body trembles beneath my touch.

'Where are you?' the man grumbles, and I can sense he's stirring to full wakefulness.

Urgently, my knees complaining at the position they're in, I grip Coenwulf, and clasp him to me, the strain in my body from reaching and lifting making me want to stuff my hand in my mouth as well. His body is rigid, which at least helps. I think he's pissed himself with fear as a fresh waft of urine reaches my nose.

'You little shits.' The man must smell it as well. 'I've bloody told you to go outside to piss.'

Carefully, I place Coenwulf beside his brother. I want to tell him to go outside, to take the horse and leave here, but what if there are others outside, disturbed by what's happening inside the shelter?

And then a fresh set of white eyes surges up before me, the warrior's gasp of shock assuring me he didn't know I was there. Hastily, I bring the almost blunt seax up to stab him, but he's quicker than I am. What sort of fool, I manage to think, sleeps with a blade that sharp when there are small children beside him?

The edge of his seax is so sharp, I see it even in the gloom. But it's his mouth that concerns me as I duck below the blade, landing on my arse, legs tangled beneath me. If someone comes at me from the slit entranceway, it'll take me too long to get upright to defend myself. I'll die here in the damp furs of children too young to know where and when to piss.

I want to roar my rage, but he's just one man. If I shout, others will come to his assistance, and I won't be able to win free for myself, let alone the two small children I swore to their mother that I'd protect.

There's nothing for it, as I hear him suck in air to call for help. I leap forward, wary of kicking the children but knowing I have no choice. Spreadeagled, I sprawl on top of the man, sending him back so that his head thuds against the hard ground beneath the furs.

I smell the blood rather than see if I've cut him or he's cut me. I stab down to where his heart must beat, but my hand encounters nothing but the furs. With my other hand scrabbling through the furs, I realise I'm lying on his legs, not his head, and reach upwards frantically, desperate to find his chest.

But it seems I've managed to stun him. He makes no attempt to counter my actions, and finally I work out where he is in relation to my seax and slice the blade into his chest. The hot gush of blood touches my hand, and the scent is ripe enough to drive away the stink of piss that permeates everything.

Breathing heavily, I run my hand over his mouth, eager to assure myself that he's dead. And he is. Thank god.

I suck in a much-needed breath, my hand once more feeling through the furs, seeking the man's seax. But my hand stops on something hard and wooden, and I pull it clear. I can't tell what it is, but I'm sure it's the wooden horse that belongs to Coenwulf. Beside it is another object, clearly metal, but what exactly, I don't know. I scoop them both into my hands. I think of seeking the man's seax but I know I've taken too long. I need to get out of the canvas and back to Eadburg.

Hastily, I return to Coenwulf and Coelwulf. Both children seem well, although Coelwulf's soft snores have stopped.

'Did you kill the bad man?' Coenwulf hiccups in fear.

'I did, yes,' I pant, and then remember the toy. 'Here, did you want this?'

He takes the toy from me but doesn't speak. His eyes remain fearful.

'Take me to Eadburg,' he mutters, thumb in his mouth, or at least, that's what I think he says.

'Come on then. But wait a moment.' I can't just emerge from the tent. I must ensure no one has heard the ruckus from inside. Slowly, endeavouring to hear over the drumming rain and eager to be gone before Coelwulf fully wakes and begins to cry, I poke my head through the ripped canvas.

The fire's entirely gutted. The rain still thuds in a terrible torrent, and I squint into the impenetrable darkness, hoping to see no one and fearing what I'll do if there's someone there.

A movement and I'm gripping my seax tightly, wishing I'd been able to find the dead man's blade, only a whiff of horse breath merges with mine, and I remember the animal.

'Come on,' I urge Coenwulf, as I stand, and add whatever object I've found to my weapons belt to explore later. Perhaps it might tell me whom these men were. Now, I just need to get away from here and join Eadburg and Brute. And then make it home to Kingsholm, where I hope the children will finally be safe.

25

It's easy to seat young Coenwulf on the horse. It's damn near impossible to do anything with Coelwulf. Hands slick with the gore of the dead man, the child slippery and stinking of piss, threatening to wake, I'm once more hobbled.

And the longer it takes to get sorted, the more likely that one of the captors will wake and realise what's happening. That their precious cargo is missing and their comrade is dead.

'Come on,' I eventually huff. 'Hold the horse's neck,' I encourage Coenwulf. He does as I ask one-handed, gripping his toy with the other. I intended to mount up behind him, but it's unachievable with Coelwulf. And I think he's less likely to cry out if I'm holding him. However, he's a dead weight. I never thought such a young child would weigh so much.

'This way,' I encourage the horse, holding Coelwulf one-handed to direct the animal. It would be better if the animal had a name, but I don't know what it is.

The smell of damp smoke fills my nostrils. I risk glancing up, but the night remains black, the canopy of trees above my head doing nothing to stop the incessant rain from falling into my eyes.

Disorientated momentarily, it takes me precious time to remember where I've left Brute and told Eadburg to go and join him. But then I reorientate myself. I'm left with no choice but to lead us all directly through the camp, skirting the smoking remains of the fire. I'd like to think it was easier to see, but it isn't. The shadowy trees call to me, but first I have to manoeuvre myself and the horse around the ropes of the tents. Or rather, just me. The horse walks with confidence I admire, the steps gentle with the precious load perched atop it.

Realising the horse is a better guide than I am, I step behind the animal, following the swish of its tail until we're some distance from the camp. Not that I relax. We've still got a long way to go. I might have only killed one man to accomplish this, but that's not an advantage. When they realise their comrade is dead and their horses stolen, they'll come for us. I need to reach Eadburg and Brute before that happens.

The weight of Coelwulf seems to increase with every step I take. Despite the terrible rain, I'm sweating. It's far easier to heft a shield or a sword than to carry this bulky child. At least, I think, he seems to have returned to sleep. I can't have him crying out. He's too young to understand the trouble that would cause us.

On legs growing heavier and heavier, I follow the horse until I realise we're going the wrong way. The horse is returning to where its fellow animals are, and I must reach Eadburg. Hastily, I step in front of the animal.

'This way,' I urge it, and for a moment I fear it will argue with me. Some sound from close by, not a cracking twig, because nothing could snap in this wet, but something else encourages the animal to follow me to where I hope I'll find my allies.

Eventually, I have to stop and look at my surroundings. Have I erred? Did the horse know the way after all? I don't recognise any of the trees I walk beside. They all look the same, from what I can see. Some have pine needles and delicate firs, others are denuded, and others still cling to their golden leaves, which flash white in the darkness.

'Bloody hell,' I explode, only to hear the unmistakable sound of footfall. I turn, expecting to see someone following me from behind, but it's impossible to tell from where the noise comes. My hand lingers on my seax, as I consider how I'll fight with a child in my arms. I must, I caution myself, remember not to use him as a shield. I look at the horse. I wish I could slap it on the rump and send it to Eadburg, but of course, it doesn't know where she is. And neither, it seems, do I.

'Bloody hell,' I repeat more softly. Once more, my heart thuds in my chest. I knew the task was far from complete, but now it feels even further from being accomplished. If the enemy warriors come at me, I'll stand no chance. I might, I appreciate, be able to ensure Coenwulf remains free, provided the horse obeys me, but what of Coelwulf? And he was the child who lived when Lady Cynehild died. It's him I must ensure lives through this.

I hear more steps coming closer. I'm sure of it. The tread is soft but unmistakable. Whomever it is moves carefully, desperate not to make any noise. I look down at the sleeping child in my arms and across to where Coenwulf is half-asleep atop the horse, although remaining upright. The animal, wise eyes on a long face, seems to understand my predicament.

Should I mount up? Should I abandon the children here, and rush with the horse to somewhere else, hopeful that the children won't be found and I can return for them later? That seems like a terrible decision. I can't rely on Coelwulf to keep quiet. If he wakes, he'll cry. I know it. And Coenwulf is too young to protect his brother. He has only a wooden horse.

Impatiently, I turn my head, seeking some way to go, some answer to my problems, but it's unachievable. All is blackness or grey, the trees impossible to see from an arm's length in front of my face.

I thought I'd rescued the children. It seems I've merely brought about their death somewhere else.

'Icel.' The word's harsh while remaining soft, a steadying hand on my arm. 'Come on,' Eadburg urges me. 'You're almost there.' I sag in relief, bending to follow her as she joins Coenwulf and the horse, and quickly directs the animal to where she wants to go. I'm unsure how she's managed to creep up on me, but then, the rain is loud, my heartbeat thuds in my ear, and I have to hear over the noise of three people breathing, not just me.

I can still hear my heart thudding in my ear, and the sweat down my back could cure a fish, but at least I'm not alone any more, with two children and only a blunt seax. And one horse.

Eadburg moves swiftly, her confidence assured, and the soft nicker from Brute assures me I'm nearly at his side, despite the penetrating darkness of night.

'Here, give him to me,' Eadburg demands as soon as possible.

Brute watches with his interested eyes. The two other horses stand, heads hanging low, allowing the water to wash down their necks. I pity them the rain, but I feel just as sorry for myself.

'He stinks,' she mutters. I open my mouth to defend myself, but I'm just grateful to have his weight removed from my arms. Now, should the enemy attack, I'll be able to fight them off without worry that I might forget and use Coelwulf as a shield just because I hold him with my shield arm. 'Come on, little man,' she coos to him. I'd caution her not to wake him, but it's too late. I realise his eyes are wide open but that the presence of Eadburg soothes him.

I can't tell what she's doing in the darkness. I reach out to Coenwulf.

'Are you well?' I demand from him, forcing my voice to be gentle.

'Yes,' he speaks around his thumb, but I understand all the same.

'Do you need to pee or anything? We have to begin our journey home straight away.'

'I did already,' his upset voice mutters.

'It doesn't matter. It happens to everyone.' I hope to console him. Hastily, I run my hands along the bodies of the other horses. Brute will be the fastest, I'm sure of it. And the horse upon which Coenwulf is already mounted will also be fine. I'm concerned about the other two. The one is bent-backed, and the other might be limping slightly, but it's not truly possible to tell in what little light there is.

'I'm ready,' Eadburg announces, her shuffling at an end. 'Will I ride with Coelwulf or Coenwulf?'

'Who can you manage easiest? We can bind Coelwulf to you, but not Coenwulf.'

'Then I'll take the youngest. I'm not the best rider, as it is.'

I agree with her decision but don't say as much. 'You should use the horse Coenwulf's on. Here, young man, come with me. You'll ride Brute with me.'

A shrill shriek erupts from him, but he quickly stuffs his thumb in his mouth.

'Have you heard stories of Brute?' I ask him conversationally. I don't have time for this, but I must soothe him. 'That was when he was younger. Now, he's as staid as your father's mount.' I hope such words will stop him from worrying, but then wince at mentioning his father. That was cruel, and I should have known better than to do so.

'So, he won't go too fast then?'

'Not with me and you, no. He'll do as he's told.' There's iron in my words that I hope my horse hears. We've come all this way. It would be bloody typical if he did something regretful now, but we do have the other horses.

Quickly, I grip Coenwulf, and eyeing Brute firmly, place him on the saddle there. There's no saddle for Eadburg. I'd put Brute's on her horse, but then I'll struggle to ride him, and the saddle is too large for the other animal. I consider what Eadburg's doing. Only then she turns and faces me triumphantly. I should have done this when I gathered Coelwulf to me. She has him held tight to her body, using only a piece of fabric she must have taken from one of the horses. He's held firmly in place there, but she still needs to mount. I also notice that while there's no saddle, there is another piece of cloth over the horse. At least she'll have something to stop her skin from rubbing with the movement of the animal.

'Here, I'll help you,' I urge her, offering my hand for her foot.

'Oh,' and I hear contrition in her voice. She's forgotten about this part of the process. It takes longer than it should to get her on the horse. I'm sure Coelwulf must have been squashed, but he makes no complaint. As soon as she's mounted, the animal pliant beneath her, I hasten to Brute, and carefully settle behind Coenwulf. He tries to shuffle forward to allow me more room, but I hold him tight.

'Stay there. There's more than enough space for the two of us.'

With the leading ropes of the other two horses in my hand, I turn to Eadburg.

'You know the way better than I do,' I grudgingly admit. She's easing herself into position on the horse.

'Then, follow me,' she chuckles softly. I want to relax, as she seems to have done, confident now that she has Coelwulf in her arms that we can manage to escape, but I remain fearful. For someone terrified of horses, she's certainly taken to riding well. Perhaps, after all, Edwin had taught her to ride, but the fear of Brute made her forget. I wish I knew.

I've stolen the children, dispersed the horses, and killed a man. Yet there are still many more of those warriors out there, and we're a bloody long way from home, with no food left, and little to give the children succour until we return to Mercia. We can hope, when they wake, that the enemy will think to find the lost children north from here, but I believe they'll soon realise what's happened. After all, with so many horses and warriors to protect the children, they must be expecting retribution from Mercia.

And even when we return to Mercia, who'll be waiting for the children? And what will they say to explain what's happened to them? I remember the object I took from the canvas. Perhaps that will hold all the answers I need.

With the branches leaving trails of wet to pool down my shoulders and back, I focus on keeping Eadburg in sight. If I lose her, I'll never find my way out of the woodland in the dark.

Our progress is frustratingly slow, but the sound of the rain covers our departure, and finally we win free from the trees. Not that it's daylight beyond the woodland. The sun might have risen, but the clouds remain so low that it could still be night. The rain continues to fall in a torrent, and in moments I'm as wet as I was when I first climbed into the tent to find the children.

I'm aware that young Coenwulf sleeps before me, his head resting on my right arm, his body slumped against mine. He feels so fragile and delicate. How, I think, could anyone mean the two children harm? I find it frightening how easy it would have been to kill them. Perhaps I should be grateful that they allowed the boys to live, despite bringing them so many days north of Mercia.

I'd like to encourage Brute to greater speed, but in the dank day, it's as dangerous as during the night.

'We should go faster,' Eadburg whispers to me, as I draw level. Coelwulf sleeps as well, his cheeks pink against the grey of the day.

'I know, but the roads will be slick and no doubt running with water and mud. And you have no true saddle, only the lead reins of the horse to guide him with.'

The two other horses finally lift their heads. I feel them tugging the lead ropes that I clutch in my hands. I eye them. Both animals look miserable. Whoever rode them here wasn't kind to them. The one, I'm sure, must have been used to carry supplies and not a person. Its coat is rubbed in places, revealing red welts where the skin has been broken. I'd like to tend to the wounds but now isn't the time.

'So, can we go faster or not?' Eadburg asks anxiously.

'A little. No more than a trot. Let me know if you feel your horse start to slow. He's better than the other two and will have more stamina.'

She nods but bites her lip, looking back the way we've come. 'Will they come after us?'

'I imagine so. It's just whether they've found their mounts or not. But, come on, we should hurry as much as we can.'

With my neck itching from being wet, then damp, then dry and then damp again, I grip Coenwulf more tightly, wishing I could trust the horses to follow us without the ropes, but I can't. Encumbered with child, two horses, and no means of reaching my seax for Coenwulf sleeps on my arm, I give Brute a gentle nudge, and he lumbers to a trot.

The sound of his hooves over the uneven stone surface resounds too loudly, but there's nothing for it. We must make more haste.

26

We ride all morning. The clouds never lift, although eventually the rain stops falling. I don't think I've ever been as wet. We stop twice to water the animals, and to allow us all to stretch our legs. There's no food for the children, and I can tell they're hungry. When we ate the last of the bread and cheese, I knew we'd be in trouble. But, then, I hadn't expected to travel so far north. I had no idea of the location that Wynflæd told me to find, only that it was north. In fact, I still don't know if I've reached that location. There are precious few people in this region, and none of them seem keen to share the names of their holdings.

Coenwulf holds his complaints, gripping his wooden horse tightly. Coelwulf, so much younger, doesn't know to stop grouching, and eventually I call a further halt, convinced I've seen a bush ripe with late berries that we can eat.

'Here.' Eagerly, I pull them clear from the barbs of the bush and hand them to Eadburg. She takes them and aids Coelwulf to get them in his mouth. His eyes brighten at the unfamiliar taste, as dark, red juice drips down his chin. Coenwulf takes his fill as well, and as I work my way along the bush, I'm aware of the horses bending to pull at the grasses. I even see Brute helping himself to one of the berries. I can hardly wait to see what colour his shit will be after that.

Not that the berries are that filling, but they're something, and mean we can eat without having to ask any of the few people we see working in fields, or trying to dry out after the deluge. We might be instantly recognisable, should our enemy ask these people if they've seen us, should they think to come south, and I'm doing my best to keep others safe from trouble.

'Will we make it to Chester tonight?' Eadburg asks me. She's released Coelwulf from his sling and now he clings to her skirt, pulling himself up and down with a smile on his face. He's not yet walking, but it won't be long, I'm sure of that. He seems to be robust. I feared for him last night, but perhaps I shouldn't have done. With the chunkiness of childhood, he seems stronger than his older brother who, I note, has begun to lose the chubby cheeks of babyhood.

'No, not a chance. We're still too far from Chester. And, even if we reach there, I don't believe we should risk visiting the place. Our only hope is to get to Kingsholm. There, the people who're loyal to Lord Coenwulf will protect his sons, even in his absence.'

'So you don't mean to seek out the king, then?'

'No. I still don't understand what's at play here. The children will only be safe at Kingsholm and nowhere else.' As I speak, I'm reminded of the item I found in the canvas. I reach into my weapons belt, and pull it forth. It's a brooch, of that I'm sure. Made from gold, and festooned with flashing rubies. It glints even in the dull day, and I show it to Eadburg.

'Did you see them with this?'

She reaches over and grabs the brooch, her eyebrows furrowed in thought. 'No, I didn't. It looks like a family heirloom.'

I nod along with her. She's right, it does, and I don't miss that the rubies are truly eyes on the brooch, the creature, an eagle, I'm sure of it, seeming to look right through me.

I suppress a shudder. This is an expensive item, and it speaks of the family who've taken the children, or so I think. This is something fit for a king, or a family descended from kings. Once more, my thoughts turn to Lord Beorhtwulf. Is this his hand at play, as I suspected? Is this some means of payment for his warriors, or is it something that must be handed over, along with the children, to prove the identity of the warriors who captured the children? I wish I knew. It worries me though. Not having the brooch, but knowing that those involved have something this valuable, means they're wealthy. They can afford to pay a great deal of coin to accomplish their goal, whatever that is.

I eye the children. Were they to be killed, far from Mercia and where their bodies couldn't be found, or did someone want them alive? To what ends, I'm unsure, although, well, they could be thinking far into the future when both children are men and can claim Mercia as their own.

Eadburg nods as she realises that I don't trust the king with the children, and looks unhappy about how much further we still need to travel.

'We need food,' she cautions, her hands sticky with the juices of the berries.

'I know, but we can survive. It's the children I worry about.'

'They'll get poorly bellies if we offer them nothing but berries,' she cautions, as though I'm unaware of that.

'We all will,' I mutter darkly. I swig water from my water bottle and offer the same to Coenwulf. He drinks eagerly. I really look at him in this unguarded moment. His clothes are heavily soiled, and there's a rip running from his neck down his chest. Beneath it, I see a welter of green and yellow bruises, and my fury returns. Whomever these men were, they're lucky to live still. But I don't think they will for long. Once I've returned the children to Kingsholm, I'll seek them out. I must know the truth of what happened here. I need to understand who was at fault. Perhaps Ealdorman Ælfstan will be able to help me with that. He'll know to whom the emblem I have belongs. I place it back in my saddlebags. 'Did you hear the names of the men who took you?'

I realise I've not really asked her what she knew, too determined to find the children.

'Well, yes, but no one I recognised. The men had the usual sorts of names. I heard them mention one name a lot, but he was clearly not there with them. Maybe that was who they were going to meet?'

'What was the name?' I ask, hopeful of finally getting some answers.

'Wulfnoth,' she announces confidently.

'Wulfnoth?' I repeat, trying to determine if I know anyone with such a name, but I don't. It's unusual enough that I would remember someone called that, I'm sure of it. And then Eadburg distracts me from my musings.

'So what now?' she questions.

'We carry on as long as we can and while we can see. Is your horse well? We can put you on one of the others?'

'He's fine. I'll keep him. I'm used to his gait.' Eadburg yawns around the words and I appreciate how little sleep we've had. It's all well and good for the children, they can sleep while we guard them. But Eadburg and I can't sleep on the horses.

I nod. She's right. The other two horses don't share the same rhythm as the one she rides.

'Come on then. We can get further today. I'm sure of it.' But all the same, fear niggles along my spine. We do need to get some sleep. But where? I don't know anyone here. I don't trust anyone, and I'm sure, no matter that we scattered the horses, our enemy will be following us soon enough.

Eadburg nods, but I can tell she's unhappy as she yawns again.

I glance over my shoulder, suddenly feeling like we're being watched. But there's no one there. Not at the moment. I don't know how long that will last.

We could, I consider, hide close to the rocks, but despite the remnants of the stone road we follow, there's enough mud on it for the hoof prints of the horses to be clearly seen. Wherever we go, we'll be easy to track.

We need more people to be about, to confuse the tracks we leave, but with the weather as bad as it is, that's not likely.

'Mount up. Let's be on our way.'

Coenwulf's eager to ride once more, but Coelwulf's unwilling to be bound to Eadburg after his moments of freedom. Face streaked with the purple and reds of the berries, his chunky legs kick out. After long moments, when even Eadburg's stern voice doesn't make him obey, I realise I'll have to have him before me.

'Here, you take Coenwulf, and I'll have Coelwulf.' The thought fills me with trepidation, but we've tarried too long already. Eadburg looks as unhappy as I feel but mounts up, bunching her skirts around her legs and revealing long, pale legs over the blanket that covers her mount's back. I move Coenwulf from Brute to her animal. The horse moves uneasily under the greater weight but settles. I then turn to Coelwulf. 'Come on then.' I heave him into my arms, mindful of holding him too tightly. If Coenwulf's bruised then no doubt Coelwulf is as well. With more luck than skill, I manage to settle myself in the saddle, with Coelwulf wriggling before me. I can't see his face, but Eadburg surprises me by laughing, the unexpected sound a source of delight amongst the stresses and strains of the last few days.

'You should see him,' she giggles. 'His mouth is wide open, his teeth stained red. If he were any older, and you weren't behind him, I'd think he'd battled his enemy and vanquished them.'

'I just hope he sits still,' I grumble, not finding any enjoyment in the feel of him before me. I don't know where to hold him, or how to hold him. I can see why Eadburg bound him to her. His legs are too short, his arms lacking the reach to take hold of the reins, and Brute is much taller than Eadburg's horse. I fear he'll tumble to the ground and be crushed beneath my horse's hooves should we have to hasten on our way.

But Brute, for all his difficult nature, settles with the youngster behind his neck. I loop part of the rein around Coelwulf, binding him to Brute and then to me in such a way. It's far from secure, but I can direct Brute with my knees. The reins are there for when he startles and dashes onwards. I don't believe he'll be doing that. Not at the moment, anyway.

Aware that what daylight there is is beginning to fade, I encourage Brute on. I've no choice but to allow the other horses to follow on if they will. I can't hold Coelwulf as well. I reach over and loop the lead ropes over their necks.

I watch them as Brute moves on. Neither animal seems keen to follow, and I give them up as lost. I should perhaps have sent them running into the wilderness that surrounds us rather than leave them there for our enemy to find. But then, just as I've given up on them, I hear hooves, and turn, expecting trouble, only to find both of them rushing to keep up.

That solves one problem for me.

We ride on. The day grows dark, for all it was hardly light at all. Coelwulf relaxes before me, and I find I can keep a firm hold on him, after all. We ride in silence, other than the beats of the horses' hooves and, eventually, I jolt awake, and return to my musings of who is responsible for stealing the children. I wish I knew whom

Wulfnoth was. It wasn't the name that Wynflæd whispered to me. No, that was Eamont.

Overhead, the thick clouds of the last day have finally cleared, and the brightness of the moon and stars ensures we can see well enough to continue riding. Eadburg sleeps, as does Coenwulf. I reach over to touch her shoulder when I fear she might slide from the horse's back. She wakes, sees me and immediately looks guilty.

'Sorry,' she mumbles, yawning around the word.

'It's not a problem. I've been watching you.' The horses have slowed to a walk. We all need some rest, but where still remains a problem. I can't see anywhere that would provide shelter enough for me to protect the children, Eadburg and the horses, should our progress be being tracked. But my eyes are gritty and I can barely sit still any more, my legs thrumming with the pain of being deadened for a long time now.

'We need to stop,' she cautions me.

'I know we do,' I murmur. 'It's more the where that I don't know.'

But, as though summoned, something rears up before me, and I glower at the black maw of the cave. It'll have to do.

'Over there.' I direct her up a steep incline, eyes peering all around me, eager to ensure no wild animals will attack us while we sleep.

The cave itself is partially obscured by huge rocks but if I can see it by moonlight, then anyone else will be able to. It's also well known because when I dismount, holding Coelwulf as securely as I dare, I see the remnants of fires and the detritus of men and women who've used the cave before.

'Get some sleep,' I urge Eadburg and the children. I've hardly finished speaking, and the three of them are curled up on the hard ground. The horses merge together, the two slower animals taking the opportunity to lie down, whereas Eadburg's horse, and Brute, remain standing.

I yawn, reaching for my seax and finding comfort in the blunt blade. I've still not retrieved my treasured stolen eagle-handled seax from Eadweard and Wulfred, who I must assume still have it. The loss of it is upsetting and unsettling. If someone should understand the intent of the eagle handle, I could be in trouble, especially if Eadweard and Wulfred have given it to this Wulfnoth, whomever he is. If I've interpreted the brooch correctly, and his intent behind taking the children, then he knows the significance of my seax's emblem.

I talk to myself, aware I need to stay away. I stand to the side of the cave, and then I walk across it, and then I stand beside Brute, but at some point I must slump to the ground and sleep.

When I wake to the distressed cries of the horses, my hand reaches for my blunt seax, and I'm on my feet immediately. It's still night-time, and the clouds have returned, obscuring the moon and stars. I strain to hear what's upset the horses, and then I see it. Yellow eyes glinting, the wolf slinks towards the cave.

It seems one of the cave's inhabitants has returned.

And he's hungry.

27

'Wake up, Eadburg,' I call to her, not caring if there are others close by who might hear my words as well. 'Eadburg, wake up.' I'm working my way closer to where she lies, blunt seax in hand, but never taking my eyes away from the wolf. The animal, air blowing before it, watches me with disinterest. I wish it were the same animal that I met outside Hereford, the one that seemed to have some connection to the Wolf Lady, but it's not. This creature is younger, more lithe, and its eyes glow orange.

Eadburg rouses quickly, a squeal on her lips as she realises my concern.

'Get the boys off the ground, and hand one of them to me.' I can't risk looking away from the animal to reach for Coenwulf or Coelwulf. I'm daring it to attack me, my thoughts returning to the wolf who aided me in the woodlands close to Hereford. I can't imagine this beast will be as helpful.

A sleepy Coelwulf is placed in my arms while I listen to Eadburg hastening Coenwulf to stand.

'With me, towards the horses.' Blunt seax still menacing, and with Eadburg behind me, we move to where Brute's watching while the other three horses complain against their tethers. I'm just glad I thought to secure them for the night, or they'd be long gone.

I listen to Eadburg calming the animals, and then, what feels a lifetime later, she calls to me.

'We're ready.'

'Then go, and take the two other horses with you. I'll be along shortly.'

The wolf continues to growl, orange eyes wide in the darkness, but it's stayed far enough away that I don't believe it means to attack us. I almost think it wants me to leave without any trouble. Hastily, I fumble for Brute behind me, lifting Coelwulf upwards, hoping he'll be able to grab Brute's mane and stay upright, until I can mount behind him.

I feared our enemy would catch us, but I also appreciated that wolves must inhabit these lands. Now, I need to get away from here without the wolf attacking.

A sudden movement, as I finally turn aside from the animal, and I try to mount up, only I mistime the action, and instead have to reach for Coelwulf or risk him falling. Now I can hear the sharp tapping of the animal's claws over the stones. Sweat beads my face, but I seek calmness, and once more try to mount. This time, my leg swings easily over the saddle, Coelwulf remains upright, and just as the wolf emits a long, bowel-loosening call for its fellow animals, I'm encouraging Brute to move on more quickly than I should.

I don't risk looking behind me. I don't need to. My hearing is alert to the noise of other animals joining the wolf, and sharp yips fill the night air.

How I've escaped again, from the clutches of a wolf, I don't know. I'm grateful as I catch up to Eadburg and the other horses. Her face is pale in the dull light. Coenwulf is again slumped in sleep, but Coelwulf wriggles before me because I've not managed to secure him as I did before.

Once more on the roadway, I take a moment to tangle Coelwulf in the reins and settle myself.

'Are you well?' I call to Eadburg.

'Yes, now. But will they follow us?'

'I doubt it. We've nothing for them to eat.'

'Other than ourselves,' she squeaks, and the sound brings a grin to my tight cheeks.

'Perhaps you. The boys will be little more than a mouthful.' An outraged shriek erupts, but I realise she's smiling as well.

'Bloody hell,' she gasps, a while later, when I feel the tension in my shoulders disperse. 'That was too close.'

'It was, yes, but we've survived that obstacle, and you did get some sleep.'

'Yes,' she confirms. 'Did you?'

'Evidently, yes, for the wolf crept up on me as well.'

'I'm grateful something woke you.' I am as well, although I don't really know what it was. I'm sure the animal could have moved more stealthily if it had wanted to. Maybe, I consider, it didn't fancy eating small children and a muscly warrior.

'We'll ride until daybreak,' I confirm, trying to decide how long that will be. But the clouds are too low and filled with fury. And then, just when I think it can't get any worse, the heavens open, and once more we're covered in rain. It falls so hard, I can hardly see in front of my face. However, the rain has one advantage. It'll cover our tracks from any who think to hunt us, even stirring the muddy hoof prints of the horses.

But it's miserable going. The rain sheets into my face, and Brute's head dips lower and lower. I have a cloak, but it's already swirled over my shoulders, and it doesn't help, not when the rain is coming from the south, instead of the north.

Before me, Coelwulf begins to cry, his sounds soft and filled with misery. It's almost as though he doesn't want to complain, but is left with no choice.

Ahead, Eadburg's head is also down, and every so often I hear her softly singing to Coenwulf. I consider what I could sing to Coelwulf. All the scop songs I know are concerned with war and death. With the Viking raiders, or warrior kings who died many winters ago. I can offer him nothing, but as it seems to be calming Coenwulf, I do think to softly hum the tunes I know. The sound begins deep in my chest, reverberating into the small body held tight to me. It must work, for his cries cease, and I think he sleeps.

Our horses make their way through the settlement with the hound and the woman, but only a mournful cry disturbs the slumbers of those beneath thatch roofs and behind firm walls. I would welcome joining them, but any attempt would be met with force at this time of the day, I'm sure of it.

A hazy grey light begins to turn the world from shadows and blackness to the monochrome of a new day. But the rain doesn't let up, and even I'm hungry now. The berries from yesterday feel like a distant memory.

The smell of woodsmoke slowly permeates my thoughts, and I squint, wishfully hoping that we might be close to somewhere that we can shelter.

I don't believe we've outrun our enemy, not yet, but the weather, and our steady gait southwards, must be giving us some chance of escaping them.

I ride closer to Eadburg. Her eyes shine at me from a face etched in cold, her lips almost blue.

'We'll have to stop,' I call to her. Ahead, the settlement of Chester is finally coming into view. I didn't plan on seeking shelter inside its ancient and tumbled-down walls, for fear the red-haired woman might be there, keen to alert someone to our presence, but there's no choice.

We're too cold and hungry to continue. I risk wounding the children further, and I won't do that. But I do wish I knew more people inside Chester other than young Godfrith and the man at the tavern when I stopped there on my journey north. If I knew the lord here, perhaps I could seek protection from him, but so far from the heart of Mercia, half of the inhabitants perhaps don't even know whom King Wiglaf is, let alone Lord Coenwulf.

'I know,' Eadburg exhales swiftly. I consider what to do, but really, there's little choice. I won't separate us and place us in danger by being apart.

'We ride in together,' I urge her. 'I have some coins, and we have the horses we could sell, if necessary.' I don't want to go to the same tavern as before. Yes, Godfrith would aid us, but what if that red-haired woman is still there? I can't help feeling her interest in me was far from benign. She might know who Wulfnoth is. She might know how to get in touch with him and then we'd be chased back to Mercia. I consider if she did follow me northwards as I attempted to reach Eamont. I'm not sure anyone has been following me, not in the terrible rain, but I suppose it is possible.

'A meal and a fire can't cost the same as a horse?' Eadburg questions me.

'It depends if the people here know who we are and what we're doing, but I hope not,' I agree, and direct Brute towards the gate I exited through on my journey north. The guards watch me approaching from beneath the shelter of an arch where the gate has been opened. At least, I think, it's the time of day when visitors are welcomed inside.

'A grim day,' a rough voice calls to me, but the speaker makes no effort to bar our entrance.

'It's been raining for three bloody days,' the voice of the other guard answers querulously. I don't recognise either of them. I hope they don't recognise me either.

'Where can we find warmth and a dry roof?' I call to them, hopeful of the name of a different tavern.

'You want Æthelgyth at the Broken Ship,' the first man calls, pointing along a road that veers towards the west. 'She has a soft spot for the youngsters, poor woman,' he continues. I consider what he means by that, but I'm already turning Brute the way he directs.

The street's quiet. No one thinks it a good idea to be out in the deluge. With relief, I see a battered sail ahead, hanging limply in the dank conditions, its white linen dyed to yellow and showing some emblem that I can't determine while it's tangled by the storm.

The sound of the horses' hooves occasions a startled face to peer through a doorway, closed, and then opened, but protected by the eaves of the house.

'Oh my goodness,' a stick-thin woman calls, a cloak over her head. 'Oswin, hurry and help these poor people with their horses.' An audible groan greets her words, but I'm dismounting, gripping Coelwulf as I go. I hasten to take Coenwulf from Eadburg, and place him on the mud-churned ground. Only then does Eadburg slide from her horse. By then, poor Oswin, a man, not a boy as I first thought, has grumbled his way outside, entirely covered by a sealskin cloak more likely to be found on the back of a shipman than a stableman in a tavern.

He startles on seeing Brute, a slow smile spreading over his face.

'He's a fine specimen,' Oswin mutters.

'He is, yes, but damn feisty when he's not drenched and miserable.'

'Aye, well, I'll see him well cared for.'

Thinking nothing of it, Oswin gathers the reins of all the horses and leads them to the other side of the street, where I realise a stable stands beneath the shelter of the stone wall.

'Come in, come in. Look at you all. It's not a day to travel.'

Æthelgyth's words are kindly meant, but I don't miss the sharp look she gives me on glimpsing the warrior's belt around my waist.

The heat greeting us is welcome, and quickly we all remove cloaks. Eadburg, after appraising Coenwulf and Coelwulf, and realising that we're alone in the tavern, removes their tunics and trews, leaving them in little more than cloths over their arses, revealing the starkness of the bruises that cover their small bodies. I grumble low in my throat, wishing I could fight the bastards who did that to them here and now.

Coelwulf crawls towards the fire while Coenwulf clutches his wooden horse, eyes wide in a pale face.

Æthelgyth bustles around beside the hearth, watchful, spooning a meaty pottage into four wooden bowls, and handing them to the three of us able to feed ourselves. Coenwulf takes the bowl eagerly, tipping it so he can eat. But Æthelgyth eyes Coelwulf with interest.

'A fine-looking babe,' she acknowledges, face shadowed. I consider what grief she carries with her. 'Come here, little man, and I'll help you.' I watch her as she carefully moves aside morsels too big for his small mouth. He eats eagerly, and I realise I can still see the vestiges of his last berry meal on his chin.

'I won't ask questions,' Æthelgyth murmurs as she feeds him. Eadburg helps Coenwulf, forcing him to use a spoon instead of tipping the food into his belly. 'But we hear strange things in these parts of lost children and Mercian thieves. I take it these are them?'

'Perhaps,' I offer after too long has elapsed. I don't know what to say. I don't know whom she is. At that, the door creaks open, and my hand reaches for my blunt seax, but it's just Oswin. He grumbles beneath his breath, as he swirls the sealskin cloak from his back and hangs it close to the door to drip there.

'Bloody rain,' I hear him mutter as he glances at us. 'Your horses are tired, but I've given them what they need. They require some rest, though. And one of them has a wound on his foreleg. Looks nasty, so I've packed it with some herbs I know.'

'My thanks,' I call to him, hoping Æthelgyth will say nothing further. But, of course, she does.

'You look too young to be the mother of that boy.' Æthelgyth indicates Coenwulf with her chin, her eyes on Eadburg's. 'And neither of you look the sort to beat young babes.'

'She's not my mother.' Coenwulf saves us from having to say anything, and I wish I'd cautioned him before we came inside. 'My mother's dead, and my father's gone away. This is Eadburg. She looks after me, at home. With her mother.' He says 'home' with obvious relish, and Æthelgyth nods along with him, although Eadburg hisses at the reminder of her dead mother.

'So he's not your father?'

'Icel?' Coenwulf gurgles. 'He's a warrior. Have you seen his horse? Brute is a fine animal.' Æthelgyth continues to nod along with him, and I feel a slither of worry worm its way along my spine.

'I did see Brute. And he is a mighty fine beast.' Oswin enters the conversation, having helped himself to a bowl of pottage.

'So, you're returning to your home?' Æthelgyth questions. Coenwulf has taken his wooden horse to Oswin's side, proudly showing it off. Oswin admires the wooden animal. I consider then whom these two are. Are they partners or is Oswin Æthelgyth's servant? It's impossible to tell.

'We are. But the weather's against us.'

'Only the weather?' she queries, her tone deceptively light.

'Perhaps not, I admit.'

'And you bring trouble to my door?'

'Potentially, yes. But it was that or brave the elements for longer, and that imperilled the children.'

'Aye, it did,' she confirms. 'But you'll be safe here for a while. The horses aren't visible from the street, and few come this way. Those at the gate know I only welcome families into my tavern. The men who fight and drink themselves insensible aren't to savour the delights of my cooking, or my ale. Now, you can rest here all day. Oswin told me this morning that the rain would clear by tonight, didn't you, Oswin? That old sea leg of yours?'

'The damn thing aches when it's going to rain, but it doesn't hurt too much today.' Oswin winks as he speaks. 'I'm sure we'll be dry in no time at all.'

'My thanks,' Eadburg finally speaks.

'There's a room through that curtain, and it has beds for all of you. And there's warm water to clean yourselves with. While you rest, I'll prepare some food for you to take with you. I'll wake you when it's time to leave.' With that, she collects Coelwulf in her arms and gives him a hearty cuddle, as she carries his nodding head towards where she indicated.

'She's a good woman,' Oswin speaks into the sudden silence. 'She'll see you right,' he confirms, and then ambles to his feet as well. 'Excuse me, young man, I must get back to the bread.'

I share a glance with Eadburg, but she's too tired to talk.

'Get some rest,' I urge her, and she takes Coenwulf's hand and leads him after Æthelgyth. I take a moment to take a calming breath, and rub my hands over my eyes and shabby-looking beard. I must look a fright, but this journey is far from over, no matter how secure I feel beneath the eaves of Æthelgyth's tavern. All the same, I step towards her as soon as she's back in the main room.

'A red-haired women, at the other tavern, saw me leave here a few days ago. Is she likely to mean me trouble?'

Æthelgyth's eyes narrow at that. 'No, the poor woman sells her body to fill her belly. I doubt she means you ill. And, she's unwelcome here. But, should I see her while you rest, I'll send her on her way, and have Oswin ensure she doesn't mean you harm.'

I feel more relaxed knowing the red-haired woman's story, although I do still fear she might be selling more than her body. But the memory of her reminds me of someone else.

'There's a boy, at the other tavern. He has no mother or father,' I say urgently. 'I gave him coin for a cloak and new shoes, but winter is coming.'

Æthelgyth nods at my words. 'I know him, yes, a sad story. I thought the monks cared for him,' she adds.

'Not enough,' I caution, and her lips twist in thought. 'He's good with horses,' I offer as though this might sway her.

'I'm sure he is.' She smiles, although her eyes remain sad. 'I'll see if Oswin can find him. Now, sleep, before you fall over.' And, with that, she moves away, without a backwards glance, and I follow Eadburg and the children.

If only we could be assured of such a warm welcome at Tamworth, then I could drastically reduce our journey time, but I can't. There's too much at play. I find my hand clutching the brooch one more time, and wish I knew more about the person who had it – the man I killed in a canvas somewhere in the far north who had been in charge of the two children.

28

I don't think I'll sleep, but I do, and a hand on my arm wakes me when I'd still rather be asleep.

'The rain's stopped,' a familiar voice says to me, and I startle awake, opening my eyes on Æthelgyth.

The children wake quickly, as does Eadburg. I'm astounded when Æthelgyth hands Eadburg two small tunics for the boys to wear and two cloaks as well.

'The others are fit for burning,' she mouths, and once more, I recall the words of the gate man that morning. Stepping into the main room of the tavern, a tantalising smell of pottage and pork almost has me salivating. There's still no one else there other than Oswin, and I consider how Æthelgyth makes enough coin to keep the place free from the heavy drinkers. I fumble in my pouch, pleased to feel the weight of coins there. I can pay handsomely for this brief oasis of peace she's given us.

We eat once more, and then I stand, ready to go. From outside, I can hear the sound of heavy rain, but abruptly, it ceases, and Oswin grins.

'I told you, woman,' he calls to Æthelgyth.

She rolls her eyes, even while helping young Coenwulf with his cloak. 'Aye, you did. A pity your damn leg can give you no inkling of when enemies might attack Chester.' The pair have an easy camaraderie, and I find myself pining for Wulfheard, Oswy and the others. With them at my side, I'd have felt far more assured of outrunning whoever must be chasing us. When Ealdorman Ælfstan bid me travel to Kingsholm ahead of the rest of the men, I doubt he anticipated I'd find myself in Chester and halfway to Strathclyde.

'My thanks.' I reach out to grip her hand, a heavy weight of coins in mine. She takes them without even looking and leans towards me.

'Keep them safe, no matter what,' she murmurs. I swallow against the sudden desolation in her words.

'I will. I gave my oath to their mother.'

'Then you're a good man. I'll pray for you,' she offers before bending, kissing both children on the cheek, and purposefully moving back to the hearth. Her back to us, she doesn't watch us leave.

Outside, rain drips from the roofs, and pools in the wooden gutters along the street, but it's stopped falling from the leaden sky. Oswin beckons me over to the stable. I'm greeted by the sight of all four horses, bright-eyed and eager to resume our journey.

'A fine horse, that one,' Oswin confirms. 'Feisty, as you say, but he knows his worth.'

I grin, reaching out to rub my hand along Brute's nose. His nostrils flare at my touch. The stables are warm and dry, not even a trace of water dripping from the tightly woven roof above our head.

Hastily, we mount up, and I see that Oswin has found a saddle for Eadburg which will make it much easier for her. Eadburg takes Coelwulf, wrapped tight to her body, and I have Coenwulf, who can sit well enough himself in the saddle. And then I look to the other horses. A bandage is wrapped around the leg of the one with the bowed back. Her eyes, while keen, also show some fatigue.

'Can you keep her here?' I ask Oswin. 'She's been badly used.'

'I can, yes. She'll do nothing but be pampered, I assure you. As will that boy when I can entice him here. I've found him, be assured. It'll help Æthelgyth to have someone young about the place.' He nods while speaking, and the thought cheers me. Better he's not here to see us leave, but at least we can resume our journey, and I needn't fear Godfrith will succumb to the coming winter weather.

'My thanks.' I reach over to grip his forearm. 'My sincere thanks,' I repeat before releasing my grip and leading Brute from the stable, another handful of good Mercian coins slipping into his hand. I feel refreshed and filled with confidence, as opposed to fear. Let whoever is chasing us come at us. I know I can fight to hold them off now.

Without a backwards glance, we retrace our steps to the gate and emerge into the dull shades of dusk. It's different men on guard duty, but they call farewell to us all the same, without any hint that they might be conniving with those hunting us. Apprehensively, I glance north but see no sign of anyone following us. Perhaps, after all, we might make it home before we're overtaken by the boys' captors.

I regret that thought. We rejoin Watling Street south of Chester, and ride all night, taking advantage of a rapidly clearing sky and a slice of moon to light the way. But we've not gone fast. The horses are rested but still tired from their exertions.

As dawn breaks, the hills to the west greet us, and I'm pleased to be somewhere familiar. Only then, as we pause to relieve ourselves, drink and allow the horses some time to nibble at the grasses, I hear the sound I've been dreading ever since retrieving the boys from the woodlands in the far north.

From behind, the thunder of many hooves sends birds flying high into the sky, denizens of the woodlands, scampering for safety. Squinting back the way we've come, I can't quite see the horses, but there's no other reason for horses to be racing anywhere at this time of the day. They must be hunting us, taking advantage of the clear night, as we've just done.

'Quickly, mount up,' I call to Eadburg. She grips Coelwulf tightly, hands fumbling with the knots to secure him to her. I thrust Coenwulf into the saddle and follow him, ensuring Eadburg's mounted.

I'm unsure where we can seek refuge, but now isn't the time to worry about that. We just need to keep ahead of them and, if possible, slip into the woodlands closer to the Welsh kingdoms. I don't know them well, but I do know a man and two small youths can hide out there for months at a time. My uncle taught me that. It might be harder with two small children and Eadburg, but I've not come so far to lose hope now.

Eadburg, so scared of the horse when I first asked her to mount Brute, bends low and encourages her horse onwards at a speed that Brute struggles to match for a few moments, now that she has a proper saddle. The other horse is quick to follow. The three animals take advantage of the better road construction here to thunder onwards. I can still just about hear the horses coming from behind, but we're certainly maintaining the gap, if nothing else. My biggest fear is that, at some point, the way ahead might be so clear that they can see us. That'll encourage them to ride all the faster, and we can't go any more quickly than we are. Well, Brute could, but I'm not leaving Eadburg behind. Or Coelwulf. Lady Cynehild bid me protect her sons, and Edwin urged me to keep the woman he loves safe. I need to do all of those things.

Once more, I wish I had Wulfheard and Oswy beside me. Ealdorman Ælfstan as well. I'm convinced he could stop those behind from chasing us. He might even be able to bring them before the king to answer for their crimes, provided the queen or her son isn't involved. I consider where he is. He must have arrived at Kingsholm long ago. Is he seeking us, or is he waiting for me to reappear? I wish I knew.

We hurry onwards. The day grows brighter, but the horses eventually slow, only not before I've led them off the side of the road. The ground's churned with the hooves of many horses. Someone must have camped here and not long ago. The mud that's formed has allowed huge impressions of the horses' hooves to remain visible, but where those horses are now, I don't know. In fact, we've seen no one all morning. We've only heard those chasing us. For a moment, I consider what might have happened in my brief absence from the heart of the kingdom. Could the Viking raiders have attacked? Could King Ecgberht have breached the southern borders again? But that's not my concern. The children and Eadburg are.

'This way,' I direct Eadburg, thinking to take advantage of the churned ground to hide our departure from the road. She follows on behind, as does our single spare horse. Immediately, we're shrouded beneath the boughs of huge trees, and in no time at all the way behind us is as dark as night, obscured by the sweeping branches overhead.

I slow Brute so that we don't risk colliding with the lower branches or trunks of the trees. The ground's uneven and spongy, with a fine mat of rich needles embedded with the mud. All sound is muffled as I calm my racing heartbeat.

I strain to hear the hooves from Watling Street, but it's impossible. It's as though we've stepped into another world beneath the trees. There's no one here but the horses, us, and a few small animals that scamper beyond our reach. I don't want to think we've evaded them. I hastily dampen down the spark of hope that surges within me. If the sound of our movements is masked, then the same will apply to those behind – if they were following us, and I'm sure they must have been.

Young Coenwulf, lulled by the slow gait of Brute, slumbers in front of me. I stifle a yawn as well. Turning behind, I realise that I've lost sight of Eadburg. I turn Brute frantically, fearful that we've become parted. That I can't see the other horse either assures me that I've lost them both, although how I don't know.

I hear something scurrying closer, and my hand reaches for the blunt seax. I breathe a sigh of relief when it's the stray horse that emerges from the trees behind me, followed by Eadburg. I see the problem quickly. Eadburg sleeps on the horse's back, head lolling from side to side, Coelwulf silent in her arms. At least he's quiet while he's asleep. His high voice won't give away our location. And Eadburg needs to sleep. She still mourns the loss of her mother and has yet to return to Kingsholm and tell her siblings. I pity her with such sorrow.

'Good horse,' I encourage the one leading the way. Brute touches the other animal's nose, and I consider waking both riders, but there seems little need. They should sleep while they can.

The day advances slowly. I direct Brute in a direction I hope is south when we're deep within the woodlands. I know the treeline won't run to Kingsholm and that, at some point, there'll be rivers and streams to cross, but with the woodlands closing in around me, I allow myself to relax. No one can attack us here. There's hardly room for the horses to pass between the trees, let alone a man with a blade to hand. And if they come in a group, they'll stand no chance.

Eadburg wakes with a yawn and gasps at where we are as she eyes the late afternoon sunlight falling through the dense canopy overhead. I offer her a smirk on meeting her gaze.

'Good sleep?' I call to her. She smiles shyly and bends to check on Coelwulf. He still slumbers. The last few days have taken their toll on everyone. I yawn again. The indeterminate colours of the woodland are fading quickly to darkness. 'We should camp,' I say softly, fearful that if I speak too loudly, I'll disturb the wildlife letting us pass without squawk or shriek to give us away.

'Yes, we should,' she confirms. 'You can get some sleep then. Do you think we're any closer to Kingsholm?' I'm glad Eadburg doesn't ask if we're still being followed because I'm unsure whether we are.

'I don't know. I think our progress will be meandering, as opposed to straight, but at least we're concealed.'

'I just want to get home,' she sighs, dismounting carefully, as I've already done, to lead Brute to a stream.

Coenwulf is on his feet, rubbing his eyes with one hand, his wooden horse clutched in the other, as he looks around in surprise.

'Here you go, little man,' and Eadburg also places Coelwulf on the ground. His brother goes to him and holds out his hands so that the chunky babe can stand upright, although I don't think he can walk yet. I know a moment of sorrow for Lady Cynehild. She should be here to witness this, not me. Indeed, these steps should be taken before his father and mother.

'I do, too,' I confirm. 'The sooner we have armed men to protect the children and you, the better. I hope Ealdorman Ælfstan will be there. He said he'd meet me at Kingsholm when we parted.'

'But we still don't know who these men are who chase us,' she persists. 'We don't know who this Wulfnoth is. I mean' – she retracts some of her statement – 'I know what the men looked like who captured us. I'll never forget their faces, but we don't know why they did what they did and why Eadweard and his allies are involved.' Her voice is filled with anger and sorrow, no doubt her thoughts turning to her mother. I've no answer for her. We don't know whom they are or what they hope to accomplish, which is a problem.

'We'll find out,' I confirm, thinking of the words Wynflæd said to me, naming Eamont, and my suspicions. And of the brooch we have. I'll have to send word to Ealdorman Ælfstan if he's not waiting for me at Kingsholm. He needs to understand what's happening. He might also be able to help me. And if I need to seek out the king, then I will. I believe whatever's going on is concerned with the succession. Not for the first time, I consider my role in that, only to dismiss it. I might know my identity now, but few would believe it. And other than Wynflæd, I don't believe anyone could confirm what Lady Cynehild said to me. The queen, and Lady Ælflæd, would certainly deny it. I'm sure of that. And Lord Wigmund. I shudder to think what his reaction might be. Not that he could wound me, but he has allies aplenty and they could make my life very difficult with their slights and obstruction.

We eat some of the bread and cheese given to us by Æthelgyth, and then I settle to sleep, having handed Eadburg my blunt seax, just in case there's trouble. I think it'll be impossible to get any rest but the thrum of the woodland encloses me. I feel safe and protected.

A shrill shriek has me startling upright. I turn, eyes wide, unsure what's happening as I blink grit from my eyes. I hear the horses moving uneasily where we left them to graze on what they could find near a stream. Only another loud shriek splits the air, and I turn again, eyes wild. That cry is from a young child. Fully upright in a heartbeat, hand reaching for my seax, which I've forgotten I'd given to Eadburg, I hear the gruff voices of men moving quickly away.

'Icel.' Young Coenwulf cries my name in his high voice. I'm standing, looking for anything I can use against the children's captors. How they've managed to creep into the camp without me realising, I don't know, but they have. And now the yells of both children reach me, but they echo, and I don't know from where they come. I rush to Brute, who remains beside the stream, unsure what he can do to help me, but knowing I need him. My foot kicks something and I look down and see Coenwulf's wooden horse. Hastily, I retrieve it, slip the three horses loose from where we tied them up, and bite my lip.

Where's Eadburg? She's not here. My eyes alight on a stretch of red in the mulch of the woodland floor, and my heart thuds in my chest, my mouth filled with bile, as I bend to collect the almost-blunt seax I gave to her. It shimmers with someone's blood, but I don't know whose.

Someone was wounded here. I pray it wasn't the children or her.

'Help me,' I urge Brute. Eyes alert, he sniffs the air, but it's the other horse that none of us has ridden which strides out confidently once more. The animal is clearly used to finding its own way.

'Follow him,' I urge my horse, taking the other animal with me as well. The horse moves with surprising speed. I can't determine whether we travel towards the west or east because I've become turned around, but the horse follows the continuing screaming of the children with unerring ability. I look for Eadburg or for some sign that someone wounded came this way, but the horse moves too quickly to truly see. And the cries of the children urge me to greater speed.

'Damn the bastards,' I mutter to myself. Dawn isn't far off. The sky is edged with an autumn morning's soft purples and pinks. I just wish it would hurry up and get light enough to see better.

The horse continues, tail flashing from side to side, tension evident in how it sometimes stops and then startles forwards again. It's more like a hound on the hunt than a horse, but I don't pause to consider how it knows which way to go.

In half the time it took us to reach where we spent the previous night, I emerge into a clearing close to Watling Street. Ahead, I can see a collection of men on horses, and here the horse I followed emits a shrill neigh, and one of the other animals turns to look at it, despite its rider's commands.

I can see the children enclosed in the arms of two men as they turn to see why the horse makes such a noise, but there's no sign of Eadburg. Have I left her behind in the woodlands? Was she bleeding to death, and I did nothing to help her?

I turn back, uncertain, thinking of Edwin, but my oath is to the children, first and foremost. As much as it pains me to think about it, she might be dead already. The children yet live, and I need to get to them before these men can take them north again.

Ten of them are milling around on horses, seemingly trying to decide which way to go. My arrival occasions no comment other than from the man whose horse moves towards the spare animal. Whatever he does, his horse won't obey him, even when he dismounts and yanks the animal hard with the reins.

If I wasn't so worried about the children, I might laugh at the sight of him falling over as the horse rushes to a gallop and thunders towards me.

'Get here, you bastard,' the man cries. I'd like to think I know him, but I don't. He wears a cloak that covers his clothes, and although I see the flash of blades at his waist, it gives me no idea of his identity or where he's from.

And then another horse rushes towards me, and Brute only just swerves aside. The rider comes with his spear before him, and I feel it graze my shoulder as my eyes open in shock on recognising one of Eadweard's cronies: Mergeat.

Damn it.

Mergeat turns his horse, eyes blazing with fury.

'You damn shit,' the man huffs. 'Days it's taken us to get here, and we don't have days to return before we're supposed to hand the children over. And you killed Wulfgeat, you turd. Wulfnoth won't be happy about that.'

I startle at his words. I didn't realise he'd been in the north. Not that I know him well. But, if he was in the woodland, then perhaps Eadweard was as well. I'd thought him run away, with his coins from Tamworth, but potentially not.

His face is covered in a rough beard, but the spear's finely made. The horse easily takes his directions, turning quickly to come at me again. I have nothing but the blunt seax, and I'll never be able to counter the spear with that. I realise I've lost the shield I did have. I don't know where, and now isn't the time to worry about where I left it, no doubt in the woodlands where I slept last night.

Added to which, the horses are already turning northwards, the two children with the men, I consider if Eadweard, Wulfred and the others of their gang are amongst them. Coenwulf cries my name again, only to be cut off with a wet slap that makes my blood boil. His soft tears turn my heart to iron as I hear the harsh crack of male laughter.

Ignoring Mergeat, who tries to knock me aside, I rush at the other man, who I realise was also at Kingsholm with Eadweard. He's still unseated and out of sorts from the horse rushing southwards. The horse that Eadburg rode follows them quickly. I hear rather than see them, as they make their escape.

Within sight of him, I lean over, seax ready to stab. He sees me at the last moment, and his mouth opens in shock, just in time for my blade to slide into his mouth. He dies with a gasp, and a plume of hot air touches my hand. Quickly aware Mergeat has turned his mount towards me, I jump free of Brute and attempt to take all the blades the dead man has: a seax, a sword and even a war axe are held on his weapons belt. I'd hoped they might be my blades, but they're not. My fingers fumble, the rumble of the other horse getting closer and closer, making my movements too slow.

I grab the man's abandoned shield instead of anything else, and as Mergeat nears me and Brute moves aside, I hold the blade of the bloodied seax before me. Mergeat's spear attempts to knock it aside, but I spin away so that the spear misses me. I manage a glancing blow on Mergeat's thigh.

He howls with rage, turning the horse in such a small space to come back at me, I almost can't believe it. I thought Brute could turn on a Mercian coin, but this animal doesn't even need that much room. The spear threatens me again. Brute's in the way now. I slap his rump to urge him to move, but my horse defies me, rearing on his back legs and kicking out with his front two. Mergeat, expecting my shield, not my horse's hooves, absorbs all of the impact on the left side of his body. But his spear is on the right. His grip falters, his movement already underway. The spear comes perilously close to my ear, and I feel it as a chill wind against my neck.

'Bastard,' I growl, turning because, despite the wounds he's taken, the fight is far from over. I bend quickly, the flash of the dead man's war axe reminding me that I have more than one weapon. Quickly, I pull the dead man's axe into my left hand, half an eye on Mergeat and his mount. The horse is a fine one. I don't recognise it from Kingsholm. Is it perhaps part of the payment for becoming involved in abducting the children?

I don't want to kill the horse, but I will if it gets in the way. Brute rears once more, but the axe is already in flight. It flies through the air, and the man turns into it to avoid Brute's hooves.

The thud impacting Mergeat's forehead is horrifying, but I don't watch. I want the seax the already dead man carries. With it in my hand, I reach for Brute, thinking to calm him, but he's ready for me. Mergeat slowly falls from his horse, leg tangling in the stirrups, landing on his spear with the axe still embedded in his head. The horse, frightened, hears the welcome nicker of the other animals that have fled south and hastens to follow them, Mergeat's head thudding against the stones of the road.

I wince, but the rest of my enemy are already hastening northwards once more.

'Bastards,' I murmur low in my throat. The name of Wulfnoth on Mergeat's lips assures me that he's to blame for this. Well, he and Eadweard, who's in this up to his neck. I need to stop them before I lose Coenwulf and Coelwulf again. I grip the dead man's sword before mounting, and yank the war axe from Mergeat's shattered skull with the loud shriek of iron on bone.

Brute flees northwards, his hooves thundering against the stone of the road. Ahead, I see the men notice they're being chased, urging their horses onwards. One of them lingers as he looks over his shoulder. No doubt, he considers where the two men are who were supposed to stop me, but they're both dead and the horses are gone. I meet his eyes, glower at the man who's also one of Eadweard's allies, and growl low in my throat as he hastens northwards once more.

Crouched low over Brute's long neck, I slip Mergeat's seax into my weapons belt, and the sword as well. The warriors' horses are good, but nothing can truly beat Brute when given his head. He rushes after them, his eyes more able to avoid the pools of lying water than mine and the few holes in the roadway. All the same, I don't believe we're getting closer. The landscape passes in a whirl of green and brown, the colours of autumn and Winterfylleð starting to predominate.

And then, when I think Brute can't go on at such speed much longer, one of the leading horses falters, and then another. Their riders try and urge them onwards, but both animals have limps. The damn fools have ridden them too hard. I watch as the children are exchanged between those with the lame horses and those who can still ride, and then Brute's rearing up before the two stranded men.

Ahead, the others are escaping, but there are only six of them once I've dealt with these two. I consider the best action to take. Should I avoid them? Take my time to kill them or allow Brute to rush into them? With no real thought, both of those things happen. One of the men, sword extended, thinks to stop our headlong dash, but Brute barrels into him, sending him and his sword clattering against the stone roadway, his head thudding with a wet sound. With a shriek of outrage, the other man tries to spin out of my way, but the sword's ready in my hand, and it ploughs through his neck, not even stopping us. I note that I know neither of these men. Perhaps they belong to Wulfnoth.

Again, I bend low over Brute's neck. I'm breathing as heavily as he is, and a white lather is forming on his neck. I can't keep pushing him like this, but neither can those I follow. Their horses will collapse. I have to hope it's before Brute does.

The road curves ahead, and for a moment I can't see them, and then, when I can, I realise that there are now only four riders. But no sooner have I thought that than a clatter of stones hitting the road brings me to my senses. One of the missiles strikes my leg, another hits Brute's long neck, and he pulls up quickly. I wince at the pain, but only one of the riders threw the stones. Now, another of the men appears before me, perhaps even rearing up from the drainage ditch as I once did in Kent.

'You'll die for this, you interfering bastard,' he cries, his words edged and sharp. He's not Mercian.

He carries a lethal-looking war axe, and he's close enough to menace Brute. I glimpse the two horses, heads down, panting behind a clump of bushes, and lash out with my borrowed sword again. I miss the man as he veers away from my wild strike. Another shower of missiles hits Brute, and me. Brute dances out of the way, sidestepping to avoid the blows. As he does so, he collects the man who tries to attack me. Unaware of what's happening, Brute's back legs knock him sideways, and as he struggles to balance, I pluck the war axe from his hand and use the butt to knock him fully to the ground.

Growling in my chest, I turn back to the man who thinks to attack us from such a distance. A small rise is giving him all the help he needs. Brute eagerly hastens towards him, responding to the squeeze of my knees. Still, missiles aim at us, some of them only clumps of mud and grasses now, but he has eerily good aim. With the sword in one of my hands, and the war axe in the other, Brute thunders towards him, head down, and all I need do is stab down with the long reach of the sword as the man tangles his own legs in haste to get away and Brute knocks him.

I leave him, gurgling bright red blood through his whitening lips, and return to the first man. He's down but not dead, his chest rising and falling. I pause and consider my next actions. I could wake him and demand to know what's happening, or I could kill him.

Looking at the winded horses, I rush to them and remove their saddles and release them from the rope that holds them firm to the tree. I can't do anything else for them, not at the moment, but both animals walk to the road, bend and drink thirstily from the gurgling drainage ditch and a large puddle close by. I eye them, but my fight is on the road ahead. With barely a thought, I bend and take the seax from the unconscious man and use it to slice across his throat.

Now there are only four of them. I'm convinced Eadweard and Wulfred are amongst them. And they do have the children.

In the time it's taken me to kill the men and release the horses, those who went on ahead are out of sight. I push Brute onwards, and as tired as he must be, he eagerly takes my command. The ground flows beneath his hooves as I consider the weapons I now have. It's a pity that none of them is my seax. Not that the war axe is bad or the seaxes I've taken. Or the sword. And at least the seaxes are sharper than the one Wynflæd gave me.

I spare a thought for Eadburg once more, hoping she lives, although I'm fearful that the enemy must have killed her and hidden her body. I don't want to consider that she lives but is cut. I hope she's either escaped or is dead. The other option is too distressing. With all my knowledge of healing, I should have been able to find her and ensure she lived.

Overhead, the sun disappears behind black clouds, and I fear it means another storm. Hunched over Brute, I huddle inside my cloak and try to drive some warmth into my cold limbs. I've not eaten all day, and there's no time now. My mouth's dry as well. I spit aside the taste of blood, unsure if it's mine or one of the men I killed, and then ahead, I hear the cries of warriors and look up. Only for my heart to sink.

29

There might only have been four men racing northwards, but they've been joined now by a group of at least another ten. Where they've come from, I don't know. Maybe they were waiting for them. I'm unsure whether these are the men I first stole the children from. They all seem to have horses, which I wouldn't expect if they were. But then Mergeat implied he'd been in the north. Not for the first time, I consider just how many people are involved in this.

I rein in Brute, when I can still see them, but far enough away that a spear can't be thrown at me or my horse, for some of the men do have spears, as Mergeat did.

The frightened eyes of Coenwulf meet mine. I think he'll cry out to me but he's crushed in front of a large man on a grey horse that paws angrily at the ground. The beast seems ferocious, and there's something about the man that appears familiar, although I can't think why. I consider if this is Wulfnoth. Although, if he is Wulfnoth, then these weren't the men in the north. It was Wulfnoth they were journeying to meet. Wasn't it?

I look for Coelwulf, and see him, almost lifeless, in front of another large man, where he's been tied to him just as Eadburg did, only this man has been much less tender in his ministrations. Their horses seem fresh, and I realise that the four racing horses are to the side of the group, their riders dismounted and coming towards me.

'Arse,' I exclaim. It's easy to see what the plan is here. They've tried to stop me from following, but now they mean to sacrifice the four men in exchange for the children. And I recognise those four men. Eadweard and Wulfred, Forthgar and Deremann from Kingsholm. The rest of the men who beat me up and left me for dead last winter.

I try and smile at Coenwulf, but his face is white and terrified. I note a livid bruise forming on his young cheek. Damn the bastards.

'Give me the children, and you can leave with your lives,' I call to the men. I'm out of all other options. It's time for some bluff.

'You and whose army?' the man who holds Coenwulf demands to know, his voice deep. I already hate him. His familiarity makes my skin crawl, for all I've never met him before. I'd have remembered him. I'm sure of that. He's distinctive. His height makes him perhaps even taller than Horsa.

It's enough that he crushes Coenwulf, but his booming voice, rich with derision, makes me grit my teeth. If I could kill him now, then I would. I don't even want to know his identity or why he's doing this.

'They're coming on behind,' I try to deceive, although I don't know why. It's clear to everyone here that I'm alone.

'You bloody fool,' he rumbles towards me. 'Kill the pestilent cock.' I realise then that Eadweard, Forthgar, Deremann and Wulfred have been advancing on me while I've been looking at the children and wasting my time talking to the man in charge of abducting them. Eadweard looks delighted with the order. Arse. I notice that he has my seax blade at his waist as well. I growl low in my throat. So, he was the one who led me astray and had me tied up. I didn't think I could despise him more than I do, but somehow, I find even more of my fury directed at him.

As I hear heavy hoof beats pounding their way north, I focus on the immediate danger. They all wear byrnies and have a good collection of weapons to hand, but not shields. Brute eyes them with the same unease that I do. He's already saved me more than once today. I can't expect him to keep on putting himself in danger, so I slide from his back.

I have the war axe I took, three seaxes, one blunt and two sharp, and the sword that I hold before me. It's not my favoured weapon, but its reach is long. Brute, despite my intentions, remains at my back.

'Go,' I urge him when the slap to his rump doesn't produce the desired result. 'Go,' I try again, but then there's no more time for Deremann and Forthgar come against me. I can't believe their blatant attack here, in the middle of Watling Street. Anyone could see them and intervene, but they're smug bastards. Deremann smirks at me, revealing that four of his front teeth are missing. Forthgar has a snub nose, more akin to a pig than a man. They also have a collection of scars that mar their faces. Deremann seems to be looking down, his cheek pulled tight. Forthgar has vivid red marks running over his nose, making him appear branded.

But they're quick. Deremann rushes me with a seax in his hand; Frothgar follows behind, a war axe in his. Wulfred stands with his spear pointing at me, a smirk on his face. I can't see Eadweard. I assume he thinks to attack me from behind; only Brute's there. I'd look but there are three men before me, and only one behind. I'd sooner protect myself from the three than the one, even if that one is Eadweard.

I counter Deremann's seax with the sword and Forthgar's war

axe with the stolen axe. If the men look surprised that I have their ally's weapons, they don't show it.

Both men hurry to get to me, but my sword keeps Deremann at bay. Forthgar shows less caution, but watching both men simultaneously is difficult. I'm unsurprised when I feel a blow land on my arm. Wulfred thinks of slicing me with his spear while I'm distracted.

'Arsehole,' I roar at him.

I lurch backwards, only to encounter Brute's broad back. He nickers, but not in welcome. As I try and move further back, he attempts to stand where I am. Slowly, I realise we're rotating. I take my three warriors with me while Brute attempts to evade the reach of Eadweard. I can hear his heavy breathing coming from behind.

'You don't want to do this,' I call to them all, knowing it's useless but trying anyway. 'The king will have you killed for this.'

I'm unsurprised when it's Eadweard who responds, his voice rich with derision.

'The king! The king doesn't care, and we'll have our coin and need never step foot in Mercia again once you're bloody dead and have stopped messing everything up. The king has shown himself to be weak. He should have had Lord Coenwulf and his by-blow killed when he had the opportunity.'

Perhaps, I consider, I erred here. It would have been much easier to ride through these men to follow where young Coenwulf and Coelwulf are being taken. Not that I have time to curse myself for a fool.

Wulfred thrusts the spear closer, coming up against my rusty byrnie, which is now even more rusted after days in the wet. My cloak might keep the rain from it, but the damp air is another matter entirely.

The impact is hardly felt, but now Forthgar almost has his war axe free. Quickly, I circle my arm, dropping it low so that the two axes disentangle, and I'm chopping at his neck as he tries to make the same move on me. He's just out of grasp, for I fear to step into his reach in case the spear punctures Brute's side.

'Damn it,' I huff as the seax opens a line down the small area of my arm visible beneath the byrnie. The heat of pain makes me irrational, and without thought, I move forwards, head lowered, and thrust it against Deremann. His nose erupts in a welter of blood and gristle even without my helm. He drops down, the spear that was almost resting on his shoulder following him.

I step into the gap, stamping down with my feet as Deremann moans on the floor. I grip Wulfred's spear. From here, the spear can't hurt Brute. I have my hands on it, just about to wrench it from Wulfred's hands when Forthgar's war axe whistles too close to my neck. I jerk backwards, knocking into Brute, who's about as forgiving as a rock wall at my back.

I'm breathing heavily, the wind taken from me, but far from done.

I jerk the spear, hoping to make Wulfred rear backwards or risk losing his teeth like Deremann. But his grip remains firm. I kick Deremann down on the ground again, wishing I'd done more than break his nose. When he stands up, and he will stand up, he'll be pissed off.

The seax whispers close once more, but I swing my war axe to meet the blade. My sword's on the floor. I dropped it to grab the spear, and now I'm not sure that was a good bargain to make, especially not when Forthgar surges upwards holding his war axe, and I can't risk bending to grip my sword again.

'Shit,' I mutter to myself. I'm thinking of all the times I fought Oswy and Wulfheard, Garwulf and Frithwine, but I'm not convinced it's fair to compare this to then. I'm entirely outnumbered, with no hope of anyone coming to my assistance. I don't want to think that Eadweard will best me, but it seems increasingly likely, making me even angrier. As does the knowledge that it's not truly Eadweard. He's left Wulfred, Forthgar and Deremann to complete the task. He's already sacrificed Mergeat and the man whose name I don't know as well, and all in the name of coin. He's no better than a bloody Viking raider bastard.

With Brute pressed tightly to me, I don't have room to move. Even evading the advance of the war axe and seax put Brute's life at threat.

The group of us has turned so far now that I'm facing the way I came and can no longer see the horsemen riding north or Coenwulf trying to look at me, head turned, from where he's once more being stolen away.

I growl low in my throat. This isn't going well. And with Eadburg missing, and Wynflæd only knowing the name of Eamont far to the north as my destination, if I die here, on Watling Street, I don't believe anyone will ever know what befell the children, despite my words that others were following on behind. Eadweard will run from here, his saddlebags filled with the coins Cuthred saw him being given in Tamworth, although by whom I'm still not sure, and the children and me will be lost for all time.

Desperation fills my thoughts. I can't die here. I won't allow it. And I won't let Eadweard be the one to end my life.

I meet Deremann's seax with my retrieved seax, the spear forgotten about. Its point still faces downwards, caught between the men advancing on me. I've no idea what Eadweard's doing. Brute turns with me. I wish Brute was Oswy or Wulfheard. Yes, he has his hooves and a nasty bite on him, but we can't shout one to another as I might do with those warriors I've fought with for many winters now.

Sweat beads my face as the two war axes face one another, and while I'm engaged with that blade, I'm aware of the spear coming closer once more. I veer backwards, and it just misses my face because Wulfred's angle's too tight. Any moment now, he'll realise, and I won't be able to counter his move by just moving my head. And Forthgar leers at me with the war axe, the stink of him filling my nose as I try and break free from where the two axe heads have become entangled. If Wulfred and his spear isn't cause enough to worry, the seax also flashes before me.

'Four men to kill one, you bastards,' I roar, thrusting forwards with the war axe, risking dropping it so it comes free from my foeman's blade. I free my war axe, but not quickly enough, as I feel the burn of a cut on my thigh. Wulfred has realised his mistake and stepped further and further back, thrusting the spear just to the side of Forthgar.

'Four men to kill one Mercian busy-body, yes,' Eadweard bellows in response.

A howl erupts from my mouth, and with it, I hear an answering whinny from Brute. If Eadweard's hurt my damn horse, I'll kill him. But first, I've got to stay alive.

Another burn shudders along my body, this one on my right cheek. I see the blood well from the cut below my eye. I'm just grateful that it didn't take my eye. I raise the war axe to counter Deremann, but he's too quick, and I feel another cut on my chin. Forthgar with the war axe is even closer now. I step back, trying to focus around the pain, expecting to encounter Brute's resistance, but it's not there. Belatedly, I hear the rumble of his hooves over the cobbled road and appreciate that he's finally taken my command to flee. That means Eadweard, who was menacing him, is now behind me.

I swirl my arms, war axe in one hand, seax in the other, but there are four blades against my two, and I'm entirely alone. There's no one to witness this as I stab and slash, but my blood runs more freely for every blow I strike. Not only my arm, cheek and chin but my thigh, calf and even a glancing blow on my back.

I can feel myself weakening. Tears of frustration mingle with my blood and sweat. I lick my lips but taste only the salt of my exertions.

'Why did you take the children?' I cry, determined to have answers before I succumb to this attack.

'They threaten the kingship. And they're weak and useless right now,' Eadweard cries. 'And what are two young lives? No one will mourn them. And there are others who would rule in their place.'

His words are gratifying to hear, and yet I still don't truly know who's behind all this.

'What's at Eamont?' I try again. If he's shocked that I know the name, he doesn't mention it.

'None of your damn business,' he growls, his attack more frenzied.

More and more, I feel myself weakening. My thoughts turn to the children. Who will find them? Will anyone even care? And I think of my uncle, bleeding his last to defend me. Did he do so for this? I don't believe he did. He wanted me to live to fulfil my destiny, and I want the children to live to fulfil theirs, but it's becoming increasingly unlikely that any of us will be able to do so.

It'll be the small child of Lady Ælflæd who becomes king one day, provided he becomes stronger. Unless, of course, whoever is behind this also means to threaten the weak boy.

Not that any of it should concern me. I'm fighting for my life. Why should matters of the future be a concern for me?

Yet I battle on. I've not given up yet. I won't accept that this is my fate. My seax blade is slick in my hand. The war axe matted with the hair and skin of my enemy. I see Deremann falter, the toothless man with the seax, but the other three remain strong and overwhelming, even the arsehole with the broken nose.

A blow rings resoundingly around my head so that it pulses with the impact. I struggle on. Lashing out wildly. I can hear someone shrieking and roaring and realise it's me. My chest is tight, my heart beating wildly as though I've run from Tamworth to Lichfield and back, and still, I'm being overwhelmed.

'Hurry it up,' Wulfred calls. 'If we don't catch them, you know the bastards will leave us, and take all the coin.'

With his words resounding in my ears, I think to spur myself onwards. They have somewhere to be. Perhaps if I just delay them, they'll tire of this and leave me alone.

Only then, there are two hands around my neck, squeezing, pulling tighter and tighter. I kick and thrash, wild strikes with both blades failing to have any impact because Wulfred, Forthgar and Deremann pull away, their blades glistening with my blood, a reminder of my failure to kill them. And slowly, my struggles lessen, my wild blows falling away, my arms too heavy to lift as I struggle against that bastard, Eadweard. I drop my seax and reach for his hands, but mine are slick with blood and sweat and even with both hands I can't grip his or pull him away.

I'd sob, but I can't even hitch a breath to do so, and slowly the world turns black.

30

I cough and retch, the world around me black, trying to remember where I am, why my body aches and why the bed I lie on has more stones in it than straw.

My throat's raw, the cough sending spasms of pain ricocheting up and down my body to add to all the other hurts and pains.

'Brute,' I try to call, but the sound that comes from my throat is more whisper than shout, and it only makes me cough again.

I'm lying on my face, I think. It feels like pins from the blacksmith's forge stabbing into my face. I can't feel my arms, and I don't know why. I try to move upright, try and see where I am and what I'm doing. And then it all comes back to me.

Young Coenwulf and Coelwulf. Where are they?

And then more comes back to me.

Why am I alive?

With too much haste, I attempt to sit upright, but my arms still won't work. I end up flopping like a fish out of water, my face once more grazing whatever I lie on. My eyes close with the pain, lights flashing behind them. I try to take a deep breath, to will myself upright, but it only makes me cough, and then a thousand other hurts make themselves known. Tears form in my eyes but I can't sob. That would hurt too much.

Instead, I close my eyes and try not to think about everything that aches or pulses, throbs or just makes itself known. I don't think I should feel my tongue, but even it feels huge in my mouth. Huge, and dry, and that sends me into another coughing fit.

Tears continue to fall, and I don't know how. I feel as dry as a husk.

Once more, I will myself to serenity, hoping to find some part of myself that can help me accomplish this. Even without Brute, I must get to my feet. I need to rescue the children. I swore an oath, and the thought of breaking that sends a fresh wave of grief flooding me.

I've failed. I know I have.

But I can't fail. Not now.

I open my eyes, resolved. No matter what. I'm going to get upright. I'll not allow Eadweard and his cronies to triumph. Or this Wulfnoth, whomever he is.

My hands and arms are no longer numb. Now they tingle and hurt all the more. I put some pressure on them, once more feeling the sharp bite of whatever I'm lying on beneath them. It might as well be a thousand blades. That's how pointed the ground is.

With a howl of rage, more akin to a wolf calling for its pack, I make my way onto my bunched knees. A whole host of fresh agony suffuses my body. The hot burn of fresh blood oozing from my many cuts fills my nostrils. I think my eyes are still shut, but they're not. It's night. The moon and stars are obscured by thick cloud with the howl of the wind finally making itself known as a shudder of cold runs through my body.

I focus on my breathing, on trying to tame the agony, but it's no good. Everything hurts. My lips are thick. My stomach aches as though a herd of cows have trampled over me. My knees, well, they feel as though they've been scoured with the very blades beneath my hands.

I reach out, determined to decipher if I'm on the side of the road, or inside a cave or some such. But there's too much air around me, the wind ruffling my sweat-drenched beard and cheeks. Its bite is as sharp as a knife. Reaching out behind me and realising that there's firm ground there, I swivel on my knees to sit on my arse.

I'm panting by the time I've accomplished that. My back aches now, but my knees are no longer as sore, for all I'm sure I must be bleeding from them. My hands snake up towards my neck. I'm remembering Eadweard's hands around me. I'm recalling the sensation of being unable to breathe. Panic makes my chest heave as I relive that moment, but a sharp stab of pain and a warm sensation over my arm and stomach recalls me to the even more frightening reality of now. I've lived through that, but now I need to survive what else they did to me, or my death might have occurred then.

I'm wounded. I'm alone. I've lost my horse and all of my supplies, and I'm shivering. I have no cloak, no means of getting warm and absolutely no chance of seeing where I am. It's just too damn dark. There are nights I wanted it to be so dark, but now, when I need the moon's light to see by, it's abandoned me. And I do feel abandoned.

Once more, panic threatens to envelop me. I'm shivering from cold and fear. And I know, for Wynflæd has told me enough times, that this is a deadly combination.

I force my hands away from my neck, instead examining the cuts I remember taking to my chin and cheek. Both feel as though they've started to scab over. They're filled with filth and muck, but there's no water for me to clean them, so I leave them alone. I have other concerns.

Gingerly, I feel my byrnie and then lower my hands to my belly, forcing myself back to expose it further. Just where my tunic rides free from my taut belly, I can sense the stickiness of a wound. With my hand, I try and determine just how bad it is. It seems to be a good hand long, and it's certainly gaping. I thrust my little finger into it to gauge how wide the wound is, only to feel fresh blood pooling from it.

'Damn it,' I curse. I have only the clothes I'm wearing, and it's bloody frigid, but the wound is a bad one. Running my other hand along the top of my trews, I sense they're sodden with blood and not piss, as I first thought.

Perhaps, I reason, I could do something with my tunic. But no. I'd need to remove it to do that, and I can't. Unless…

My hand scurries to the side. Have they left me with my weapons? I could cut it free. But I find nothing in the close vicinity, and I daren't risk moving any more. I've no idea how much I've bled. I might feel weak from blood loss, but it's impossible to tell with all my other aches and pains. For now, the agony is making me sharp. I appreciate that it might be masking my true state.

With nothing for it, I reach as far forward as I can, prepared to rip my trews to give me something to stem the bleeding. But there's no strength in my hands. I can't rip my trews, and the movement brings a fresh wave of sweat to drip down my nose.

And I've discovered another problem in the process: the cloth of my right trew is stuck in place, no doubt due to bleeding there as well.

My arms shake as I lean backwards. Perhaps I should tear my tunic after all. But no, I've no strength to rip anything.

Defeated, I consider my options. None of them is good, and it's proving impossible to do anything in the dark. Perhaps, I realise, it would be better to just be asleep until dawn breaks. But I can't guarantee I'll live until then.

A shriek of frustration leaves my mouth, making my throat ache as I realise this is futile. I'm alone. There's no one to help me. I don't even know where I am. It doesn't matter how much healing skill I once had because it's impossible to implement any of it. I'm thirsty. I'm in pain. I'm cold. Perhaps it would have been better to die with that bastard's hands around my neck. No one with any honour should kill like that. But Eadweard thought to murder me in such a way. He wounded Brute, he must have done for my fierce horse to leave my side. Eadweard thinks he's killed me. Thoughts of Brute have me worrying all over again. The children. Eadburg. Brute. Wine. Me. If I die here, what will happen to them all?

I grit my teeth. It's impossible to tell how much of the night has passed, but I imagine much of it for it to be so utterly dark. I've no choice but to wait for the morning, if I live to see it. Come the morning, I'll be able to decipher where I am and determine all of my wounds. Come the morning.

Fearful of my belly wound bleeding more, I pull my knees up to my chest and curl into a ball, arms wrapped around my legs. It's uncomfortably tight, but it's the only way I can keep warm and, perhaps, arrest the bleeding. I don't think I'll sleep, what with the blades digging into me, my aches and pains, but at some point I must, because when I wake, driving rain stinging my eyes, it's daylight, and I can see just how precarious my position is.

What I thought were blades sticking into my back are the sharp angles of stones as I lie in what must be a quarry, but a long-abandoned one. There's a sharp edge at my back, down which is a much deeper hole. I'm only grateful the bastards didn't shove me into it as I waken, uncurl my tight, unresponsive body, and try to work out what I should do first.

My body trembles, the rain driving what heat I've been able to generate from it. My clothes are wet, and my hair as well. My hands, which were no doubt bloodied and bruised, look white as dead fish as I examine them. Once more, I grit my teeth, around the thousand different hurts and aches, opening my mouth to try and catch some of the streaming rain to cleanse my mouth and aching throat.

I attempt to stand, swaying alarmingly as I do so. Once upright, I teeter worryingly towards the sharp drop. But there's something close by that I want. A part of the quarry has been worked, but not the area above. It'll allow me to get out of the driving rain if nothing else. Resolved, I stagger forward one step, and then another, knowing that while I'm upright, all of my wounds have the opportunity to bleed once more.

I know my leg bleeds, but I'm not sure about my belly wound.

The distance, which I thought was little more than three horses' lengths, threatens to undo me. It's just too far. I'll never make it. I pause, catch my breath, choke on my crushed throat and then sway. The rain stings my eyes and every hurt on my exposed body. I find a wolf grin on my face. With the force of it, it might clear the muck from my cuts. It hurts like driving sleet, but it spurs me on.

All the same, I need to get out of the rain.

Again, I sway alarmingly from side to side. I look down at my feet, urging them onwards, but they seem wedged in place. Instead, I lean forwards until I almost tumble over, and then my feet finally move, urging me onwards. I make it, the sharp overhang immediately stopping the rain from pelting me. It feels as though I've stepped from outside into a hall with a fiercely blazing hearth. I allow myself to enjoy the sensation, but I'm no fool. I know how dangerous thinking like that can be.

I stand there, catching my breath and looking into the sheeting rain. I can't see Watling Street from here. I can't think they'd have taken the time to move my body far, but all the same, I don't know where I am. I recall Watling Street being bounded mostly by woodland and fields, not a quarry.

Once more, I feel blood seeping from my belly wound and realise it's time to do something about it. Checking my face, I can feel the scabs have moved with the onslaught from the rain, but hopefully, they'll start to seal themselves again now that I'm out of it. Glancing down, I eye my right leg. The cloth's welded tightly to it. I won't be able to remove that, but somehow, and I'm sure it wasn't like that last night, the cloth of my left trew is almost hanging off anyway. I bend and rip it fully off, the biting stab of the cold hitting my skin as my arms protest the movement. Stretching upwards and wincing as I do so, I hold it against my belly wound. Somehow, just doing that makes me feel better. But I'm far from assured of living through this just because I've managed to stem the flow of fresh blood.

Panting, I consider my next objective. I need to move and find people who can help me. But the night made it impossible to see, and the low clouds letting lose their barrage of rain now obscures everything.

I suck my bottom lip, tasting salt and blood once more. I need something to drink. I'm aware I've not pissed for too long. My body, already too dry, will be suffering even more. It's so damn frustrating. The rain is falling in buckets, but I don't have one to hand to capture the water.

Perhaps I should just be pleased to be out of the torrent. I lean back, feeling the marks where the stone's been carved from the wall behind me. Some of it almost feels smooth. I'd run my hand along it, but I don't want to. I'm starting to shake again; this time, it is with the cold. My clothes are drenched. My tunic is stuck to my skin.

I can't go on like this. It might seem madness, but I must get out of my wet clothes.

Growling low in my throat, I force myself to consider removing my byrnie. No matter how I look at it, it's going to hurt. I can allow it to hurt and then recover, or I can ignore the issue, feel warm for a while, and then die in agony because I'm not warm at all, but rather shivering to death.

There's no choice to be made there.

But the wall of the quarry might help me. Leaning against it, I use my numb fingers to release the catch on my weapons belt. It falls to my feet with a loud clang, rubbing against my makeshift bandage as it falls. When my byrnie's removed, I can use the belt to keep the bandage in place.

Leaning back, I allow the quarry to take the weight of my byrnie, lowering my legs in the hope that I'll be able to wriggle out of it like a snake. For a moment, the pain in my knees is too great, and nothing seems to be happening. I almost give up the task but then feel the rusty byrnie start to lift from my shoulders. I continue, and eventually it slips over my head, and I'm beneath it, almost sitting on my arse once more.

I consider staying there, legs before me. But I'm still cold, far too cold. I bend low, moving my body out of the way from where my byrnie will fall, and with relief, hear it thunk to the ground. The next part will hopefully be easier.

Arms juddering, I grip the bottom of my tunic, my eye catching the livid score along my arm, which I think was my first wound, although it might not have been. I've forgotten the order in which I received them. With a grunt of effort, I lift my tunic free from my back, releasing the scent of my wounds and filth, so that I almost gag. The fact it's wet doesn't help either.

A shiver runs over my body, but my eyes catch on the site of the welter of purpling bruises over my chest. I can't imagine my back looking any better.

I work quickly then to secure the strip from my trews in place around my belly wound. I still don't risk looking at it. It's wide but not necessarily deep. While I might stink, I don't smell the shit of the grey coiled ropes inside my belly.

I breathe, once more licking my lips, conscious that when my tunic went over my head, it knocked my facial wounds.

I gaze at my trews, but there's so little of the one leg left that I can't see it will help me to remove them. And, of course, the other side is stuck to my leg anyway, a wound having bled there since yesterday. At least, I consider, I assume it was yesterday. It might be that I was knocked out for longer than that.

What then shall I do now? The options are remarkably few. I can wait here. I can walk out in the rain and see if I can find someone. But I have only my trews and boots to keep me warm, and although I'm glad to be released from my byrnie, I'm still bloody cold.

A whimper leaves my mouth as I tighten the belt around my makeshift bandage.

I'm still buggered. I can't deny that.

Lips trembling, aware I need water, but that even cupping the rain in my hands will result in me being drenched, I hunker down, wincing at the pains as I sit down once more, naked back to the rough stone face, and close my eyes.

I can't do anything in the rain.

I'll sleep awhile.

31

Next time I wake, I know the sun is out, and the rain's stopped, but I find it impossible to open my eyelids. I'm curled tightly in a ball, like a hedgehog keen to evade its hunter but missing the prickles.

If someone attacked me now, I'd have no way of defending myself. I lick my dry lips, dreaming of water, the sound of running water nearby. But it's not enough. My eyes won't open.

* * *

My violent shivering wakes me next, and it's night-time. Or at least I hope it is. My eyes open, gritty and itchy. I'm still curled in a ball. In fact, I think it'd be too hard to uncurl now. My body's adopted this new position. Like dogs who know their time has come, I've chosen the position I mean to die in. I can't escape from this. I'm finished. Hazily, I think of Eadburg, and how I failed her. Of Edwin, and how I failed him. Of Wynflæd, and how I failed her. Of Lady Cynehild, and how I failed her. A broken sob cracks from my sore throat as I consider the two young boys, Coelwulf only just starting to walk. I've failed them more than anyone. Is this all my life was ever meant to be? I'd rage with fury, but I'm just too tired.

* * *

Next time I wake, I'm warm. A soft smile touches my cheeks. It won't be long now. I consider muttering a prayer to God, but it's all I can do even to think the words of the familiar prayer. I don't much agree with his idea of heaven anyway. I think, perhaps, it would be better to go to Valhalla and feast for eternity. But I've no weapon to hand, so that's not going to happen either. I decide to enjoy feeling warm.

Only then I'm aware of voices. They're saying my name. Or so I think. The sound comes from far away.

'Bloody hell. Let me see him.' I smile again, recognising Oswy's voice. I didn't think I'd hear his dulcet tones ever again. It's strange to realise I'm hallucinating him.

Only then I feel hands on my body, a sharp stab of something and I want it to stop.

'What's he saying?' I hear someone else ask. I think it's Wulfheard, but I might be wrong. What's happening to me?

'Gibberish,' Ealdorman Ælfstan confirms. I can hear the concern in his voice. And then Wulfheard speaks again.

'Are you sure you know what you're doing? We should take him to Wynflæd.'

'There's no bloody time for that,' Oswy huffs and, whether I will it or not, my eyes open on the strangest scene I've ever witnessed.

There's a fire in front of me. I can see the welcome reds and yellows dancing on the end of thin sticks and larger pieces of wood, the superheated blue of its heart assuring me this fire's been burning for some time. It's what Wulfheard, Oswy and Ealdorman Ælfstan are attempting that concerns me more.

'What are you doing?' The words don't sound as though they come out of my mouth. My tongue's so dry it's stuck to the roof of my mouth, and it's an effort to work it loose. Perhaps, I realise, I should greet them with more warmth, but I'm worried about their intentions.

I can tell that Oswy's nervous, his eyes peering down at me and something glinting in his hands.

'Gibberish, but Maneca, hand me the water.'

Gentle hands lift my head above my shoulders, but still, I hiss with pain. Swallowing is torture as I allow the cool fluid inside my mouth. I drink as much as I can, but the beaker is removed too quickly, Maneca snatching it away from me when it's still more than half full.

'What are you doing?' I manage to say this time. Ealdorman Ælfstan, hovering over me, is the one to speak.

'Oswy will stitch your wound.'

'What?' I squeak, meeting the troubled eyes of the man I saved inside Londinium. 'He doesn't know what he's doing.'

'He's watched you perform the task more than enough times,' the ealdorman dismisses. I feel my eyes widen.

'And?'

'And what, Icel? You're lucky we found you. And you're bloody lucky that Oswy is prepared to try this, or you'd be dead by now.'

I eye Oswy, where his lips are pursed in thought, the needle in his hand flashing with all the malice of a bloody seax. 'Is he?'

'What?' Wulfheard demands.

'Is he prepared to try?'

'He has the needle, doesn't he?'

'Yes, he does, but looks like he's about to gut a pig, not stitch me back together.'

Oswy looks at me, with an arched eyebrow. 'For that, little runt, I might just leave you with a message.'

Without further pause, he plunges the needle into my wound, and I shriek, bucking upwards against the pain as Oswy rears backwards, the needle, or so it feels, embedded in my skin.

'Hold his damn legs still,' Wulfheard orders everyone, the words of the ealdorman subsumed beneath his commanding tone. 'Cenred. You're a big bugger. Get over here and hold his leg. Maneca, take his arm. Ealdorman, you can take the other one. Ordlaf, get the other leg. Now, hold him, or Oswy can't stitch him, and then he'll bloody delay us even further.'

'What?' I squawk as rough hands seize my extremities. I try and move, but the men have me held firm. Oswy's going to do his worst, whether I like it or not. 'Not so bloody deep,' I say instead, trying to be reassuring. I'm aware of others in the campsite and the gentle nicker of horses. It's daylight, but it's bitterly cold. Someone has given me their cloak, the fur collar lining making my nose tickle, but I fear to sneeze while Oswy has his iron embedded in my stomach.

'Like this?' Oswy queries, as I feel the searing pain of my flesh being stabbed with the needle, the pig's gut running through me so that I have to grit my teeth against the painful and disorientating experience.

'How the hell do I know?' I huff, sweat beading my face.

'Yes, like that,' Wulfheard intervenes.

'Small and neat,' I offer again. The pain is immense. I finally understand why the men I treat can never rest easy as I stitch them back together.

The movement of my flesh being tugged is horrific. Instead, I distract myself.

'How did you find me?'

'We came looking,' the ealdorman offers.

'Why?'

'Wynflæd.' It seems then that my fears no one would know where I was were ill-founded. The ealdorman must have gone to Kingsholm, and then to Tamworth.

'So how did you find me?'

'Brute.'

'Did you find him? Is he well?' I attempt to move my head to look, but there are too many people crowding around me to see.

'Of course we found him, or we'd never have found you. He led us straight to you.'

'But he left me?' I feel my forehead wrinkle, only that hurts, so I stop doing it immediately.

'Well, he came back. Poor sod. He was nudging you and you were insensible. Without him, you'd be dead.'

The thought is far from consoling. Still, I wish I could see Brute. My nostrils flare at the familiar stink of heated iron, and I brace myself for what will come next. I've been burnt enough times to know this will hurt.

'I take it you didn't find the boys,' the ealdorman continues first. And now I close my eyes, remembering my failure. While Oswy mutters to himself, and I really fear what he's doing, I think about the last time I saw young Coenwulf wedged into the saddle of the man I think is Wulfnoth.

'I did. I had them.' My voice is broken, the words only just audible even to my ears. I don't want to say them. I don't want to admit to everything I've done wrong. 'But they found us. In the woodlands. There was a woman with me. Eadburg, you met her at Kingsholm. I don't know what happened to her. They killed her mother, but she escaped. She might still be there, not as lucky as me to have Brute to find her, and they took the children away. North again.'

With my eyes closed, I can't see the expressions on the faces of those who help me, or rather, hold me prostrate so that I can't buck and twist against Oswy's less than gentle ministrations. But I hear the heavy silence all the same, and then I feel hands tighten on my arms and legs and I know the worst is to happen.

The pain of the heated blade is like nothing I've ever experienced before. Sweat beads my face as I twist and buck, my roar of outrage so loud I can hear nothing else.

Only when the blade has gone do I open my eyes, sympathy on the faces of those who slowly release me, a look of shock on Oswy's face as he thrusts his seax back into the heat of the fire.

'Do you know who has them?' Wulfheard asks gruffly, when he believes I'm able to answer once more. Perhaps they put the tears that fall from my eyes down to Oswy and my wounds. But I know better.

'Eadweard and Wulfred are involved. But I didn't recognise the man who has the children. A huge man. He rode a huge grey steed. I heard the name Wulfnoth, but I don't know if that was him.'

'It was,' Wulfheard responds angrily. I also hear the others muttering to one another as well, as though they too know who the man is. And still, the pull and twist of the needle is busy at its work. I wonder how big the wound is. I mean, I knew it was large but Oswy has been at the task for a long time now. Only then I feel his hands moving down my leg. He's finished. I breathe more deeply, and feel the tension on my arms and legs ease.

'Why does he want the children?'

'Because the bastard has a black heart and will sell his soul to the highest bidder. But I know where he's going.' At this, I open my eyes and glower at Wulfheard. He wears a smile that presages someone's death, and I shudder at the likeness I see there. I've seen that expression on another man's face, and I feel my forehead wrinkle in consternation.

'Wulfheard—' I open my mouth to ask, but the ealdorman interrupts me.

'We'll go after them as soon as we've got you somewhere safe. And we'll send someone to hunt for this woman.' And my thoughts spiral and I forget what I was going to ask him.

'I'm coming.' I grimace as even saying the words hurts.

'You're not,' the ealdorman replies immediately.

'I bloody am. I don't care if I die.'

'And you will,' Oswy offers, meeting my eyes with his, but he's grinning as he says it.

'Just get on with it, and then we can get going,' I urge him. I'm unsure how many other wounds he needs to tend to, but suddenly, I'm impatient.

'You need to eat and drink,' Ealdorman Ælfstan grudgingly acknowledges. For some time, I've been aware of the smell of something cooking close by. I thought it was Oswy using the herbs to heal me, but perhaps it's a meal. My belly rumbles with the thought of food.

'And sit up,' Oswy glowers, but still he grins.

'And piss,' Wulfheard joins in by repeating my oft-spoken cautions to the men when I tend to them.

'And get some clothes on,' Maneca cackles, and I appreciate that I am, under the fur, entirely, bollock, naked.

32

Sitting is an agony. Standing is sweet torture, but at least I'm reunited with Brute, who comes, with his inquisitive nose, to knock me as I finally release my vivid yellow stream into the nearby undergrowth. I hear the others talking about me, and Oswy hovers close enough to wrinkle his nose at the acrid stench. And, of course, to grab me when Brute's reunion is overenthusiastic and I threaten to tumble into the undergrowth, along with my piss.

'You stink enough without adding to it,' he cautions me, a firm hand on my arm, just about keeping me upright. 'You need to step aside.' He smacks my horse's rump and Brute, teeth bared, snaps at him, causing me to wobble once more as Oswy moves to evade the crotchety animal.

I smirk. Pleased to see my horse.

'Are you wounded?' I ask Brute, and Oswy startles at that.

'I didn't...' Oswy begins.

'I know,' I mollify, using Oswy's firm arm and Brute's own back to allow me to check my mount for injuries. Brute ran. There must have been a reason for that, when he'd stood at my side for so much of the fighting.

Limping, my right leg burning where Oswy's sewn the flaps of skin together, I run my hands along my horse, but as I make my way around his head and to the left side of his body, it doesn't take much investigating to discover why my horse did what he did.

Eadweard appears to have tried to skin my horse. Above his front left leg, a wide cut glimmers red in the daylight, the skin loose, although the wound seems shallow. I wince to see it, and Brute, with his usual mild temper, rears backwards from me, and this time I sway so much that I have to take three rapid steps forward just to stay upright. As Brute's hooves hit the ground, a thud of agony echoes around my body, just to add to the unpleasantness of it all.

'Bloody hell,' Oswy offers, reaching out with his hand as though to touch the wound. Brute repays him with another snap of his teeth. It's a good job that Oswy has the reflexes of a warrior or he'd be missing a hand.

'Come on, boy.' Brute allows me closer, but still backs up away from me. 'I need to see,' I find myself explaining to him, only to cough, painfully, the sound more akin to a stone being pulled over gravel. Brute startles at the noise, and so do I, which makes my stitches and burned flesh twinge. 'Damn it,' I murmur when I can speak again. Oswy's come back to me, and the commotion has also brought Wulfheard and Ælfstan.

'Poor bugger,' Ælfstan murmurs. His words are soft and filled with sympathy for my horse.

'Aye, that'll have made him run,' I confirm. I cursed my horse for leaving me, but I can see exactly why he might have done so. Such a wound would have terrified him. I mean, he runs from a bloody butterfly.

'Will he let Oswy tend him?' Ælfstan queries.

'I doubt it. I'll have to do it.' I'm unsure how. Standing is agony, and my body thrums and shivers beneath the fur cloak that wraps me, but if I want to join the march north, there's little choice.

'Boiled water?' Oswy queries.

'Some linens?' Wulfheard also adds.

'Pig's gut,' the ealdorman concludes, and once more, tears form in my eyes.

I've missed my fellow warriors. Yes, they don't know my identity. But here, with these men, I couldn't give a damn about my birthright. This, I believe, is where I'm meant to be. But only when I've rescued the children, returned them to Kingsholm, and ensured they're never in danger again. And that, I admit, might not be as easy as it should be.

* * *

By the time I've tended to Brute, with the aid of every single member of the war band doing something, I'm exhausted and breathing heavily. My neck still stings, and sometimes my voice is softer than a whisper, and at other occasions it's louder than Oswy in battle. I never know what I'm going to get and, as such, everything disconcerts me.

The day's starting to draw in, and that frustrates me. We need to be going north. I don't know, and neither do the others, just how long's passed since I last saw the children. Wulfheard might be confident he knows where the children are being taken, but what if he's incorrect?

'We need to go,' I urge the ealdorman as we settle before the fire. Well, they do. I'm standing. It's too painful to keep getting up and down. Not that standing is exactly a delight. My leg wound means I limp, and if I don't hold my arm in just the correct position, it throbs. Whatever Oswy's done to my belly wound, and I daren't look, it's not currently hurting too much. In fact, it's the scratches on my hand and face that throb. I've not been able to bathe, but I'm wearing Oswy's spare tunic and Maneca's extra trews, and while they smell faintly of both men, I certainly feel more like myself. After all, my boots are mine.

'We'll eat and then move on. I'm sending Kyre and Landwine ahead. They're going to scout and search for our prey.'

I eye the two men who stand quickly and make their way to the horses. I trust them both, but I must admit, should they find the children first, Coenwulf and Coelwulf will probably be more terrified of them than the men who've captured them.

'How many of them were there?' Kyre questions me, returning to the fire before leaving.

'At least fourteen. I don't think I managed to kill any of Eadweard's cronies who attacked me.'

'Wouldn't know. We don't know where that was.'

'But it was on Watling Street,' I announce, confused. I would have expected there to be some sign of what happened.

'They cleared it up then. That's probably why they moved you as well. They didn't want to leave any obvious signs of their passage.' I shudder at those words. I've killed many warriors in my time, but I'm not sure I've ever done so with the cold-blooded intent these men showed. Certainly, apart from the dead men my uncle killed, and which I forced over the steep incline to ensure the wolves stayed away from my wounded uncle, I've never moved the dead, apart from to bury them.

'We'll keep our eyes peeled,' Landwine murmurs. Both men seem buoyed by the task they've been assigned. As I've come to expect from these warriors. They show no sign of fear even though they might be riding into a great big bloody fight.

'Eat up, young Icel,' Wulfheard urges me. The pottage is delicious, but it's as though I've forgotten how to eat. I'm so tired, and the aches that plague me, even when I swallow, make it hard going.

'You're not going anywhere until you clear that bowl, and even then, you might not be able to mount.'

I've been considering this for some time. But I'm joining them. I don't care how. I'm going.

'I'll walk if I can't ride,' I mutter grumpily.

'You might just be at this rate. Now, eat up, buttercup.'

Growling, and then wishing I hadn't, I hasten to eat, despite how painful it is. I also drink as much water as I can. I still feel dry, and my lips are cracked and sore. I know better than to lick them, but I don't have any salve to rub over them, and so I keep licking them, and that only makes them sorer.

And then there's no more time to procrastinate.

Brute's wound has been tended to as best I could. Given time to rest and recover, I believe he'll be fine, but of course, neither of us has that time. We need to ride on.

Speaking softly and hoping my voice doesn't crack, I run my hand over my horse's back, assessing how I'm going to mount without too much pain. As I recall Waldhere saying to me after the attack on the Isle of Sheppey, once I'm mounted, it might not prove possible to dismount. I might just stay there, hoping the others can return the children without my aid. I don't know if I can hold a seax, and certainly, the thought of wearing a byrnie fills me with shuddering fear. It'll hurt, no matter what. But I must get the children, and my seax, back from Eadweard.

I lead Brute to a handy tree stump and set about mounting, grateful that the others are all busy with other tasks to watch me. Or so I think.

Sweat beads my face, slipping down my back, and still, it's an agony to lift my leg. It doesn't help that I can't grip Brute where I might normally because of his wound.

'Hurry up, Icel. The children will be older than you by the time you get your leg over your horse.' Wulfheard's words are as reassuring as he intends them but it spurs me onwards. Eventually, with some help from Brute, who almost seems to bend at the knees to aid me, I'm finally mounted. I'm absolutely buggered. But I'm on my horse. Now I just need to ride as well.

Ahead, Ealdorman Ælfstan calls his men to order.

'Ride alert to everything. We only found Icel thanks to Brute. These bastards might be hiding the children even better than that.'

'But I doubt it,' we all hear Wulfheard mumble.

'Aye, we all doubt it, but all the same. Let's not allow such assumptions to blind us to the possibility.' There's censure in the ealdorman's words. I consider if I've missed something between the two of them. Have they fallen out in recent days, and I've only just noticed?

But, as Brute steps out, favouring the right side of his body and so making his gait unsteady, the agony that thuds through my body is other-worldly. Whatever's happened between the ealdorman and Wulfheard becomes irrelevant. It's too much effort just to stay seated on my horse.

We ride. Well, I hang on. The others ride, Oswy concerned beside me, his face twisted in consternation and fear. Eventually, I can't help myself. Despite everything, a chuckle blossoms from my mouth.

'What's so damn funny?' Oswy growls.

'Is that what I look like when you lot ignore all my advice?'

'Like what?'

'A mother hen, fussing and biting my tongue.'

Swift fury descends over Oswy's face, the coming night casting his craggy features into a stark contrast of shadows. Only then his face transforms, and he grins. 'Yes. That's it. A mother hen. You always look like you're going to offer us a pillow to take our ease.'

I chuckle again. It's better than bloody crying, which is what I'd like to be doing.

At the sound, I feel Brute relax; suddenly, he's galloping, as usual. It seems, in a moment of levity, both of us have managed to forget our wounds. I only hope it lasts.

33

It doesn't. We ride all night, slower because, while the moon is bright, it's still dark and we need to be careful. We don't see Kyre and Landwine, which means that our prey are still out there. The anger of what they've done goes some way to making me forget my aches and pains, but it's not enough to drive them entirely from my mind.

I stay where I am when the others dismount to water the horses and relieve themselves. Brute doesn't object, and it makes it much, much quicker for all involved.

We continue throughout the next day as well, and I know I sleep in the saddle, Oswy ensuring I don't fall to the ground. We've slept, but only for a small amount of time, making use of the cave where I met the wolf with the children. No wolves trouble us, but the moans and whimpers in my sleep have upset the others. The ealdorman is grim-faced, but it's Wulfheard who's the most sullen, and I'm unsure why. I want to ask, but I don't. I'm loath to draw attention to myself, or I fear they'll leave me.

I order Oswy to find me some moss, wild carrot leaves and dandelions, using the moss on my wound, and adding the dandelions to the pottage we eat when allowed the time to cook it. I'd ask for more, but I know he won't be able to find it. I've already had to stop him adding poisonous mushrooms to the pottage once.

On the second night, we stop in the woodlands where I first found the children, and I discover I can dismount more easily. One of the horses we released finds us during the night, startling Osmod on guard duty, but in the morning, I greet the animal warmly. I hope the others have found their way to some food, perhaps even to the settlement we passed with the hound and the woman. I must have slept through that part of the journey.

Kyre returns to us, his face tight with fury, when we've travelled for half another day.

'We've found them,' he growls, his hand hovering close to his seax.

'Where's Landwine?' Ælfstan demands.

'Watching to make sure we don't lose them. Although, they're hardly hiding,' Kyre complains. His face is twisted, and he keeps licking his lips as though he can taste vengeance. 'They're in a hall, with a fire blazing and men on guard duty around it. They're waiting for someone.'

'Someone with the silver coins to pay the bastards, I imagine.' Wulfheard's furious face has, somehow, become even more twisted with anger.

'Yes, and they're coming today, at some point. We need to get the children before they arrive.'

'How many enemy warriors?'

'I've seen fourteen of them so far, but not the big bloke that Icel spoke about, Wulfnoth. They have horses, but of course, if they escape, they'll miss their rendezvous with whoever's coming to pay them.'

'He won't run,' Wulfheard confirms, as though he knows it for a surety. I'm curious about whom this man is and why Wulfheard knows him so well. Sometimes, I realise, I forget that all these men had lives before I knew them.

'Lead on,' the ealdorman informs Kyre. 'We'll scout the place out and decide what to do then. I don't care if we kill 'em all, as long as the children survive.'

I turn to face the rest of the men I now call friends, even if I know they can kill with their little fingers. I've fought at their side many times, but I've never been the one in stitched-up pieces. Neither, I realise, have I been the one with a huge stake in what was about to happen. The knowledge now is disorientating. Never before have I needed to rely on my fellow warriors as much as I do now. It's a sobering realisation, yet it's not one that worries.

We're the men of Mercia, and if we're fighting to retrieve Mercians from whatever enemy has them, then it doesn't matter if they're children or adults. They're all bloody Mercians.

* * *

Ealdorman Ælfstan sends others to assist Landwine in assessing the hall that the enemy have the children locked up inside. When they return, expressions are grim.

'We can't take the horses.' Kyre is firm on that, as is Oswy. I don't look at them as they say this. I might be able to ride, but running or walking is almost beyond me. Still, I'm not going to be left behind.

'They'll hear us coming if we take the horses,' Oswy echoes again, not looking at me.

'There are two big buggers at the front who actually have their wits about them. The rest, I couldn't say for sure. We've not seen the children, but we've heard them.' Kyre bites down on the rest of that remark, and I consider why. But perhaps it's best if I don't know. For now. I'll kill the bastards, all of them.

'We can circle the property. There's low wicker fences surrounding it. There are pigs in one of the fields, mind. We don't want to make them squeal.' A grin splits Oswy's face as he finds some amusement in that. Ealdorman Ælfstan's face is set in a grimace as he considers.

'Then we split our force. Icel, if you think you can make it, you stay closest to the horses. If we have to run from here, I want you to stand more than half a chance of reaching Brute.' His words are far from reassuring.

'Cenred and Oswy, you stay with Icel. Godeman, Kyre and Osmod, you take the far side. Waldhere, Ordlaf, me and Wulfheard will take the front. The rest of you, it looks like you have to contend with the pigs.'

I would grin at the unhappiness on the faces of Maneca, Uor, Wulfgar and Landwine, but I'm too busy trying to dismount. I'm too slow. When my right foot hits the ground, I think I've done it, only for the delayed pulse of pain to send stars dancing before my eyes and my balance to fail me just as my left leg hits the ground. Somehow, I've also managed to hurt Brute as well, for he veers forwards leaving me with no support.

I hit the ground, jarring my teeth, belly wound, head and everything else as well. Not for the first time, tears fall from my face. I wish none of the men had witnessed that, but I know I've not been so lucky. Strong hands on my arms, and Oswy is beside me, Wulfheard to the other side. I wait for them to tell me to remain behind as they right me and pretend not to see my tears.

'Take this.' Oswy thrusts a seax into my hands as soon as I'm upright. 'You need something to kill the scum with.' I almost choke on his kindness, gripping the well-formed blade hungrily. I've lost too much while trying to track down the children.

'And this.' Wulfheard thrusts a war axe into my other hand. I have my weapons belt, and I've been given my rusted byrnie. My weapons belt is already in place around my waist, but not my byrnie. With fumbling hands, I reach for it, where it's waiting for me, rolled on Brute's back. I wince at the weight, realising how weak I am. It's only been a few days, but my strength has been stolen from me.

Before I can make a further arse of myself trying to shrug into it, the two men are there, taking the weight from me and forcing it over my head. Raising my arms hurts, but it's nothing compared to the feeling of tightening my weapons belt over it, with the added heft of the blades. My belly hurts, but it's only one of so many other aches that they've all merged together.

'You look like a...' Oswy's voice trails off as he eyes me.

'Trussed pig,' Wulfheard offers sourly.

I hold my tongue and limp to where I can empty my bladder. I do, at least, manage to stay upright this time.

Again, I think someone will ask me if I'm sure about this, but no one does, as I limp to where the rest of the men wait. Some of them are clearly impatient. But not all of them.

They eye me, Cenred most carefully.

'Just remember which end to stick 'em with,' is his helpful advice, and then Kyre is leading the way. I follow on last, Cenred and Oswy with me.

Everyone steps carefully, and I try and copy them, but it's difficult with my limp. I try to put weight on my right leg, but it thrums with a nausea-inducing pain, so I continue limping.

I look the part. What I'll be able to accomplish, I'm unsure, but prepared to try. And really, I'm more concerned with ensuring the children recognise me as someone who's come to help them.

I watch the rest of the men scrambling to where they've been told to wait. At some point, the ealdorman alongside, Waldhere, Ordlaf and Wulfheard veer aside, to the settlement's entrance. Ælfstan offers me an appraising glance, but Wulfheard, head down, makes his way without looking at me. I can't help fearing for him. Something about this warrior who has the children means more to Wulfheard than it does to me. I hope he behaves himself. I hope he doesn't take too many chances. I wish one of the others had the stones to tell me what it was.

Overhead, bird call drowns our steps, the harsh cawing of blackbirds high in the trees. Not the best omen, but whether for those we're going to attack or for us, I can't determine.

Through the trees, I catch sight of the hall, and despite the birds, can hear the harsh shriek of young Coelwulf through the wooden walls of the building. My heart thuds loudly in my chest but Cenred and Oswy are no fools.

'Wait for the signal,' Cenred urges me. 'Or die because the others aren't ready yet.'

I nod, but my throat's dry once more.

I run my hand over the borrowed seax and war axe, dreaming of ripping into the flesh of the men who thought to try and kill me. That steadies me. Coelwulf might be distressed, but he won't be for long. Soon I'll have him safely on the way back to Kingsholm, even if when he gets there, he'll have no father to welcome him home. He will, at least, be somewhere safe. Or so I hope.

The day drags. I grow impatient, and thirsty, the raging pain making my head pound in time to my heart. Cenred, beside me, is calmer, his eyes sharp, whereas I'm hazed by pain. I fear my movements will be too slow to attack. Yet the ealdorman has allowed me to remain with the rest of the men. He's a cautious man most of the time. He must trust my abilities, as does Wulfheard. Either that or Oswy's told them that I'm going to die from my wounds regardless and they've decided to allow me to die on the edge of a blade rather than in agony on my deathbed. Either way, I take comfort in knowing the probable outcomes and don't ask Oswy, where he waits with me as well.

I can't see the two men guarding the settlement's approach. It is, as the advance party said, a good place to build a hall. Very secluded for those who don't want to play much part in wider events and who want somewhere defensible as well. There are walls surrounding the settlement, but they're deceptive, woven from hazel, and I can see no ditch, although I might be wrong about there being one. Perhaps, I realise, I should have listened more closely when Kyre was reporting to the ealdorman.

In contrast, the hall's walls are made with thick trunks, the wattle and daub that fills the spaces between fresh and glistening. Whoever lives here is wealthy. But there aren't many outbuildings. My thoughts return to the monastery on the Isle of Sheppey. There were many outbuildings there. Some for the sheep. Others for the monks to sleep within. Perhaps, I consider, those are to the far side of the main building, for I'm sure that someone such as this wouldn't allow the servants, slaves or animals to share the living space with them.

'We go when we get the signal,' Cenred reminds me as I wait impatiently.

'And what is the damn signal?' I ask in a harsh whisper.

'You'll know it when you hear it,' Oswy counters.

'So what, there isn't one?'

'There's always one. You just don't always know what it is. It depends on the circumstances. We can't all bloody hoot like an owl when it's broad daylight.'

I don't know why Cenred mentions an owl, and I feel my forehead furrow.

'Look,' Cenred continues. 'We use an owl sometimes, and of course, none of the daft gits have thought of that until now, so, you know, we'll know it when we hear it and not before.' I nod, lips twisting, as I lick at their cracked surface. I fear they might never feel normal again. Certainly, the women who work in the king's hall in Tamworth won't be looking to kiss me anytime soon. Not that I want to kiss them. Or maybe I do. I don't know and dismiss the thought to focus on what I'm supposed to do.

Only then, a sound thrums through the air. I look to Cenred and Oswy, and they look to me.

'What the hell was that supposed to be?' The call, perhaps meant to be some sort of trill, has the distinct sound of Wulfheard behind it.

'Bloody arseholes,' Cenred complains, checking his weapons belt before striding out from the shelter of the trees, followed by Oswy. Ahead, the fence waits for us, but it takes no time for Cenred to slice through it with his seax. 'Why did they bloody bother?' he grumbles, more to himself than to me.

Cenred doesn't wait for me. Oswy forces his way through, and by the time I happen upon it, my right leg making me wince, both have disappeared. I thrust my arm through it, the pieces of the fencing having knitted back together as though they'd never been forced apart.

'Hurry up,' Oswy hisses. I realise that I'm going to get as much sympathy from Oswy as I've so far received from Wulfheard. Biting my lip, thinking only of the children, I follow the two warriors through.

I glance left and right, considering where the rest of the men are, but I can't see them. Neither, from what I can hear, does it seem that the alarm's been raised. I reach over and touch Cenred's arm.

'Was that the call? None of the others are here.'

'They know what they're doing. Come on. Keep up.'

Cenred moves swiftly, Oswy following him. The fencing that we've come through doesn't allow immediate access to the hall. Instead, Cenred has to force a path through another line of fencing, and then a final one. It's time-consuming, but I still don't understand why they've taken the time to build it when it's about as much use as melted cheese.

It slows us, yes, but only a little. Through the third fence, and I'm finally greeted by the site of the hall and my fellow warriors. The strange bird call must have been the signal, after all. Wulfheard, I see, is already engaged in a fierce fight with someone. Their cries reach me, as does the clash of iron on iron, but it's not the huge man I saw on the horse. That'll annoy Wulfheard.

'Stop dallying, and hurry up,' Cenred urges. Oswy already has weapons ready in his hand. I appreciate then that while there's fighting to the front of the hall, we're faced with the hall itself. The doorway is wide open. I don't know if my fellow warriors have forced it open or if it's just like that. From inside, I can hear the cries of Coelwulf, and they're growing in intensity, and my stomach fills with a leaden weight. If they've done anything to him, I'll kill them all.

With renewed vigour, I hasten to a crab-like run, Cenred and Oswy beside me. Cenred's steps are light compared to mine, and I know he purposefully slows his pace to keep in time with me. Oswy is swifter. He stops at the door, hand blocking our path, as he tries to glimpse the interior. The smell of food cooking stirs my stomach, but that doesn't mean everyone inside doesn't have a blade to hand, ready to kill the enemy.

'Come on.' Oswy moves forward, expecting Cenred and I to stand beside him, and I do, but Oswy's movements are more fluid than mine. I see what I don't want to see as my eyes adjust to the darkness.

A man, who I think is Wulfnoth, holds the two children tightly while wearing a gloating grin. I see the glimmer of iron in his hand and know he means to kill them, given the opportunity.

'Well, well, well, it seems you didn't die, after all.' The words are pointed, aimed at me, and also, I realise, at the shocked expressions of Eadweard and Wulfred who thought to have killed me.

'Give me the children,' I urge him. 'They don't belong to you.' I'm impressed my voice is firm as Cenred and Oswy stiffen beside me. No doubt they're doing a quick assessment of our chances of retrieving the children alive.

The sound of fighting can be heard from outside, but inside, there are more than fourteen men, so our two sides aren't evenly matched. And, of course, the bastard has a blade at the children's throats.

Coenwulf, eyes wide, smiles on seeing me, but the enemy jabs his blade closer. He howls in fear. I'm unsurprised. I'd do the same in his situation. Coelwulf, meanwhile, is held in a tight grip, but he struggles against it. His harsh shrieks would put an eagle to shame or the pigs, knowing they're about to be slaughtered.

Eadweard, Deremann, Wulfred and Forthgar quickly regain their senses, weapons to hand, and move to encircle Cenred, Oswy and me. Apart from Eadweard, they all look like I managed to land a few cuts and blows on their faces before they overpowered me. That makes me smirk. The other men hang back. Perhaps they don't need to act unless these four fail in their attempts to kill us.

'Give the children back, Wulfnoth,' I try once more. 'And you might live to see the sunset.'

'And you and who else are going to see to that? Those men outside? I know them, and I don't believe they're anything to worry about.'

Cenred and Oswy have their eyes on Eadweard and his allies. I take some pleasure in seeing the cuts and abrasions on their faces and exposed arms. I'm glad I gave as good as I got, even if, in the end, they thought they'd won. I'm pleased I didn't just give in to them.

But, as the warrior speaks, there's a crash from outside, and the roar of angry voices. I recognise Ordlaf, and Maneca, Wulfheard and the ealdorman. And every man in that hall looks to the door as though the wall might disappear and reveal to them what's happening. All apart from the man I face. He's heavily scarred. And still, I think I should know him.

'Kill them,' he says, the tone counter to the command. He sounds almost bored.

Eadweard, Wulfred, Forthgar and Deremann advance quickly then. They can't entirely surround us, because the door remains at our backs, and I jab with my seax, frantically trying not to overbalance, as Eadweard skips closer. He laughs at me, spittle flying from his mouth, the smell of ale on his lips, my eagle-headed seax in his hand.

Somehow, my seax hits home, raising a thin line of blood on his left arm. I grimace, trying to find my courage and strength to reclaim the children for a second time even though these men nearly killed me. I try not to look at the boys, no matter their cries. Once I've killed these men, I'll be able to console them. And I will.

Eadweard yelps at my blow and comes at me quickly with my stolen seax. I counter his blows with my blade, curling my left fist, keen to knock his nose aside and have him blinded by the pain. He must sense my intent and jabs out with the seax towards my hand. I smirk, ramming my seax handle into his nose instead. The sound of Eadweard's nose collapsing is audible, and he spits aside blood that runs between his thin lips and into his mouth. Using my elbow, I also knock his forehead, and he stumbles backwards. Unable to stop my forward advance, I follow him, one hand seeking something to steady myself with, but there's only him.

I grab for Eadweard, and follow him down with a heavy thud that reminds me of all my hurts, and sends me into a stabbing frenzy. My body over his, I rear up on my arm and gore him repeatedly, his chest rupturing with each blow despite his byrnie. He tries to counter the attack, but I'm too quick. He's barely raised the stolen seax to counter my blows when his arm crashes to the wooden floor. He's dead, and yet I can't stop spearing him. The feel of his blood on my face spurs me on.

'Bastard,' I shout, my voice raw and strained.

'I think he's bloody dead, Icel.' Oswy's words finally permeate my hearing. I glance up to him, and realise he's fighting two men. One of the others is curled in a ball on the ground, bleeding copiously. I try to stand, but my legs are twisted, and my hands slip in the slickness of Eadweard's blood.

'Here.' Wulfheard is suddenly there, his hand on my arm, pulling me upright. Oswy no longer faces Wulfred and Deremann but only Deremann, Wulfred swaying on his feet, but the light has left his eyes. He's dead before he hits the ground. Cenred has taken on Forthgar.

He bends and takes my eagle-headed seax from Eadweard's lifeless hand, and I welcome the familiar feel of my blade in my hand.

'Kill them,' Wulfnoth rears. I hear Wulfheard's exhalation as more foemen come to meet the attack. These seem to be more seasoned warriors, their blades shimmering in the light from the hearth fire, but we now outnumber them. I'm pushed aside by the rest of my fellow warriors, busy with the task of killing the enemies who believe stealing children is acceptable. And my eyes alight on the man who still holds them.

Somehow, I forge a path through the fighting, being knocked here and there, but staying upright all the same. The man doesn't see me until I'm close to him, Coenwulf almost reaching out to touch me.

'Get back,' Wulfnoth menaces. 'Get back to Wulfheard and his pathetic warriors, or I'll butcher these children.'

I don't glance behind me, as he wants me to do. I know that

Wulfheard and the rest of the men are winning the fight. Wulfnoth speaks with bluff and thinks to use the children to stay my hand. It won't bloody work.

Coenwulf watches me fearfully, but Coelwulf still strains against the tight hold of this man, the seax in his right hand, close to Coenwulf's neck. It gives Coelwulf much more room to cause problems.

I consider how best to approach this. I don't want either boy wounded, but Wulfnoth evidently believes I'll play nice and not just attack him. But Wulfnoth's wrong. I'll slice him. I'll risk Coenwulf getting cut because I know I'll be able to heal him if the worst should happen. I take a breath, test my stance to ensure my wounded leg won't fail me, and then, as I lurch at him, Coelwulf, using all of his baby teeth, snaps down on Wulfnoth's exposed hand.

Wulfnoth shrieks, dropping Coelwulf heavily to the floor, who doesn't even seem to notice as he crawls towards me with a gurgle of delight. I jump over him, my seax stabbing down and into the thick seax-holding arm of the man still wincing over the bloody mark on his hand. Coenwulf screams, the sound shocking, but not one of pain, rather one of rage as the blood of his captor gushes over him.

The man's grip on the seax falters, and it's all the opportunity I need. I wrench Coenwulf free, pulling on his arm and knowing I'll leave a mark but not caring. Better a bruise than dead.

With him in my arms, I glower at the other man. His triumph has slid from his face, like wax from a candle, and he's exposed.

'Leave him,' I hear Wulfheard holler. 'Leave him, Icel. He's for me to kill.' Wulfheard speaks with no delight, only conviction. I risk turning, and appreciate that all of the enemy warriors are dead and that Ealdorman Ælfstan cradles Coelwulf in his arms, a strange look on his face, almost as though he's never held a child before.

'Who is he?' I demand from Wulfheard, chest heaving. I want to kill him. I want to use my seax blade with Mercia's eagle emblazoned on it to kill the man who thought to deprive Mercia of her young eaglets.

'A traitor, and always has been,' Wulfheard responds, moving past me and offering nothing further. I hobble backwards, keen to unite the two brothers and not to be a part of whatever vengeance Wulfheard means to exact from the man who stole the children.

'Who is he?' I murmur to Ealdorman Ælfstan, as I reach over and run my hand through Coelwulf's fair hair, as the clash of iron on iron reverberates throughout the hall.

'He's his brother,' Ælfstan admits in a soft voice, and now I understand why he looks at the children as he does. Brothers. But not necessarily allies.

'Why?' I hear Wulfheard demand from his brother as they fight, seaxes twisted together, their fists doing most of the damage. Wulfheard is certainly winning, despite the difference in height between the two.

'Why not, brother?' the other man taunts.

'Who paid you?' Wulfheard demands, but his question is only met with derisive laughter, as the crash of blade on blade intensifies.

'A nastier piece of dung you'd be hard-pressed to find,' Ælfstan continues, as though we talk of small matters, and not two men fighting to the death. 'He has no love for Mercia, or her kings. Some even say he was involved in the murder of King Coenwulf's son near enough twenty years ago.'

I gasp at that. If Coenwulf's son had lived, his brother, Coelwulf, would never have become king. My father would never have usurped him, and the last ten winters need never have happened.

'Aye, Icel. The bastard has a lot to answer for, and Wulfheard is the man to ensure it's done properly. He's waited a long time for this.' While I think to shield Coenwulf's eyes from what's happening before me, he struggles free, and I allow it. After all, he should see this for himself. He might never feel safe again unless he knows his captor has been killed.

And he is being killed. Carefully, precisely, Wulfheard overpowers his brother. With a soft gasp, that could almost be mistaken for a sob, Wulfnoth lies bleeding, one eye missing, his nose broken, and Wulfheard's seax through his neck, cutting off his air with the wet gurgle of a cask of ale being run dry. Wulfnoth's dead, and yet I can't help thinking, we still don't know who paid him, or indeed, any of the men, to capture Mercia's children.

34

It takes more than ten days to return to Kingsholm. Ealdorman Ælfstan leads the way, grim-faced. He's content that Wulfheard killed his brother. But he's dismayed not to know who was the power behind the attempt on the lives of the children, if indeed, that was the intention all along, which appears likely from what Eadweard said to me.

It seems to me, at least, that Lord Wigmund is implicated, but Ælfstan cautions me to silence. He says not enough is known. I disagree with him, but I hold my tongue. For now.

On the journey, Wulfheard is silent. The children are gregarious, and when we seek shelter in Chester for two nights, Æthelgyth cares for them with all the joy she showed previously, and I'm delighted to see young Godfrith with her and Oswin. He shows me his new cloaks and boots with pride, his new tunic and trews as well.

My thoughts turn to Eadburg, time and time again. I fear she's dead. I believe it's my fault, but I only receive an answer when, with the first snowstorms, we ride through the gates of Kingsholm. We find the place hunkering down for the winter months, and Eadburg's there, being tended to by young Lady Cynewise, returned from Tamworth, with some of the king's warriors, on the orders of Lady Ælflæd. I also suspect Wynflæd's involvement as Cynewise greets me with a smile and a gabble of new knowledge about moss.

Perhaps, after all, my thoughts towards Lady Ælflæd have been blackened by her association with Lord Wigmund, and the precariousness of her position as the sister of a traitor, and wife to the king's son.

Not that Eadburg is well. She's as scarred as I am. While I limp and groan, Eadburg suffers from a deep wound forged through her back. The bastards thought to kill her, and they would have succeeded, if not for the aid of the Wolf Lady, who somehow found her, nursed her, and ensured she was returned to Kingsholm. The woman is powerful in the same way as Wynflæd. I think I'd like to know more about her. When the seasons change, I'll return to Hereford. I'll ask her more about the wolves. I feel I should know about them. And also about her. I would like to know how she came to live as she does. I've used the woods to hide in many times. I can only think she runs from a destiny as momentous as mine might have been.

Eadburg sobs on seeing the children, and they on seeing her, and while all are sombre for the death of Eadburg's mother, as are Eadburg's siblings, even the youngest, not much older than young Coelwulf, there is also much joy. The small children have survived. It's a miracle worthy of one of the priest's sermons.

'Icel.' Ealdorman Ælfstan summons me, two days later, to sit beside him before the hearth. It's piled high with wood, blazing merrily. Outside, the snow has continued to fall. A surprisingly early snowstorm that presages a bleak winter. We're lucky we arrived when we did. If not, it would have been an even more difficult journey here. And it was already hard enough with all our wounds and two small children.

'Ealdorman.' I incline my head, wishing I didn't still feel the crushing weight of Eadweard's fingers at my throat as I do so. It's a constant reminder that not even his death has yet banished.

'Sit with me,' Ælfstan urges me.

We're alone. The other men are in the stables, assisting Pega and Hatel with the increase in the number of horses that must be tended. It's more awkward than it should be, but eventually I'm settled, my right leg before me, my belly stretched slightly backwards to prevent the healing wound from catching and, worse, from itching where it rubs against my trews.

'You did well. I owe you an apology for taking you from the children, dismissing your concerns, and for not hastening back to Kingsholm when you came alone. If they'd died, I'd never have forgiven myself.'

I don't feel I need to add that I wouldn't have forgiven myself either.

'It seems, whether it's men telling you should be the king's commander, or men trying to steal away small children, that you're somehow more closely linked to the ruling house of Mercia than I would have thought possible for someone such as you.'

His fierce eyes blaze into mine. If he's hoping for a confidence, I can't give him one. I must keep my secret. I've seen how much trouble it can cause two small boys. With my reputation as a warrior it would be so much worse.

'I've urged you, in the past, to be careful. To watch what you do, and now I would reiterate that, young Icel. Mercia's enemies are gathering, and as you know only too well, it's not just external enemies, but internal ones as well.' His words are solemn, edged with a warning. 'The king ages. Those who wish to rule after him grow in power and influence. Some, it seems, are more than willing to kill for the chance to rule,' he continues. His voice thrums with intensity. 'Lord Beorhtwulf is a problem. I suspect his ultimate involvement in this, as does Wulfheard. Mind, his brother would sell his soul to the highest bidder, so it is possible it was someone else. I don't suspect Lady Ælflæd.' He says this more softly, eyes alert to those close by. 'I do suspect her husband, and his mother. The queen fears her queenship will be fleeting, and like other Mercian women, especially those associated with Winchcombe, she means to shore up her support and supporters.' I can tell the ealdorman has given the matter a great deal of thought. I nod along with him. I can't deny any of his concerns.

I should have sought out the king, but I've not been able to. Not yet. Perhaps when the snow clears I'll return to Tamworth. Perhaps I'll even inform him of my parentage. No, I could never do that, I realise. I don't want anyone to know. Not now. My future is set. The soft hand of young Coenwulf steals into mine, a cheeky grin on his honey-smeared face, Coelwulf tottering behind him, with Lady Cynewise holding the youngster's hands to keep him upright, and as much as I want to fear the future, I can't. Not when it might just rest in the hands of these two small boys, and their fierce aunt.

Only time will tell.

HISTORICAL NOTES

This story is mostly fictional, but for fans of the later books which feature Icel, I felt it necessary to build the relationship he shares with both Coenwulf, who we don't really get to know well, and certainly his younger brother, Coelwulf. I also thought it was an excellent way to hold a mirror to his uncle's actions when Ecgberht of Wessex attacked Mercia, and stole Icel away to the borderlands with the Welsh.

As I've said many times before, events in Mercia at this time are not at all well documented. But there is a storm brewing, and I always think it's good to set it up firmly beforehand.

I've always found the title of Northumbria confusing for the area of northern England, but that does indeed seem to be the correct term for all land north of Mercia, once the smaller kingdoms had been merged into the larger ones. It is as simple as my characters say: Northumbria was land north of the River Humber. On occasion, the term Southumbria was also used for all land south of the River Humber. Such huge rivers gave reasonably permanent border features between kingdoms, although, of course, they were on occasion overwhelmed.

The four main roads of Saxon England are well known: Watling Street, Ermine Street, Foss(e) Way and Icknield Way. There are also other well-known roads, such as Dere Street, running through Northumbria to the kingdom of the Scots. There was also a road running north from Chester and through Cumbria towards Carlisle, Akeman Street, and a road running from London towards Winchester, and also one running from London towards Kent are also known. It is believed that the Roman roads were still utilised throughout this period, if not often repaired.

ACKNOWLEDGMENTS

Thanks, as ever, to my editor, Caroline, for a few gentle nudges with this one, and everyone at Boldwood Books for your huge enthusiasm for these tales set in the distant past. A special shout-out to Ross, who has to contend with my 'made-up' words, and inability to get slaughter field, any more and slaughterhouse quite right.

To my fellow authors, thank you for all your support. Elizabeth R. Andersen, Eilis Quinn and Kelly Evans, I'm looking at you there. Also to Donovan Cook, J. C. Duncan and Peter Gibbons, my fellow Boldwood authors, for your encouragement.

And a huge thank you to my other half and (adult) children, for moving 'around me' so that I could get *Protector of Mercia* finished in time. And I'm sorry I have quite so many heavy books.

To my readers, thank you for continuing to enjoy my tales set in Saxon England. I appreciate you and hope you continue to enjoy my stories.

ABOUT THE AUTHOR

MJ Porter is the author of many historical novels set predominantly in Seventh to Eleventh-Century England, and in Viking Age Denmark. Raised in the shadow of a building that was believed to house the bones of long-dead Kings of Mercia, meant that the author's writing destiny was set.

Sign up to MJ Porter's mailing list here for news, competitions and updates on future books.

Visit MJ's website: www.mjporterauthor.com

Follow MJ on social media:

twitter.com/coloursofunison
instagram.com/m_j_porter
bookbub.com/authors/mj-porter

ALSO BY MJ PORTER

The Eagle of Mercia Chronicles

Son of Mercia

Wolf of Mercia

Warrior of Mercia

Eagle of Mercia

Protector of Mercia

The Brunanburh Series

King of Kings

Kings of War

Boldwood

Boldwood Books is an award-winning fiction publishing company seeking out the best stories from around the world.

Find out more at www.boldwoodbooks.com

Join our reader community for brilliant books, competitions and offers!

Follow us
@BoldwoodBooks
@TheBoldBookClub

Sign up to our weekly deals newsletter

https://bit.ly/BoldwoodBNewsletter

Printed in Great Britain
by Amazon